COWBOY TOUGH

She turned in her seat to face him. "If it hadn't been for you I don't know what I would've done. I probably would've gone crazy."

"Nah, you're a fighter and Corbin, he's a coward." A dead coward if Jace ever got his hands on him. Okay, Jace wouldn't really kill him but he'd like to make him suffer.

He leaned across the cab and kissed her. Just a sweet peck on the cheek, but Charlie turned and took his lips, cupping the back of his head with her hands to kiss him deeper.

Jace reacted and kissed her back. Long, slow, and thoroughly. When she didn't resist, he kept going.

She tipped her head back against the seat and he went in for more, drunk on the taste of her. Her hands came around his neck and he pressed her deeper into the seat, bruising her lips with his, winding his hands through her hair. Kissing her into tomorrow.

He shouldn't have. It was wrong on about a thousand levels.

Yet, he couldn't seem to stop himself. She felt so good—curvy and warm and feminine—and responsive, returning his kisses with equal passion. He could make her feel good too. Take the hurt away if she'd let him...

Books by Stacy Finz

The Nugget Series
GOING HOME
FINDING HOPE
SECOND CHANCES
STARTING OVER
GETTING LUCKY
BORROWING TROUBLE
HEATING UP
RIDING HIGH
FALLING HARD
HOPE FOR CHRISTMAS
TEMPTING FATE

The Garner Brothers
NEED YOU
WANT YOU
LOVE YOU

Dry Creek Ranch
COWBOY UP
COWBOY TOUGH

Published by Kensington Publishing Corporation

Cowboy Tough

Stacy Finz

LYRICAL SHINE
Kensington Publishing Corp.
www.kensingtonbooks.com

LYRICAL SHINE BOOKS are published by

Kensington Publishing Corp.
119 West 40th Street
New York, NY 10018

All Kensington titles, imprints, and distributed lines are available at special quantity discounts for bulk purchases for sales promotion, premiums, fund-raising, educational, or institutional use.

Special book excerpts or customized printings can also be created to fit specific needs. For details, write or phone the office of the Kensington Sales Manager: Kensington Publishing Corp., 119 West 40th Street, New York, NY 10018. Attn. Sales Department. Phone: 1-800-221-2647.

Lyrical Shine and Lyrical Shine logo Reg. U.S. Pat. & TM Off.

First Electronic Edition: February 2020
ISBN-13: 978-1-5161-0926-5 (ebook)
ISBN-10: 1-5161-0926-0 (ebook)

First Print Edition: February 2020
ISBN-13: 978-1-5161-0927-2
ISBN-10: 1-5161-0927-9

Printed in the United States of America

Chapter 1

Jace Dalton pulled to the side of the road, rubbed the bristle on his chin and tried to remember whether he'd shaved that morning.

It had been that kind of day.

He checked the clock on his console. Five. Not so late. Then again he'd been up since dawn.

He let out a loud yawn, exited his vehicle and crossed the two-lane road, one hand lazily resting on the butt of his service weapon. He stuffed the other in the pocket of his down jacket.

There was a CR-V parked on the wooded shoulder, perilously close to the road. In less than an hour it would be dark and a motorist coming around the bend might not see the SUV in time. From a distance, the vehicle appeared vacant, though it was hard to tell.

The nearest services were a good five miles away and Highway 49 was three in the other direction. He hadn't seen anyone hiking along the roadside, at least not in the direction he'd come from.

As he got closer, he walked around the hood of the car to get out of the line of traffic and peered through the fogged windshield. The driver seat was in a reclining position. Something resembling a bundle of clothes lay on it. He blew out a breath that turned white in the cold and tapped on the passenger window.

The bundle moved, and his hand reflexively gripped his gun tighter.

"Unroll the window, please. And put your hands on the steering wheel where I can see them."

The window came down and a pair of brown eyes stared back at him. That was all Jace could see because the person was covered in a hooded coat and wrapped in a blanket.

He leaned in the window and scanned the back seat and the trunk area, which was packed with suitcases, clothes, cartons, and overstuffed garbage bags. It looked like someone's entire apartment.

How long the vehicle had been on the shoulder like that was anybody's guess.

"You can't park here," he said. "There's a campground six miles down the road, a motel off the highway, or a shelter in Nevada City."

California's homeless problem had spread from the big cities to the state's rural areas. While Dry Creek hadn't attracted too many vagrants, its neighboring towns had seen an influx. Jace didn't know why they came here. In late January, the Sierra Foothills weren't a particularly hospitable place for someone living out of a car or on the streets. Temperatures dipped into the twenties. And just up the road, where the elevation reached 2,500 feet, they got snow.

"Okay, I'll go." The voice was barely audible but distinctly female.

He took a few steps back and when the woman made no move to leave, he leveled his gaze at her. He'd meant what he'd said. She couldn't stay here. He was about to give her directions to the shelter but noticed she was clutching her stomach.

"Are you okay, ma'am?"

She nodded.

"Ma'am?"

"I'll leave now." Her eyes welled as she reached for the ignition.

Jace couldn't let her get on the road if there was something truly wrong. He hadn't smelled alcohol on her breath or seen any signs of drug use. But clearly there was a problem.

"Ma'am, I'm going to have to ask you to step out of the car."

She doubled over. "I...don't...think...I...can."

He reached in the window, opened the door, and tried to lean across the passenger seat. A pile of clutter was in the way. "What can I do to help you?"

She didn't answer, just continued to grip her midsection. He spotted an open box of saltine crackers on the floor and a bottle of carbonated water. Maybe she had a stomach flu.

"Is there someone I can call?" he asked, hoping there was someone local.

"No." She wrapped the blanket tighter around her and tried to sit up straight and adjust herself in the seat. "I'll be okay...just need a few seconds."

That's when he saw the blood. A small pool had settled in the seam of her seat. He'd missed it before when the folds of her wool coat had draped over the chair.

"Ma'am, you're bleeding."

She whimpered. "I think I'm having a miscarriage."

He dragged his palms down his legs and observed her for a few seconds, trying to assess what to do next.

As a patrol cop he'd helped deliver a baby in the back of a pickup once. He'd also seen his fair share of gunshot and knife wounds. Auto wreck injuries were his bread and butter. But never a miscarriage. Not ever.

He crouched down. "When did the bleeding start?"

"I'm not sure." She grimaced. "The cramping about thirty minutes ago, that's when I pulled over."

The closest hospital was twenty minutes away in Auburn, only a little bit farther than the nearest firehouse. He could get her to the emergency room faster than waiting for an ambulance and didn't think moving her himself was any more dangerous than leaving her by the side of the road until the paramedics could come.

"I'll take you to urgent care, okay?"

"No," she protested. "There's nothing anyone can do."

Her reaction seemed odd to him. Shouldn't she want help? He couldn't force her to go, but he couldn't leave her here like this, either.

"Maybe there is," he said. "Maybe they can save the baby."

She darted a glance at him, her eyes shining, and he saw it. Hope.

"Okay." She started to open her door but he stopped her.

"Let me come around in case of cars." Even while he'd been focused on her, a few trucks had whizzed by. Besides the campground, there were more than a dozen homes off the windy road.

"My SUV," she said suddenly. "I can't leave it here. Everything I own is in it."

"I'll get one of my deputies to park it at the station."

She shook her head. "No! I'll drive myself."

There was no way she could drive in her current condition.

He walked around the front of the CR-V, took her key from the console, locked the door, and hid the fob in the dirt. "It'll be safe, I promise." He scooped her out of the vehicle before she could object and found her purse next to the box of saltines.

She started to struggle, gasped, and clutched her stomach again.

"Put your hands around my neck," he said. She wasn't much heavier than his fourteen-year-old, but he wanted to give her something to hold on to.

Her hands were ice-cold, and he made sure to secure the blanket around her as he settled her into his front seat. "I'll get the heater going."

Her eyes were closed but she wasn't asleep, just checked out.

"You with me?"

She nodded but he was starting to worry. He got on the road, called the hospital to let them know he was coming, and flicked on his light bar. He left the siren off because he didn't want to scare her.

The second call was to dispatch a deputy to fetch her car. Then to Mrs. Jamison. He briefly explained the situation and asked her to drop the boys at Cash and Aubrey's house. His cousin and his cousin's fiancée lived on the ranch, just a short walk from Jace's. If they weren't home, his other cousin, Sawyer, would be.

"You have children?" she asked when he got off the phone.

"Two boys. Travis is fourteen and Grady's nine." He glanced over at her. Her eyes were still closed and her arms were wrapped around her middle like she was literally trying to hold herself together.

"That's nice," she said, slowly rocking back and forth.

"We'll be there soon. Are you sure you don't want me to call someone?" Her husband? A relative?

She jerked and her hand clenched the edge of the blanket. "I'm sure."

"All right." If she was homeless, Jace suspected she had no one to call. The world was filled with tragedy. In his line of work, he saw it every day. Still, to be alone like that… "What's your name? I'm Jace. Jace Dalton."

She didn't answer, and to Jace it seemed like she was somewhere else entirely. Lost in the physical pain and the emotional anguish of knowing she was likely losing her child.

Jace drove in silence, leaving the woman alone with her thoughts. He was out of his depth on what to say anyway and hoped that his quiet presence gave her at least a small measure of comfort.

By the time he pulled up to the emergency room, the sky had turned dark and moody. When he opened his door a gust of wind hit him and the air smelled pungent. The forecast predicted showers, but it felt more like a storm.

An orderly met them at the ramp with a wheelchair and Cash lifted her out of the passenger seat. A rust stain now covered the part of the blanket that had been tucked under her bottom. She was still bleeding.

"My purse!" She snapped out of her trance and held her hand to her chest. "Oh God, I left it in my car."

Jace registered that she was wearing a diamond wedding ring and filed the information away for later.

"I got it. It's right here." He dug the handbag off the floor of his back seat and placed it in her lap, noting that, like the ring, the purse looked expensive.

They went inside, where she was quickly whisked away.

"Evening, Sheriff." The desk clerk waved.

"Evening, Kay." Other than a woman with a small child, the waiting room was nearly empty. The hospital served three counties and there were times when the emergency room's small lobby was standing room only. "Slow night, huh?"

"It's still early." She motioned behind her where the exam rooms were separated by a wall. "You waiting, or do you want us to call someone?"

"Nah, I'll hang out for a while." Jace didn't know if they'd keep her overnight. He supposed if they released her he could always have a deputy shuttle her to her car. But he didn't feel right about leaving her alone.

There was a hat rack by the double glass doors and he hung his Stetson, then took a chair near the television, where he scrolled through his phone. Cash had texted that he and Aubrey had the boys. His family was good that way. As the Mill County sheriff, his schedule was often unpredictable.

About fifty minutes later a pregnant couple came through the door. Jace overheard the man tell Kay that his wife was cramping, which turned his thoughts back to the woman. He still didn't know her name.

He wasn't so sure anymore that she was homeless. The handbag and the plaid pattern of the blanket reminded him of a designer brand that Mary Ann used to go nuts about and cost roughly a month of his sheriff's salary. Then there was the wedding ring. He didn't know how he'd missed that the first time.

No, not homeless.

A more likely scenario was that she was moving, which would explain the cartons and clothing. The Honda had California plates, but he didn't recognize her being from around here. Then again, her face had been mostly obscured by her hood.

Jace found the TV remote and flicked on the news. The pregnant couple had been escorted to one of the exam rooms, leaving only him and the lady with the child in the waiting room. He glanced over at her to make sure she wasn't bothered by the sound of the television. She smiled, fluffed her hair, and tried to strike up a conversation, when one of the emergency room docs came through a pair of swinging doors.

"Sheriff." He nodded at Jace and motioned for him to follow him back to where the exam rooms were.

They went inside a small office with white walls and generic pictures of Gold Country. The doctor shut the door. Jace took a seat and the doctor wheeled a stool to the countertop desk.

"You know anything about the patient you brought in?"

Jace had seen the doctor a few times before. Unfortunately, as a cop and a father of two young, rambunctious boys, he was more familiar with the ER than he wanted to be. Still, he didn't remember the doc's name and had to look at the tag on his white lab coat.

"Nope. I found her in her vehicle on Lakewood Road. She okay?"

"She suffered a second-trimester miscarriage, which isn't all that common. But not unheard of. There's no indication of an infection. We're running tests for chromosomal abnormalities, but my suspicion is trauma. A beating, to be precise." He paused and locked eyes with Jace to see if he understood.

"She was assaulted?" Jace didn't know why it surprised him. He'd been in law enforcement more than a decade. Still, there hadn't been any bruises Jace could see, just the blood from the miscarriage.

The doctor shifted in his chair. "There are physical signs of injuries consistent with abuse. Her back is black and blue with contusions and she has a hematoma on her left leg, as if someone pummeled or kicked her repeatedly. And her demeanor...She doesn't want us to call anyone, refuses to give us access to her medical history, and won't supply us with a home address."

"What about medical insurance?"

"She claims she doesn't have any."

That, in and of itself, wasn't hard evidence. A lot of people didn't have medical insurance.

"Her name?" Jace asked. "Did she give you that?"

"Charlie Rogers." The doctor lifted a brow. "I suspect it's not real since she won't give us an address. She does, however, have a driver's license with that name."

Jace snorted. With Photoshop and a piece of heavy card stock he could be Buster Posey. But why a fake ID? Unless she was trying to disappear, which was nearly impossible in this day and age.

"Is a social worker talking to her?" Jace asked. It was protocol.

The doctor pinched his lips together. "She refused."

"I'll talk to her." But if she'd already refused to talk to the doctor, Jace didn't expect he'd have any better luck. It wasn't atypical for victims in these types of cases to refuse to report their abusers. "Are you releasing her tonight?"

"We'd rather not. She's passed most of the fetus and placenta. I gave her something to pass the rest and for the pain. But she should be monitored. She says she doesn't want to stay."

No one could force her to.

"Let me see what I can do," he said, though a female social worker would've been better equipped. He grew up on a cattle ranch and was raised by a rough-and-tumble cowboy. Needless to say, Jace didn't have a lot of finesse in these situations.

And the woman had just lost her child.

"I'll check to see if she's ready for a visitor." The doctor left the office and Jace went in search of a men's room.

He took a leak, washed his hands and face, and checked his phone. Grady had sent a miss-you emoji, which probably meant Cash or Aubrey had given him a nine-year-old's equivalent of a time-out for misbehaving.

He went outside, leaned against the wall, and called his cousin. "Everything okay?"

"Yep, we just had dinner. How 'bout you?"

Jace couldn't remember the last time he ate. Breakfast maybe. "I'm gonna be a while. The boys behaving?" They were probably celebrating Mrs. Jamison's last day. They'd managed to run her off too.

"They're good, Jace. They did their homework and are now watching TV. Why don't we keep them overnight and get them to school in the morning?"

Jace looked up at the sky. Lots of angry clouds. A storm was definitely coming, he could feel the electricity in the air and smell the sharp scent of ozone. "If it's not too much trouble, I'd appreciate that."

"You got it."

He signed off and went back inside.

"Doctor Madison says you can go back," Kay told him. "She's in exam room five."

Jace passed through the double doors again and the duty nurse waved to him from behind her station. "When are you taking me dancing, Sheriff?"

"As soon as I learn how to two-step." He winked, crossed the floor, and knocked on number five's curtain.

"Come in," came a weak voice.

When he got inside, she was gathering up her coat and purse from the chair. She was pale and her eyes were ringed with deep, dark circles. But even in her pallid condition, she was beautiful. He could tell that right away. Not the kind of woman he was usually drawn to, too understated. She was a little younger than him, maybe in her early thirties, with long dark hair, almond-shaped brown eyes, and a slight overbite. She seemed petite but it was hard to tell in the oversized scrubs she had on.

"Mrs. Rogers"—his eyes slipped to her ring again—"you mind if we talk?"

She rested a trembling hand on the exam table. Jace got the impression she was using it to hold herself up.

"I would like to get to my car now, please."

"It's securely parked at the station, about twenty minutes away. Nothing will happen to it. Why don't you sit down for a second?"

She did, but Jace suspected only because standing was difficult.

"You can't drive in your condition." He pulled up a chair and straddled it. "The doctor thinks you should stay here, let the nurses monitor you."

She didn't respond, staring vacantly at the wall.

"I'm sorry, Mrs. Rogers. I'm terribly sorry for your loss." He started to reach for her hand and thought better of it.

She swiped at her eyes. "I need to go." Her voice was barely above a whisper.

He tilted his head so they were eye level. "You're safe here."

She shakily got to her feet, clutching her purse, coat, and a plastic bag with her soiled clothes to her chest. "Please…take me to my car."

There wasn't a whole hell of a lot he could do to keep her here, short of arresting her.

"Ma'am, I have to ask you a few questions first. Okay?" He looked at her, hoping to compel her to sit back down, even though she was dead set on leaving. But to where? That was the question.

She let out a huff of frustration, waited a beat, and finally took the doctor's stool in the corner of the exam room.

"Is your home safe?" he asked softly, knowing he sometimes came off gruff and he didn't want to frighten her. Although he'd been trained in how to handle victims of domestic violence—and that's what he thought she was—he'd only done it a handful of times.

"Yes," she answered quickly, not meeting his eyes.

"Is there someone in your life who makes you feel unsafe?" He tried to make eye contact with her, but she lowered her gaze to her short brown leather boots.

"No." She swallowed and lifted her chin defiantly. "Why are you asking me these questions?"

He took a deep breath and, in that instant, decided to take off the kid gloves. "Are you being abused, Mrs. Rogers? Because Doctor Madison thinks you are…He thinks it's the reason for your miscarriage." She started to protest and he held up his hands. "No one's judging you, Mrs. Rogers. All we want to do is keep you safe."

She started to respond but clutched her stomach instead. "I have to use the restroom." She winced while trying to unfold herself from the stool.

He jumped to his feet to help her but she rejected his hand. "I'll meet you in the waiting room."

In essence, she was telling him his Q&A was over. He watched her leave the exam room, hunched over in pain, then scooped up the rest of her belongings and made his way to the lobby.

He waited by the glass doors. It was raining now and even from inside he could hear the wind howling.

"It's really coming down," Kay said.

The waiting room was as quiet as when he had gotten here. An elderly man now sat in the place where the mother and child had been.

"Yep, looks like we're in for a soaker." He stared out the window, thankful that his SUV was still parked at the curb.

The woman...Mrs. Rogers...emerged a few minutes later and Jace joined her at the desk. She signed a release form and paid her bill—in cash. Jace watched as she counted out more than a thousand dollars. No wonder she'd freaked out about her purse when they'd first arrived.

He grabbed his hat off the rack, helped her with her coat, and held his own over her head as they rushed outside to his vehicle. "Not a good night to be out on the road," he said, hoping she would see the foolishness in him taking her to retrieve her car.

She responded with stony silence and wrapped her arms around herself.

"Cold?"

She nodded. He cranked up the heat, then pulled out of the parking lot onto Highway 49. The rain was coming down in sheets, lashing his windshield. He turned the wipers to full force and still had trouble seeing the road in the glare of the headlights from oncoming traffic.

He slid her a sideways glance. It was difficult to see in the dark, but under the glow of an occasional streetlamp her face still appeared ashen. "You okay?"

"Yes," she said, then took a long pause. "Thank you for waiting for me."

Once they got out of Auburn the constant pelting of rain made visibility worse. Afraid of hydroplaning, Jace took the road much slower than he usually would. Next to him, she sat motionless, perhaps asleep.

About halfway to Dry Creek, she stirred. "I'm sorry I kept you from your family."

"It's part of the job," he said. "How about you? Do you have someone expecting you tonight?"

She didn't answer. No surprise there, but he wanted to open the line of communication and hoped that away from the hospital she might feel more comfortable telling him what was going on.

A bolt of lightning lit the sky, followed by a clap of thunder. Beside him, he felt her tense.

"Mrs. Rogers, why don't you let me take you to a motel? Even in the best of circumstances, it's not a night for driving. I can have a deputy deliver your car."

She silently rested her head against the passenger window and let out a long, low sigh. "All right."

He'd like to think that she'd finally come to her senses, but was more inclined to believe that she just didn't have the wherewithal to drive in this weather after what she'd been through. He should've been more persistent about her staying overnight at the hospital. The idea of her being alone in a hotel room didn't sit well with him, but he supposed it was at least something.

"There's a place about three miles from here," he said. "Nothing fancy, but it's clean and family operated." The Goldilocks Motor Lodge. He'd gone to high school with the owners' son.

"Okay. Thank you." Her voice sounded broken.

Up the road he took the turnout to the motel, a long row of stone cottages that hadn't been updated since the '90s. There was a pool in the courtyard where the wind had blown a deck chair onto the cover.

He pulled under the wooden porte-cochere over the office. "I'll go inside and get you a room, if that's okay?"

She nodded but followed him inside the lobby anyway. There was a fire going in the woodstove at the other end of the room and a wreath left over from Christmas.

Nell was working the desk. She raised her head from the book she was reading and looked curiously at Charlie Rogers's blue scrubs.

"Evening, Sheriff. Miserable outside, ain't it?"

"Yep, but we could sure use the rain."

"Ain't that the truth."

"Nell, Mrs. Rogers here needs a room."

Nell shook her head. "'Fraid we've got no vacancies. Between the weather and that Teddy Bear Convention in Nevada City, we're all booked up."

Shit, he'd forgotten about the International Teddy Bear Convention at the Miners Foundry. It was an annual event and brought thousands of collectors to Gold Country, including historians from all over the world.

"You know if the Prospector Inn has rooms?" It was more expensive than the motor lodge and off the beaten path, but it would serve.

"Nope. They've been sending folks here."

Okay, well that posed a problem. There were a number of B and Bs in the area, but he suspected most of those were full too. He could call around, but typically the local innkeepers turned on their answering machines after eight.

"There's the Swank," Nell offered, and Jace silently groaned. Back in high school they used to call it the Skank, and unfortunately it hadn't changed since then. The motel, an old Howard Johnson's from the 1950s, was off 49, next to a bar that catered to bikers.

"Thanks, Nell, we'll check it out."

They got back in his SUV and he sat there for a few minutes, considering the options. Everyone stayed at those Airbnbs now, but he didn't know anyone with a room to rent. He blew out a puff of air, knowing he was about to break one of his hard-and-fast rules of never taking the job home with him. But in this situation he didn't see any way around it, other than to drop her off at the station and let her sleep in one of the jail cells.

No way would she make it to Roseville where lodging was plentiful. Even in good weather, the Sacramento suburb was forty-five minutes away, and she was in no condition to drive. It hadn't escaped him that on the short ride from the hospital, she'd gone from bad to worse, stooping over in her seat and holding her belly.

He started the engine for the heat and turned to her. "I live in a big house with five bedrooms. The guest rooms are in a separate wing. It's warm, it's dry, it's safe, and it's relatively clean. And it looks like it's your only option."

Her eyes grew wide and she wrung her hands. "We're strangers."

He waved at the raging storm outside. "It's strangers or that." If it was anyone besides himself he might not be so cavalier about a woman going home with a man she didn't know. "May I be blunt, Mrs. Rogers? Staying in the home of the county sheriff appears to be less risky than whatever... whoever...you came from." He gave her a pointed look.

She swallowed hard and gave an imperceptible nod. The poor woman could barely keep her eyes open. He suspected it was the painkillers.

Jace pulled away from the Goldilocks Motor Lodge. The turnoff to Dry Creek Road was five miles away and they drove it in silence while the rain turned to hail pellets the size of bullets. With only her soft breathing in the background, he wondered if she'd fallen asleep.

As he climbed his muddy driveway, the motion lights on the garage went on.

She lifted her head and became suddenly still. He wasn't sure if it was her reaction to the grandeur of the ranch house or a statement about how unsettled she was with coming here.

"It was my grandfather's," he said about the house, trying to be conversational to put her at ease. "He left the ranch to me and my two cousins when he died."

"It's lovely," she said quietly.

"Come inside." He pulled his hat down lower on his head and got out. The dogs must've wandered over to Cash's to keep watch over the boys. They usually greeted him with exuberant barks and bathed him in slobber.

He went around to her side. She bristled when he touched her arm but reluctantly let him help her out. Either she'd accepted that he wouldn't hurt her or was too weak to resist. They went through the mudroom and he flicked on the light in the kitchen.

She stopped and glanced around the room. Mrs. Jamison had cleaned because the usual pile of dishes was no longer in the sink. Jace remembered the flowers in the back seat of his SUV. He'd have to deliver the bouquet to her house in the morning.

"You want something to eat or drink?" he offered.

She sagged against the center island, clutching her purse, and he noted she was still pale.

"Thank you, but I'd just like to go to bed now." A little color rose to her cheeks, reaffirming the awkwardness of staying in a stranger's home.

"Let me show you to your room." No one had used that wing of the house in a while. Jace hoped it wasn't too dusty.

He guided her through the great room, flicking on lights as he went. She studied her surroundings as they made their way to the guest wing. Jace thought she was mapping out an escape route. He was about to tell her she was safe here and realized how empty those words would sound. He continued through a long hallway where a series of Western landscapes hung on the wall, and pushed open a door.

"You'll be in here." He made room for her to cross the threshold and her eyes immediately flicked to the French doors that opened onto the porch. "The bathroom is through there. Help yourself to anything you need."

"Thank you."

He started to leave, then stopped at the door. "Mrs. Rogers, if you tell me what you're up against, the law can get involved. We can go to the DA and press charges."

She stared down at the hardwood floor but said nothing.

Chapter 2

Rays of light bounced off the walls, and Charlotte slowly opened her eyes. For a few panicked seconds she thought she was home in San Francisco, next to Corbin. But slowly, the events of the past few days came back to her and she reflexively rested her palm on her stomach.

Her baby was gone.

She closed her eyes again and took a few deep breaths, refusing to let herself cry. There would be time for that later. Time to mourn the loss of her child, the loss of life that had been growing inside her for fourteen weeks. But now she had to figure out how to get her plan back on track.

She rolled to her side, where a bronze clock in the shape of a horseshoe sat on the nightstand. Three o'clock. No, that couldn't be right. She got off the bed and padded to the chair where she'd left her purse the night before and checked her phone.

It was dead.

There was an outlet next to the chair and she rummaged through her purse, found a charger, and plugged the phone in. That's when the door squeaked and she whipped around, shielding her face.

"Who are you?" A young boy stood in the doorway. He had to be the sheriff's son. Same blue eyes and dark hair. Even his stance—thumbs hitched inside his jean pockets—was the same.

"Char…Charlie, Charlie Rogers. And you?"

"Charlie's a boy's name." He came deeper inside the room.

"Not always." Despite herself, she smiled. He had a smudge of dirt on his nose and she yearned to wipe it clean. "Do you know what time it is?"

He shrugged. "School gets out at two thirty and that was like a long time ago."

She glanced back at the horseshoe clock, then at the French doors. The blinds were down but there was a good amount of light streaming though the spaces between the slats. She walked over to the window and peeked outside. It had stopped raining but it was definitely late afternoon, judging by the sun's location.

"Why are you here?" he asked, eyeing her blue scrubs with interest.

"I got sick last night and your dad found me by the side of the road. All the hotels were booked for a convention, so he brought me here."

"Oh." He didn't seem to think it was odd that his father brought home a total stranger in hospital clothes. Perhaps the sheriff did stuff like this all the time.

The weirdest part was that Charlotte had managed to sleep soundly in a stranger's house—or anywhere for that matter. Maybe it was her overwhelming grief or the medication the doctor had prescribed. But for the first time in more than a year she felt rested.

She gazed outside again. As far as she could tell, her CR-V wasn't out there and she needed to get going. Meredith had warned that it was never wise to stay in one place too long, especially this close to San Francisco. What was it? Three hours away maybe. Even less.

It seemed like she'd just passed Sacramento when the cramping had started. She'd gotten off Interstate 80 looking for a restaurant, and the next thing she knew she was on a backcountry road and had had to pull over to the shoulder.

The little boy sat on the edge of the bed. Looking at him, her heart hurt. She could actually feel the muscle aching, like a constant throbbing. It made her want to roll up in a ball and go back to sleep.

Davis. She'd secretly named her baby after her mother's maiden name. Davis.

Can't think about that now.

"Do you like video games?" the boy asked.

"Uh, *Pac-Man* maybe. Does that count?"

She scanned the room, looking for her boots, and spotted her clothes and underwear neatly folded on a trunk at the foot of the bed. Someone had laundered them. The sheriff's wife, she hoped.

She interrupted the boy, who was going into great detail about something called *Dragon Quest*, which she assumed was a video game. "Where's your mom?"

"She moved away when I was a little kid." He hitched his shoulders and looked away.

Okay, there was obviously something more to that story. "Who's watching you?" The boy couldn't be more than nine years old.

"My brother, Travis. He's feeding the horses. I'm in charge of Sherpa and Scout, they're our dogs."

"How old is Travis?" Maybe he could take her to her car. Hadn't the sheriff mentioned their ages? Probably. But now she couldn't remember.

"Fourteen. His birthday was two weeks ago. My dad took us to see the PBR at the Cow Palace. Travis wants to be a professional bull rider when he grows up but my dad says he'll get his brains knocked out. I kinda agree."

Somewhere, a phone started ringing and the little boy bolted down the hallway, only to return a few minutes later.

"My dad wants to talk to you." He handed her a cordless phone and took off back down the corridor.

"Hello," Charlotte said.

"I tried to call you a couple times today on my landline. It's been a crazy day…a shooting outside Chesterville."

"Oh my." She couldn't imagine having that kind of crime in such a bucolic area but supposed it could happen anywhere. "Were people hurt?"

"Nah, it was just a pellet gun. But these two yahoos have been going at it all week over a damned fence and things got out of hand. In any event, I've been short on deputies to get your car over to the ranch. I'll drive it over myself as soon as I can, no more than an hour. Promise."

"Okay." It would give her time to take a quick shower, which she desperately needed, and to call Meredith. "Thank you, Sheriff. For letting me stay…for everything."

"Not a problem. Have you thought any more about what I said…about pressing charges?"

She paused, trying to compose herself. "There's nothing to press charges for. Whatever the doctor told you is wrong…"

There was silence on the other end of the phone, then, "It's up to you, Mrs. Rogers. See you in about an hour." He hung up and she let out a heavy sigh.

She should've left Corbin months ago, when she'd first found out she was pregnant. Charlotte sat on the edge of the bed and rested her face in her hands. God, what had she done?

You don't have time to beat yourself up, she told herself, got to her feet, and checked her phone for a signal. She locked the bedroom door and went inside the bathroom to call Meredith.

"Where have you been?"

Charlotte put the lid down on the toilet seat and sat down. "I lost the baby, Meredith."

"Oh boy." Meredith expelled a long breath and Charlotte could hear her thinking. She wasn't prone to strong emotions. It was probably why she was so good at her job. Calm, cool, and so damned collected that sometimes Charlotte wondered if the woman even had a pulse. "Where are you now? Please tell me not in San Francisco."

"No, not San Francisco." The truth was Charlotte only had a vague idea of where she was. After everything that had happened, the details were fuzzy. All she remembered was exiting off the interstate to find a restaurant with a clean bathroom because something hadn't felt right, and winding up on a county road. "Near Auburn, I think. That's where I went to the emergency room."

"Oh God, you didn't give them your real name, did you? And what about payment? Don't tell me you used a credit card or gave them your insurance information."

"I paid cash and used Charlie Rogers. But Meredith, the doctor saw the bruises and took X-rays and pictures. He told the sheriff who brought me in."

"He had to," Meredith said. "He's required by law. What did you tell the deputy?"

"Nothing. I told him the doctor was mistaken. But, Meredith, this is where it gets complicated. I'm at the sheriff's house now. I was in no shape to drive last night, the local hotels were all booked, and I had nowhere to go."

"He took you home? Oh, Charlotte." Meredith was moving around now, Charlotte could practically hear her pacing. "Let me think about this for a minute. First of all, do you feel safe?"

"Yes, I think so. The sheriff—I think he's the actual sheriff—seems decent. He has two children. But he's pushing me about my home life... about the possibility of pressing charges."

"Don't tell him anything. At this point we can't trust anyone, even a cop. And especially not an elected official. If indeed he's a sheriff, he's an elected official. What's his name? I'll do some research."

Charlotte squeezed the bridge of her nose, trying to remember. The realization that she didn't even know his full name hammered home the insanity of the situation. She was running from one man only to go home with another, whom she knew absolutely nothing about. "Dalton, I think. I believe the hospital staff called him Sheriff Dalton. He told me his first name, but I can't remember it now."

"Okay, let me see what I can do with that. When did you leave, Charlotte, and why didn't I hear from you on Monday?"

"Hold on a sec." Charlotte got up, turned on the faucet, and splashed water on her face. "I'm back." Corbin stayed home from work on Monday and didn't leave the house until late Tuesday morning." He did what he always did, ingratiated himself by making her breakfast in bed and sending obscene amounts of flowers to their apartment, until she forgave him.

"So you didn't leave until Tuesday? Oh boy. You never would've made it to Boulder on time, even without the extra complication."

Charlotte wanted to scream. *Complication?* "I just lost my baby, Meredith!" But Meredith was only trying to help. Only trying to save Charlotte's life. After a year of refusing to see the truth, Charlotte had finally grasped the danger she was in. And Meredith knew it too.

And now, the miscarriage would serve as a constant reminder of the mistakes Charlotte had made.

"I'll have to make other arrangements for you," Meredith said. "The job in Boulder won't wait. There might be something in Kansas City. Can you hold tight with the sheriff until I get back to you?"

"I don't know him, Meredith. I still can't believe he took me home with him. I'm a complete stranger. For all he knows, I'm a serial killer."

Meredith snorted. "Anyone looking at you would know you're not a serial killer."

It was the truth, but Meredith didn't mean it in a good way. What she was really saying was that Charlotte was so beaten down that anyone looking would only see weakness. Someone to pity, not fear.

"Just one more night," Meredith said. "Just enough time for me to find you another job and another host. A hotel will leave you vulnerable. Staying with a cop...well, for right now, while you're still so close to San Francisco, is better. Just don't tell him anything."

"How do I know he's not a psycho?"

Meredith didn't answer right away, then said, "You don't. But my gut tells me he's less of a psycho than Corbin."

"What if he won't let me?"

"If he asks you to leave, call me and we'll figure something out. In the meantime, whatever you do, don't use your real name or your credit cards. Cash only, until we can set up something under Charlie Rogers. You hear?"

Meredith had already been able to work wonders with getting Charlotte the Honda and a phone. Neither could be traced, not even by Corbin, who had tentacles all over the state.

"I won't. Call me as soon as you have something."

"I will." Meredith signed off.

Charlotte checked the time again and jumped in the shower, letting a glorious spray of hot water sluice over her. For a guest bathroom it was large and luxurious. Under different circumstances she would've taken the time to really appreciate the hammered copper fixtures and vintage clawfoot tub.

The house turned her thoughts to her host. She'd been in no condition for him to make an impression, yet he had. The cowboy hat, the boots, the stunning blue eyes, and his gentle kindness. They'd all left a mark.

She hurriedly dressed in her clean clothes while a pack of dogs barked outside. Drawing the blinds open, she saw that it wasn't a pack but two dogs, circling her CR-V while the cowboy sheriff got out of the driver's seat. Charlotte watched as he alighted from her car and crouched down to scratch one of the hounds behind its ear. The dog licked his face and he wrapped it in a hug, nearly knocking his cowboy hat off in the process.

Nope, the sheriff wasn't likely a psycho or a serial killer.

She found her way to the kitchen, taking in more of what she hadn't been able to see the night before. The place was huge, with endless windows and sweeping views. The kitchen had marble countertops, industrial-sized appliances, and a large center island. But what made the room all the more breathtaking were the tall open-beam ceilings and the enormous hand-crafted deer-antler chandeliers that hung from the iron trusses.

It looked like something you'd see in Wyoming, and nothing like the densely spaced rows of painted ladies in San Francisco.

The sheriff came through the mudroom and hung his hat on a hook by the door. She waited by the kitchen island, unsure of what to do. What was the etiquette for asking a man she didn't know if she could stay another night?

"Good afternoon." He bobbed his head at her as soon as he entered the kitchen. "Your car's in the driveway just the way you left it."

"It looks like the storm's over."

"Yep." He peered out the window and looked up at the sky. "Where you headed, Mrs. Rogers?"

"Call me Charlie, please. Colorado," she lied. "I have people there."

"Colorado, huh?" He said it like he didn't believe her, which was ironic because that's where she'd originally been headed.

Now, it was wherever Meredith could find her a job and a place to live. The trick was never staying in one place too long. For the women who had, it hadn't ended well. Meredith had relentlessly drummed that into Charlotte's head like a hammer on an anvil.

"Uh-huh." She was just about to make up a place. Denver, Aspen, Colorado Springs. But the boy she'd met, and another whom Charlotte could only assume was the brother—same beautiful blue eyes—came running into the kitchen.

"Whoa, slow down, kiddos." The sheriff wrapped his arm around the older one's shoulder and Charlotte flinched. It only took her a second to realize that it was an affectionate gesture and she quickly collected herself. But she'd learned the hard way that affection could turn to violence on a dime.

"Travis won't let me ride his minibike," the younger one complained.

"What's wrong with yours?"

"It's out of gas, remember? You said you would get me some, but you never did."

"Been a little busy, buddy. Travis, let Grady ride your minibike."

The older one, Travis, bleated, "Daaaaaaad," like he was in a great deal of pain.

"I'll tell you what: Either you share or no one rides."

"That's not fair."

"Whoever said life was fair?" The sheriff tossed her keys on the counter. Charlotte noted that, unlike the day before, he wasn't wearing a uniform, just a pair of jeans and a Western shirt. His badge was on his belt and for some reason seemed a lot taller and broader today than he did yesterday. When Travis filled out he'd be the spitting image of his father and too good-looking for his own good.

Travis started to stomp off and the sheriff tugged him back by his T-shirt. "Did you say hello to Mrs. Rogers?"

Travis turned to her. "Hi. Are you our new babysitter?" He wrinkled his nose.

"No, she's our guest," the sheriff answered. "You have homework?"

"Math."

"Then get to it. You too, Grady, no minibikes or video games until you get it done."

"Yes, sir," both boys said in unison and rushed off, leaving Charlotte alone with the sheriff.

The sheriff scrubbed his hand through his hair, then turned his attention to Charlotte. "Did you get something to eat?"

"Uh, no. I'm embarrassed to say that I only woke up a little while ago." She sat on one of the stools because she was feeling a little shaky. It was either the aftereffects of the medication or the overwhelming toll the last few days had taken on her. And it wasn't going to get any better. Meredith had drawn her a pretty clear picture of what Charlotte was up against.

"It'll be another hour or so before dinner, but there's plenty of snacks." He walked inside a pantry the size of a San Francisco bedroom and returned with an armful of choices. Everything from chips to cookies. "Pick your poison."

She couldn't help herself and laughed, then chose a package of peanut butter crackers. "Thank you, Sheriff."

"Jace. Just call me Jace."

"Okay." She tore open the plastic and took a nibble of the cracker, trying to remember the last time she ate. "Your sons are lovely."

"Lovely?" He raised a brow. "They've run off five babysitters in a little over a year. The last one left yesterday, though she stuck it out for eight months."

"Why? They're adorable." Of course Charlotte had spent all of five minutes with them. For all she knew they were holy terrors. The eldest had seemed to have a skosh of an attitude. But didn't all kids that age?

"They're good boys as long as they're not home alone together, then they're liable to kill each other." He grinned to show he was exaggerating. "You like lasagna, or do you have to hit the road?"

She cleared her throat. "About that: I was hoping it wouldn't be an imposition if I stayed another night." She couldn't believe she was asking. The whole idea of holing up in a stranger's house in the middle of nowhere was surreal. Twelve months ago, no one, least of all her, could've imagined she'd be in this position. But here she was. Fighting to stay safe and asking a man she didn't know from Adam to extend his hospitality. "I'm assuming the hotels are still booked and I could use another day to recuperate. I could pay you."

Jace didn't say anything at first, just scrutinized her as if he was trying to read her intentions. The sheriff clearly had a suspicious nature. Either that or she was as transparent as tracing paper. She was leaning toward the later.

Then again, he was a cop.

"Daaaaaaad!"

Jace slipped past her and stood between the kitchen and the great room. "What?"

"Travis ripped my shirt."

Jace tipped his head back and seemed to be praying to the ceiling. "Both of you, in here, now!"

Charlotte shrank back, having a Pavlovian response to the yelling.

The boys came rushing in, both shouting over each other.

"Look what he did." Grady pulled the sleeve of his shirt away from his arm to show a tear in the seam of the shoulder. "It's my favorite shirt, Dad, and he ruined it."

Jace picked up his hand and she held her breath, waiting for it. The slap. The punch. The kick. But it never came. Instead, he appraised the rip with his fingers, testing the fabric to see how bad the damage was.

"I can fix it," she blurted, and three pairs of eyes turned to her.

"You can?" Grady stared, pleading.

She moved closer to examine the damage. It was a simple repair. Ten, fifteen stitches would do it. But it was knit material and she'd need her serger to do the job properly.

"Just have to get my machine out of the car." She scooped her keys off the counter where Jace had dropped them.

He walked out with her. It was nippy without a jacket, though her oversized sweater would've been plenty warm enough for overcast San Francisco days. It was colder here and the air was crisper and cleaner, especially after yesterday's rain. Everything smelled fresh, like wet pine needles, oak bark, and grass. Cows dotted a distant field and she gazed out over the land to have a look. It was quite a front yard, rolling hills and trees for as far as the eye could see.

There was also a creek. She'd seen it in the glow of his headlights on their drive in and had heard it from her bedroom during the night. It curved around the back of the house, snaking its way up the side.

"It's breathtaking," she murmured.

"Yep." He shoved his hands in the pockets of his jeans and gazed out over the distance where a split-rail fence listed like a stooped old man.

To Charlotte it was part of the ranch's rustic charm. Same with the weathered barn with its chipping red paint and sagging roof. So much inspiration here that she'd almost forgotten why she'd stepped outside in the first place.

"It's back here." She pressed her fob and lifted the tailgate. The bags, boxes, and luggage—well, it was a wonder she could fit it all. And still, she'd left so much behind.

"Let me help you with that." He hefted one of the suitcases and placed it on the ground while she rummaged through the piles to find her sewing equipment.

"Got it." She started to lift the serger from the back and he instantly took it from her and still managed to shove the suitcase back into her trunk, one-handed.

"That all?"

"Just this." She held up her sewing basket and followed him back to the house.

He put her machine down on the breakfast table and watched as she lifted off the case. "Are you a professional seamstress?"

She'd never thought of herself that way, but come to think of it, she sort of was. "I used to own a store where I sometimes restored or repurposed old furniture, including redoing the upholstery."

After she said it she feared she might've given away too much. Then again, stores like hers were a dime a dozen. Even the cleverest detective would have a hard time narrowing that vague clue down.

"Where was the store?" he asked, trying to sound conversational rather than investigative. She knew better.

"Sausalito." It was the first place that popped into her head and the kind of town that would've embraced a store like hers as much as Noe Valley had. Still, Sausalito was a little too close for comfort. Just over the bay from Corbin.

If she wanted to truly disappear without a trace, she'd have to learn to be a better liar.

"What happened to it?"

Now she'd hemmed herself in. "Nothing," she lied. "It's still there. Just a different owner. I sold it ten years ago."

He looked at her like he was estimating her age and wasn't buying it. Ten years ago, she would've been twenty-five. Silicon Valley was full of twenty-five-year-olds who'd sold Fortune 500 companies, let alone a single-proprietor luxury home-store.

"Where did Grady go?" she asked, hoping to change the subject.

"Grady," he hollered. "Mrs. Rogers is ready to sew your shirt."

Grady appeared a few minutes later, holding the shirt in his hand, topless. His small, concave chest made her grin. And his eyes, shining with hope, gave her a little kick in the chest.

How long had it been since she'd sewn? The sudden memory of why she'd quit filled her head and she bit down hard on her lip, tasting the salty, metallic flavor of blood. She licked it away and focused on her task, trying not to think about her store and why she'd had to let it go.

It took her several minutes to load her cones and thread the machine. Travis came in the kitchen and he, his father, and brother gathered around the table to watch her mend Grady's shirt. It was just a long-sleeve Henley, with a brand name that Charlotte didn't recognize across the chest. For whatever reason it was special to the boy.

Though it had been a while, maybe six or seven months, it felt good to have her foot on the pedal and her hands guiding the fabric under the whir of the machine. It was a simple repair job but it made her remember what it used to be like to be productive. How the pretty slipcovers and window treatments she made had filled her with pride.

"Sweet," Travis said as she sewed a series of flatlock stitches along the seam of Grady's sleeve.

"You better thank Mrs. Rogers for saving your bacon. Otherwise, you would've had to dip into your allowance to buy Grady a new shirt," Jace told Travis.

"Thank you, Mrs. Rogers."

"You're welcome." She turned the Henley right-side out and called Grady closer to have a look. "See, just like new." She demonstrated that the tear was now a perfect seam.

"Thank you, Mrs. Rogers." He clutched the shirt to his chest as if it were the most important thing in the world and dragged it over his head.

Then, he wrapped his arms around her and gave her a great big hug. For a moment she froze, shocked by the contact. As he clung to her, something in her chest moved and her eyes welled with tears.

"Hey, buddy." Jace pulled him back and mussed his hair. "You and Travis go finish your homework, okay?"

The boys filed out of the kitchen.

When they were out of earshot Jace said, "Sorry about that. When he's not chasing off babysitters, he can be clingy."

She pretended to laugh, but the hug had shaken her. It had been a painful reminder of what she'd lost. And yet, the connection had stirred something inside her. Something that gently plucked at a lifetime ago.

A life before Corbin.

"No worries." She packed up her serger and basket and started to take them to the car.

"You can stow them in the mudroom until tomorrow," he said, and pulled a frozen lasagna out of the freezer.

"So it's okay if I stay then?"

"The room's yours," he said, yet she sensed a hesitation on his part. And why wouldn't he be reluctant? She was no one to him.

"Thank you. I'll leave first thing in the morning." She hoped by then Meredith would have a new arrangement for her.

He nodded and turned on the oven. "You planning to open a new store in Colorado?"

He was digging again. She supposed she would've done the same if he was a stranger in her home.

"Yes, as soon as I find the right location." A store would be the first place Corbin would look, Meredith had warned. No, Charlotte would have to take the kind of jobs Corbin would never suspect. Jobs she'd never done before.

"Can I help with that?" She pointed at the lasagna.

"Not much to do other than stick it in the oven." He reached inside the fridge and pulled out a bag of ready-made salad. "And pour this in a bowl."

"I could set the table."

"Sure. Plates are up here." He nudged his head at one of the upper cabinets.

She found linens in a drawer and carefully folded each cloth napkin into a rosette. It was something she'd learned from her sister, Allison. From one of the cupboards, she gathered four glasses. They were cobalt blue and quite pretty. She assumed the dining room was too formal and began arranging the placemats on the breakfast table. Out of the corner of her eye, she caught Jace watching.

"Is something wrong?" She should've asked about the dining room. It was presumptuous of her to think they'd be more informal.

"Nope, nothing wrong. You've got a flair for that kind of stuff, don't you?" He bobbed his head at her table arrangement, lingering on the rosettes.

She'd done nothing special, really. "You have nice dinnerware." The plates were different, a pattern Charlotte had never seen before. Each one was embellished with what appeared to be a cattle brand. "Are they family heirlooms?"

"They were my grandmother's. Her parents had them custom made. That was their ranch's brand."

"They're amazing."

Jace chuckled but the laugh sounded hollow to Charlotte.

"What's so funny?" she dared to ask.

"My ex-wife hated them with a passion. We fought about those plates more times than I can count."

"But they're your family's history," she said and immediately wished she could take back the words. His problems with his ex-wife were none of her business. Furthermore, the woman was entitled to her opinion. It had been her house too, after all.

He shrugged. "That was my thinking, but she wanted something more modern." He pulled out a square plate covered in bright geometric patterns. "Now tell me, would you want to eat off this? It gives me vertigo just looking at it."

Admittedly, it wasn't her taste. She preferred the family heirlooms—anything with history that told a story. But to each her own. "It's a very popular style."

He grunted something unintelligible but didn't seem the least bit angry that Charlotte hadn't taken his side. She considered asking about the ex, remembering what Grady had told her, but didn't want to wear out her welcome by prying. Perhaps Jace had been a terrible husband and the wife had fled with just the clothes on her back.

The ex certainly hadn't taken her dishes.

The oven dinged to signal that it had reached the right temperature, and Jace slid the lasagna in and got to work on the salad. She found flatware and finished setting the table.

"How long have you been sheriff?" A benign enough topic, she presumed.

"Six years. I was appointed when my predecessor left midway through his term for health reasons, and was elected two years later. I'm up for reelection in June."

Be careful.

Meredith had cautioned her about politicians. Corbin's father was about as connected as anyone got. Even in small rural counties.

"How's that going?" she asked, just to hold up her end of the conversation.

He waggled his hand from left to right. "I wouldn't call it a slam dunk. But I'm by far the best guy for the job. In the six years I've been doing it, crime rates have dropped significantly."

She got the sense that it wasn't just a stump speech, that he was probably pretty good at his job. Judging by how he'd treated her, Sheriff Jace Dalton cared about people. Then again, first impressions could be deceiving. Hadn't she learned that the hard way?

"I wish you luck," she said.

"Thanks. If it doesn't work out I can always ranch full-time." He shrugged.

"What exactly does that entail?" She'd seen the cows in the field and had no idea whether they were for milk or meat or were merely pets. Her experience with farm animals was limited to television.

"My two cousins and I run about a hundred head on Dry Creek Ranch. My grandfather used to run a lot more, but the drought killed us." He gazed out the window where the sun had begun to set. The days seemed shorter in the country.

"What do you do with the cattle?"

He turned away from the window and rested his back against the sink. "Breed 'em and sell their calves at market. Beef prices are good right now, though that could change. For us it's just a sideline. But eventually we'd like to grow the operation."

"It sounds like you and your cousins are continuing the legacy."

"Yep." A corner of his lip tugged up in a half grin and she saw a great deal of pride shining in those startling blue eyes of his.

He was an interesting man. A single dad and, from the looks of things, raising his two boys alone. Sheriff, cowboy, rancher. Handsome enough to turn heads but seemingly oblivious to his own appeal.

Maybe. Perhaps he knew just how good-looking he was and didn't care.

He grabbed a bottle of dressing out of the fridge and went back to tossing the salad. She made herself busy filling a water pitcher she found in one of the cupboards.

"Charlie?" He cleared his throat. "You ever planning to tell me what's really going on here?"

She hesitated for a beat, wishing she could trust someone in his position and that Corbin wasn't above the law, then answered in one word. "No."

Chapter 3

Jace climbed out of his pickup, travel mug in hand, and crossed the south pasture to the barn. He could see his breath hanging in the morning air. Little white puffs.

"You bring some for us too?" Sawyer eyed Jace's mug.

Jace's cousin appeared to need more than coffee this morning. A double shot of espresso or eight more hours of sleep.

"Nope. Were you up all night or is this a new look?" Rumpled, bloodshot, and generally resembling a bag of shit.

"Deadline. Give me that." Sawyer pulled Jace's cup out of his hand and took a swig. "Shit, hot." He waved a hand over his tongue.

Cash shook his head, rested his boot on the bottom rail of the fence, and hung his arms over the weathered wood to stare out at the cattle grazing in the field. "What's up with the CR-V in your driveway? New babysitter?"

"Long story, but the short version is no, not a babysitter. A woman I found on the side of the road."

Cash and Sawyer's heads jerked up at the same time.

Cash spoke first. "What do you mean you found her on the side of the road?"

Jace stuck his hand under his hat and scratched his head. "Medical emergency. She was having a miscarriage."

"Ah, jeez." Sawyer rubbed his eyes. Even when he wasn't working on a book all night, six in the morning wasn't his best time of day. Typically, Mr. Globe-Trotting Journalist didn't make an appearance until after nine. That's when he showed up at the ranch house to root around Jace's refrigerator because he hadn't gotten around to buying his own groceries.

Over the last year, he'd been embedded with troops in Afghanistan and was writing about the war.

"That's awful," Cash agreed. "But it still doesn't explain why she's at your house."

"All the hotels were booked, on account of the Teddy Bear Convention at the Miners Foundry, and she was in no condition to drive." Jace proceeded to tell his cousins about the emergency room visit, the doctor's suspicion that someone had been knocking Charlie around, and how he'd come to a similar conclusion.

"Wasn't there anyone she could call?" Cash asked. "If not, there's got to be a women's shelter somewhere around here."

There was one in Chesterville, run by the Unitarian Church, Jace had learned yesterday. Apparently his undersheriff sat on the board.

"She denies being abused." Jace shrugged. "She says she's on her way to Colorado to open a business."

"This woman have a name?" Sawyer asked.

"Charlie."

"Charlie?" Cash squinted his eyes to block the sun.

"Charlie Rogers. I ran her license plate and the name checks out. Though the address comes back to a San Francisco nonprofit called Rosie the Riveter Foundation. According to the description on its website, it helps underprivileged women build careers."

"And run away." Sawyer handed Jace back his travel mug. "That would be my guess, anyway. Sounds like a story I did a few years back about an underground web of networks that help women escape their abusive homes. She say anything about a husband?"

"Nope. When I asked her who we should call, she said no one. But she wears a wedding ring with a diamond the size of one of our steers." Jace stuck the mug on a fence post and joined Cash at the railing. "I tried to get her to press charges but she's adamant that nothing's going on. She's leaving today, so not much more I can do."

"I still can't believe you brought her home." Cash gave Jace one of his incredulous FBI stares. He'd left the Bureau last year and had taken a job with the California Department of Food and Agriculture investigating livestock thefts. But he still had the whole fed thing going. Everyone and everything was suspect.

"I felt sorry for her." Frankly, his whole reaction to her had been out of character. He'd been drawn to her in a strange sort of way. She was beautiful, to be sure, but it was something else. Something less tangible.

"That's not like you." Cash blew on his hands, then shoved them in his jacket pockets. "Hell, if you took in every person you felt sorry for, you'd have a houseful." This woman must've really gotten to you."

"Like I said, she was in no shape to drive, especially in yesterday's storm, and she's leaving today. We gonna talk about the tax bill?" Along with the ranch, their grandfather had left them with an outstanding property tax bill the size of California.

Sawyer crossed his arms. "We have until April. Why do we have to do this at the ass-crack of dawn?"

"Because April is only a little more than two months away," Cash said. "And we've put it off long enough. Either we file for another extension and rack up more interest, putting off the inevitable, or we talk to a real estate agent about selling. Maybe we could split the property in half, sell off the back forty and keep the rest."

"No!" Jace and Sawyer said in unison.

"Dry Creek Ranch is our birthright, not Dry Creek Ranch lite. For Chrissake, Cash, some goddamn developer will wind up buying it and turning it into a bullshit planned community with country manors." Jace put finger quotes around manors.

The local developer—i.e., Jace's former best friend Mitch Reynolds—had already tried to buy Beals Ranch, their neighbor's property, in a fraudulent deal to put in an eighteen-hole golf-course community. It was a long, complicated story. But the CliffsNotes version was that Jill Beals Tucker and her brother, Pete, had conspired to force their parents into a short sale of the land in exchange for a kickback from Mitch. Jace had uncovered the scheme and the fallout had been an ugly mess, counting the breakup of Jill's marriage to Jace's other best friend, Brett Tucker.

Most folks in the community didn't know the full extent of the scandal, including the fact that Jill and Mitch had been having an extramarital affair. A lot of the details had been covered up to spare Brett's and Jill's parents the humiliation. But there had been plenty of collateral damage to go around.

Even to Jace himself and Cash's fiancée, Aubrey, who at the time had been weeks away from marrying Mitch.

"Grandpa would turn over in his grave," he continued.

"We've been talking about this since summer, Jace. Between Grandpa's back taxes and our current property taxes, we're looking at close to two hundred thou. You tell me how we find that in the budget and Sawyer can go back to bed."

"Not by selling," Sawyer said. "Can't anyway. Not without Angela signing off."

Jace and Cash exchanged a glance. Sawyer's sister had been missing for five years. It wasn't unusual for Angie to take a few months' hiatus from the family. But this time, she'd vaporized like the tule fog in November. Grandpa Dalton used to say that Angie danced to the beat of her own drum. Jace, who loved her like crazy, thought his grandfather was being kind. Flaky was more like it. She lived a high-risk nomad's life, hooking up with fringe groups, traveling to remote corners of the world, and getting involved with weird causes.

No one had ever voiced it out loud, but being a family of law enforcement types, everyone but Sawyer had thought it.

Angela was likely dead.

An exhaustive search and an open Los Angeles Police Department missing-persons investigation had turned up nothing. Not a body nor any clues to her whereabouts.

Despite the lack of leads, Sawyer had never given up trying to find his sister, harboring what Jace thought was false hope that she was out there somewhere, alive and well.

What about the cattle?" Sawyer returned to the topic of taxes. "How much do we stand to make when we bring our calves to market?"

"Not enough," Jace said. "We'd be lucky to come up with a third."

"A third is better than nothing." Sawyer, the eternal optimist. Of course, unlike Jace and Cash, he'd grown up with wealthy parents and did plenty well on his own, especially without a family to feed. But even he didn't have that kind of cash lying around. "I could hit up my folks for a loan."

"I don't want to do that," Jace said. He loved Uncle Dan and Aunt Wendy like they were his own parents, but when you started borrowing money from family, things got weird. Besides, if he and his cousins wanted to keep the ranch, they had to pull their own weight. This wasn't a one-time deal. New year, new property-tax bill. And the amount on five hundred acres of prime California real estate was nothing to sneeze at. If they could at least get caught up, though, they might be able to manage the biannual payments.

Maybe.

"We're once again at an impasse, I see." Cash threw his hands up in the air. "You don't even want to see if the county will let us break off some of the property to sell? You could keep the house, Jace. Sawyer could keep his barn loft and Aubrey and I the property where the cabins are, so we can build."

It wasn't just the house, though Jace hated to uproot his sons. They'd been through enough, losing their mother, and the ranch house was the only home they knew. But unlike Cash and Sawyer, Jace had grown up here. After his parents and baby brother died in a car accident, his grandparents had raised him. Dry Creek ran though his veins like blood. And ranching was his heritage—a way of life for four generations of Daltons. Without the acreage, the ranch would amount to a gentleman's farm and everything his grandfather had worked for would be gone.

"I'll cash out my 401(k) before I'll split up the ranch." The truth was, his retirement plan didn't have all that much money in it, but at least it was a start.

"And pay a huge penalty and get taxed up the ass?" Sawyer said. "Nah, we'll figure something out. Maybe my book will get optioned for a movie and Bradley Cooper will play me."

"Yeah, more like Danny DeVito," Jace tossed back, and Cash laughed. They needed to keep Sawyer from getting a big head. It was bad enough he was the best-looking of the three of them.

"I guess we're right back where we started." Cash toed the dirt with his boot. "I've got to get to work, so let's adjourn yet another fruitless meeting."

"What time is it?" Sawyer grabbed Jace's wrist and checked his watch. "I better motor too. I need to make it to Sacramento in time to catch a flight to New York."

"What's in New York?" Jace asked. He'd been hoping that Sawyer could watch the boys. School was closed for a teachers conference. Although Travis was old enough to look after his younger brother, the two of them left to their own devices were trouble.

"Meeting with my agent and then catching the train to DC to do some interviews for the book. I'll be back by next week, so don't do anything rash while I'm away."

Jace turned to Cash. "What are you doing with Ellie?" Cash's little girl was a year younger than Travis.

"She and Aubrey went to San Francisco last night to go dress shopping for the wedding."

"Your wedding isn't until June."

Cash shrugged. "According to the magazines Aubrey reads, now's the time to buy the dress. Hey, what do I know? I'm just along for the ride."

Bullshit. Jace had never seen his cousin happier. And Aubrey, she was so freaking in love with Cash it made Jace nauseous. He fervently hoped their marriage worked out better than his and Mary Ann's had.

"You got someone to watch the boys?" Cash asked.

His family was more than aware that Mrs. Jamison had quit. Jace was pretty sure Travis kept a secret scoreboard stashed under his bed of how many babysitters he and his brother had run off.

"They should be okay for the day." If Jace restricted their movements to the house and the immediate yard, they couldn't get into too much mischief. "I'm working on getting them into an after-school program until I can hire a full-time person."

He desperately needed someone to shuttle them to their various activities, fix them supper when he couldn't get home in time, and do light housekeeping.

"Good luck with that." Sawyer bobbed his chin at Jace. "Grady and the barn mouse incident have become the stuff of legend."

Jace's youngest had dropped a rodent down one babysitter's shirt. "Mrs. Jamison handled them just fine."

"Then why'd she quit?" Sawyer laughed. "You think it was because they called her Yoda?"

Jace fixed Sawyer with a look. "Don't you have to get to the airport?"

"I was just leaving." He headed to his Range Rover and Jace and Cash watched him drive away.

"I better run too. A ranch in Rough and Ready got hit a few days ago. Three hundred sheep."

"Shit, that's a lot of mutton. At least it sounds more exciting than my day. I have to meet Tiffany about the new campaign slogans." He groaned. "Good times."

Cash elbowed him in the ribs. "Let's hope Mill County has a short memory."

"You talking about that crap last summer with Aubrey dumping Mitch because of Jill? Everyone's over it." Jace waved his hand in the air dismissively, got in his truck, and drove the rutted trail back to the house.

The CR-V was still in the driveway when he pulled in, which didn't surprise him. Charlie was probably fast asleep. At dinnertime yesterday, he thought she might open up. But she'd stuck with her original story. None of it rang true to him, not even the part about going to Colorado to open a store. It was perfectly plausible, but his gut told him she'd made the whole thing up.

He wished she would trust him with the truth. Otherwise, his hands were tied.

By the time he got home from work this evening, she'd be gone. Hopefully, she'd go somewhere safe, somewhere where she could have a good life and leave behind whatever trouble plagued her.

The boys were in the kitchen eating cereal when he got inside. Grady had the same shirt on that Charlie had mended for him the night before. "Hey, buddy"—Jace tugged on the Henley—"let's wash this, okay?" "It's clean." Grady got up and put his bowl in the sink. "Smell it." "Nah, I don't want smell it. Go put another one on and I'll throw it in the machine before I leave."

"Can I go to Ruben's today?" Travis asked. "He got a new PlayStation."

Jace didn't care much for Ruben. He thought he was a spoiled brat and a bully and would prefer that Travis hang out with his other friends. But he'd made it his policy to let his sons figure these things out for themselves. "Not today, bud. I want you and Grady to stick to home and go no further than the driveway." He got down a bowl, filled it with cereal and milk, and took a big bite. "We clear on this?"

"Yes, sir," both boys said at the same time.

"I'll try to get off early and we can have dinner at the coffee shop. How does that sound?"

"Can we have waffles?" Grady asked. The kid could eat waffles morning, noon, and night. And Jimmy Ray, proprietor of Dry Creek's sole restaurant, made the best chicken and waffles in the state. Hands down.

"Sure." Jace lightly squeezed the back of Grady's neck. "Whatever you want, kiddo. Now go put on a clean shirt. Travis?"

"I guess, but I'd rather go to Ruben's. Can't I just go for an hour?"

"I need you around here to look after your brother. Okay?"

Travis acted put-upon, but nodded.

"Come here." Jace called his eldest over. "Thank you for manning up."

"You're welcome." Travis shuffled his feet.

Jace tried not to lean on him too hard. Ever since Mary Ann left, Travis had designated himself the family caretaker. It was a lot of weight for one skinny kid to carry.

"No minibikes today, okay?"

Travis rolled his eyes but tacitly agreed. Grady was too busy spinning around on the barstool.

"Good morning." Charlie came into the kitchen, carrying an overnight bag.

She had on a pair of jeans and another oversized sweater. He suspected she was probably still showing a little bit from the pregnancy. What was different today was makeup. Not a lot, just some eye stuff that made her brown eyes look even larger and a little color on her cheeks.

Again, he was struck by how pretty she was.

He scanned her left hand and noticed the ring was missing.

"Thank you for your hospitality."

"Have some coffee and breakfast before you hit the road."

"I couldn't impose any more than I already have."

"No imposition," he said and got up to make a fresh pot of coffee. "I have to get going, but I'll load up your car before I go."

"That's not necessary."

"Your sewing machine is heavy." He patted one of the barstools, signaling for her to sit. "It's unlocked, right?"

"Yes, thank you."

He took her duffel and grabbed the machine on his way through the mudroom. When he came back in from loading her CR-V she was getting two mugs down from the cupboard.

"I've already had mine," he said. "But help yourself. There's eggs in the fridge and bread for toast, or if you'd prefer, cereal." He pointed to the half-full box of Cheerios that was still on the counter. "I'm gonna take off."

"I can't thank you enough." She walked him to the back door.

He stopped and gave her a long look. "Are you safe?"

Her eyes fell to the ground. "Of course." But her hands were shaking.

He hesitated, tempted to tell her to stay until they could stop whoever was hurting her. But as long as she was reticent to tell him what was really going on, there was nothing he could do. "Do you have a solid plan?"

This time she met his eyes. "Yes."

"Good. But if you change your mind and decide to get the law involved, you know where to find me." He slipped her his business card. "Safe travels, Charlie."

She nodded and stood at the open door while he drove away.

It hit him as soon as he reached the highway that he would never see her again and a strange kind of melancholy set in.

* * * *

Charlotte made herself an egg and sat at the breakfast table to eat. When she got on the road she wanted to keep going until she reached Utah. Then, maybe, she could stop looking over her shoulder. At least for a little while. But it was so cozy here in this big, mountain house that it was a little tough to leave.

The ranch was so off the beaten path that it made her feel safe, even though it was too close to the Bay Area.

Grady left the kitchen, came back several minutes later wearing a different shirt, and was clutching an old sock in his hand.

"Mrs. Rogers, can you sew this with your machine for me?" He handed her the worn sock, which on closer inspection was a handmade sock puppet. A cowboy sock puppet, to be exact. The wool had faded to a light gray, the felt cowboy hat was slightly askew, and the poor thing was missing an eye. The toy seemed too young for a boy his age.

She assessed the puppet's empty eye socket. "Do you have the other one, Grady?"

"No. Can you just make one?"

"Not like this." It was a sew-on wiggle eye from a craft shop. But a black button might do the trick. A winking cowboy. "Let me go out to my car and see what I can find in my sewing basket."

She could do it by hand and it would only take a few minutes.

"I'll come with you." He leapt up and with his hand hit the top of the door frame separating the kitchen from the mudroom.

"May I finish my breakfast first?"

"Sure." He sat his butt on the table next to her plate of eggs.

"Where's your brother?" The last time she looked, the older boy had been moping around the kitchen, like he'd lost his favorite dog.

"Being a butthead because he can't go to Ruben's."

She presumed Ruben was one of his friends. It certainly wasn't her place to look after him, but she knew Jace was in a bind as far as babysitters, though the boys were probably old enough to take care of themselves. The least she could do was keep an eye on them until she left.

She got up, found his room, and knocked on the door. "Travis, is everything okay?"

"Yeah," he called.

"May I come in?"

No answer. But a few seconds later she heard footsteps and his door swung open to a large room with a full-size bed, a beanbag chair, and rodeo posters covering the walls. "I'm on the phone."

"Oh, okay. Sorry to disturb you."

She headed back to the kitchen when he called, "I thought you were leaving."

"Soon." Clearly she'd worn out her welcome with at least one of the Daltons. "Come out and say goodbye when you finish your phone call."

Back in the kitchen, Grady was standing on the kitchen counter reaching inside one of the upper cabinets.

"What are you looking for?"

"Candy. My dad keeps it up here so we can't get into it."

"Hmm, sounds like you're breaking the rules, then." She hated to be a buzzkill, but it was sort of early for candy.

"It's okay, he won't care."

She arched a brow, doubtful. But why stop him? He'd just eat it the minute she left.

Charlotte took her plate to the sink, where a pile of dishes was starting to resemble the Leaning Tower of Pisa, and washed them all. And because she couldn't help herself, dried and put them away as well.

"You ready to see what I've got in the back of my car?" she asked Grady, who was now shooting wadded up Starburst wrappers across the room with a rubber band.

"Let's do it." He thumped his chest and she hid a smile.

By the time they got to the car, Charlotte wished she'd remembered her coat. Grady, who only had a T-shirt on, seemed oblivious to the weather.

"How come you've got so much stuff back here?" He sat on her bumper as she rummaged through her basket.

"Uh, because I'm moving. How about this?" She held up a black button about the same size as the existing wiggle eye.

"That'll work. Where are you moving?"

"Kan—Colorado." She'd almost forgotten what she'd told Jace the night before. Lying had never been her forte. Perhaps if she'd been good at it, she would've managed to hide her pregnancy from Corbin. "Let me just find a needle and some gray thread."

She got what she needed and they walked back to the house; rather, she walked. Grady ran, jumped up and down the back porch stairs, then walked across the railing as if it was a tightrope, nearly giving her a heart attack.

"Where's the sock puppet?" It wasn't on the kitchen table where Charlotte had left it.

"I threw it away," Travis said. He was leaning against the sink counter, eating a banana.

"It's mine, Travis. Not yours." Grady pushed him aside, opened the cabinet door, and dug through the trash until he found it.

"It's stupid." Travis shoved him and grabbed the puppet, holding it over Grady's head.

The next thing Charlotte knew, the two boys were on the floor, brawling. They were yelling and slugging each other. For a second, she disconnected, blocking out the noise. The hitting. And just as quickly she remembered she was the only adult in the room.

"Boys, stop it! Stop it now."

They either ignored her or couldn't hear between the punching and shouting.

She raised her voice. "Travis. Grady. If you don't stop it now, I'll call your father."

That got their attention. Travis rolled off Grady, who got an extra jab in before crawling across the floor to retrieve his sock puppet.

"Look what you did," he whined. "You pulled out the other eye and the hat's off. I hate you, Travis."

"It's a stupid puppet for babies. You're not a baby anymore, Grady, so grow up."

Grady began to cry. "Mom made it for me and you ruined it."

And there it was. The boy loved his mother. The woman clearly wasn't around anymore, but the puppet still was. Charlotte felt her chest squeeze.

"I can fix it, Grady. I can make it like new."

He looked up at her with big blue eyes and wiped his nose with the back of his hand. Then he turned to Travis and socked him in the arm. To Travis's credit, he didn't hit his brother back. Still, there was resentment there. The older boy's entire body fairly vibrated with it. It didn't take a psychologist to decipher who the anger was directed at. And it wasn't Grady.

She held her hands out to both boys and helped pull them off the floor. They were solid kids and still weak from her miscarriage, she staggered back from the effort.

"Let me see the puppet, Grady." She held her hand out and assessed the damage. Not too bad. The hat needed to be reshaped, but other than that a few strategical stitches would put it to rights. "I need to make another trip to the car, and I need an iron. Who's going to get me the iron?"

"I will," Grady said.

Travis walked out with her to the CR-V and waited while she gathered up her basket. She'd need to replace both eyes now and reinforce a small tear. The machine wasn't necessary, but she needed a darning needle, a matching button, and some interfacing for the hat. Over the years of working on upholstery projects, she'd amassed a collection of sewing notions. There was bound to be something in her basket she could use.

Sock puppets didn't come up too often in her line of work. But she'd do her best for Grady because the puppet obviously held a great deal of sentimental value. Travis took the basket from her and carried it to the mudroom door. He reminded her of his father.

Charlotte had proven to be a lousy judge of character, but from all outward appearances, Jace Dalton was a gentleman. A caretaker.

"You shouldn't fight with your brother," she said, not that he had any reason to listen to her. Besides the fact that Charlotte was an outsider in his home, she was hardly the voice of authority.

Travis stopped before going inside. "She's never coming back, and the sooner he gets that through his dumb head, the better."

"Your mom?"

He didn't answer, just trudged inside, leaving her basket on the table.

"Thank you, Travis."

He rolled his eyes and went to the living room where the TV went on. Grady returned with an iron.

"Do you need the board?"

"Uh—" Charlotte searched the kitchen. The granite countertops would probably be fine with a towel as a cover, but may as well be safe. "Sure. Why not?"

He dashed out of the room and returned a short time later with an ironing board and set it up next to the table. She caught the time on the oven clock and cringed. She should've been on the road an hour ago. It was a nine-hour drive to Salt Lake City, the first stop before Kansas. At this rate, she'd be driving well into the night.

She focused on stitching up the small tear first, careful to keep the threads from unraveling more. It was a simple job, but she was intent on erasing any trace of the tear. The next step was finding two matching buttons in her bag of tricks.

"What do you think of these?" she asked Grady. They were silver instead of black, but she had two of them.

"They're good."

She grinned because he was easy to please. He also couldn't stand still. He was constantly moving or climbing things, or bouncing up and down.

She snipped the remaining threads holding the puppet's cowboy hat and put it to the side while she sewed the eyes on. The felt cowboy hat would require a little more work, including some blocking with the iron.

"When did your mom make the puppet?" she asked. Since he'd been the one to bring it up, she didn't think it was a taboo subject.

"When I was a baby. She made one for Travis too, but he hates his."

"Does she come to visit often?" Now she was probably sticking her nose where it didn't belong, especially given all her own secrets.

"She lives in France." He sat in the chair next to her and pulled it so close they were bumping elbows. "Have you ever been there?"

"Once." It was a long time ago. She'd been on summer break from college and had backpacked across Europe with two girlfriends. One Paris flea market, and that's all she wrote. Charlotte came home filled with plans to open a store complete with everything from home furnishings to handmade linens.

"How about you?" she asked Grady.

"No. My dad says I can't go until I'm older."

Charlotte was betting it had nothing to do with Grady's age. "Well, that'll be nice."

Grady hitched his shoulders. "She might come visit here soon."

"That's great, Grady."

He didn't say anything and she returned to working on the sock puppet. Charlotte found an outlet for the iron, waited for it to get hot, and began reshaping the hat.

"The mail's here." Grady jumped up and shot outside like a bullet.

Out the window, she watched a UPS truck chug up the driveway but remained focused on the hat. The shape was coming back, and if she tacked the side with a small stitch it would hold better than it had before. She turned off the iron and sat down at the table to sew the hat on the puppet. Then her work here would be done.

She glanced at the clock again. If she didn't report to Meredith soon, her friend would send in the National Guard. With a few more stitches, she tied off her thread, snipped all of the loose ends, and held the puppet up to admire her handiwork.

"Pretty good, if I do say so myself." Charlotte packed up the rest of her supplies and went off to find Grady so she could show him the end result.

"Grady," she called from the door. "Come see the puppet."

She slipped outside and walked around the house to find him. The UPS truck was gone and on the front porch were two packages. But no Grady.

Charlotte opened the front door and called to Travis, "Have you seen your brother? He went outside to greet the delivery driver and now I can't find him."

Travis begrudgingly got off the couch and wandered over to the door, where he cupped his mouth and yelled, "Grady!" He slipped his bare feet into a pair of cowboy boots that had been sitting in the entryway and joined Charlotte out on the porch. "Grady!"

He gazed out over the yard and let out a snort. "God, he's such a dork. He's over there."

Charlotte turned in the direction Travis pointed and saw Grady by the split-rail fence, rolling on the ground with one of the dogs. At first glance, she thought he was playing with the pup. But something about his position didn't look right. He was balled up in the dirt and rocking from side to side as if he was in pain.

"Grady." She ran down the porch stairs and sprinted toward him. "Grady, are you okay?"

Travis followed her and they reached Grady at the same time. He was clutching his arm and moaning.

"What happened?" She crouched down to have a closer look. "Move your hand away so I can see."

He moved it just enough for her to see that his arm was bent and swollen.

"I'm going to call my dad." Travis raced back to the house.

Charlotte didn't know whether it was okay to move him but it appeared that only his arm was injured. "What happened?"

"I was climbing on the fence and fell off. It hurts."

"Show me where."

He pointed to his arm and tried to sit up. The dog was licking his face and Grady grabbed it around the neck with his uninjured arm to hoist himself up.

"Does it hurt anywhere else?"

He shook his head and she brushed his hair away from his forehead. He felt hot and she was starting to panic. What if he had a concussion or was hemorrhaging?

Travis came jogging back with his phone in his hand. "Dad's secretary is trying to find him. Uncle Sawyer and Uncle Cash aren't answering their phones."

They needed to get Grady to the hospital. At the very least his arm looked broken. She considered calling 911 but suspected it would take forever to get an ambulance out here. The drive had taken thirty minutes or more from the emergency room the other night. Granted, there'd been a storm, but it was still a haul.

"Are you okay to get in my car?" She looked at Travis and together they were able to stand Grady up. "Is Auburn the nearest hospital?"

Travis nodded. His face was so pale, she worried that by the time they got there, both brothers would need urgent care.

"Let's get Grady to the car. Then, Travis, I need you to run inside and grab my purse."

They were able to walk Grady the few yards up the driveway and help him into the passenger seat. The back seat was cluttered with luggage. Charlotte cleared out enough stuff to make room for Travis and shoved it in the cab of Jace's truck. Someone had dropped off his police vehicle in the morning and he'd taken the SUV to work. Thank goodness he'd left his pickup unlocked.

Travis came back with her purse and they took off to the main road. "Do you know how to go?" She looked in her rearview mirror and again Travis nodded. The other night she'd been too out of it to remember the directions.

"Turn right here. At the stop sign ahead make another right. I'll tell you what to do after that."

"In the meantime, leave a message for your dad and tell him we're on our way to the emergency room."

She could hear Travis in the background as she concentrated on the road. Grady was hunched over, holding on to his arm, quietly sobbing.

From her purse on the floor came the ring of a telephone. Meredith. If she didn't answer, she'd officially be MIA.

Charlotte let it go to voicemail.

Chapter 4

Jace ran across the parking lot and nearly collided with a man in a walker. "Sorry, sir."

He tipped his hat and kept going. By the time he'd gotten the message about his kid's accident, Grady had already been seen by an emergency room doc and an orthopedist.

Jace was in charge of the well-being of an entire county, yet he couldn't keep his nine-year-old out of harm's way.

Kay was manning the front desk again. She didn't bother with a greeting or pleasantries, just ushered him through the double doors. There were a few familiar faces at the nurses' station. Usually, he stopped to shoot the breeze and flirt a little. This time, the charge nurse pointed at a room and Jace lengthened his strides.

Behind the curtain, he found a crowd.

"Dad!" Grady sat at the edge of the exam table with Travis hunkered over his arm. "Sign my cast."

Jace wrapped an arm around him and pulled him in for a hug. "How's he doing, Doc?"

The doctor rolled closer to the exam table on his stool. "Just waiting my turn to sign the cast. Looks like bull riding is out this year." The doctor winked. "It's a clean break. Should heal just fine as long as this young gun follows my instructions, which includes not climbing fences or trees. Right, Grady?"

"Yes, sir."

Travis handed the doctor a marker and he scrawled something on Grady's neon-green cast.

"Look what I have." A nurse wandered in with a basket of stickers and a blow-dryer. "Every cast needs a Casttoo. Pick one and I'll set it for you."

Grady pawed through the assortment, settling on a decal with red and yellow flames. "Can I have it here?" He pointed to a spot high on his forearm.

"You bet." The nurse removed the adhesive back and stuck the tattoo on the spot, then used the blow-dryer to heat seal it.

The doctor shook Jace's hand and went off to see the next patient. While the boys focused on Grady's new cast art, Jace locked eyes with Charlie, who sat tensely in the corner.

"I'm sorry," she mouthed as if this was somehow her fault.

As of this morning, she'd been in a hurry to get far away from whoever was chasing her. Yet, she'd put the plan on hold to take care of his kid. His ex-wife couldn't be bothered to be there when her sons needed her. But this haunted waif of a woman, a virtual stranger, had.

The knowledge of that made something move in his chest.

He nudged his head to signal for her to follow him outside, where they could have some privacy. She trailed behind him to the waiting room.

"He went outside to greet the UPS driver," she said in a rush. "I should've been paying more attention. I can't believe I let this happen. I—"

"Whoa, slow down. This isn't your fault. Grady could have the Secret Service guarding him and he'd still get himself into trouble. Besides, it wasn't your job to watch my kid. I'm sorry you had to deal with this, but I'm sure the hell glad you were there. Otherwise, with me out-of-pocket all day, it would've fallen to Travis. That's a lot for a fourteen-year-old to handle."

She let out a long breath, the strain of the day evident in her face. Drawn and tired.

It was almost four thirty. A little late to head out to wherever it was she was going.

"Why don't you stay another night?" he said. "Traffic will be bad, everyone heading up to the snow for the weekend. You'd be better off leaving Saturday morning."

She didn't say anything at first and Jace got the impression she was contemplating her options.

"Thank you for the offer, but I'll have to check with my friends in Colorado. Excuse me for a few minutes." She disappeared around the corner and appeared to be heading for the restroom.

Jace stood there for a beat, staring after her. She was beautiful to be sure, but there was more there, starting with the fact that she'd put a nine-year-old's well-being above her own.

Substance.

The least he could do was look out for her another night.

"Dad?" Travis tugged on his shirt. "Can we go home now?"

"Yep, just have to wait for Mrs. Rogers to come back from the bathroom."
He draped his arm around the back of Travis's neck. "Then we can blow
this joint. How's your brother doing?"

"He's a dork, like usual. But Grady didn't break the rules, Dad. He
stayed in the yard."

"You his lawyer, now?" His sons fought like hell, but they always had
each other's backs, which gave Jace some solace. He was raising them
right. He hoped.

Mary Ann's leaving had left them with scars. And not a day went by
that Jace didn't blame himself for that. What kind of husband must he have
been for a mother to up and abandon her children and give Jace full custody
without hesitation? Had life with him on the ranch been that unbearable?

Jace dropped by the nurses' station to see if he needed to sign any
paperwork.

"We've got you on file and speed dial, Sheriff," the head nurse joked.

Last winter, Travis had been in with a busted ankle. In June, Grady
had tangled with a bee hive, puffing up like the Goodyear Blimp after
being stung more than a dozen times. Nope, they were no strangers to the
emergency room.

"Okay, then I'll round up my posse and get out of your hair," he said.

"You can stay as long as you like." She winked and started to say
something mildly suggestive, when Charlie appeared. Except for Kay,
it was a different crew than Wednesday night, so no one recognized her.

"We're good to go," he told her and gathered up Grady.

In the parking lot, they made a plan to head back to the ranch. Travis
went with Charlie so she wouldn't have to drive alone, and Grady came
with him.

"Meet you there," he said, noting that ever since Charlie had come back
from the bathroom she'd seemed twice as distressed as when she'd left.
Jace suspected it had something to do with that phone call to Colorado.
The woman had secrets, that's for sure.

She confirmed his suspicions when they got home and said she'd take
him up on staying another night. Apparently her friends weren't waiting
up for her.

One more night, he told himself. It was only one more night. *Why'd
you ask her to stay if you didn't want her to?* It was a question he didn't
want to examine too closely.

"How 'bout dinner?" He grabbed a few steaks out of the refrigerator. Technically it was too cold to grill, but beef tasted better on the barbecue.

"I'll wash up and help," Charlie said on her way to the guest room.

"Hey, Travis, go feed the horses," he called into the great room where the boys had turned on the TV. "Hurry up, son, before it gets dark." Travis grumbled but acquiesced.

Grady came in the kitchen and hopped up on the counter. "Dad, can I go over to Uncle Cash's and show Ellie my cast?"

"Ellie and Aubrey are in San Francisco. You can show your cousin tomorrow, how 'bout that? In the meantime, what did the doctor say about you climbing up on stuff?"

"Oh yeah." Grady got down, using his good arm. "Did you see my sock puppet?" Grady grabbed the old toy off the table and stuck it under Jace's nose.

Mary Ann had made each boy one when they were toddlers and used to put on little shows, making the boys laugh until they were doubled over. Jace would stand in the doorway of Grady's nursery, watching while his throat grew thick.

It had been years since he'd seen the puppets. "Where did that come from?"

"Mrs. Rogers fixed it for me. She sewed on new eyes and made the hat better."

Jace hadn't been aware the puppet needed mending. In fact, he didn't know the boys still had them. "That was nice of her." He examined the two silver buttons and remembered Charlie hunkered over that complicated sewing machine of hers, sewing Grady's shirt, and grinned.

"You still play with the puppet?" Jace would've thought Grady had outgrown sock puppets years ago. The only toys the boys seemed to care about anymore were video games and their minibikes.

"No," Grady said, and clammed up.

Jace didn't want to embarrass him, so he left the topic alone. Grady went back to the great room to watch TV and Jace rummaged through the pantry to find a side dish, settling on a box of mac and cheese. Not exactly adult food, but the boys liked it. So did he, to be truthful.

Charlie joined him a few minutes later. She'd changed into a pair of exercise pants and another sweater, this one slightly more fitted than the last one. Her hair had been tied up in a haphazard bun with loose strands curling around her face. And those big dark eyes …

He liked looking at her. Could probably do it all day.

"Thanks for fixing Grady's sock puppet." He let his gaze fall from staring at her face and focused on seasoning the steaks to keep from making them both uncomfortable. "I didn't know he'd held on to it."

"He said his mother made it. I suppose it holds sentimental value."

"Yep" was all he said. When it came to Mary Ann, there wasn't much to talk about. He'd loved her and she'd left him.

"She lives in France, huh?"

He stifled a laugh. "For now. Tomorrow, who knows?" He tried for a smile. "She travels a lot."

"For her job?"

"Nah, she picks up work as she goes. She always wanted to see the world and that's what she's doing, I suppose."

"What about the boys?" When Jace's silence stretched on, she dropped her head. "Uh, I shouldn't have asked that. It's not my business, please forgive me." She got that high-pitched tone that he noticed affected her speech patterns whenever she was nervous.

"You were just being curious, Charlie." He turned to meet her eyes. "The boys are with me." Mary Ann hadn't asked to see them in the three years she'd been gone. Occasionally, she'd send a birthday card or a little trinket she'd picked up. Sometimes she asked Jace to send pictures. But that was it.

"Oh…I see. Well, you've done a very nice job with them."

He snorted. "I don't know about that. But I do the best I can. After today I'll have to double my efforts to find a full-time babysitter. Someone with superpowers, preferably. Grady's the most accident-prone kid I know, and Travis is getting to that age where he wants to spread his wings, not look after his baby brother."

"And why did the last one leave?"

"Maybe because she overheard the boys calling her Yoda." He said it almost to himself, but Charlie laughed. The sound of it stuck in his head like a sweet country song.

"Seriously? Come on, why did she really leave?"

His lips tipped up even though it was anything but amusing. "Because old age and a hyperactive nine-year-old and a headstrong fourteen-year-old don't mix. The kids wore Mrs. Jamison out."

"Oh, come on, they're not that difficult. Grady is a sweetheart and Travis was amazing when his brother fell."

Jace's chest filled with pride. "Don't let Grady hear you call him a sweetheart. He already has a way with the girls, and I don't want it going to his head." His lips slid up. "And Travis has got his own issues. But yeah, they're both pretty terrific."

Her eyes watered and Jace felt like a jackass, talking about his kids when she'd lost hers. "I'm sorry, Charlie." He'd never been good at expressing himself, especially when it came to things like grief. Mary Ann used to accuse him of being too stoic. "Words have never been my strong suit, but what you're going through...I'm just really sorry."

"Thank you." She blinked back a tear and quickly pulled herself together. "What can I do here to help?"

"Salad," he said, relieved to move on. He found a bagged one hiding in the back of the fridge and tossed it to her. He pointed her to the cabinet with the wooden salad bowl and went outside to fire up the grill.

Jace waited for the coals to get hot, enjoying the tranquility. Charlie was getting to him. He tried to chalk it up to the fact that he felt sorry for her. But he knew better. He was taken with her quiet beauty in a way he hadn't been with any other woman. Yes, there were women he slept with. All single, consenting adults who were looking for a few hours of intimacy and, like him, nothing more.

But Charlie wasn't single, and physical attraction was as thin as a marriage license. He'd learned that the hard way.

"Do you need help out here?"

He turned, surprised to hear her voice. "Nah, I'm good. It's cold, you should go inside."

She hugged herself and came down off the porch into the backyard. "This is quite a setup you have." She gazed around, taking in the log gazebo, the stack-stone fireplace, the smoker, and grilling station under the strings of twinkling lights.

"We raise beef and like our grilling." His late grandfather would've barbecued every meal if he could've. Something about Dalton men and an open fire. "My grandfather built the outdoor kitchen. I added the Weber because the woodburning barbecue takes too long when I need to feed two hungry boys in a hurry. And using a gas grill"—he laughed—"that would be sacrilegious."

"It's beautiful." She continued to take in the backyard.

"It is." He nodded. The whole ranch was. The place was engraved on his heart. "My ancestors came right around the Gold Rush. Since then, it's been a series of ups and downs for Dry Creek Ranch, but we've always managed to hang on."

"Resilient, huh?"

"I guess you can say that. How about you?" He held her gaze. "Where do you come from, Charlie?"

They both knew he wasn't asking about geography. She'd already established that she'd lived in the Bay Area.

There was a long pause. "Nowhere I want to talk about. I just want it behind me."

He shoved his hands in his pockets. "What's in front of you?" Because it sure the hell wasn't Colorado. He'd been in law enforcement long enough to know the tells of a lie when he heard one.

"Honestly, I don't know yet."

"I can help you, Charlie." It was his job, he told himself. But the damned truth of it was, his reach only went as far as Mill County. Not the Bay Area or wherever she was running from.

She didn't say anything, just stood hugging herself in the cold, her nose turning red. "If you've got this"—she nudged her head at the Weber—"then I'll go inside and set the table."

He watched her return to the house. Tomorrow, she would go and he'd be able to shake whatever this was he was feeling. Infatuation? Lust? Just plain old yearning for something other than loneliness?

He put the steaks on the fire and when they were done took them inside to let the meat rest. "Travis, Grady, wash up. Suppertime," he called into the front room.

Charlie was putting the finishing touches on setting the table, including using a few of his grandmother's old canning jars as candle holders.

Hmm, he never would've thought of doing that, but the table looked nice all lit up that way. "You learn that at your store?" Jace bobbed his head at the jars.

"Um, maybe." She seemed to think about it for a while. "I've just always been obsessed with repurposing old things to make a room pretty. It's my way of preserving history, I guess."

"Well, you're spoiling this house of bachelors." He tore open a box of mac and cheese to nuke in the microwave.

"Thank you for letting me stay another night."

He waited for the timer to go off and took out the piping-hot mac and cheese, brushing by her on his way to the table. She was slighter than he'd originally thought. One of their newborn calves could knock her down.

"After you rushed Grady to the hospital I'd say we're even." But he wasn't keeping score.

"We're eating without you," he yelled to the boys.

They bustled in, loud and boisterous. He pulled out a chair for Charlie. The kids and ranch might be a zoo, but there was still room for some courtly gestures. They ate while Grady regaled them with tales of the day's adventure. The kid had a flair for the dramatic. And with each telling, the story got bigger and more detailed.

Jace looked across the table at Charlie and found her smiling. He caught her eye and winked. After dinner the boys did the dishes. Everyone pulled their weight on the ranch, even Sawyer, who'd grown up having a maid, a cook, and a driver.

"You want a glass of wine, a beer, or a cup of coffee?"

"Uh, a glass of wine would be nice."

He went to the refrigerator and found the bottle of white one of his deputies had given him for Christmas. "A guy I know made this. He owns a small vineyard a few miles from here. I can't vouch for whether it's good."

He opened the bottle and poured each of them a glass. "Let's take it into the study." It was the one room in the house the kids hadn't taken over, even though they liked to do their homework in there.

Jace took the chair across from Charlie and propped his boots up on the oversized ottoman.

Charlie sipped her wine and gazed around the room. "Another great space. This entire place is breathtaking."

"Thank you. It was my grandparents' heart and soul. My cousins and I hope to pass it on to the next generation."

"Travis and Grady are lucky boys."

Jace liked to think so. But ultimately it would be their choice whether to tether themselves to the land or to sell. You couldn't force the ranching way of life down a person's throat, they had to crave it like water.

"Did you grow up in the Bay Area?" he asked.

"No, Portla—" She stopped, realizing she was about to say Portland. But Jace hadn't missed it.

Oregon or Maine? He didn't detect a Maine accent, but she could've lost it when she moved out West.

"I was a navy brat," she said. "Grew up everywhere."

It was a nice save and possibly true, but he wasn't buying it. Just like he wasn't buying Charlie Rogers was her real name. Either she was in the witness protection program or, like Sawyer said, was trying to disappear. He was betting on the latter.

"That so?" He stretched out his legs. "Is that how you wound up in the Bay Area?"

Her eyes narrowed. "How about we not do this and talk about you instead? What did you do before you were sheriff?"

"I was a cop for Roseville PD. First patrol, then detective. And I've always been a rancher." He clasped his hands behind his head. "What else do you want to know?" Perhaps if he talked about himself, she'd open up.

"Why'd you become a cop?"

"My uncle was a cop and I looked up to him. And my parents and younger brother were killed by a drunken driver, which I suppose also influenced my career decision." He'd been a little kid at the time they'd died, but even so, he'd never fully recovered from losing his entire family in one fell swoop. No one did, he supposed.

"That's awful," she said. "I'm so sorry for your loss."

"It was a long time ago. How about you? You close with your folks?"

Before she could answer Grady cracked the door, came in, and leaned over the chair, resting his head on Jace's shoulder. "Dad, my arm itches."

Jace pulled Grady in for a one-armed hug. He could tell the kid was on overload and sensed a meltdown coming on. "Not much you can do about it, buddy, except stay cowboy tough." Grady buried his face in Jace's chest. "I think we should get you to bed, kiddo."

"But it's not even ten o'clock and it's Friday. We get to stay up late on Fridays."

"Aw, bud, not this Friday. It's been a long day and you should get extra sleep to help that arm heal faster. You want it to get better, right?"

"I guess." Grady rubbed his eyes.

Jace rose, lifted Grady off his feet, and turned to Charlie. "Give me a few minutes to get him settled."

She got up and stretched her back. "I think I'll turn in early too."

A rush of disappointment filled him. Despite her evasiveness, he'd enjoyed talking with her. Looking at her. Hell, he'd enjoyed just being in a room with her.

"I'll take these to the kitchen." She swooped up the two wine glasses and left the den.

It was probably for the best, he told himself. If she wasn't going to let him help her, there wasn't a whole lot left to say.

Chapter 5

Charlotte sat in the middle of the bed, checking her texts. Nothing from Meredith yet. If Charlotte couldn't get to Kansas City by tomorrow there would be no job waiting for her. And since the drive took at least two days, Meredith was trying to line something else up. She hadn't been happy when Charlotte had called from the hospital.

Not happy at all.

But what should Charlotte have done? Leave Grady alone with a broken arm to fend for himself? No, that hadn't been an option.

She kicked off her shoes and leaned against the pillows, pulling the blanket over her lap.

The wine had gone to her head and the buzz felt nice. If Jace didn't win his bid for reelection, he could always become an innkeeper and turn the place into a bed-and-breakfast. The sheriff was an excellent host. And an excellent father, from what she could tell. He was also extremely appealing.

Too appealing.

Charlotte had discovered the hard way that if something seemed too good to be true it usually was. Jace's ex probably had a lot to say on the matter. Why else would a woman leave her handsome husband, her two beautiful kids, and this glorious ranch?

In the morning, she'd leave too, which was a blessing in disguise. Everything about this place had gotten too comfortable and safe. And Charlotte couldn't afford to grow complacent. Not where Corbin Ainsley was concerned.

Two years ago, he'd walked into her store. Until then, she hadn't believed in love at first sight. But Corbin knew how to make an impression.

"That's some window display you've got there," he'd said in a voice so deep and sexy that it had given Charlotte chills.

Browsing the shop, he'd stopped to examine a china hutch she'd refinished in black chalk paint and had filled with a collection of vintage cups and saucers. "Nice." His smile had turned her inside out.

He'd been so good-looking—tall, blond, and rangy like a runner—that she automatically searched the room for a wife or girlfriend. But it had only taken five minutes of light conversation to ascertain that he wasn't married or in a serious relationship. He'd flirted so outrageously that it had been a little hard to take him seriously.

On his way out of the shop, he'd flipped her a business card. "Ball's in your court."

She'd peeked at the card. "Corbin Ainsley, Attorney-at-Law," it said in raised letters on a linen background.

Eight days later, she broke down and called him. On their first date, she'd expected to be disappointed. Since living in the Bay Area, her dates had consisted of an accountant who made sure to split the bill exactly down the middle, even though he'd had twice as many cocktails as she had. A coder who still lived in his parents' basement. And a television reporter who constantly stood her up to chase stories.

But Corbin was attentive, charming, self-deprecating, and when it came time to pick up the tab, he slapped his gold card down and slid her regular old Visa back across the table. When she tried to tell the server to split the bill, Corbin threatened to have him fired if he did.

"That's not fair," she'd said. "I asked you out."

"Yep." He'd smiled. "Best day of my life."

Looking back, it was a pretty unctuous thing to say. But she'd lapped it up like a kitten with a bowl of cream.

Two days later, he took her dancing at the Starlight Room. They were the youngest people in the lounge and they laughed until she thought she'd have an accident on the parquet floor. Afterwards, he'd kissed her and she saw stars.

The next time she saw stars, he'd smacked her in the face.

It was six months after their dancing date and he'd asked her to move in with him. She told him she wasn't ready for that kind of commitment, that they hadn't known each other long enough.

What do you mean, no? I thought we had something here. Something real.

We do, but moving in together is a big step. And call me old-fashioned, but my parents wouldn't approve.

Your parents? What are you, eighteen, Charlotte?

Of course not, but now I feel like you're pressuring me.
Pressuring you? I love you, I want to start our life together. Is that so
wrong? Only someone warped would think so.
Warped? Now you're being an asshole.

They'd fought, both saying mean and hurtful things. When she got up to walk away, he pulled her back and slapped her. Stunned, she sat on his couch, her face stinging from his open hand.

He broke down and sobbed like a child, begging for forgiveness, saying he didn't know what had come over him. *I'm a lawyer, for God's sake, not a barbarian.* He apologized profusely, swearing he'd been consumed by love and fear of losing her.

She believed him, and two weeks later subleased her apartment.

The first four months at his place were like a honeymoon. They ate breakfast in the sunny nook off his kitchen, watching the sunrise over the bay before they left for their respective jobs. Even though Corbin's office was in the financial district, he'd make the trek across the city twice a week to visit her at the store and take her to lunch. Sometimes it was in a fancy restaurant, other times just a taqueria with a few weathered picnic tables. But it was always romantic.

After work, she would race home so they could have dinner together. Their biggest dilemma was whether to eat takeout or dine at one of the many cafés or bistros near their apartment, or settle in for a meal cooked at home. Afterward, they spent the rest of the night in bed, making love until they fell asleep.

By the fifth month, things began to change. Subtly at first. Corbin became more critical, sometimes to the point of being hurtful. The house was too messy, Charlotte's cooking was lackluster, she worked too much. Charlotte thought it was the strain of his job talking. His caseload had increased and there was a lot of pressure for him to put in ten to eleven hours a day.

Although he was always in the office, he wanted Charlotte home. At first, she thought he was looking out for her, making sure she didn't suffer from burnout. But as the owner of a small business with only a few employees, she didn't have the luxury of keeping banking hours. Besides running the store and keeping the books, she had to scout thrift stores, garage sales, and flea markets for new merchandise, and restore the pieces she found.

It was hard work but she loved it.

To compromise, she started bringing projects home so she could at least be there when he left the office. But he complained that her paints and fabrics cluttered the apartment. When she tried to set up the spare room for her sewing, he accused her of taking over his home.

His home.

But she couldn't argue. Corbin was indeed shouldering the entire mortgage. She'd offered to pay her share, but he wouldn't hear of it.

You just focus on us, baby. I'll take care of the finances.

She wasn't altogether comfortable with the arrangement, but her friends said she was crazy. The house was in his name, therefore his responsibility. And who, after all, wouldn't want to be taken care of?

She, for one.

But to keep the peace she went along, chipping in by doing the cleaning, laundry, and cooking. Occasionally, she'd surprise him with a first-edition book or a small gift she'd picked up during her buying excursions. He always made a fuss over the presents and a big show of putting them in a prominent place in the apartment.

But he soon started to grumble that her buying trips were interfering with their quality time together, which was ludicrous because he was gone more than she was. When they fought about it, he'd relent, then give her the silent treatment for days on end, like a spoiled child. Eventually, she reduced her scouting expeditions to once a month, which wasn't nearly enough to keep the store fresh with new merchandise.

Later, he balked at her working weekends. The shop was busiest on Saturdays and Sundays and she really ought to be there.

Weekends are for us, babe. I kill myself Monday through Friday just so I can have Saturday and Sunday with you. And what do you do? You run off to that little store of yours.

Again, she gave in, convincing herself that he was right. If they couldn't at least carve out two days a week together, how would their relationship ever survive?

When she'd taken him home to meet her parents and Allison, he'd been distant to the point of rudeness. She confronted him about it and he instantly became defensive.

They're the ones who made me feel like an outsider. Your sister is a real cold fish. No wonder she's still single. The woman is so jealous of you it makes me sick.

Jealous? She's not jealous. Al's had plenty of boyfriends. I don't know what you're talking about.

That's because you're a kind person and only want to see the good in people. Take it from me, your sister has a lot of resentment for you.

You're wrong. Allison's not only my sister, she's my best friend.

No, that's where you're wrong, Charlotte. I'm your best friend. No one knows or loves you like I do.

The notion that Al was jealous of Charlotte was ridiculous, but her dislike of Corbin was palpable. Even Charlotte's gracious and demonstrative parents were reserved when Corbin was around. Charlotte blamed it on the fact that Corbin was a high-powered attorney and a senator's son with a sense of entitlement. It wasn't his fault, it was just the way he was raised. Charlotte wished her family could understand him the way she did.

But that wasn't to be. Corbin actually enjoyed antagonizing Al, to the point where Charlotte looked for excuses to duck out of holidays and other family gatherings. She even bagged out on her cousin's wedding, which Charlotte had been looking forward to because it was in Portland and an opportunity to stay the weekend with her parents.

This new man in your life seems to demand an awful lot of your time, dear.

We've just got a lot going on, Mom. Between my store and Corbin's job, we barely have time to breathe.

Her baby sister was less diplomatic about it.

I don't get you, Charlotte. The way you let him push you around... well, it's gross. He's gross. Pompous and bossy... abusive. I think he's intentionally trying to drive a wedge between us. Why are you letting him?

They fought about it and Allison hung up on her. Charlotte was hurt while Corbin was outraged, accusing Al of trying to break them up.

She's so jealous, she's trying to turn you against me.

Charlotte shrugged it off. A few days later, Al called her at the store.

Why aren't you returning my emails? We need to talk about this, Char. I don't like the way he treats you.

What emails? I never got an email from you.

Corbin probably got into your laptop and deleted them.

Now you're being absurd. Corbin would never do any such thing.

Are you sure? I certainly wouldn't put it past him. The guy is a total control freak. How can you be so blind when it comes to him? He threw an absolute shit fit the last time we were all together because you wanted to spend the day with me, trawling garage sales. He's possessive and acts like he owns you. Does he hit you, Charlotte? I think he hits you.

Of course not. Are you insane? If I didn't know better I'd think you were jealous, Al.

Jealous? I'm worried about you is what I am. You're not the same anymore. You're always canceling trips to see us, and when Mom and Dad wanted to come to San Francisco to visit, you came up with that bullshit excuse about Corbin's father coming to town. Why couldn't they come at

*the same time? It wasn't like Mom and Dad would monopolize you. Not
like someone else I know.*

When Corbin came home that night Charlotte told him what had
happened. His response was to forbid her from talking to her sister ever
again.

Don't tell me who I can and can't talk to.

That was the second time Corbin hit her. This time, he slapped her hard
enough to leave a bruise on her right cheek. She ran to the bathroom and
locked herself in, only to hear the front door slam. Corbin didn't come
home that night. Charlotte would've left the next morning, except a home
pregnancy test confirmed her suspicions.

Charlotte was carrying Corbin's child.

She hung on for the sake of the baby. And because she believed Corbin
was a good man at heart, a man who simply had anger management
problems. But together, they could conquer anything.

Charlotte now knew that she'd been beyond naïve. An innocent who'd
grown up in a gentle home where abusers didn't masquerade as loving,
caring soul mates. As the situation got worse, it became very clear to
Charlotte that you can't change a person, especially a man as deeply
insecure and troubled as Corbin Ainsley.

All she could do was escape him.

She checked her phone again, got up, and changed into her pajamas. It
had been three days since she'd fled San Francisco, and yet bedtime still
made her anxious.

For a second, she considered calling her parents. Her warm, nurturing
parents. But it was the first place Corbin would look for her.

Ultimately, it had been because of her parents' relationship, sweet and
enduring, that she'd refused to marry Corbin. As soon as he'd learned
she was pregnant, he'd insisted that they set a date. It was the only time
she'd defied him, her last shred of resistance. In return, he'd left her on
the floor, battered and bloody.

*Why don't you just stick a stake through my heart, Charlotte? You know
I'll never let you go. Without you, there's nothing. I'm nothing. You're mine
and I'm yours. Forever.*

Him, him, him, until Charlotte was nothing. Oh, she was wrong—she
was something, all right. She was Corbin Ainsley's possession. And the
child she carried—his heir—was the prize.

That's when she knew she had to leave. She'd only made it three hours
away, but with every mile she'd driven, his voice roared over the noise of
the freeway.

I'll never let you go, Charlotte. I'll never let you go.

* * * *

The ringing of a phone startled Charlotte awake. A quick glance at the clock on the bedside table said nine o'clock. She'd slept in again.

She swung her legs over the bed and swiped her phone off the bench where she'd left it to charge.

"Meredith?"

"He reported you missing this morning."

"Oh God." Charlotte pressed her hand against her forehead. "What are we going to do?"

"Calm down. We knew this would happen."

She was right. They'd prepared for the inevitability that Corbin would go to the police. But now that he had, she was panicking. "How do you know for sure?"

"I have people at SFPD," Meredith said. "He claims you're unstable, that you suffer from depression and that he's worried about the baby."

"Oh God," she repeated.

"He'll want to be careful, Charlotte. Getting the police too involved could backfire on him."

True, Corbin's father wouldn't like the attention. But no way would he let her disappear. "What if we got word to him that I'd miscarried... threaten him with what happened?" In her heart, though, she knew it wouldn't stop him from coming.

I'll never let you go.

There was silence on the other end of the phone and Charlotte could practically read Meredith's thoughts. *He'll kill you.*

"He won't believe you," she finally said. "And if he does, we both know that abusers need to be in control. He'll blame the miscarriage on you, turn it into something you did to spite him, and want to punish you for it. That's the way they work, Charlotte."

Charlotte squeezed her eyes closed. This was never going to end. "Will the police send my picture out?"

"We're trying to keep that from happening. It's not illegal for an adult to voluntarily disappear. We just have to make sure the right people at SFPD understand that you're sane and don't want to be found. We deal with this every day, Charlotte. There are good people in the department, good people who work with us."

"Meredith, do you understand how connected he is, who his father is?"

"I do. It's just one more hurdle we have to overcome, but it's not insurmountable." She paused. "I need you to listen to me, okay? You've come this far, don't get cold feet now." Meredith waited for Charlotte to respond and when she didn't, said, "Charlotte, do you hear me?"

"Yes." Charlotte sank into the bed again. The smell of bacon wafted under her door and she could hear the sounds of a household waking up. "I'm not getting cold feet." But she was terrified.

"Good," Meredith said. "How much do you trust this sheriff you're staying with?"

"I don't know." How could she, she barely knew him. "He seems trustworthy, but so did Corbin. Did you find out anything about him?"

"Only what you know. He's sheriff of Mill County, a small area of roughly fourteen thousand people wedged between Placer and Nevada Counties."

"And he's a father of two young boys," Charlotte added, because based on the way Jace was with his sons, she had to believe he was a good man. "Why?"

Meredith exhaled. "Because I need you to stay there a little while longer. Just until we see where we are with SFPD and I can find you a new gig and a temporary place to live. Unfortunately, you keep blowing opportunities on that front."

Charlotte knew Meredith hadn't meant to sound harsh or unsympathetic. Meredith moved heaven and earth to keep women safe from their abusers, a job that took more fortitude than it did bedside manners. Charlotte got that and thanked the lord she had Meredith on her side. But what she wanted seemed too much to ask. It also defied logic, given that she'd been reported to the police as an unhinged, missing pregnant woman.

"I can't keep imposing on him," Charlotte said. "Besides, wouldn't he have access to the missing person's report? Aren't these things shared statewide?"

"Not necessarily, and when they are, they go into a huge database, not on the back of a milk carton. And yours won't even make it into the database if we can discreetly let SFPD know that you're not a missing person and you're no longer carrying Corbin's child. You're going to have to work with me here, Charlotte. For the moment, it's better for you to stay put until we get this sorted out."

"All right." She knew Meredith was only trying to help, even though asking for what amounted to charity didn't feel right to Charlotte.

"I'll suss out the situation with SFPD and send you an update as soon as I can. I only wish we had someone in your sheriff's department who worked with our network. But we don't." Meredith hung up in that brusque way of hers.

Charlotte continued to sit at the edge of the bed. How the hell had she gotten here? She'd never considered herself a weak woman, a woman susceptible to an abusive partner. Before Corbin she'd never been mistreated, had never suffered from low self-esteem or exhibited any of the other textbook risk factors.

Yet here she was, running.

In the distance, a television went on and Charlotte heard clinking sounds coming from the kitchen. She quickly showered and dressed and made her way to the kitchen, where she found Jace and his sons eating breakfast.

"Morning." Jace got up and placed another setting on the table. "You hungry?"

"I could eat." The kitchen smelled heavenly, like comfort food.

The oven dinged and Jace pulled out a sheet of biscuits that had baked to a golden brown.

"You made those?" she asked, surprised.

He held up a Pillsbury can. "Me and the doughboy."

She smiled. Without even trying, the sheriff could charm. So could Corbin, she reminded herself. Like a snake-oil salesman.

"Sit by me, Mrs. Rogers." Grady waved her over with his cast and pushed out a chair for her with his foot.

"How's the arm?" she asked.

"Itchy but good."

Jace put a basket of the biscuits on the table and began frying up a new package of bacon. "You want eggs?"

"I'll make it." She got up and took over.

He pushed a mug and a container of milk in front of her. She fixed her coffee to taste and sipped, appreciating the jolt of caffeine, despite another night of sound sleep. The ranch was restful. More restful than she was used to.

"You don't work on weekends?" She had no idea what a country sheriff's schedule was like. But she wanted to ask him about staying longer, when the boys weren't around. If he said no, she'd have to come up with something else. Whatever that was.

"I'm mostly on call, unless there's something big going on. Then I go in. You taking off for Colorado soon?"

"I wanted to talk to you about that." She nudged her head at Travis and Grady, who were in deep conversation about who could eat the most biscuits. "Should we wait until after breakfast?"

He raised his brows in question. "Okay."

"Does anyone else want eggs?" she asked, averting eye contact with him.

"The boys already ate." Jace plucked strips of bacon from the fry pan and drained them on a napkin-covered plate.

"That isn't all for me is it?"

Jace shrugged. "It won't go to waste."

He was in jeans today. They were more faded and worn than the pair from the other day. And his shirt was a blue, long-sleeved pullover that matched his eyes and stretched across his chest, emphasizing his build.

A man that size—that strong—should have made her nervous. Yet, he didn't scare her at all.

They sat at the table and she ate while Grady gave a detailed story about a boy at school who ate bugs. Ants. Flies. Even stinkbugs. Charlotte had no idea what a stinkbug was, but got the general gist that it wasn't something you'd want to eat, based on Travis's gagging noises.

"Hey"—Jace put a firm hand on Grady's shoulder—"how 'bout we not talk about this while Mrs. Rogers is eating?"

The conversation hadn't affected her appetite in the least. For the first time in months, she was starved. Even pregnant, she'd mostly eaten to nourish her baby. "I ate crickets once."

Both boys swiveled around in their chairs with eyes big as saucers.

"You did?" Grady looked absolutely delighted by this revelation. "Did you like it?"

"Uh, I didn't dislike it. For the most part I remember it being crunchy and salty."

"Why'd you eat it?" Travis asked. "Was it like a dare?"

"Nope. I was in Thailand on a buying trip for my store. It's pretty common snack food there. They eat fried crickets like we eat potato chips." It was one of the best trips she'd ever been on. Just her and her sister, Allison, exploring the beauty of Southeast Asia.

Allison. Oh, how she missed her sister.

"Seriously?" Travis seemed truly impressed. "Can you buy them on the internet?"

"I'm sure you can," she said.

"How long ago did you go to Thailand?" Jace asked.

"Two years ago." Her shop had just been chosen by *San Francisco Magazine* as the best home goods store in the Bay Area.

"Two years ago? Didn't you say you sold it ten years ago?"

She blanched, instantly realizing her mistake. "I sold that store, this was a different one." Of course he'd see right through the lie, but she'd boxed herself in.

He had the decency to let it go. That was the thing about Jace, he appeared to be quite decent. And here she was taking advantage, lying to a man who only seemed to want to help her. But the rules were the rules: no social media, no contact with her family, no confiding in anyone.

Even cops.

She finished eating breakfast and cleared the dishes, hiding behind the busywork from Jace's watchful gaze. But then the boys ran off and it was just them, alone.

"What did you want to talk about?" he asked.

Asking for things, for favors, and especially help, had never been easy for her. Charlotte had always thought of herself as an independent woman who would rather work out life's trials on her own. That's why she still didn't understand how she'd let Corbin in so deep that he'd succeeded in completely controlling her. With his constant belittling, her courage had taken a hit and now she was forced by her awful circumstances to beg a near-stranger to let her hide in his home for another day or so. And she had nothing to give in return other than money. But he'd rejected it the first time she'd offered to pay for a room.

Perhaps she had something else to give. And without stopping to weigh the complications, she blurted out, "Hire me. I can take care of the boys for a week, giving you time to find someone permanent, in exchange for room and board."

A week?

She didn't have a week. But anything shorter would've been a transparent plea for help, and she needed to feel in control again. She needed to feel like she had worth, instead of being dependent on others to save her from this wretched mess she'd gotten herself into.

He came over and stood by the sink, where he gave her a hard look. The one thing she knew with certainty about Jace Dalton was that he wasn't a fool. His instincts about her had been spot-on so far. And he evidently had a good memory.

Didn't you say you sold your store ten years ago?

No, he wasn't a man to be played. Not that she wanted to dupe him. She liked his boys and everything about this ranch. It would be no hardship for her to stay for a week, though Meredith would likely say otherwise.

"I thought you had people waiting for you in Colorado." He folded his arms over his chest.

"The situation has changed and I find myself with a free week on my hands." It was a partial truth. "And it seems to me you could use a little help around here." She glanced at the pile of breakfast dishes in the sink and remembered the clutter in the great room where the boys left everything from an old banana peel to a mound of video games on the coffee table.

"I could," he acknowledged, then stood back for a second, eyeing her. "You need a place to stay, Charlie?"

He'd seen right through her proposal. Even so, he was considering it. She could see it plainly in his wavering smile. It was no secret he was desperate for childcare.

She nodded, unable to keep up the charade and knowing it was futile anyway. "It would be a win-win for both of us."

"Would it?" He scrubbed his hand through his dark hair. "I don't know who or what you're running from, Charlie. Can you guarantee it won't touch my family?"

Yes, Corbin had too much to lose, including his father's money and backing. Besides, he was a coward at heart, turning his tongue-lashings and fists on defenseless women behind closed doors. He'd never cross someone like Jace Dalton. Corbin was more likely to buddy up to him so he could persuade him that Charlotte was a nutjob.

"It won't touch your family." She was the only one at risk.

"I'll have to think about it," he said. "Can you wait until this afternoon?"

She nodded because what choice did she have?

Chapter 6

Grady came into the kitchen, turning Jace's attention away from Charlie. "Can I go over to Uncle Cash's and show Ellie my cast?"

"Sure," Jace said. "You should call first, though."

Grady grabbed the landline while he raced around the mudroom. The kid couldn't stand still even for a second. Jace could hear him telling someone the entire story of his accident. Cash. Aubrey. Jace couldn't tell who Grady was talking to. Honestly, he was distracted by Charlie.

She finished the dishes in the sink and was tidying up the kitchen in a pair of slim black pants and a red turtleneck. He wasn't an authority on fashion—far from it—but her clothes looked expensive. Tailored to her petite figure and made from the kind of quality fabric you'd find in the high-end department stores Mary Ann used to drag him through when they were married.

It didn't take a crack detective to figure out that Charlie Rogers had fled money. Everything from her new car to her trip to Thailand spoke of privilege. Yet, she wasn't above getting her hands dirty—pitching in on KP or fixing food at mealtimes.

When Grady had taken his tumble, she'd been the one to rush him to the hospital and stay by his bedside. The boys appeared to like her, though that wouldn't stop them from running her ragged. And she seemed reliable and above all, responsible, despite her reticence to talk about her past.

Still, until he knew more about her situation, would he be putting his sons at risk?

"Dad, Uncle Cash says I can come over." Grady hung up the phone.

"Okay, but put on real shoes, not those slippers. Where's Travis?"

"He's talking to a girl on his phone."

A girl? When the hell had that happened?

From the side of his eye he caught Charlie's lips curve up. She folded the towel she'd been using and left the kitchen. He presumed she was returning to her room.

"When you get back from Uncle Cash's, I thought we'd go to town and have lunch at the coffee shop." He had to pick up his new campaign signs from Tiffany's house and wanted to hit Tractor Supply for a few watering troughs. The old ones were rusted.

"Okay. Can Mrs. Rogers come?"

"Sure, if she wants to come." It wasn't as if he planned to kick her out today. Or even tomorrow, for that matter. But letting her watch his kids... he didn't know how prudent that was.

"What about Uncle Sawyer? Can he come too?"

"Uncle Sawyer went to New York. I don't think he'll be home for a few days."

"How about Ellie, then?"

"If Ellie wants to come, she's welcome to join us." Grady would include all of Dry Creek if Jace let him. The kid liked to collect people and keep them close, which Jace assumed had something to do with Grady losing his mother when he was five. "But, Grade, we're good with just the three of us, right?"

"Yup." Grady tugged on a pair of boots from the mudroom. "See ya." He flew out of the door so fast that Jace hadn't had time to tell him what time to come home.

He shook his head and went in search of his eldest, who sure enough was lying on his bed, talking on his phone. Travis abruptly hung up as soon as Jace popped his head inside the bedroom.

"Who was that?" he asked.

"No one." Travis swung his legs onto the floor and quickly stashed the phone in his nightstand.

Jace raised a brow. "No one, huh? It sounded like someone to me." He rubbed his chin. "Do we need to have a man-to-man?"

Travis rolled his eyes. "No. Don't be weird, okay."

Jace chuckled and sat on the edge of the bed. Travis's room reminded Jace of the year he'd wrangled at a dude ranch in Wyoming, where he'd slept in a bunkhouse with a dozen ripe cowboys. Who knew one fourteen-year-old's room could rival the smell?

"Nothing weird about girls," Jace said. "Anyone I know?" He knew pretty much the whole damned town. And if he didn't know this young lady in particular, good chance he knew her parents.

Travis hitched his shoulders. "Tina Kline."

"Tina Kline with the sorrel mare who came in first place in last year's barrel racing competition at the Dry Creek Junior Rodeo?"

"Yeah. Now don't go saying anything to her."

Jace threw his hands up in the air. "Now would I do something like that?"

"Yes. We're just friends, Dad."

"Friends are good." Jace prayed it wasn't the kind of friendship where benefits were involved. He'd had a couple of those himself and they didn't tend to end well, especially for a fourteen-year-old with raging hormones. "Let's keep it that way for a few more years, okay, Trav?" He maintained eye contact with Travis to make sure he understood without embarrassing him.

"Yes, sir."

"Good." When had Travis gone from being a tyke to a young man? As much as he missed that little boy who used to follow him around the barn, he sure admired the young adult Travis had become. "On to other business, then. You've got to clean this room, kiddo." Jace got up. "It reeks and looks like your laundry basket blew up. After you've made a good dent, we're going to town for chicken and waffles. So giddyup."

Jace hiked the quarter mile to the horse barn. Tomorrow, he planned to move some of the herd to one of the back pastures where the grass had grown thick and tall from the rain. They were having a wet year, which Jace never took for granted. Here in the foothills—the entire state of California, for that matter—it could go from waterlogged to parched in the swish of a horse's tail.

He gazed out over the horizon. He loved these five hundred acres as much as he'd loved his grandfather. Nothing but fields and hills and trees and sky for as far as the eye could see.

He could hear the creek in the not-so-far distance. In summertime, he and his cousins had fished and swum until their lips turned blue. Now, his boys and Cash's daughter, Ellie, did the same.

This was and always would be home. He just had to figure out a way to pay for it.

Just as he got to the barn his phone rang. He checked caller ID and picked up. "You want me to get Grady out of your hair?"

"Nah." Cash laughed. "He's entertaining us with stories about his ER visit. Where are you?"

"At the horses."

"I'll meet you there in five."

Cash probably had a cattle-rustling case he wanted to kick around with Jace. When Jace had a law enforcement conundrum, he did the same with Cash.

He draped his arms over the corral gate and let out a loud whistle. Amigo's ears perked up and the gelding crossed the pasture to hang his head over the fence so Jace could scratch his nape. The horse nickered and nudged his nose against Jace's pocket.

"I don't have anything for you today, boy. Tomorrow." He patted Amigo's neck.

A flock of birds burst from the trees and Jace turned to see Cash coming down the hill. His cabin was the same distance to the barn as the ranch house. Jace pulled down the brim of his Stetson to keep the sun out of his eyes and searched his pocket for his Ray-Bans, only to come up empty-handed.

"Morning," Cash said, and joined Jace at the fence.

Jace checked his watch. "Not anymore."

"Guess not." He grinned, looking like a man in love.

"You oversleep?" Jace ribbed.

"Something like that." Cash rubbed Amigo's forehead. "I hear Jacob Jolly hired a campaign manager out of Sacramento."

This wasn't news to Jace. His opponent had a big war chest. According to rumor, a lot of the local pot farmers were making big contributions to Jolly's campaign. Pot was legal in California and Jace didn't have anything against farmers. What he did have a problem with was taking money from big business of any kind. And pot farming was a huge business.

"I heard," he said. "Is that what you wanted to talk about?"

"Nope, just wanted to make sure it was on your radar. I wanted to talk about this Rogers woman. Grady says she was the one who drove him to the hospital. I hadn't realized she was still here. You said she was leaving."

"Plan changed." Jace toed a dirt clod with the tip of his boot.

"Why's that?"

"She was on her way out when Grady fell off the fence. By the time we left the hospital it was late. I told her to stay another night."

Cash pinned him with a look. "You think that's a good idea?"

Probably not. "She took care of my kid. What was I supposed to do, say, 'Good luck driving these roads in the dark'?"

Cash pushed off the fence and continued to stare him down. "What's going on, Jace?" His cousin knew him better than anyone.

Jace let out a breath, watching it evaporate in the cold. "I don't know. I guess I feel sorry for her."

"Is that it? You're letting a stranger stay in your house because of pity?"

"Yeah…no…ah hell, I don't know." He felt drawn to her, which was crazy because he knew nothing about her. She was married, for God's sake. "You ever think Angie might be out there somewhere in trouble? I hope to hell someone's taking care of her."

Jace waited for Cash to let that sink in. They all loved Angie and had felt helpless when she'd gone missing. If he could save someone else… "She wants to stay another week."

Cash didn't say anything at first, and Jace could feel his cousin's judgment as sharp as a spur.

"Look," Cash finally said, "I'm not telling you to throw her out into the cold. Just be wary. Just be a goddamn cop."

Jace tried to summon enough anger to tell Cash he was a sanctimonious sumbitch. *Be a cop.* As if he needed his cousin's unsolicited advice. But he was honest enough with himself to know that Cash was 100 percent right. That if the boot were on the other foot, Jace would be telling his cousin the same thing.

He didn't respond, letting the silence stretch between them while they stared out over the land. Somewhere in the distance a cow bellowed, and Amigo's ears twitched. The chill bit through Jace's jacket and he shoved his hands in his pockets to keep them warm.

"Aubrey and Ellie have a nice trip to the city?" Jace asked just to break the stalemate.

"Yep. They stayed with my folks and managed to bring back an entire department store, even though we're already bursting at the seams in that cabin. Aubrey's partner has offered to draw up plans for a house, but I want to wait until we figure out this property tax business with the ranch."

Jace knew they had to get this done. "When does Sawyer get home?"

"Next week sometime."

"Let's talk about it then. I've got to get to town, pick up some campaign signs from Tiffany." Jace started to walk away.

"Are you planning to let her stay?"

Jace kept walking. "I don't know yet."

By the time he got home, Travis had dumped a mound of laundry on the mudroom floor. The washing machine and dryer were both going and he found Charlie folding towels and linens at the counter.

"You don't have to do that," he said, taking off his hat and maneuvering around the piles of clothes to hang it on one of the rows of hooks on the wall. He used the bootjack to pry his boots off. It was a time-honored tradition. No dirty boots on Grandma Dalton's shiny floors.

"I actually find it relaxing." Charlie folded a sheet into a tidy square.

He'd never been able to do that, at least not with the fitted ones. The elastic edges always got in the way.

"I've got to go into town. On Saturdays the boys and I sometimes have lunch at the coffee shop there. The owner…Jimmy Ray…is famous for his chicken and waffles. You interested in coming along?"

A look of pure panic streaked across her face.

"Charlie, is there a problem?"

"No. I just don't know if I'm ready to be around people yet."

Jace's bullshit meter instantly went off. She'd been around him, his kids, the hospital, without showing any real signs of distress. Sadness for the baby she'd lost, sure. But what he'd just witnessed a second ago was fear, not grief.

"You ever been to Dry Creek?" Maybe he was missing something here.

"I don't think so. Where is it exactly?"

"It's off 49, past Auburn. We turned off for the ranch the night I drove you here, otherwise we would've driven straight through the middle. It's a small town. Not more than a coffee shop, a grocery store, a post office, city hall, a Greyhound bus station, and a couple of schools. Blink your eye and you'd miss it." Whatever she was running from wouldn't find her there.

And if it did, it would have to get through him.

"I guess I could come," she said, hesitant.

"Let me gather up the herd. In the meantime, you can leave the rest of that for me." He gestured at the basket of clean laundry. He'd gotten behind with the wash since Mrs. Jamison had left.

"It's no big deal," she said. "And the least I can do. Look, I didn't mean to put you on the spot before. If you're opposed to me staying another week, I totally understand. I would be just as cautious if I were you."

He leaned against the laundry counter and met her gaze. "I just need the day to mull it over. It would help if I knew what your situation is, though." He was starting to sound like a broken record. But it was her secret to tell and she obviously had her reasons for holding out on him.

She nodded but, as suspected, didn't offer any new information. "Thanks for your consideration."

He went to check on Travis and called Cash's cabin to let Grady know he'd pick him up on the way to town. They made it out of the house in a record ten minutes. Travis climbed in the back of the king cab and Jace signaled for Charlie to take the front passenger seat. She'd put on a woolen hat and a pair of sunglasses. If she thought it was a good disguise, she was wrong. The beanie did nothing to hide all her silky brown hair. And the shades only emphasized her heart-shaped face.

When he reached Cash and Aubrey's he tooted his horn and Grady came running outside with Ellie.

Jace unrolled his window. "You coming with us, El?"

"No. We're going to look at a horse today." Ellie came up to the driver's window and leaned in to wave to Travis and her gaze fell on Charlie.

"This is Mrs. Rogers." He tweaked Ellie's nose and she and Charlie exchanged hellos.

"What kind of horse?" Jace asked. Ellie and Cash had been looking for a fancy show horse for more than a month, so Ellie could ride dressage. The quarter horses on the ranch were for cutting cattle, not contests. He'd been teasing her about it for weeks.

"You know what kind, Uncle Jace." She rolled her eyes.

"Where is this horse you're looking at?"

"Nevada City. Dad knows the people."

"Well, good luck. Make sure you tell her Amigo's the head honcho in the stable." He gave her another tweak.

Cash's daughter had only come to live with them on the ranch last summer when her mother had died of breast cancer. It had been rocky at the start, but Ellie had fallen in love with the Daltons as much as they'd fallen in love with her.

"I will." She stood next to the front porch, waving, as they drove away.

"Aunt Aubrey said Travis and me can be in the wedding," Grady said, and continued to talk their ears off all the way to Tiffany's house.

"I'll just be a few minutes." Jace hopped down from the cab. "As soon as I load up the campaign signs, we can go eat."

Tiffany's house was on one of the most prestigious streets in Dry Creek, which wasn't saying all that much. But the homes on Deer Lane were what Jace called mini mansions, with a lot of slick landscaping, swimming pools, and three-car garages. Most of them were built by Mitch, who lived a few doors down from Tiffany.

Tiffany's garage door lifted and she came out onto the driveway wearing half of Fort Knox around her neck. Her jewelry was kind of legendary in Dry Creek. Gold chains as thick as lassos, pendants as big as Jace's fist, and earrings the size of the chandeliers at the ranch house. Her husband was loaded.

He used to own an insurance agency near Sacramento, sold it for a bundle, and they'd decided to retire to the country. Tiffany whiled away the time doing volunteer work. For some reason she'd taken a shine to Jace and had appointed herself his campaign manager.

"You brought the whole family." She blew air kisses at the boys, who lowered their eyes, pretending to find something inordinately interesting on the back-seat floor. When her gaze landed on Charlie, her eyes widened. "Aren't you going to introduce us, Sheriff?"

Jace walked Tiff to the passenger door and Charlie lowered her window. He introduced the two, and after sensing Charlie's discomfort managed to lure Tiffany away with campaign talk. Her sole experience in politics was running one successful campaign for an obscure candidate's bid for the state legislature. Now, she thought she should have her own political talk show.

But she was a hard worker and even better, her services were free. Because unlike his opponent, Jace didn't have deep campaign coffers. Most donations came in as fungible goods. Homemade muffins from the Mill County Cattlewomen for a campaign rally, wine from a local vintner for a meet and greet, and once, Bobby Briggs lent them his Santa Maria open-pit adjustable barbecue for a tri-tip fundraiser. Jace had provided the beef.

They'd managed to raise a whopping $865.82.

Tiffany put her hand on his arm and pulled him farther from his truck and out of earshot of the others. "The polls aren't looking too good."

"What polls?" The primary wasn't until June and no one did political surveys in Mill County. Jace didn't know why because it would be real easy. Pollsters could call every household in Mill County in less than three hours.

"I've been conducting my own and …" She stretched her bottom lip wide, leaving a smudge of red lipstick on her two front teeth. "Not good. Those shenanigans last summer left a bad taste in voters' mouths."

"Shenanigans? Are you talking about that bullsh…nonsense with Aubrey and Mitch?" Aubrey and Mitch's breakup had been as explosive as the Fourth of July and the rumor mill had put Jace square in the middle. By now, he would've thought the good folks of Mill County were over it. "You telling me that people still believe I stole Aubrey from Mitch? Give me a damn break. She's marrying my cousin, for God's sake."

"Don't shoot the messenger." Tiffany put her hands on her hips. "I warned this would come back to haunt you."

"What?" he raised his voice. "I didn't do anything wrong." It was Mitch and Jill who'd been screwing around.

"Of course you didn't," she said in a voice that sounded a lot like recrimination to Jace. *Of course you didn't.* "But people believe what they want to."

It was absurd.

"Exactly what kind of poll did you conduct?"

"Okay, maybe it's not what you would call the true definition of a poll, but I've been taking the pulse of the county." Whatever the hell that meant. "And there's mixed feelings about you. Sally Reynolds has never forgiven you for her son's breakup with Aubrey and has made it her business to bad-mouth you all over town. And Jacob Jolly is popular around here. Everyone loves Jolly Hardware."

Yeah, especially the pot farmers.

"First of all, I didn't break up Mitch and Aubrey. I didn't have a damn thing to do with it, though I'm glad she dumped his ass. Sally should thank her lucky stars her son's not doing five years hard time in a state prison, instead of harping on his failed engagement. As for Jolly, he has zero experience in law enforcement, unless you count the year he dressed up as McGruff at the Halloween festival at the Mill County Fairgrounds."

"Jace, as your campaign manager it's my duty to give you the facts, whether you like them or not. We've got to ramp up our campaign, schedule more engagements, maybe get you on *This Week in Northern California*."

Jace had never heard of it, but was pretty damn sure whatever it was wasn't interested in the Mill County Sheriff's race.

"You're probably the hottest sheriff in America," Tiffany said. "I shouldn't have any trouble getting you oodles of television exposure."

Jace looked up at the sky, holding on to his patience. "Tiff, no television appearances. Let's just run a good, honest campaign. Okay?" He didn't wait for her to answer. "I'm going to load up the signs now and then feed my kids."

"Fine." She folded her arms across her chest. "It's your political funeral, not mine."

She led him inside the garage, where he grabbed a stack of placards. Before he could walk them back to the truck, she cornered him.

"Who's the woman?"

"Charlie?" He wasn't about to get into details. "A friend."

"What kind of friend? I've never seen her around here. Does she live in the county?"

"She's just passing through, Tiffany."

"Are you sure? I might be able to work with that." She bobbed her chin in the direction of Charlie. "I couldn't help but notice that she's quite attractive, though it was difficult to tell for sure with those sunglasses on. If you two were, say, about to get engaged, that could erase the whole Aubrey issue."

"There is no Aubrey issue, Tiff. And I'm not about to get engaged. So you can put that idea out of your mind like, say, yesterday. Gotta go."

He quickly stashed the signs in his pickup storage box and backed out of the driveway as fast as he could.

"Jeez, Dad, it took you forever," Grady whined. "I'm so starved I could eat two orders of chicken and waffles, plus two mud pies."

Jace's lips quirked. The kid had eyes bigger than his stomach. "We'll see how you feel after your first order."

"Was there a problem?" Charlie asked.

"Nah. Tiffany likes to talk."

He took a shortcut through the residential part of Dry Creek to Mother Lode Road, slipped into a parking space in front of the coffee shop, and cut the engine. The restaurant had been a mainstay of Dry Creek since his grandfather was a boy. Sometime in the '80s, Jimmy Ray and his wife, Laney, took it over. They were getting on in years but nothing seemed to slow them down, though the restaurant could use a fresh coat of paint and the grease-stained pictures of cattle on the walls needed to be put out to pasture.

Still, the old-style diner was Jace's home away from home. It's where he and his grandfather had Saturday lunches at the counter together for nearly thirty years. It's where he'd continued the tradition with his own sons. Same for celebrations. Junior rodeo and high school football game victories. And gatherings with the local cattlemen to discuss the price of beef.

Jimmy Ray's restaurant, which as far back as Jace could remember was simply called the "coffee shop," was the epicenter of life in Dry Creek.

Laney was at the cash register, ringing up a customer, when they came in. Jace greeted her with a wave and hung his cowboy hat on the coatrack. He pointed to an empty booth in the far corner and she nodded, letting him know it was okay for them to sit there.

Charlie glanced around the dining room. Jace couldn't tell if she was turning up her nose at the restaurant or was merely curious. She hadn't struck him as a snob, but based on her wardrobe and the fact that she'd owned a fancy store made him think she was used to restaurants with white tablecloths that didn't serve truck-stop food.

"It doesn't look like much, but my cousin Sawyer, who's a total foodie, eats here nearly every day," he told her as they squeezed around the booth. The boys took one side, leaving Jace to share the other bench with Charlie.

"It certainly smells good." She ogled the baked goods in the case, sounding genuine, then studied the menu.

"I'm getting chicken and waffles, a side of fries, and an Oreo milkshake," Grady announced, going up on his knees to get the attention of a boy from his class who was sitting with his parents across the room.

"Hey, buddy, sit down. You're not at home, okay? You can talk to your friend later."

Grady flopped down on his butt, practically landing in Travis's lap. Travis pushed him and Grady started to sock his brother back when Jace reached across the table and grabbed his fist.

"Behave or we're going back to the ranch," he said in a low, menacing voice reserved for handling tough situations while on patrol. Flipping on the badass usually—not always—worked on the boys too.

Charlie shrunk back and everyone got quiet.

He put his hand on her leg the way he would with a spooked horse, then quickly realized he shouldn't be touching her and pulled it away.

"We Daltons are loud, but it's all bark, no bite," he said apologetically. A man in his position couldn't afford to be too soft or too sensitive. Still, he didn't like to see her scared. Not of him.

She pretended she didn't know what he was talking about, a serene smile affixed to her face, replacing the abject fear he'd seen only a few seconds ago. "I can't decide between the chicken and waffles and the chicken fried steak."

The boys shouted, "Chicken and waffles!"

"They're both good," he said, tempted to brush a stray strand of hair back under her hat.

Her cheeks were rosy from the cold and she'd taken off her sunglasses. Two ranchers sitting at a table across from them had checked her out as they'd come in. Jace wasn't sure if it was because Charlie was nice to look at or if they were curious. Other than Aubrey, he hadn't been seen with a woman at the coffee shop in recent history.

"Since Travis and Grady like the chicken and waffles so much, I'll go with that." She closed her menu.

Laney came over to take their orders and wasn't subtle about her interest in Charlie, giving her, then Jace, a thorough examination. He could've sworn he heard her hum approval. Great, between Laney and Tiffany the whole town would have him engaged by tomorrow.

"Where's your manners, boy?" Laney slapped Jace on the head with her order pad.

His reflexes kicked in and he moved before she could smack him again. "Charlie, this is Laney. She and her husband, Jimmy Ray, have owned and operated the coffee shop since dinosaurs roamed the earth."

She pretended to take another swing at him, winking at the boys. "Pleased to meet you, Charlie. Where you from? I haven't seen you around here before."

"I'm just passing through on my way to Colorado."

Laney didn't miss the way Charlie had sidestepped the question and wasn't about to let it go. Jace could see her getting her interrogator on and jumped in before she put Charlie under the hot lights.

"Hey, Laney, you think we can get something to eat before my kids starve to death?"

"They don't look like they're starving to me." She rested her hands on her hips. "What can I get you hooligans?"

There was a chorus of "chicken and waffles." Grady also asked for French fries and a shake.

Laney shook her head, then her eyes lit on his cast. She'd missed it when they'd first walked in, focusing instead on Charlie. "Little man, you could eat the north end of a southbound polecat. Now what on earth happened to your arm?"

"I broke it." Grady told her the story of how he fell from the fence, adding sound effects for color. Then he segued back to lunch. "Want to bet me ten bucks I can eat it all?"

She put her hands back on her hips. "You're on. I'll bet you a slice of my chess pie."

"Yes!" Grady stood on the seat and waved his cast in the air.

Charlie laughed. For a moment, the sadness was gone. And Jace got a little lost in her deep brown eyes. Maybe spellbound was more like it.

Laney cleared her throat—she wanted the rest of their drink orders—and Jace was forced back to earth.

And that's when he knew he'd let her stay the week.

At the back of his mind there was Angela. But even if his cousin had never gone missing, Jace didn't have the stomach to throw out a woman in trouble. It wasn't in the Dalton DNA, or the cowboy creed, or the reason he'd gone into law enforcement.

But he'd keep his eyes on her. And that right there was the problem, because from the moment she'd arrived in his life he hadn't been able to take his eyes off her.

Chapter 7

On Monday, Charlotte woke up bright and early. Jace had given her a week's reprieve from running, and she planned to earn her keep. After a quick shower, she dressed, put up her hair, and even applied a little makeup before going downstairs.

By the time Jace came into the kitchen, she had the table set, the bacon sizzling, and a bowl of pancake batter waiting.

"You're up early." He poured himself a cup of coffee.

"Ready for some breakfast?"

He noticed the griddle and the maple syrup out on the counter. "Pancakes and bacon, huh? That's Sunday morning food."

She couldn't tell whether he was pleased or being critical. Yesterday was Sunday, and they'd had eggs and sausage.

"Would you prefer something else?" She started to cover the batter bowl with cellophane.

"Hell no." He grinned and she felt something in the pit of her stomach stir. Relief, she told herself. Relief that he wasn't angry. "I love pancakes. I just never have time to make them on weekdays."

"Well, you don't have to worry about it now. I've got you covered." She turned the flame up under the griddle. "What would you like me to do while the boys are at school?"

"Some laundry would be good, but for the most part the time is yours. They need to be picked up at three and Travis needs to be run over to a junior rodeo meeting. He can show you where it is. Grady has to do his homework before TV, video games, or anything else. He'll try to tell you otherwise. Stand tough or he'll run roughshod over you.

"And, Charlie, the job comes with a salary, not just room and board."

"No salary. I mean it. I'm just happy to be here." And she was. A week without running.

She poured four large dollops of batter onto the pan and waited for the pancakes to form tiny bubbles before flipping them over.

Jace walked down the hallway and yelled to the boys, "Rattle your hocks."

What an odd expression. Charlotte assumed it meant that the boys should hurry up. It was getting late.

"Your pancakes are ready." She stacked them on a plate and served him at the table.

He called one more time to the boys and tucked into his food. She stood by the range top, watching him out of the corner of her eye. He buttered the front and back of each pancake with great efficiency, then doused the stack with syrup.

"Mm, these are great," he said around a bite, cutting another with the side of his fork, eschewing the knife.

She liked watching him eat. Heartily and without self-consciousness.

"Oh, I forgot the bacon." She quickly plucked a few strips from the pan onto a plate she'd lined with a paper towel and served him the pieces.

"Thank you," he said. "Aren't you going to sit down and eat too?"

"As soon as I feed the boys."

On cue, they bustled in, sniping at each other. Jace looked up from his plate, lifted an eyebrow, and they immediately stopped fighting.

"We're having pancakes?" Grady joined Charlotte at the range and sniffed the bowl. "I love pancakes." He did a little dance and wrapped his arms around her waist for a hug.

Travis stole a strip of bacon from the pan. "We're gonna be late."

"And whose fault is that?" Jace motioned for both boys to sit down.

Charlotte made them each a stack of pancakes and brought the rest of the bacon to the table.

"Mrs. Rogers is going to take you to school and pick you up." Jace pinned Travis and Grady with a look. "Be sure to mind her, you hear?"

Both boys nodded. She just prayed that no one broke any more bones on her watch.

Jace finished his breakfast, loaded his plate and mug into the dishwasher, and took off for work. Charlotte, clutching a mug of hot coffee, watched from the window as he climbed into his police vehicle and drove away.

She'd been both surprised and relieved when he said she could stay. Now, she'd have to break the news to Meredith. Charlotte had promised Jace she'd give him seven days of employment and she planned to stick to her word, even if Meredith found her housing and work in another state.

"You guys almost ready?" she asked, glancing at the clock.

"Yeah." Travis brought his plate to the sink. "Can we pick up my friend Ruben on the way?"

Jace hadn't said anything about carpooling. But what harm would it do to shuttle one more kid?

"Sure," she said. "Where does Ruben live?"

"He's on the way. I'll show you."

She noticed Grady got real quiet. Something told her he wasn't too thrilled about Ruben. Perhaps he wanted his big brother all to himself.

"Bundle up, boys." The forecast was predicting temperatures in the forties.

Like his brother, Grady cleaned up after himself and followed Travis into the mudroom, where he collected his backpack. The boys went to different schools and Charlotte had been instructed to drop Travis first at Dry Creek High.

She grabbed her keys and purse and herded the boys out the door. "You ride up front with me, Travis."

He directed her to Ruben's house, which sat at the end of a tree-lined driveway on Dry Creek Road. An attractive woman about Charlotte's age jogged down the porch stairs and came around to the driver's side of Charlotte's CR-V.

"Hi, I'm Kelly. You must be Mrs. Jamison's replacement."

"Yes." Charlotte introduced herself, leaving out the fact she was only a temporary replacement.

So far, it was safe to show her face around town. This morning, she'd checked the internet on her phone to make sure there weren't any missing-person posters of her floating around.

Hopefully, Meredith could prevent the police from putting out anything formal. But it was a free country. Corbin could use social media to spread the word of Charlotte's disappearance, even offer a reward if he wanted to.

If he did, she and Meredith would have to come up with a plan B.

"Where in heavens did Jace find you?" Ruben's mom was all smiles but Charlotte detected a whiff of rivalry coming off the woman like too much perfume. There wasn't a wedding ring on Kelly's finger, so maybe she was a single mom, hoping to snag the equally single Jace Dalton.

Charlotte was certainly no threat; in a week she'd be gone.

"We're friends," Charlotte said. "I'm just visiting and helping Jace out until he finds a permanent situation."

Ruben got in the back seat and Charlotte waved goodbye.

She had barely pulled out onto Dry Creek Road when Grady let out a yelp.

"What's going on?" She glanced in her rearview mirror to find Grady holding his head. "Are you okay?"

"Yeah," he said. But the hesitance in his voice told her otherwise.

She switched her gaze to Ruben and saw an altogether too familiar gleam in his eye. The gleam of a bully who'd just enjoyed taunting his prey. "Would you like to change places with your brother, Grady?"

"That's okay."

She glared at Ruben and said to Grady, "Say the word and we'll pull over."

He hunched his shoulders and for a second she was torn over what to do. Travis and Grady started talking and she decided to leave it alone for now. She managed to find the high school without Travis's help and dropped the two older boys off.

"Come up here with me," she told Grady. "I don't know where the middle school is."

He undid his seat belt and instead of getting out of the car and coming around to the passenger side, he climbed over the seat.

"Careful, Grady."

He fastened himself in and pointed her in the right direction, telling her who lived in every house they passed. The running commentary went on for a few miles.

"Grady," she interrupted, "what's the deal with Ruben?"

"He's a butthead."

"Did he hit you?"

Grady didn't respond at first, then said, "He was just horsing around."

"Do you like it when he horses around or do you let him get away with it because he's your brother's friend? Because you don't have to...and you shouldn't. Travis wouldn't want you to."

"Travis thinks I'm a baby." He fidgeted in his seat.

"Travis is your brother and he wouldn't want anyone to mistreat you." Perhaps if she'd been straight with Allison, she and her sister would be on speaking terms today. "Besides, I don't think you're a baby, nor does your father. So if someone is picking on you, you have to speak up. Okay?"

"Okay." But he didn't sound too convincing.

No, it would be up to her to keep tabs on this Ruben kid while she was here. Grady told her where to turn for the middle school and she joined the line of cars waiting to drop off their kids. For a small town the queue was long.

"You have everything?" she asked as the car ahead of her moved up just enough for Grady to safely get out of her SUV.

"Yep." He opened the door and scurried out, using his one good arm to heft his backpack over his shoulder. "Thanks for the ride, Mrs. Rogers."

"I'll see you here at three."

She turned around and drove through the residential area from which she came, putting off the inevitable task of calling Meredith. She'd do it when she got back to the ranch.

Even though it was the first day of February, some of the modest homes in the neighborhood still had Christmas lights hanging from the eaves. The yards were tidy, though. And Charlotte noticed that nearly every driveway was home to a pickup or two.

She enjoyed looking at the houses, the homemade wreaths that covered the front doors, and the backyards that pushed against acres of open space where cows and goats grazed.

Impulsively, she detoured off the main road onto one of the side streets. She remembered it from the time they went to Jace's campaign manager's house. Up the hill was where the big homes were. *The Pacific Heights of Dry Creek*, she thought and laughed to herself as she took her time climbing up the hillside.

It was lovely, with sweeping views of the mountains and pine trees, and of manicured front lawns and big iron gates. But nothing compared to Jace's ranch.

Yesterday, she'd gone with him and the boys on a short walk on the property. They'd followed the creek to the horse barn and the sights had taken her breath away. The land went on until it seemed to reach the sky, making everything seem minuscule in comparison. And the air...oh the air...she just wanted to gulp it in.

Charlotte had never considered herself a country girl, but she could get used to living in a place with wide-open spaces.

She passed Tiffany's house, recognizing the fountain in the front yard, and ventured farther up the hill. At the top, she took another road that seemed to head out of town. The homes were spaced farther apart and the more she descended, the smaller they got. Some of the houses looked downright dilapidated, with old farm equipment strewn across the property. She passed one with a yard sale sign hanging from an old chain-link fence.

Old habits were hard to shake, and she found herself turning down the driveway to a barn that looked like it was about to topple over. Half the metal roof was gone, and what remained didn't appear watertight. She got out of her CR-V and was greeted by an elderly man. He was stooped over, carrying a bucket, wearing a pair of overalls.

"Hello." She pointed in the direction of the sign. "Are you still having the yard sale?" Charlotte didn't see anything spread out on the lawn, or what passed for a lawn.

The place looked like a rundown farm that had probably been quite nice at one time. There was a series of outbuildings and a large cottage with a big front porch. In the distance, she heard bleating. Goats, sheep, she wasn't sure.

The man didn't say anything but indicated that she should follow him. Charlotte let him take the lead. They went inside the barn, which appeared to be in better shape than she'd originally thought. It had a dirt floor, and animal stalls lined two walls. The middle of the barn was open and stuffed with junk.

"Everything in here has gotta go," he said. "I'll make ya a deal. But you've got to clear it out yourself." The old man put down his bucket and straightened his back to give her a thorough appraisal. He didn't seem too impressed with what he saw. "I don't think that little van of yours will do the trick."

A semitrailer wouldn't do it.

At first glance, she took the piles of debris for a lot of ancient farm equipment. But from the side of her eye she caught something that looked interesting.

"You mind if I explore a little?"

"Knock yourself out." He picked up his bucket again. "I've got to feed the livestock." And with that he disappeared.

Charlotte didn't know where to poke first. There didn't seem to be any organization, just a dump pile of things. Despite the disarray, she couldn't wait to get started. This used to be her drug of choice, scrounging through people's discarded goods, looking for hidden gems or pieces she could repurpose and make shiny and new.

She rolled up her sleeves and got busy, steering clear of the mechanical parts. There was a rusted wheelbarrow that if sanded and repainted barn red would make a gorgeous planter. A couch that was stained and frayed and half the stuffing eaten by critters. But the wooden frame was the way they used to make things in the old days, solid as rock. With new cushions and a custom slipcover, it could be beautiful again. There was a corrugated metal trough that could easily be converted into a garden fountain, and a wagon wheel that was begging to become a chandelier. A rusty iron fence that with a little TLC would make a beautiful headboard for a bed. And a barn door with peeling paint that Charlotte rather liked just the way it was.

Two hours later, she'd started a pile that would take a good-size moving truck to get home. And that was the thing, she didn't have a home. She didn't have a store to sell any of this stuff from, nor a workshop to refurbish any of it.

"You've been busy."

Charlotte had been so caught up in sorting that she hadn't noticed that the farmer had returned.

"I have." She smiled and turned to the pile she'd assembled. "How much do you want for this?"

He sniffled and pulled a handkerchief from his back pocket to wipe his nose. "I'm selling it all, the whole barn full, for a thousand bucks."

"I only have use for what I've collected here." It was a ridiculous assertion because she didn't have a use for any of it. Yet, she couldn't seem to let it go. The couch, the wheelbarrow, the antique nightstand, the rest…it all called to her. The items needed someone to nurture them back to life.

The man scrubbed his hand through his wiry hair and stared at her rag-tag assemblage. "What're you gonna do with it?"

"Make it good again."

He toed the metal trough with his worn boot. "Good again, huh? I don't see it, but I like the spirit of it." He stuck out his hand. "Milt Maitland. And you are?"

"Charlo…Charlie Rogers." She shook his gnarled hand.

"I'll tell you what, Charlie Rogers. You haul it away and it's yours. Free."

Free? She'd never had that happen before. Still, taking it would be crazy. An *I Love Lucy* episode. Not only didn't she have the means to haul it away, but how the hell was she going to take it with her when she left in a week?

"We've got a deal," she heard herself say, despite the utter absurdity of it.

Whatever it took, Charlotte was going to make every single abused and neglected piece in the pile beautiful and useful again.

Chapter 8

Jace had a difficult time keeping his mind on work. Twenty times he'd wanted to pick up the phone and call Charlie to see how her first day on the job was going, to discuss dinner, to tell her where the thermostat was in case she wanted to adjust the heat. And twenty times he put the phone down before punching in her number.

Pretty screwy because he'd never looked for excuses to call Mrs. Jamison.

And make no mistake about it, dinner…the thermostat…were exactly that. Excuses. But Charlie Rogers was a mystery he wanted to unravel, which was a dozen wrongs on so many levels, starting with the fact that he liked having her in his house. And he shouldn't because she wasn't here to stay.

Still, it had been a long time since he'd had a woman to come home to. Someone to talk to about his day, who did fussy things to make the dinner table special.

Yesterday, when they'd all walked to the horse barn together, he'd liked the little sighs of wonder she'd made at every tall tree. How excited she'd gotten when they'd spied a few deer drinking from the creek. The way she'd timidly fed Amigo a slice of apple and laughed when the gelding's lips moved over the palm of her hand.

His boys liked her too. Whether that meant they would refrain from terrorizing her this week, only time would tell.

Annabeth tapped on his door, pulling him from his thoughts.

"Cash is in the lobby."

"Yeah? Send him in." Unlike Sawyer, who never met a closed door he wouldn't walk through, Cash paid attention to small things like protocol.

And gatekeepers like Annabeth. Jace supposed it was a leftover from Cash's regimental FBI days.

Today, though, he looked about as much like an FBI agent as Jace did a banker. A snap-down Western shirt, jeans, boots, and a Stetson.

"The cow-cop job seems to be working well for you." Jace propped his boots up on the desk and leaned back in his chair.

"Turns out it was a good decision." Cash's lips hitched up.

Damn right it was. Jace had helped him get the job with the Bureau of Livestock Identification after his cousin had been senselessly fired by the FBI. Now he rode around in his truck all day, investigating livestock thefts and monitoring cattle sales.

"What's up?"

"Want to go lunch?"

Jace sat up straight in his seat. This was the first time Cash had ever popped in out of the blue for social reasons. "Everything okay?"

"Of course. A guy can't eat?"

Jace got his hat and shearling jacket off the rack. "Coffee shop?"

Cash laughed. "Where else would we go?"

They crossed Main Street to Mother Lode Road, stopping a half dozen times to say hello to various townsfolk. Grandpa Dalton had been bigger than life and his memory still hung large over Dry Creek. Even though Jace was a grown man and the county's top cop, with two sons of his own, in the eyes of the town's residents he was merely Jasper Dalton's grandson.

And that was okay with Jace. Because in his eyes there'd been no finer grandfather than the old cuss. And no finer cowboy.

Laney managed to find them a table amid the packed restaurant. Neither of them required a menu, knowing every dish by heart. They got the weekday special: a steak sandwich with a side of fries and a frosty mug of homemade sarsaparilla, another one of Jimmy Ray's specialties. It didn't hurt that the special was called "the Jasper" after Grandpa Dalton.

Jasper had ordered that same meal for three decades on the days he came to the coffee shop for his cattlemen klatch. Some of the same old codgers were still coming and still eating "the Jasper" special.

"Sawyer home yet?" Jace pulled a paper napkin from the holder and spread it across his lap.

"I think he's getting in sometime today. I noticed that CR-V is still in your driveway."

"Yep."

"I'm going to violate my self-imposed rule and ask: Is there something going on between you and this woman?"

"Nope. Like I said, she's married. And even if the guy's a son-of-a-bitch, which I'm pretty sure he is, I'm a moralist bastard."

"But there's something there?"

Jace let out a wry laugh. "Like what? She's running from something, won't tell me what it is, and has one foot out the door. So no, there's nothing there." He played with a packet of sugar on the table.

Everything he'd said was the truth. What he'd left out was that for the first time since Mary Ann had left, a woman had stirred more than his sex drive. Cash was smart enough to let it go but not stupid enough to believe he'd been wrong. Because there was something definitely there, at least on Jace's part.

Something fruitless.

Laney brought their food and they ate in companionable silence.

"You want to be my best man?" Cash asked, when both of them had eaten their last French fry.

"Hell yeah, but what about Sawyer?"

"Ring bearer." They both laughed. "Him too. Aubrey says it's the new millennium and anything goes."

"Two best men, huh? Works for me. Does that mean we're both responsible for throwing the bachelor party?"

"Aubrey says bachelor parties are out."

"Of course she does." Jace snorted. "Anything to suck the joy out of life."

"Hey, she's your best friend." Cash drained the rest of his sarsaparilla. "Just a barbecue with friends and family would be good. But don't put Sawyer in charge of it. He'll turn it into a production…get Gordon Ramsay to cater it and Keith Richards to play."

Jace chuckled. "Yeah, he's kind of douchey that way."

The lunch crowd began to filter out and Jimmy Ray came out of the kitchen to say hello. He pulled up a chair at their table.

"You two look like trouble. Who was that pretty lady you had with you the other day? Laney thought she was real fine."

"Just a friend," Jace said, trying to quell any rumors, even if it was useless. Folks here liked to talk.

"A friend, huh?" Jimmy Ray poked Cash in the shoulder and winked. "Tiffany says it's more."

Bless Tiffany's lying heart. "Tiffany's wrong. She's a friend, Jimmy Ray, and she's just passing through on her way to Colorado."

"That's too bad." Jimmy Ray shook his head. "It would've taken you off the market. Too many women hanging their hats on getting a blue-eyed Dalton, not leaving any left for the rest of us."

"Last I looked you were married," Jace said.

"Are you kidding me? Laney would throw me over in a big-city minute for one of you fellows."

"Watch out for Sawyer. He's got his eye on her," Cash said. Laney was roughly the same age as their late grandmother.

Jimmy Ray threw his head back and laughed. "I'd pay him to take her off my hands."

The old man was full of shit. Laney and Jimmy Ray might fight like cats and dogs but they'd been together longer than Jace had been alive. When Jimmy Ray had his triple heart-bypass, Laney closed the restaurant and never left his bedside. Ten days she held vigil.

That was love for you.

Cash took care of the bill and they walked back to the sheriff's department together.

"Light day?" Jace grabbed his messages on his way to his office.

"Yep. I'll probably swing by Tractor Supply to get Ellie a saddle blanket."

"You bought that fancy horse?"

Cash nodded. "It was love at first sight. Unfortunately, my wallet isn't feeling the romance."

"The kid deserves some spoiling after what she's been through. Plus, taking care of a horse builds character."

"I've never seen her this excited. She was up before dawn and at the barn by sunrise to fuss over the mare before school."

"The mare have a name?"

"Sunflower."

Jace snorted. "What the hell kind of name is that for a horse?"

"The one the previous owner gave it." Cash checked his watch. "I better get going. I promised we'd go for a ride after Ellie gets out of school. You need anything from Tractor Supply?"

"I'm good. Enjoy your ride. I'll be down at the barn later to check out this Sunflower."

After Cash left, Jace settled in to catch up on paperwork but found his mind straying to Charlie again. Pretty soon, she'd be picking up the boys and ferrying Travis to his meeting. He started to pick up the phone and just as quickly put it down. She didn't need him micromanaging her.

Instead, he started nosing around on the internet, more than likely a worthless endeavor. If Charlie had given him a fake name, which he was pretty sure she had, there wouldn't be anything to find. So he focused on the Rosie the Riveter Foundation. The nonprofit maintained a low profile in cyberspace. Jace couldn't find any news stories on the place, nor much of anything else. The website was also short on information. There was a photo gallery of women at various jobs with testimonials about how the foundation helped them find work. But something about the pictures, the stilted smiles and the uniform settings, made Jace think they were staged.

He called the phone number on the homepage and got a recording. *"Thanks for calling. Please leave a message and someone will get back to you shortly."*

Sawyer had probably been right about the foundation being a front for an organization that helped women disappear. Why else would Charlie's car registration come back to the address, unless they were helping her maintain anonymity?

He called up the National Missing and Unidentified Persons System on his computer. But without having a real name or knowing whether Charlie had even been reported missing was a lot like searching for a stray calf in a wildfire. About 600,000 people went missing a year. He'd learned the significance of that staggering number when they'd first started searching for Angie. So to simply peruse photos would take weeks, even months.

Fed up, he went back to his paperwork. Ten minutes into it, he picked up the phone. Jace had a friend at San Francisco PD. They'd gone through the academy together in Roseville. After a year on the force, Chris got a job in San Francisco, where his girlfriend was going to dental school. Last year, he'd made sergeant and was working property crimes.

It was a long shot but worth a try.

"Hey, long time, no see," Chris answered, obviously recognizing Jace's number. "You still sheriff up there?"

"For now. How's life in the city?"

"Good. Just bought a place in the East Bay. How 'bout you? How's that big ole ranch of yours?"

"A handful but I wouldn't trade it for the world. You got a couple of minutes for me to pick your brain?"

"Of course I do. What's up?"

"You ever hear of a nonprofit called the Rosie the Riveter Foundation? It's on South Van Ness, I think in the Mission District."

"It's not ringing a bell. Why, is it in trouble?"

"No. It claims to help disadvantaged women find jobs…get them back on their feet. But rumor has it that it's one of those underground organizations that assist women in escaping abusive relationships. I've got a situation here where something like that might be useful." Out of respect for Charlie's privacy, he didn't want to give too much away.

"You try calling over there and introducing yourself?"

"No answer. But I figure they might be leery of someone they don't know, even someone in law enforcement." Or especially someone in law enforcement. These kinds of groups liked to fly under the radar.

"You want me to do some asking around?" Chris said.

"I'd owe you one."

"A weekend fishing at that ranch of yours should do it."

"You've got it." Jace would welcome a visit with his old friend.

"You ever hear from Mary Ann?" Chris asked.

Jace took a long pause. "Last I heard she was still living in France with that dude she met in Costa Rica."

"That sucks, man."

For the boys, yeah it sucked. "It is what it is."

"You seeing anyone? Diane's got a lot of single friends."

Jace laughed. "Maybe after that weekend fishing I'll come to San Francisco, see your new place and meet some of Diane's friends." It wouldn't kill him to get out every once in a while and meet some women he hadn't gone to preschool with.

"Sounds like a plan. Give me a day or so to do some poking around."

"Thanks, Chris. I appreciate it."

Jace worked until six and went home. The boys' boots, jackets, and backpacks were lined up neatly in the mudroom and something coming from the kitchen smelled amazing. Best of all, he didn't hear the television turned up to an earsplitting volume or "I'm going to kill you" being yelled from anywhere in the house. Unless aliens had landed and kidnapped his family, all seemed right with the world.

"Anyone home?" He wandered into the kitchen to find Sawyer sprawled out at his breakfast table and Charlie stirring a pot on the stove.

"We're here." Charlie reached up to grab a stack of plates from the cupboard and Jace watched Sawyer follow her with his eyes until his gaze rested on her ass.

Behind Charlie's back, Jace stuck his palm under Sawyer's chin and snapped his cousin's mouth closed. Sawyer lifted his shoulders apologetically.

Charlie turned around and brought the plates to the table. "You have a good day?"

He started to say that no one had died and decided to save the gallows humor for his cousins. Sawyer might not be a cop but he was a journalist. Same off-color jokes. Charlie probably wouldn't appreciate them. Most didn't.

"Not bad," he said. "Where's Travis and Grady?"

"Doing their homework in your study. Uh, that's okay, right? If not—"

"It's fine." He took the plates from her and set them around the table. "They like to use the computer in there."

"I just don't want to do anything wrong." She went back to the stove and continued stirring.

He exchanged a glance with Sawyer. "Looks to me like you've got everything handled." He gazed around his tidy kitchen and nudged his head at the pot. "What're you cooking there?"

"Chili. Is that okay? Your refrigerator has more beef in it than the meat aisle at Safeway. I thought I'd put some of it to good use."

"Chili's great. Thank you." Homemade food, a clean house, quiet kids, he sure the hell wasn't complaining. "Everything go well today?"

"No problems," she said. "The boys were wonderful."

Sawyer choked on his beer. "Someone must've replaced them with someone else's kids."

Jace added, "No ER visits, I guess."

"Nope, though Grady is probably suffering from a sugar high. He and I went to the coffee shop to kill time while Travis was at his meeting, and he had two pieces of carrot cake and a big cookie. He swears he'll still have room for dinner."

"He will," both Jace and Sawyer said at the same time. The kid could pack it in.

Sawyer got up, leaned over the big pot, and took a whiff of the chili. "Smells great. Unfortunately, I can't stay."

"Unfortunate for whom?" Jace quipped. "Here, let me walk you out."

Sawyer responded by giving Jace the finger.

Charlie seemed somewhat taken aback. He'd have to explain to her later that this is how the Daltons showed affection.

Sawyer prepared to leave and Jace followed him out to the back porch. "How was New York?"

"Cold but productive." Sawyer bobbed his head at the house. "You failed to mention that your damsel in distress is smoking hot. Like Penelope Cruz hot."

"She's also got more baggage than a packhorse."

"Who doesn't?"

Jace gave his cousin a long, hard assessment. Despite covering two wars and crawling into the dankest corners of hell, Sawyer usually pretended that his life was a freaking rose garden. And why not? He was successful, rich, and his parents' crown prince.

But Jace knew better.

The day Angela fell off the face of the earth was the day his cousin had lost his light. He still burned bright to those who didn't really know him. But if you did, it was as if someone had replaced the sun with a fluorescent bulb.

"Yep." Jace nodded. "Who doesn't? The thing is, I'm not looking for any more to add to my already heavy load."

"No?" Sawyer jogged down the stairs to hoof it home in the dark. "Could've fooled me."

Jace stood in the cold, watching as Sawyer crossed the field to the barn he'd converted into a New York–style penthouse. His cousin had more money than he had good sense. Jace was giving Charlie a week. That's all.

He went inside to check on the boys and change out of his uniform. By the time he returned to the kitchen, Charlie had finished setting the table.

"Dinner is ready," she said and took a loaf of bread out of the oven.

The four of them ate together, Travis and Grady talking over each other until the room reached a decibel level that could turn a person deaf. Charlie didn't seem to mind that her pretty table and tasty meal were overshadowed by Grady's descriptive story of how Arnie Judson ate six fish-stick tacos at lunch and proceeded to projectile-vomit across the cafeteria.

"Hey, buddy, how 'bout we not tell that story at dinnertime?"

"But Dad, it was epic."

"Sounds like it was, but we're eating, Grady. Mrs. Rogers went to a lot of trouble to—"

"She said we can call her Charlie," Grady interrupted.

Charlie's lips curved up and Jace felt her smile right in his gut. Just one week, he told himself.

* * * *

After dinner, Jace helped Charlotte do the dishes so the boys could finish their homework.

Together, they found a nice groove, Charlotte rinsing the dishes and Jace loading them into the washer. Corbin's idea of helping was to criticize.

Charlotte, you're wasting water. Charlotte, how many times do I have to tell you to buy the eco-friendly soap, not this shit?

"The chili was delicious," Jace said. "Family recipe?"

"Uh, no, just something I made up." Once upon a time, she'd liked to cook.

Charlotte, stick to reservations. I told you my mother was a Cordon Bleu–trained chef.

"Jace?" It was the first time she'd ever called him by his first name and it felt weird. A little too intimate, even if they were living under the same roof. "I did something impulsive today and I should've checked with you first."

"Yeah, what's that?" He looked up from the dishwasher, curiosity streaked across his face. It was certainly better than the alternative: anger.

"I stopped by this farmer's house on the way home from dropping the boys off at school. He was having a yard sale and I bought a few things." She inwardly cringed. It was a lot more than a few things. "And I was wondering if I could store them in one of your empty outbuildings and if so, could I borrow your truck?"

She held her breath, suddenly realizing just how presumptuous her request was. She was only here for a week and was treating the place like her personal storage facility.

"Sure," he said, completely unfazed. "Who was the farmer?"

"Uh, an elderly man…Maitland he said his name was."

Jace stopped what he was doing and looked at her. "Old man Maitland on the other side of town? That barn full of junk?" It wasn't said as a rebuke, mostly just bafflement.

"Not junk exactly, but when I'm finished it'll be extremely saleable."

"I'm looking forward to seeing this." He didn't seem altogether confident, but at least he wasn't belittling her.

The question was, how would she go about selling the pieces without a shop or a permanent address? Online stores like Etsy would be too risky and the first place Corbin would look. She'd figure it out later. For now, it just felt good to be creating again.

"You need the truck to pick the stuff up?"

"Uh-huh. I'll be very careful with it."

"I'll pick it up for you," he volunteered. "I assume tomorrow's okay."

"Tomorrow would be fantastic. Thank you."

"I've gotta say I'm curious to see what you've got cooking here. From what I can remember it was mostly rundown farm equipment. Nothing even salvageable. Hope you didn't pay too much."

"Nope." She laughed. "It was a real bargain. Free."

"Free? You're kidding me. Old man Maitland is a tightwad. He must have a thing for pretty brunettes," Jace said and Charlotte felt her face heat.

His broad shoulder accidentally brushed against her arm as he walked to the refrigerator, and she got goose bumps. The reaction was a little startling. After she got pregnant, sex with Corbin had become an exercise in humility. Corbin had never forced her, but saying no had never felt like a viable option. Even before getting pregnant, she'd begun to detest his touch.

For a fleeting second, she wondered what it would be like with Jace, and just as quickly banished the thought from her head.

He discreetly glanced at her ring finger, something she noticed he did frequently. Her phony wedding set—thirty-nine dollars at Macy's—was somewhere at the bottom of her purse. Meredith said a married pregnant woman would be less conspicuous than an unwed one. Charlotte had thought it was overkill, but Meredith was the expert.

"Charlie—" he started to say but didn't finish.

"Yes?" she said, even though she sensed he wanted to ask a question she wasn't supposed to answer.

He leaned against the fridge door and for a moment just stood there, considering her over the rim of his beer bottle. Then he stepped toward her, stopped himself, and abruptly said, "I'm turning in for the night."

It was only seven.

He headed for his study. She heard him say something to the boys, then footsteps down the long hallway, and a door shutting. She went to her own room, where she took her cell into the bathroom.

It was time to call Meredith.

Chapter 9

The next day, after dropping Travis and Grady at school, Charlotte met Jace at Mr. Maitland's farm. Jace had ditched his uniform for a pair of jeans and a flannel shirt. It was a good thing he had, because by the time he loaded the back of his pickup with Charlotte's assortment of castoffs he was covered in dirt, dust, and rust.

"You've got a cobweb on your hat." Charlotte reached up to swipe it off his Stetson, surprising herself with her boldness.

He leaned down so she could finish the job. "It's seen worse." He stood back to appraise the pile. "I guess one man's junk is another's treasure." He climbed into the back to tie everything down securely.

Charlotte felt guilty about pulling him away from work, but she had enjoyed watching him load. There was a beauty to his efficiency—and all those straining muscles. He'd been so cheerful about it that it had lifted her spirits.

The previous night's discussion with Meredith had made for a sleepless night. Corbin was ramping up his search for her and had even taken the extreme measure of calling in his father to put pressure on the police to treat Charlotte as a high-priority missing-persons case.

Meredith would've preferred that Charlotte get as far away from California as she could. But she hadn't yet found Charlotte a place to land.

"When I do, you've got to drop everything and go. Like the wind," Meredith had warned.

In the meantime, she'd have to be even more vigilant about flying under the radar. Tough to do when she lived with a cop. Luckily, Dry Creek seemed to be an island unto itself, even if it was only a couple of hours from a major city.

"Are we good?" Charlotte called up to him.

He jumped down from the bed of the truck. "We should make it home without anything falling out."

Mr. Maitland sat on an upended bucket, watching from a distance. Occasionally, he'd shout advice. Jace would nod but inevitably ignore the suggestion.

"Do you have to get back to the office? If not, I could make you lunch." It was the least Charlotte could do. Jace had gone to so much trouble on her behalf, even if he did think she was nuts. A few times she'd caught him staring at her new pile of possessions with a bewildered expression on his face.

"I've got time for a sandwich." He patted his stomach. They'd eaten breakfast only a few hours ago, but the Daltons had hearty appetites. Grady could devour two packages of bacon all by himself.

"I'll follow you home in case the load comes loose."

He gazed at the tie-downs he'd used. "It won't." On his way to the cab of his truck, he knocked the mud off his boots and waved his hand in the air to Mr. Maitland.

Before getting into her own car she walked over to where the old man still perched on the bucket and thanked him again. "It's going to a good home."

It took him a few seconds but he got to his feet, trying without success to straighten his back. "This is what happens when you milk goats for a living."

That and age. Charlotte put him somewhere near ninety.

"All sales are final," he said in a gruff voice that Charlotte was beginning to realize was a dry sense of humor.

"No worries." She reached for his gnarled hand, gave it a shake, and started for her SUV. "I'll send pictures."

"You come back in person, young lady."

She would if she was still here.

At the ranch, she followed Jace to an old barn that had been overgrown with brush. By her last count, there were at least five barns, including a stable for the horses, on the property. This one had a south-facing window that had been boarded up with plywood. And even Jace had to give the door a few hard tugs before it would slide open.

"It just needs a little oil," he said and began unloading.

Charlotte went inside, which was only slightly better than the exterior. Cobwebs hung from the rafters like netting and dried-up bird droppings covered the wooden floor. It was dark and dusty. But it was dry and seemingly rodent-free. And it was only a short walk along the creek from the house. She could hear water gurgling from inside the barn.

Later, she planned to come back with a broom and scrub brush and set the place up as best she could to serve as her workshop.

"There's electricity." Jace pushed a wheelbarrow piled high with her various treasures into the corner and bobbed his head at a wall outlet. "I'll see if I can find a window to let some natural light in." He pointed at the boarded-up one.

She started to remind him that she was only staying a week, not to go to any trouble. But he already had and she didn't want to appear unappreciative.

"I'll help you with the couch."

They went outside and he jumped into the truck bed, lithe as a tiger. He pushed the ratty sofa to the edge of the tailgate and she took the end hanging off the truck.

"Wait for me," he said and hopped down, hefting her end onto the back of his shoulders. "I've got it."

She grabbed the underside of the other end with both hands. "I can help." But he'd taken the brunt of the weight. It was a heavy couch, well made, which is what had attracted her to it in the first place.

"You probably shouldn't be lifting things," he said.

She'd had a miscarriage, not a C-section. But his concern warmed her. Why he was single was a mystery.

"I'm fine," she assured him, and helped him get the sofa inside the barn.

He put his end down and came around to her side and lowered that end too.

"Are you?" He straightened his back. "I don't know you, Charlie, but there's a sadness about you. I see it in your eyes, even in your smile. Losing a child...well, it's got to be the worst thing on earth." He leaned against one of the open framed walls and shoved his hands in his jacket pockets. "Maybe you should talk to someone, get counseling."

"This will be my counseling." She moved her eyes over the couch, then the wheelbarrow.

He didn't say anything, just observed her with those piercing blue eyes.

And for no reason at all she said, "His name would've been Davis. It's my mother's family name. I thought it would be nice to preserve it."

"Davis is a good name. Strong. My parents named me for my late grandfather. Jasper."

"That's nice too." She turned her face away so he wouldn't see her cry. "I made him a quilt. Perhaps you know of a family in need of a baby blanket."

"Nah, you should keep it." He'd come up alongside her and touched her arm. "I'm really sorry, Charlie."

"Thank you." She turned back to him, her cheek brushing his shoulder, where she let it rest in the folds of his jacket. His arms moved around her and for a few moments he held her close. There was strength in those arms. So much strength that for just a little while Charlotte forgot to be afraid. And then, just like that, he pulled away. "I could find you someone to talk to. A professional."

"Not now, but maybe later." There wouldn't be a later but it was easier to say there would be. "In the meantime, I appreciate you giving me a shoulder."

"I want to give you more than that," he said and seemed to become flustered. "What I mean to say is I want to help you, Charlie. This thing you're running from...I could make it so you didn't have to."

She stared up at the cobwebbed ceiling. "That's the thing, Jace. You can't."

* * * *

Jace was so goddamned frustrated he wanted to kick something. Why wouldn't she just talk to him? Have a little faith? He could make whoever was hurting her go away. And he could...hold her the way a man holds a woman.

Back in the barn it had felt so damned good. And so damned wrong.

He got up from his desk and shut the door. Today was the kind of day where he wished he could go outside and do real police work—bust in a couple of doors—not push papers. He fired up his computer and did another search for Charlie Rogers, even though it was waste of time.

There were too many to count. All of them the wrong Charlie Rogers.

He went back on the NamUs website and got lost in looking at pictures of missing people for an hour. When that got old he perused Bay Area newspapers. For all he knew she'd lied about living there. Yet, her Honda was registered to the Rosie the Riveter Foundation in San Francisco.

Screw it.

He picked up the phone and dialed Chris's cell phone number.

"Speak of the devil. I was getting ready to call you."

"Yeah?" Jace perked up. "You got something?"

"You were right about that foundation. There's a detective in our domestic violence unit who works with them occasionally. Off the books, of course." While providing abused women with fake IDs might be virtuous, it was illegal. "She said she'd reach out to them for you if you need a middleman."

"Maybe." But Jace didn't want to blow Charlie's cover. Nor did he expect anyone at the foundation to provide him with information about her. "So this is the deal: I sorta lied. The woman I was talking about is probably already getting help from Rosie the Riveter. She was passing through town and I thought if I knew more about her situation I could help. By now, though, she's long gone."

"Long gone, huh?" Chris hadn't made sergeant for being naïve. But Jace could trust him. He was solid.

"Work with me here. I'm just trying to find out who she is…what she's running from."

"And you want me to find out without giving me any more information?"

That was about the gist of it. "Could you just ask around? See if any women have been reported missing?"

"I could do that," Chris said. "But I don't need to tell you how many people in this city are looking for someone. Parents looking for their adult children who have taken to life on the streets. Family members looking for their mentally ill relatives. Hell, folks get on and off buses every day here just to disappear. This is San Francisco, man. You name it, we've got it."

Jace let out a whoosh of frustration. Why had he become so obsessed with Charlie? Angie, he told himself. That's why. If he couldn't help his cousin, he could at least look out for Charlie. "I know, I know. Whatever you can do, that's all I'm asking."

Charlie had been pregnant when she'd left. In Jace's mind, a spouse would move heaven and earth to find his baby.

"You got it," Chris said. "Talk to you soon."

Jace tried to spend the rest of the afternoon focusing on budgets, reports, and the agenda for the upcoming county supervisors' meeting. But the memory of Charlie in his arms played havoc on his concentration. He hadn't been this fixated on a woman since Mary Ann.

Yeah, and look how well that turned out.

He should've gone with his gut where his ex-wife had been concerned. The more he fell for her, the more she'd acted like a caged animal ready to bolt the minute the door opened. Then they got pregnant with Travis and she was stuck. Stuck with him, is what she'd said. Stuck with Dry Creek Ranch and living in a nothing town.

Next came Grady, and she was jumping out of her skin, so filled with wanderlust that she spent half her days glued to the Travel Channel.

Everything he did to try to make her happy only made it worse. Joining the Mill County Sheriff's Department so he could be closer to home instead of commuting to Roseville. Hiring Mitch to draw up plans for a house so she'd have her own domain, instead of living with Grandpa Dalton.

Loving her until he thought he'd go crazy with it.

She'd called his love suffocating. A fortress built to keep her in. So she scaled the walls, ran as fast as she could go, and put an ocean between them.

This time around, he'd go with his gut no matter what his heart said.

The watch commander's voice came over the radio. "Hey, Sheriff. We've got a 417 at the Beals Ranch. Thought you might like to handle it."

Jace moved closer to the radio. "What's going on?"

"It's unclear, Sheriff. Apparently someone came to repossess a piece of equipment and Mr. Beals pulled a gun on him. That's all his daughter told the 911 operator."

"Is someone there now?"

"Deputy Anderson."

"Tell Anderson to keep everything under control until I get there." He rushed across the bullpen. "I'm out for the rest of the day, Annabeth. You can forward my calls to my cell."

"Okay. Be careful, Jace."

By the time he got to Beals Ranch, things had escalated. Randy had taken the man from the repossession company hostage in the equipment barn and was threatening to blow his balls off if he even so much as touched his tractor. Jill was trying to talk her father down but he wouldn't listen to reason.

"Randy, give me the gun." Jace brushed by Deputy Anderson, who'd only been on solo patrol for a few months and was completely out of his depth on something like this. "Dammit, Randy, you want to go to prison and leave your family to deal with this mess?"

"Get away, Jace. I don't want to hurt anyone, but I will if I have to."

"Over a tractor? Over a goddamn tractor?"

Randy pulled the butt of the Remington firmly into his shoulder and gripped the stock. Even from a distance, Jace could feel Anderson stiffen. He motioned to the deputy to stand down. All he needed was for the rookie to intensify the situation.

"Randy, you're making everyone nervous. Put the gun down and let's talk about this."

"Nothing to talk about. The bank ain't taking my tractor. If your grandfather were still alive he'd shoot the son-of-a-bitch too."

"No, Randy. He'd let the son-of-a-bitch take the tractor and figure out a way to get it back. Lawfully."

Randy let out a rusty laugh. "God, I miss him. We're all dying, Jace. Every damn last one of us. And you kids don't give a rat's ass about the land, about the cattle. It's all about the money." He slowly turned to Jill, keeping the repo man in his sight line. "Where's your mother?"

"She's in town, Daddy. Don't do this. Hand the gun to Jace. Please!" She stood there in a pair of hip waders and had probably been mucking out muddy stalls when the trouble had started.

The repo man inched closer to the bay opening where a flatbed truck had been parked.

"Where do you think you're going?" Randy's finger twitched over the trigger and the man stopped in his tracks.

Jace thought he might've pissed himself.

"Randy, I'm not going to ask you again. Put down the gun."

"I'm not letting him take my tractor."

Breaking every protocol in the book, Jace grabbed the barrel and pulled the Remington away from Randy, who didn't put up much of a fight. The repo man sagged against a post and took a few minutes to collect himself, then went to work on loading the tractor onto the truck.

Randy slid down the wall and sat on the ground, resting his face in his hands. Jace got down there with him.

"You'll figure out a way to get it back," he said.

Another rusty laugh bubbled out of Randy. "Next, they'll come for the livestock trailers. Damned bank. A man can't even catch his breath before they start crawling up my ass, wanting their pound of flesh. You gonna arrest me?"

"I should." Jace looked over at Deputy Anderson, who appeared stymied by what to do next. He motioned that the deputy could go.

"A man has a right to protect his property."

"Except it's not your property. It's the bank's. How deep are you in, Randy?" As the sheriff it was none of Jace's business, but the Beals and the Daltons had been neighbors for three generations. Randy's father had been Grandpa Dalton's best friend.

"Deep enough to drown. I should've sold to Mitch after that incident last summer." That incident last summer should've landed Mitch, Jill, and Pete in prison. But Randy and his wife had refused to press charges against their kids. Now, Jill was back living on the ranch, trying to make up for the damage she'd caused by shouldering some of the work.

"Can you find your way out of this?" Jace asked.

"I frankly don't know how. We're behind on our payments and taxes are killing us. It's wet now from all the rain, but another dry year and ..." Randy trailed off. "Your grandfather was smart not to throw good money after bad when the drought came. We thought taking out a second would help us hold on. Now we owe more than we make."

It was the story of the foothills.

After three years of devastating drought, you either culled your herd or went to the bank, hat in hand. As much as it had killed him to lose close to a century's worth of breeding stock, Jasper Dalton hadn't wanted to saddle his grandkids with that kind of debt. As it was, Jace and his cousins couldn't afford arrears in the ranch's property taxes, let alone monthly payments on a bank loan.

"What about debt consolidation?" Jace asked. "You talk to someone about cutting a deal with the bank?"

"Yeah, maybe I'll do that."

Jace doubted it. Cattlemen were a proud lot.

The repo man finished loading the tractor and drove away, leaving clouds of dust in his wake. Technically, he was only allowed to repossess the equipment from the driveway and had trespassed, so Jace didn't bother asking if he wanted to press charges, though he probably should've.

"Go on in, Randy. Shower up before Marge gets home." Jace got to his feet and held out a hand, but Randy stood up on his own.

He watched the cowboy walk to the house and remembered that Jill was still there. They hadn't talked since Jace had booked her into the county jail.

"Daddy wouldn't have shot 'im," she said.

"I know."

"Thank you for coming. He's been in a bad way lately and you coming and talking him down, well it helped."

He nodded and started to walk away.

"Brett's doing well."

"I know that too." Jace talked to Brett at least twice a week while Brett attended a vocational school for disabled war veterans in Sacramento.

"Are you ever going to forgive me, Jace?"

"Probably not, Jill. You cheated on my best friend with my other best friend. You stole from your parents. And you and Mitch may have ruined my chance of getting reelected with that bullshit rumor you helped spread about Aubrey and me. So no, Jill, I don't plan to forgive you anytime soon."

"Brett's forgiven me."

"Brett has always been a better man than I. He also happens to be the father of your children, so I'm sure he wants to keep things copasetic between you two." He crossed the driveway to his SUV, Jill hanging in his shadow. "Me, not so much."

"We've known each other our whole lives. You have to forgive me." She was at his passenger-side door now.

"No, I don't." He got in the driver's seat. "Go check on your dad."

On his way to the ranch, he called Cash and conferenced in Sawyer. "Meeting at my house in two hours."

When he got home there were fresh flowers on the kitchen table and something that smelled like homemade bread in the oven, and Jace let himself breathe. Seeing Randy lose it like that had stuck with him the whole ride home.

"Dad, Charlie made rocky road cookies. You know, like the ice cream. You want to taste one?"

Jace grabbed Grady in a headlock and kissed the top of his head, which was damp and smelled faintly like shampoo. "After dinner."

"What about me? Can I taste one now?"

"After dinner. Homework done?"

"Almost."

"Then giddyup, pardner."

Grady let out a groan and padded off to Jace's office. Jace assumed Travis was already in there, probably using his computer. In the dining room, Charlie had her sewing machine set up and appeared to be working on an elaborate project. There was a stack of fabric at the end of the table and spools of thread in every color on a wooden holder.

Charlie jumped to her feet as soon as she spotted him. "I'll clean it up."

"Why? Aren't we eating in the kitchen?" It seemed like she was right in the middle of whatever she was doing and it didn't make sense to put away all her materials only to drag them out again. "What are you making?" He stepped closer to have a look.

"It's a slipcover for that sofa we moved today." She began clearing off the table.

He gently touched her arm. "Just leave it. That way you can come back to it without having to set everything up again." Compared to the boys' projects, hers was neat and organized. "You had all this stuff in your car?"

"Everything but the fabric. I met a seamstress today…Wren, I think her name was…when I took Grady to soccer practice after school. She has a little shop near the field."

"Sew What," he said. "I know the place."

"She told me about this great fabric store in Grass Valley. After soccer, Travis, Grady, and I took a ride over there and I bought all this." She gazed at her pile and scrunched up her face. "I may have gone a little overboard."

"I don't know anything about how much material a slipcover takes." He wasn't even exactly sure what a slipcover was. What he did know was that nasty thing in the barn was beyond saving, but she seemed to know what she was doing.

"Not as much as I bought. But I'll make matching pillows. Dinner should be done soon." She glanced up at him, taking in the mud on his pants, and flashed a sympathetic smile. "Long day?"

"I had to talk the neighbor down. He tried to hold off repossession of his tractor by pulling a shotgun on the guy from the tow company. We wound up sitting on the ground to talk it out."

He usually kept his cases confidential and unlike the rest of Dry Creek hated gossip, but the incident with Randy had bothered him on a visceral level. He'd seen enough desperation in a man's eyes to know that Randy was hurting. Bad.

"Oh my." Charlie covered her mouth with her hand. "Was anyone injured?"

"Nah, but Randy...he's the neighbor...is in a bad way. His ranch is under water and he's struggling to hold on."

"Does he raise cattle too?"

Too. Jace had to keep from laughing. Compared to Beals Ranch, Dry Creek was a hobby farm. It didn't used to be that way. Before the drought, Grandpa Dalton ran a fairly sizeable cow-calf operation. Never as big as the Beals, but respectable.

"Yeah," he said. "On a very large scale. But it's a tough business."

"What'll happen?"

"I don't know." Jace shook his head. "The ranch has been in the Beals family for generations, so I suspect he'll do whatever he can to hold on."

"Maybe he should figure out another way to profit from the ranch." Charlie headed for the kitchen and Jace followed her.

"None of us want a development." The very thought of it made Jace queasy. The land along Dry Creek Road had always been cattle ranches. A few spreads had changed hands over the years to farmers and horse breeders, but it had always been agricultural.

"Not development." She leaned down and checked whatever was in the oven. "Just something else, something that would generate more income." Charlie straightened up. "Don't listen to me. I clearly don't know what I'm talking about."

"I think you mean something like what the McCourtneys do. They grow pumpkins and sell 'em to a big distributor in the Central Valley. But the last few years they've opened up their farm to the public around Halloween and let folks pick their own pumpkins. This year, they offered hay rides, built a maze for the kids, and set up a little country store where they sold jams, produce, and wreaths. Nick McCourtney said they made a killing. Next year, they're planning to keep it open all the way to Thanksgiving and add homemade pies to their repertoire."

"I love that." Charlie wore a big grin that made Jace's gut tighten. That smile was like the sun peeking out on a cloudy day.

He cleared his throat and spoke to keep from basking too long in that smile. "It's not as easy with cattle. Dude ranches are a dime a dozen and you need a lot of capital to build the infrastructure for that. Cabins, a commercial kitchen, enough tack for guests. The liability insurance alone is huge. There are a couple of cattlemen who let cell phone companies lease space on their ranches for towers. Besides being an eyesore, the income is only enough to keep a few lights on. The trick is coming up with something new and profitable. You got any ideas? Because we could sure use a plan around here." If they came up with something good maybe they could raise the money to pay the taxes on Dry Creek Ranch.

Surprised, she sputtered, "Me? Oh, I wouldn't know anything about that."

"Why not? You used to own a business, right?" He gazed into the dining room, where her slipcover project still sat on the table. "You're creative. That's what it takes to come up with a winning idea. Creativity."

Surprise turned to pleasure. Her expression practically glowed with it and Jace was back to staring. God, she was pretty. And nice to talk to.

"Then I'll give it some thought." She pulled a pan from the oven and pushed the door closed with her hip.

He forced himself to look away from her and focus on whatever was in the pan. "Lasagna?"

"Yes, the boys said you like it."

"Love it. Love rocky road cookies too, though until today I'd never heard of them."

"Those were a bribe to get Grady to bathe after soccer."

Ah, that explained the shampoo smell. Jace's youngest was a great many things. Clean wasn't typically one of them.

"So they've been okay, huh?" Travis and Grady seemed to like her at least.

"The kids?" Her lips curved up. "They've definitely got a lot of energy but they're good boys, just—"

"Just what?" he wanted to know.

She began setting the table. A stall tactic, Jace suspected.

"Tell me, Charlie. Whatever you've got to say, I can assure you I've heard worse."

"It's nothing negative." She finished carefully placing the flatware on each mat. Small fork, big fork. A little formal for a family dinner in the kitchen, but Charlie liked to do things up and Jace kind of liked it. It would've done his grandmother proud.

"I'm not a psychologist, but I think they act out because they miss their mother," she continued.

She wasn't telling him anything he didn't know. "Probably. Not a whole lot I can do about that." Mary Ann had been the one to leave, not him. He made sure the kids were out of earshot and said, "She used to at least call and send cards for their birthdays. She doesn't even do that anymore."

"Why do you think that is?"

Jace shrugged and stared out the window. "The ranch…the house…this town, it was never for her. But I foisted all of it on her, so she ran. She ran as far as she could go."

Charlie didn't say anything, but he could see the wheels spinning in her head. She was running too.

* * * *

After dinner Charlotte went back to her sewing. Jace's cousins came over and she could hear them talking in the kitchen. Jace was telling them about the neighbor, and then they began talking about their own financial problems. From what she could gather from the conversation, their grandfather hadn't been up-to-date paying his property taxes when he'd died, and now the three of them had to come up with the cash to make it good.

She cut and sewed and listened, realizing the direness of their situation. Though no one had said the words, Charlotte understood that they could lose Dry Creek Ranch if they weren't able to pay the bills.

Charlotte had been here less than a week, but even she could see how much Jace and his children loved this place. She couldn't fathom them losing it.

"What are you working on, there?"

She turned to find the cousin named Cash standing behind her, looking over her shoulder.

She'd met him earlier while cleaning up after dinner. He'd been cordial enough but definitely standoffish. She couldn't say she blamed him. A few days ago, she'd been a stranger. Now she was living here.

"Uh, I'm recovering a couch."

He nodded. "Jace said something about you getting a bunch of furniture from old man Maitland. My fiancée's an interior designer. She's into stuff like that." He focused on the pattern she'd made from tracing paper. "I'm sure she'd be interested to see what you've got going here."

"I'd love to meet her. Tell her to drop by the barn near the creek. That's where I'll be working on most of the projects." The last thing she should be doing was forging connections here. The less people knew about her, the better. But what else was she supposed to say? They were Jace's family after all.

"I'll do that," he said and made his way to the bathroom.

She went back to working on her slipcover, using the ranch as her inspiration. Farmhouse chic. Lots of denim, ticking stripes, burlap, and leather accents.

To be sitting in the dining room, sewing, felt oddly normal. It was as if she'd become part of the household.

Travis was in his room, probably talking to the same girl Charlotte had seen him with when she'd picked him up from school. She was no expert on teens, but Travis seemed pretty taken with the girl. She couldn't be sure but she thought she saw them holding hands.

Grady was watching TV in the front room. The program must've been a comedy because every few minutes or so, he barked with laughter. Several times, Jace had shouted for him to pipe down.

A fire roared in the woodburning stove that sat between the kitchen and dining room. Occasionally, Jace would get up from his discussion and throw in another log.

Sherpa, an Australian shepherd with one brown eye and one blue, lay under the table at Charlotte's feet. Scout was on the couch—where he wasn't supposed to be—with Grady. The entire scene could've been a painting of the perfect American family. To think Jace's ex-wife had run from here boggled the mind. But she supposed outsiders could've said the same thing about her.

Her life had once appeared a fairy tale. The big airy condo with its Golden Gate view and Presidio Heights address. The handsome lawyer, who in his free time did pro bono work for the poor and sat on charitable boards. His U.S. senator father.

To observers she and Corbin had had it all. No one would ever believe that Senator Ainsley's golden child was a possessive, verbally abusive woman beater.

Chapter 10

Thursday afternoon Jace got an email from Chris. It was only four words: *Is this the woman?* Attached was a picture of Charlie.

He picked up his office phone and punched in Chris's number. "Who is she?"

Chris chuckled. "You don't mess around, do you? According to her boyfriend, Charlotte Holcomb."

Jace looked at the picture again. Except for the evening gown and the expensive jewelry dripping from her ears and throat, it was Charlie all right.

"Boyfriend? Who is he?"

"What's this about, Jace?" Chris asked, his voice firm.

Jace didn't want to jack his friend around, yet he didn't want to give away Charlie's location either. "I think the boyfriend's been abusing her and she's on the run from him. So he reported her missing, huh?"

"A few days ago. He's a big-deal lawyer, Jace. And his father is Senator Charles Ainsley."

Jace took a few minutes to absorb that news.

Everyone in California knew who Charles Ainsley was. Before running for the U.S. Senate, Ainsley was mayor of Los Angeles and was the state's own version of a Kennedy. Women thought he was hot and guys wanted to drink a beer with him. People still talked about the time Ainsley had jumped on stage during a benefit concert to support the victims of the Wine Country fires and had accompanied Neil Young on "Rockin' in the Free World." Ainsley was no Neil Young, but Jace thought he'd held his own.

Other than that, he didn't have an opinion on the guy. But Grandpa Dalton used to say Charles Ainsley was "big hat, no cattle." Jasper Dalton had high expectations of his elected officials. Jace, not so much. Hell, a hardware-store owner with absolutely no law enforcement experience was probably going to beat Jace for sheriff just because he talked a good game.

"He says she's pregnant and suffers from severe depression and he's worried about her safety," Chris continued.

Jace had seen no signs of depression, only fear. "Did you meet the guy... Charles Ainsley's son?"

"Nope. Apparently he met with the chief personally." Chris let out a humorless laugh. "It pays to be someone in this town. Anyone else who lost his girlfriend would've gotten no further than the front desk."

Girlfriend. Jace was still trying to get a grip on the revelation that she wasn't married. Odd that Charlie had been wearing a wedding ring when he first met her.

"The dude's name?" Jace wanted to do a little research on his own. The fact that he was a senator's son would make it easier than usual. There was probably plenty of information about him floating around online.

"Let me look." Jace could hear Chris tapping a keyboard in the background. "I'm not supposed to be doing this shit."

"Yeah, I know. But it's for a good cause."

"You sure about that? Maybe the chick's batshit."

Jace could take that two ways: Chris was either questioning Jace's judgment because of his prior track record with Mary Ann, or considering the possibility that the senator's son was telling the truth. "Could be" was all he said.

"Corbin. Corbin Ainsley. Douchie name, that's for sure."

Jace laughed. "Thanks, bro. I don't figure I have to tell you that this conversation never happened."

"Nope. You and I never talked." Chris clicked off and Jace jumped on the internet highway.

Two hours later, Jace called Cash. "Where are you?"

"Over at the coffee shop, getting lunch. I spent the morning in Plumas County. It was a good twenty degrees colder and I'm still trying to warm up."

"You're a wuss. I'll be right over, order me a steak sandwich." Jace hoofed it the two blocks to Mother Lode Road.

Laney pointed to their usual booth where Cash sat, hunched over a cup of coffee and the local newspaper. "Your sandwich is coming."

"Thanks, Miss Laney." He winked and she swatted his butt with a menu.

"What're you reading that rag for?" Jace took the bench across from his cousin and grinned. It was a good little newspaper. Before people got the news on their phones or in 280 characters on Twitter, they actually read it. Now, it was mostly for old-timers.

Cash turned the paper and pointed to the picture on the front page of Ellie holding a certificate. Student of the month. "Aubrey called to tell me about it."

"Nice. Grady got menace of the year."

Cash shook his head but grinned despite himself, then his lips pressed together in a grimace. "How's the new babysitter working out?"

"That's what I wanted to talk to you about." Laney brought their food and Jace waited for her to move on to the next table before he picked up where he'd left off. "Her boyfriend reported her missing."

"What about her husband?" Cash took a bite of his sandwich.

"Doesn't have one." Jace had checked public records under Charlie's real name. "The boyfriend is Charles Ainsley's son."

"Charles Ainsley as in Senator Ainsley?" When Jace nodded, Cash let out a low whistle.

"He's a lawyer in San Francisco, handles mostly corporate cases, some economic espionage. Name's Corbin Ainsley. You ever hear of him?"

Before moving to the ranch, Cash had worked and lived in the city.

"Nah, I never worked white collar. I met the senator a few times, though. Just the usual glad-handing shit. How'd you find out?"

"I've got a few sources," Jace said. "Charlie doesn't know I know."

"You planning to tell her?"

Jace took a long draw on his sarsaparilla. "I don't know. What would you do?"

Cash eyed Jace for a beat. It didn't take a genius to know he didn't approve of Charlie living at Jace's. Domestic situations were hairy and often blew up fast. As a patrol officer, Jace would've chosen a riot over a DV call.

"I'd tell her you know," he finally said. "If you're going to designate yourself her personal protector, there needs to be open communication. For everyone's safety." He emphasized the word "everyone."

"He'll never find her here, but I hate the idea of him getting away with what he did."

"I wouldn't be so sure. It's pretty difficult to stay hidden these days. And the guy obviously has the resources to launch a full-blown search. Your friend...Charlie...a week, my ass. She's here for the long haul."

"What makes you say that?" Jace took another sip of the sarsaparilla.

"That project she's got going in the barn. That's not something you do in a couple of days."

It had struck Jace the same way. The truth was he'd been more than happy to lug the crap from old man Maitland's just for that reason. He kept telling himself it was the protective cop in him who wanted her to stay, not the man. But the man knew he was a damned liar.

"Everyone at the ranch should be alerted." Cash looked at Jace pointedly.

Cash was right. They needed to be prepared if Corbin Ainsley ever showed up. What he ought to do is drive to San Francisco and take out the son-of-a-bitch. Who the hell beats up a woman? The thought of Charlie's black-and-blue back...of her miscarriage...made his stomach pitch and he pushed his plate away.

"I'll talk to Sawyer," Jace said. "You explain the situation to Aubrey. As long as we keep our eyes open, everything will be fine."

* * * *

Charlotte was fitting her slipcover when the call came. She climbed over the couch and grabbed her cell off the window ledge. She'd given the barn a good cleaning and the place had proven to be a great workshop. Jace had hooked up a light for her. In the daytime, with the sun beaming in, it wasn't too cold.

She quickly scanned the number that flashed, assuming it was Meredith. But it was a local area code, the same one as Jace's.

"Hello?"

"Ms. Rogers? This is Leslie from Dry Creek High School. We can't reach Sheriff Dalton and Travis needs to be picked up."

Charlotte glanced at her watch, fearful that she'd somehow gotten lost in her work and had missed pickup time. But it was still early, only one. "Is he okay?" She grabbed her scarf and started back to the house at a jog.

"He's fine, but he's been suspended for two days for fighting. He said to call you."

"Fighting?" That didn't sound like Travis. He could have a smart mouth at times, especially when his father wasn't around, and he liked to challenge her. But he struck her as a fairly gentle boy.

"Yes, ma'am. Can you come or should I keep trying the sheriff?"

"I'm on my way."

On the drive to town, she contemplated whether to call Jace's assistant. He'd given her the number, saying Annabeth could always find him in an emergency on the police scanner. But Charlotte wasn't sure Travis's suspension rose to the level of emergency. Jace was used to the boys and their mischief, after all.

The high school was on the outskirts of town, near the fire department and a park where a lot of the kids hung out after school. She pulled into the visitor parking lot and went in search of the office. It was her first time inside the building. The smell—a combination of cleaning solution and floor polish—brought her back to her own high school in Portland. Though Dry Creek High was a fraction of the size, the walls, covered in student artwork, still looked the same.

The office was down a long corridor and Charlotte heard her boot heels clicking on the terrazzo floor. Travis sat on a bench right outside the principal's door, his face glued to something on his phone. Charlotte sat beside him.

"You have to check in with Hagatha before we can go," he said without looking up.

"Okay." She went inside the office, looking for whoever this Hagatha was and was about to ask the woman at the front desk when Charlotte saw the principal's name plate. Agatha Roletti.

Hagatha. She shook her head.

She introduced herself to the receptionist and signed a form to take Travis home. He was still playing on his phone in the hallway.

"Time to go," she said and nudged his arm.

He got into her CR-V without saying a word.

"What happened, Travis?" she asked, stealing a glance at him. He was being unusually quiet.

He shrugged. "My dad's gonna be pissed."

"Probably." No sense lying. She started the engine and nosed out of the parking lot. "What was the fight about?"

"Ruben was being a jerk, so I decked him."

"Ruben, the boy we gave a ride to school the other day?" The one who was antagonizing Grady?

"Yeah, he's a dick." He slid her a look. "Sorry."

She hid a smile. Jace had raised his boys to have good manners. "How did he go from friend to dick?"

He looked at her again, trying to contain his surprise. See, she could say it too.

"He picks on people. Lately, it's been this girl who everyone kind of makes fun of. She's got a big bald spot on her head. I don't know, maybe she has a disease or something. Cancer even. Usually, she wears a hat to cover it up, but everyone knows about the bald spot. They call her Eagle. You know, like bald eagle. Today, Ruben pulled her hat off and threw it across the cafeteria. Everyone was laughing while she tried to cover her head with her arms." He shrugged. "It pissed me off."

"I can see why. That was really mean what Ruben did. And humiliating to that poor girl." Charlotte had to tread lightly here. She didn't want Travis to think she was condoning fighting. At the same time, she was proud of him for standing up for the girl. "Is that why you hit him?"

"First I told him to knock it off. That just made him do more. He started rubbing her head like a Buddha stomach and everyone was laughing. She started crying and I just lost it."

"And that's when the fight started?" Charlotte stopped at the light and pulled onto the highway.

"Yeah, in front of the whole cafeteria. I would've shoved his face into the table, but Mr. Colby broke it up and sent us to the office."

"You know you can't change people with your fists, right, Travis? Ruben's a bully. I saw that the day he sat in the back seat of the car with your little brother. Violence isn't the way, otherwise you're just like him." Ruben sounded like a Corbin-in-training and she wasn't exactly sad that Travis had hit the boy. Still, she wasn't about to tell Travis that.

"My dad's gonna kill me, especially when he finds out that I'll be missing my algebra final on account of getting suspended."

"Did Ruben also get suspended?" If there was any justice the kid should be out for the rest of the year.

"He got five days because of what he did to Shelby and has to go to sensitivity training. Mr. Colby saw the whole thing."

Then why the hell hadn't Mr. Colby stopped Ruben from teasing that poor girl? That's what Charlotte wanted to know. "What's sensitivity training?"

Travis shrugged his shoulders. "I think it's like when they teach you not to be a dick to people, but I'm not really sure. What should I tell my dad?"

"The truth." Charlotte turned off onto Dry Creek Road. "Tell him exactly what you told me."

From everything she'd learned about Jace Dalton, he'd know exactly what to say to Travis. She would also bet that he would cut the boy slack for standing up to Ruben to protect a bullied girl. It showed character, even though Travis had used his fists. Getting suspended from school... well, she didn't know how Jace would respond to that. The thing was, she knew he'd handle it right because he was a wonderful father.

The best thing about her stay at Dry Creek Ranch was being reminded that good men still exist in the world.

When they pulled up to the ranch house there was an old Volvo station wagon in the driveway and a woman sitting on the front porch. One of Jace's admirers, Charlotte supposed, and a tingle of envy ran up her spine.

Travis got out of the car and waved. "Hey, Aunt Aubrey."

"Hey, good looking. What are you doing home? I hope you're not sick."

"Nope." Travis didn't say more, just brushed by her and went inside the house.

"Hi." Charlotte stood at the base of the porch and shielded her eyes. "I'm Charlotte…the boys' babysitter."

"So great to finally meet you." Aubrey came down the stairs. "I'm Aubrey, Cash's fiancée. He said you were working on some pretty interesting projects and that I should come check them out."

"Oh…right…you're the designer." Charlotte prayed that Aubrey had never been to Refind. Her store had been popular with decorators and designers across Northern California. But Aubrey didn't seem to register any kind of recognition, so Charlotte felt safe. "Come on in. How about a cup of coffee?"

"I would love one."

They went through the front door, which in the short time Charlotte had been here rarely got used. Everyone entered and exited through the mudroom.

Aubrey gazed around the living room as they walked to the kitchen. "Whoa, I don't think I've ever seen it this neat." She paused at Travis, who'd wasted no time playing video games, and messed up his hair.

"Hey, Travis," Charlotte said, and pointed to the TV screen. "This probably won't help your cause with your dad, if you know what I mean. If I were you, I'd do something to butter him up, like maybe clean your room. Just saying."

As they crossed through the dining room Charlotte heard the game go off.

"What's that about?" Aubrey asked.

"Travis had a run-in with a bully at school. He got suspended for a few days."

"Uh-oh." Aubrey made a face. "Jace won't be too happy about that."

In the kitchen, Charlotte put a pot of coffee on and found some of her leftover rocky road cookies and arranged them on a plate. Aubrey sat at the kitchen island and, like in the front room, gave the place a once-over.

"You've really whipped the house into shape."

"It wasn't anything," Charlotte said. "For the most part Jace and the boys keep it pretty neat."

Aubrey snorted. "Pretty neat? Jace has been my best friend since elementary school. Not neat. And the boys…please. Oink, oink is more like it."

"So you've known Jace since childhood, huh?" Charlotte was curious about their relationship. It seemed unusual for a man like Jace—cowboy sheriff—to be best friends with a woman.

"Played in the same sandbox and sat next to each other in kindergarten. His mother was one of my mother's best friends. When his parents and baby brother died, the whole town went a little crazy with grief. Jace was just a kid, maybe six at the time. In one fell swoop, a drunken driver took away his whole family."

Jace had had a significant amount of loss in his life. His parents, his brother, his grandfather, and his wife. It was enough to make Charlotte's heart fold in half.

"Did you know Mary Ann?" Charlotte let the question slip out, instantly realizing how audacious it was. She and Aubrey were strangers, not BFFs.

From the expression on Aubrey's face she was just as stunned Charlotte had asked. "He told you about Mary Ann?"

"Just a little. I shouldn't have said anything. It's really not my business."

"No, it's fine. I'm just surprised is all. He never talks about her. And we all tiptoe around the subject as if on eggshells. I knew her as much as anyone could know Mary Ann. She didn't like me much, and quite frankly the feeling was mutual."

The coffee was done brewing and Charlotte poured them each a cup and put the plate of cookies between them.

"Why not?" Charlotte asked. If Aubrey wanted to dish, who was Charlotte to stop her?

"I didn't like her because she broke Jace's heart. The man treated her like a queen and that wasn't good enough. Nothing—not this house, not this ranch, not Jace's job—was ever good enough. Me? She didn't like me because Jace did."

"She viewed you as a threat?" Aubrey was a beautiful woman.

"Nah, I wasn't. And Mary Ann didn't suffer from low self-esteem. Far from it. Plus, I was living with Jace's best friend at the time and despite the rumors, Jace has always been like a brother to me."

"What rumors are those?" Charlotte was probably asking too many questions, but Aubrey didn't seem to mind.

Aubrey let out another snort. "After I dumped Mitch, my former fiancé, there was a crazy rumor that Jace and I were having an affair. Ridiculous, because I'm totally in love with Cash. It was a smear campaign and unfortunately I think it might hurt Jace's bid for reelection." She looked Charlotte up and down as if she was thinking something but was forcing herself to keep quiet.

Charlotte remembered Jace's hush-hush conversation with his campaign manager the day they went to her home to pick up his campaign signs. Maybe this is what they'd been talking about. She supposed gossip was a way of life in a small town, but it would be tragic if Jace lost the reelection because of it. "Is there anything he can do to better his chances of winning?"

"He needs to up his profile. Tiffany wants him to do more community events but Jace is deluded. He thinks being a good sheriff is enough. He's a great sheriff, but unfortunately his opponent has out-raised him in campaign contributions and shows up to every festival and livestock auction in Mill County to ingratiate himself. It doesn't hurt that he also owns the local hardware store, which everyone goes to."

Charlotte wished there was something she could do to help. Jace had done so much for her. But she didn't know a lick about politics, or law enforcement for that matter. Besides, she was a nobody around here and needed to keep it that way. Any day now, Meredith was going to call with Charlotte's marching orders. It was important that she lie low until then.

"What a shame," Charlotte said. "He's such a good guy."

"Yes, he is." Aubrey gave her that odd assessment again, then briskly changed the subject. "Show me what you're working on."

Charlotte brightened. It had been a long time since she had a project to show off. "It's down at the barn. You up for a walk?"

A short time later, they crossed the field, careful to avoid the mud. It had rained the night before and a gorgeous rainbow streaked across the sky. She still couldn't believe she got to wake up to this kind of beauty. Everything—the trees, the grass, the hills—was so green it was a visual wonderland. Sometimes, especially on days like this, Charlotte wanted to spin around like a child with her arms held out. Dry Creek Ranch was so vast and beautiful it made her feel free.

Free from the chains of Corbin Ainsley.

She slid open the barn door and heard Aubrey let out a little cry of delight.

"I want it." Aubrey circled the sofa Charlotte had been working on for the past couple of days, admiring the patchwork of vintage denim and ticking stripe fabric she'd used for the slipcover and the grain sacks from Mr. Maitland's farm she'd repurposed into pillows. "I don't know where we have room for another sofa in our little cabin, but I want it."

Charlotte laughed. Aubrey's reaction was exactly what Charlotte strived for. It's why Refind had been such a success before she'd begun neglecting the store to accommodate Corbin. Eventually, business had gotten so bad she'd had to close the doors.

"I don't know what it looked like before, but it's fantastic now." Aubrey walked around the couch to view it from all sides.

Charlotte pulled her phone from her pocket and began swiping through before-and-after photographs. "It was pretty rough."

Aubrey expanded the picture for a better look. "You're not kidding. You're a miracle worker. Those flour sacks…what you've done with them…you can get a lot of money for something like this." She ran her hand against the back of the sofa.

Thousands in the city. But Charlotte didn't know what kind of prices her furniture could fetch around here.

"It still needs some alterations. The cover is a little looser than I'd like it."

"What else do you have?" Aubrey wandered around the barn, taking inventory of various projects Charlotte had started, including an old window she'd turned into a picture frame and was still waiting for the chalk paint to dry. There was a rusted milk bucket that was serving as a flower vase. "I have clients who would die for this stuff. You mind if I snap a few pictures?"

"No, go right ahead." Charlotte didn't have a lot of time left in Dry Creek, but maybe Aubrey could sell the pieces for her.

Without even thinking about it, Charlotte began walking around the barn and creating little tableaus with some of the more finished pieces. She propped an old paint-splattered ladder against the wall and hung some of her fabric remnants in such a way as to make them look like blankets. In another corner, she leaned a wagon wheel against the wall. "I'm going to do something with this eventually, but for right now I think it looks kind of cool like this."

"Whoa, you're really good at merchandising, aren't you?"

"I owned a store for many years," Charlotte said.

"Really? Where?"

She stuck with the same story she'd told Jace, which was probably still risky. Aubrey, being a decorator, might do a little research. And while Charlotte hadn't given the name of the store, someone skillful on the internet could narrow the shop down to Refind in Noe Valley.

"I can see you're really good at it." Aubrey continued to shoot photos with her phone. "If any of my clients are interested, this stuff is for sale, right?"

"Absolutely. I also do custom wo—" She stopped, realizing she didn't have time to take commissions. Not unless she worked out of her car. "I've got my hands full for now." Charlotte gazed around the barn.

"Just keep doing what you're doing. If this stuff goes over the way I think it will, you'll be plenty busy."

It was a nice visit and under better circumstances Charlotte could see herself being friends with Aubrey. Besides their mutual love for home décor, Aubrey struck Charlotte as completely genuine. She reminded her a little of Allison, which made Charlotte miss her sister even more.

Perhaps one day, if and when she stopped running, she could call her family and make amends.

Chapter 11

"After dinner, you mind if we have a talk?" Jace asked Charlie as she set the table.

They were eating later than usual because he'd had to respond to a car versus tree on Peninsula Court. No one had been seriously injured, but the teenage motorist who'd caused the accident had been driving a group of high school seniors home after a "study session" and had blown an .08 on a Breathalyzer.

It made Travis's suspension pale in comparison, though Jace wasn't too happy about that either. He was proud that his son had put a bully in his place but wished Travis hadn't resorted to fighting to do it. Even if he himself had been tempted a time or two to knock Ruben on his ass.

Tomorrow, first thing in the morning, he planned to drive Travis to Ruben's house for a conversation about bullying and fighting. Ruben's mom had her hands full working two jobs and raising that boy and his brother on her own. She didn't need the extra worry.

The best place for Ruben was at school, not sitting home, figuring out more ways to get in trouble. Jace never understood why suspending a kid was a good idea. He could think of a dozen better punishments than giving a kid a free vacation.

"Okay," Charlie said. "Is anything wrong? Should I have called you about Travis?"

"This doesn't have anything to do with Travis." Jace didn't want to get into it before the kids came in to eat. But he also didn't want to ambush her.

They exchanged glances and he saw Charlie's face fall. He was pretty sure she knew he'd figured out who she was and where she'd come from.

Good. The sooner they got this out in the open, the sooner they could come up with a plan.

Charlie pulled the roast out of the oven and Jace called the boys to supper. With Charlie, the household ran like a well-oiled machine. He didn't know how she managed to fit in her projects while keeping everything so organized, including putting food on the table and shuttling the boys to and from their activities. Mrs. Jamison had been great, but Charlie seemed to have a better rapport with Travis and Grady. As far as Jace knew, they didn't call Charlie "Yoda."

Charlie had even tried to soft-pedal Travis's suspension to him.

Of course he shouldn't have been fighting, but he was standing up for that poor girl, doing what he thought was right.

They were both on the same page there.

Travis and Grady joined them at the table. Everyone helped themselves. He might not be able to pay the property taxes, but they sure ate well on the ranch.

Grady took a big bite and with his mouth full said, "I wish I would've seen Travis pop Ruben in the face." He simulated a boxer and punched the air. "Pow!"

"Knock it off," Jace told him.

Grady put his fists down and took a bite of his potatoes. "Is Travis grounded?" he asked with his mouth full.

"That's between your brother and me. You study for that spelling test?"

"Boring. B-O-R-I-N-G. Boring."

Jace fixed Grady with a look. The kid was a smartass. Travis sat at the other end of the table, moping. Jace had taken away his phone, which meant Travis couldn't spend half the night talking to Tina. Charlie seemed to be in her own world and had barely taken a bite of her food.

"The roast's fantastic. You ought to try it."

She dutifully took a bite but her head was somewhere else, probably mentally preparing herself for their upcoming conversation.

No one but he and Grady seemed to be enjoying the meal. Travis asked to be excused and cleared his plate. Grady grabbed a cookie for dessert and ran off to play video games, leaving Jace alone with Charlie.

She got up and began clearing the rest of the dishes. Jace helped her at the sink. When they were done, he grabbed a beer and poured her a glass of wine.

"Shall we take this into the study?"

She followed him and he shut the door so they wouldn't be disturbed.

"Charlotte Holcomb, huh?"

She took a spot on the loveseat but didn't say anything while he made a fire in the woodstove.

"Your ex is looking for you," Jace continued. "He's been to the police."

From her bland expression the news wasn't anything she didn't already know.

"What's your plan?"

She seemed to contemplate whether to answer and after a long pause finally said, "At the end of the week I'll be moving on."

"Where to?"

"I don't know yet." She tried to avoid his penetrating stare by dropping her gaze to the floor.

He sat next to her and lifted her chin with his finger. "Charlie, look at me. I'm not the enemy here. I can help you."

"You don't know what you're dealing with." She shivered.

He didn't know if it was from fear or the cold. His office didn't get as much sunlight as the rest of the house. He grabbed the throw off the back of the couch and placed it around her shoulders. "The fire will get warm soon. I know he's the son of Senator Ainsley. He's not above the law, Charlie."

She closed her eyes. "I'm not so sure about that. He's crazy. I let a crazy man control me. And he won't be done until he crushes me, because Corbin Ainsley can't stand to lose, regardless of the cost. When he finds out I lost the baby, he'll blame me and he'll want retribution."

"What about your retribution, Charlie? You lost your child, for God's sake. How about some retribution for you?"

"Retribution?" she said in a near whisper, startled by the question. "I'm just trying to survive."

"You're safe from him now. He'll have to get through me to get to you. But let's put him where he belongs. Let's put him behind bars, Charlie."

She shook her head. "I have to leave. I promised you a week and I'll give you week, but I've got to go."

"That would be a mistake, take my word for it. The man has resources and he'll put them toward looking for you. I say you stay right here, get a restraining order, and when he comes calling, I arrest his ass."

"Then what?" She rolled her eyes. "First chance he gets, he'll bail out. And I'll be the one to pay. You don't know Corbin, you don't know his sense of entitlement."

No, Jace didn't know Corbin Ainsley, but he knew men just like him. Men who thought the world owed them something, men who were cowards and used their fists on defenseless women.

"I've been in law enforcement a long time." He reached over and lightly touched her arm. It was meant to be reassuring but the softness of her skin made him want to linger. They were talking about an asshole who beat her up, and all he could think about was touching her. What the hell was wrong with him? "It's your decision whether you want to keep running. But Charlie…Charlotte…you and I both know it's not the answer. You should take your life back, open another home-goods store or whatever it is you want to do. You shouldn't have to live out of a car and move from place to place, using a bogus name."

"Not completely bogus." She flashed a wan smile. "My dad used to call me Charlie when I was a girl. With Corbin I lost everything—my sense of safety, my self-worth, my self-respect. I was damned if I was going to lose my name too. So when the time came for me to change my identity, I fought to keep a little piece of it." She let out a mirthless laugh. "Charlie Rogers. There has to be thousands of them, right?"

He put his hand over hers. "No one can take your self-worth or your self-respect. Maybe you misplaced them for a time, but I have no doubt you'll find them again. No doubt at all."

Her eyes grew misty and she sniffled. "Thank you for saying that. Thank you…for everything."

"Let's get Corbin Ainsley." Jace wanted the son-of-a-bitch so bad he could taste it. "Let's get your life back."

"Why? Why would you do this for me? You're up for reelection, and Corbin's father…he's powerful. He knows everyone and can pull strings to hurt your campaign." She turned sideways on the couch and stared up at him with concern.

"Have a little faith, Charlie. I grew up here. These are good people. They want a sheriff who puts the law before politics." Despite Tiffany's so-called poll, he truly believed that. And even if Jace was wrong, he wasn't going to turn a blind eye to injustice. It wasn't the way he was built.

"Meredith says I need to leave the state, go somewhere where Corbin can't find me."

"Who's Meredith?"

Charlie went pale. "No one. Forget I said that. Please."

Jace suspected Meredith was with the Rosie the Riveter Foundation but decided to leave Charlie's slip alone. If she wanted to give Meredith cover it was her prerogative to do so. Jace had no beef with the woman. But Meredith's advice sucked.

"That's not a plan, Charlie, that's condemning yourself to life on the run."

"A life on the run is better than no life at all."

"You think I'd let something happen to you?" He looked at her for a good long time. "My plan's better."

"To get a restraining order? Then I'd have to reveal my address?"

"Not with a domestic violence restraining order. You can use the Safe at Home program. It'll give you an address to use for the purpose of court documents. We'll get a lawyer to help you fill out the paperwork." After he'd met with Cash for lunch he'd done more research, and the DV restraining order was the way to go. As soon as Corbin walked through it, which Jace knew he ultimately would, the Mill County Sheriff's Department would pounce. "Did you ever file a complaint with SFPD?" It would sure help if she had.

She pinned him with a look. "He's a prominent lawyer and a senator's son. How far do you think I would've gotten?"

At least they had the emergency-room doc's report and pictures. That would be enough to secure the TRO.

"I don't want to make trouble for you…or the boys. I have places I can go."

"Do I look like someone who scares? You're safe here, Charlie. I can't guarantee you'll be safe running. Let's do this the right way. If you don't want to report the abuse to SFPD, that's your choice. But at least get the restraining order, make a record."

He kneeled down on the floor in front of her. With her hand in his, he said, "Stay here, Charlie. Let me keep you safe."

He would offer the same to anyone under his jurisdiction. But the bottom line was, he didn't want her to go.

Ever since he'd found her on that lonely stretch of road, he'd been drawn to her. Attracted to her beauty and her quiet courage. The fact was, she stirred something in him, something that had long been dormant. And he knew if she left he'd never see her again.

He didn't believe in fate or destiny, or any of that other romantic garbage. But something told him if she decided to take off it would be a missed opportunity for both of them.

Her bottom lip quivered and her eyes pooled. "I love it here. You, the boys, the ranch, even that barn." She bobbed her head at the window, the one that faced her workshop, and sniffled. "But every expert I've talked to has said get out—even if it's just with the clothes on your back—and run. Change your identity and stay off the grid."

"That was before you had me in your court." She started to protest and he held up his hand. "Do me a favor and think about it. You promised me a week. There are a few days left, enough time to digest everything I've said. If you decide to leave at the end of a week, I'll help you any way

I can." He stood up, leaned down, and planted a kiss on her forehead. "Goodnight, Charlie."

* * * *

Charlotte sat by the fire long after Jace had left the room, thinking. She wanted to stay here with every fiber of her being. Changing towns, going from state to state, was no way to live. The ranch, on the other hand, was a haven. And Jace and the boys...she was getting attached to them. There was no question about that.

Every evening she watched the clock, waiting for Jace to walk through the door, straining to hear his truck come up the driveway. She told herself that he made her feel protected. Safe. But it was more. In the short time she'd known him, he had made her believe in herself again. Depending on her to watch his sons had given her a sense of purpose. And not a day went by when he didn't compliment her meals or her table settings, or one of her repurposing projects.

Corbin had never been happy with anything she did. Nothing was ever good enough. In the beginning, his criticisms had been small, petty swipes.

Charlotte, you call this washing? Look here, you left a spot of sauce on the pan. Charlotte, you're not really going to wear that are you? I have people to impress.

But with time, the swipes grew into verbal blows with enough blunt force to do as much damage as the physical beatings. She kept making up excuses for him, convinced that with enough love and patience he'd change. And until he did, she tried not to set him off.

Here, Jace rarely raised his voice. Of course, he didn't have to. The man had merely to cock a brow and the boys fell in line. Not because Jace was in any way scary or dictatorial, he just commanded respect from people because he gave it in return.

And her projects...if she left, she'd never see all of them through. But if she stayed, she'd be a sitting duck because it would only be a matter of time before Corbin found her. And despite Jace's good intentions, he couldn't be with her all the time. He worked long hours, keeping the entire county safe. And Corbin was the kind of coward who'd lie in wait until she was alone and vulnerable before pouncing.

It was a lot to think about. Charlotte would take the next couple of days to make her decision. In the meantime, she'd enjoy every single second of every day here on Dry Creek Ranch.

Chapter 12

By the end of the week, Charlotte had made her decision to stay. Meredith had blessed the choice with a healthy degree of trepidation.

"You're a hundred percent sure you can trust this sheriff?" she'd asked, sounding doubtful. "In my experience everyone has an agenda, Charlotte. You have to ask yourself, what's his?"

A babysitter. Jace needed one, Charlotte told herself. And he was a natural-born protector who saw a woman in need. If there was anything more to it than that, she had no clue what it was. Not once had he made an advance or done anything untoward. The sheriff was a perfect gentleman and it wasn't as if he didn't have his pick of the single women in the county.

Charlotte had watched many a woman's eyes follow him across the coffee shop on the occasions they'd eaten there. There was a group of single moms at Grady's school who'd invited Charlotte to join them for coffee at the Starbucks in an adjoining town. It didn't take long for her to figure out that their interest was in Jace, not in befriending her. The one time she'd gone to their coffee gathering, they'd plied her with questions.

"You two aren't romantically involved, right?" asked a bubbly redhead who had seemed to hold her breath until Charlotte had answered that Jace was her employer and nothing more.

"But you're living at the ranch in his big house, aren't you?" asked another one of the moms, this one a blonde with wide blue eyes, whose husband had died in a crane accident at thirty-five.

The interrogation went on for thirty minutes before Charlotte suddenly remembered she had somewhere to be and politely excused herself.

So Jace's patronage was not because he lacked female company. Any one of those women would've been more than happy to accommodate any of his wants or needs.

Whatever the reason he'd taken her under his wing, Charlotte wasn't about to look a gift horse in the mouth.

By late February, she'd assimilated to ranch life, adopting Jace's habit of getting up just as the sun was rising. After he finished his chores they would sit in the kitchen together, sipping coffee, enjoying the peacefulness of the morning until the boys woke up. She often shared the details of her latest project and he told her funny stories about his deputies or the job.

On one such morning, he talked about the back taxes on the ranch and how he and his cousins were struggling to come up with the cash.

"You don't think you'll lose the land...the house...do you?"

"Nah," he said. "My grandfather would roll over in his grave. We'll figure out something."

They sat there for a few moments, just holding each other's gaze. Charlotte reached across the breakfast table and touched his hand in a gesture of empathy.

"Have you thought any more of how the ranch could bring in more income other than the money you bring in from the cattle?"

"Nothing I'm willing to do." Jace shook his head but had held on to her hand. "I can't see Cash, Sawyer, or me running a country store." He chortled. "And I'm sure as hell not going to put in a golf course or condominium complex. Some folks have planted grapes but I'm not a farmer. It's not like Mill County is known for its wine anyway. But it is known for its beef." He stared out the window and eventually said, "We'll work something out."

Subconsciously, his thumb rubbed back and forth against her wrist. She liked the sensation of it, the way his calloused finger felt against her soft skin. There was nothing demanding in his touch, just a gentle soothing that was almost hypnotic.

But Sawyer walked through the door and broke the mood.

"You got anything to eat?"

Charlotte rose, went to the refrigerator and got out the eggs to make him an omelet.

"Charlie, Sawyer can make his own eggs."

Sawyer took the basket from her. "Sit, drink your coffee. I'll make us all something."

"God help us," Jace said.

Charlotte didn't know much about Sawyer other than he was a journalist who was working on a book and that he lived across the field in an old barn he'd converted into a loft apartment. She'd never been inside but was hoping for an invitation just to see what Sawyer had done with the place. Both Jace and Cash referred to Sawyer's home as "the New York penthouse." Charlotte wasn't sure if they were being facetious or it really was something you'd see in a big city.

But so far, an invitation hadn't been forthcoming. Like Cash, Sawyer was polite but reserved around her. She knew Jace had told them of her situation and didn't blame them for being protective of their cousin and his sons. For no doubt they thought her ex would bring trouble. Aubrey, on the other hand, had been extremely welcoming, stopping by Charlotte's workshop a few times a week to check on her progress with old man Maitland's "junk," as everyone liked to call it. On a couple of visits, she'd brought a thermos of coffee and homemade cookies and they'd made an impromptu picnic of it.

"What drags your ass out of bed this early?" Jace asked his cousin.

"That investigator I told you about called. He thinks he has a lead on Angie."

Charlotte had heard the men talk about Sawyer's sister once or twice. From what she had gleaned from the conversation, Angie was missing.

"I hope you've thoroughly vetted this guy." Jace got up from the table and poured himself another cup of coffee. "Some of these investigators have been known to come up with leads"—he made finger quotes in the air around the word "leads"—"when they think the gravy train is about to run dry."

"Of course I vetted him. I'm a fucking journalist, Jace."

They both at the same time looked at Charlotte. "Sorry for the language," Sawyer said.

She snorted. "Seriously?"

A ghost of a smile appeared on Jace's lips and he turned back to Sawyer. "What's the lead?"

"He says two years ago, Angie was living in a co-op in New Mexico. Some kind of new age thing in the desert, near Taos."

"That sounds like Angela. But two years... that's a long time ago, Sawyer. She could be anywhere by now."

"It's something to go on, though."

Charlotte heard so much hope in Sawyer's voice that she assumed it was a good lead. But when she caught Jace's eye there was sadness there, not hope. It made Charlotte wonder how many times Sawyer had gone down this road, only to reach a dead end.

"Has he talked to any of the folks in the co-op? Does it even exist anymore?" Jace pointed at the pan on the top of the stove. "Your omelet's burning."

Sawyer turned down the heat. "He hasn't gotten that far yet. He needed my authorization to go to New Mexico. I'm tempted to go myself, but I've got a deadline."

"Did you give him the authorization then?"

"Of course I did."

Jace rubbed his hand down his face. "Maybe it would've been wiser to make a couple of phone calls first. See what you could find out about this so-called co-op."

"I plan on it. But this guy's good, better than all the others I've hired."

"That's my point, Sawyer. Why is he able to dig up stuff no one else has?"

"I don't know, Jace. Why are you a better sheriff's candidate than Jacob Jolly? Why was Cash a better FBI agent than the whole damn Bureau?"

"Just do yourself a favor and check some of this stuff out before you give this guy a blank check," Jace said.

Charlotte didn't know any details about Angie, but reading between the lines she got the distinct impression Jace wasn't buying the investigator's findings. It was a shame because Angie's disappearance was obviously a great source of sorrow in the family. Later, after Sawyer left, she planned to ask Jace to tell her the full story.

That was another thing that had happened in the weeks she'd lived at Dry Creek Ranch. She no longer tiptoed around questions she had or topics she wanted to discuss, fearful that Jace would bite her head off. Jace was always patient, always happy to answer her questions about ranch life or respond to personal inquiries such as how he planned to pay the back taxes. Their conversations were always open and Jace never showed a trace of condescension, even though she knew next to nothing about cattle or law enforcement. A few times she'd even broached the subject of Mary Ann.

While he always responded in that concise, unvarnished way of his, he never said anything disparaging about his ex. He never let on that he was disgusted that she'd left two boys in order to move to France, though Charlotte could only assume he was. However bad the marriage might've been, how do you abandon your children? And, really, how terrible could the relationship have been? Waking up in the same house as Jace every morning wasn't a hardship. Not even close. He was honorable, dependable, protective...the list went on and on.

Charlotte's only insight into Mary Ann, besides the fact that she'd left her boys motherless, came from Aubrey. And according to Jace's best friend—perhaps not the most objective person—Mary Ann was simply a woman who was never happy. Charlotte had certainly known people like that—Corbin, for one—making her think Aubrey's assessment was probably the truth.

Especially because Charlotte had no evidence that Jace was an ogre. Just the opposite, in fact.

Sawyer pushed an omelet under her nose. The eggs were brown around the edges. Overcooked. But Charlotte took a big bite anyway because she didn't want to be rude. Besides, her appetite had returned in a big way since losing the baby. She'd been eating three meals a day, often packing herself the same school lunch she made for the boys to take with her to the workshop.

"Charlie and I were just talking about a way to monetize the ranch," Jace said.

Sawyer looked up from his plate, gave Charlotte a cool assessment, and went back to eating. "You mean besides the cattle?"

"Yeah. Like the McCourtney's pumpkin patch and country store."

"Last I looked, we don't grow pumpkins."

Jace smacked the top of Sawyer's head. "No, but maybe we should. I hear they're raking it in."

"Too seasonal. We need something year-round," Sawyer said, surprising Charlotte for taking her idea seriously. "Let me think about it, do a little research. Whatever we decide, though, won't pay out fast enough for us to make the back taxes. I'll talk to my parents."

Charlotte saw Jace bristle. "I told you I don't want to ask them for money."

"It would just be a loan."

"Damnit, we talked about this, Sawyer. You agreed that we'd do this on our own."

"No, you talked about it," Sawyer said around a full mouth. "I didn't agree to anything. My parents are loaded and this is our family legacy we're talking about, not a handout for a startup. They don't want us to lose it as much as we don't want to lose it."

Jace shook his head. "If you want to ask them for your share, go right ahead. But I'll take care of my own. I suspect Cash will say the same, but that's between you and him. I've got to get to work."

He grabbed his hat and vest from the mudroom and Charlotte watched him get inside his police SUV.

"He's a stubborn SOB," Sawyer said almost to himself.

"Do you really think you're at risk of losing the ranch?" Coming from the help, it was a presumptuous question but Jace had never made her feel like a hired hand. And she knew how much he valued his grandfather's bequest.

He gave her another appraisal, this one cooler than the first. She thought he was going to tell her to mind her own business but he shrugged instead.

"If he continues to be that bullheaded about it, we will. We owe two hundred thousand dollars. After putting food on the table, paying the electric bill, and keeping shoes on the kids' feet, there isn't a lot left over in a sheriff's salary. And if he continues to deny the fact that Jacob Jolly is a real contender for his job, Jace won't even have his crappy sheriff's salary."

"It's that serious?" Aubrey had said as much, but Charlotte wondered if she'd been overreacting.

Sawyer didn't respond in words, just pinned her with a look.

Oh boy. Sawyer struck Charlotte as someone who knew the score. "What should he be doing that he's not?" she asked.

"A good start would be raising money for advertising. I think he has all of a thousand bucks in his campaign fund. That won't even buy him a display ad in the Dry Creek supermarket circular. He could use some billboards along the highway, a few full-page newspaper ads, and mailers that should go out to everyone in the county. Ideally, as we get closer to the primary, he should air a couple of TV spots on one of the regional cable stations. Hell, at this point, I'd be happy if he had buttons and bumper stickers to give away. But my cousin seems to think he'll be reelected on his job performance alone. Pretty damn naïve if you ask me."

Jace wasn't naïve. Just the opposite. Being a cop all these years, he'd probably seen it all. But Sawyer was right, Jace did take the attitude that his work spoke for itself. Unfortunately, voters were often more taken with flash and disingenuous promises.

"What about holding an expensive dinner for donors?" She'd been to several for Corbin's father. They'd been tedious and the food had been awful, but they'd raised a lot of money.

Sawyer chuckled. "I don't think a fancy rubber-chicken dinner would go over too well around here. But a barbecue might. We could serve Dalton beef to remind everyone of Jace's roots in the community, charge eighty bucks a head, and Jace could mingle with his constituents. We could show a video chronicling his accomplishments. He might not raise a lot of cash, but at least he'd get himself back in the game."

Charlotte nodded. She liked the idea. "Okay, how do we proceed? Should one of us talk to Tiffany?"

Sawyer hopped off the stool and walked his plate to the dishwasher. "You better talk to Jace about it first. I'd do it, but you saw how well he listens to me. You, on the other hand…let's just say you have his ear. That's saying a lot because no one has had it for a long time." He gave her a hard stare. "I hope you'll keep that in mind. He's had enough hurt in his life; he and the boys don't need any more." With that he walked out and headed across the field to that penthouse apartment he lived in.

She didn't quite know what to do with Sawyer's statement and spent much of the day pretending not to give it any weight. When Jace got home that evening she told him about the idea for the barbecue.

"I've had 'em before," he said as he came up behind her to sniff the potato soup she was making.

The sheer size of him hulking over her should've filled her with unease. Instead, she felt cocooned. Warm and safe and aware of him in the way a woman is of a man whom she longs to be touched by. The truth was she'd been thinking of him—and touching—a lot. The revelation was as strange as her desire to feel a man's arms around her again. It had been a long time since she'd wanted intimacy.

Yet, with Jace it was all she could think about.

"After buying all the supplies I pretty much just broke even," he continued, unaware of the effect his proximity was having on her.

"Sawyer said we could use beef from the ranch." She moved away from the pot to gain a little distance and immediately felt bereft of his body heat. Funny, because she hadn't been cold before he'd walked in the door.

"Yeah, we can do that. But there's still everything else. All the fixings. Drinks. Staff. It adds up."

"Maybe we could get donations and volunteers." Off the top of her head, Charlotte could think of at least a dozen women who would be more than happy to help if it meant getting closer to Jace. And Tiffany would know others to hit up.

Jace scrubbed his hand through his hair. "I'll think about it."

"I could organize it for you," she blurted out, adding, "with Tiffany's help of course."

"Yeah?" His lips ticked up and she felt her heart bounce up and down like a teeter-totter. "I suppose we could do it at the ranch, break out some of the old outdoor heaters and build a big bonfire."

"Absolutely, though it's getting warmer." She was excited for the chance to return some of the generosity he'd shown her. And a party. She used to love throwing parties.

Charlotte and Allison had thrown a sixtieth birthday party for their mother that friends and relatives still talked about. They'd blocked off their parents' street and turned it into a park with dozens of potted trees, flower boxes, and hundreds of twinkly lights. They'd even hired street vendors and a swing band to play on a stage made to look like an old-time park gazebo.

The entire event had been magical.

"I'll call Tiffany right after dinner," she said. "I bet Aubrey would like to help too."

"Whomever you want." He shrugged but he was still smiling. "Thank you."

"I haven't done anything yet."

She reached up into the cupboard for bowls when she felt him behind her again. When she turned around, his startling blue eyes locked with hers. They just stood there like that and Charlotte was sure Jace was going to kiss her. But just like that he quickly moved away.

"Should I call the boys in for dinner?"

"Sure," she said and began setting the table so he wouldn't see the disappointment on her face. She'd wanted that kiss. God, how she had wanted it.

And what the hell was wrong with her? Kisses, touches. She'd just escaped a horrible relationship. Not more than a month ago, she'd lost a child. And now she was dreaming about Jace Dalton. No wonder she was the queen of bad choices.

Jace yelled to Travis and Grady and within a few minutes the boys swarmed the kitchen.

"Charlie, can my friend Joshua come over after school tomorrow? Please?" Grady wrapped his arms around her waist. The boy was a little charmer.

She looked at Jace, who responded, "It's up to you. You're the one in charge while I'm at work."

You're in charge.

He had no idea how much those words meant to her, how they helped restore a piece of her self-esteem. His belief in her should've been enough. It should've been everything. What did it say about her that she wanted more? So much more.

Chapter 13

Jace turned in early that night. After dinner he usually enjoyed a glass of wine and conversation with Charlie in his study. But tonight he wasn't interested in talking. What he was interested in wasn't in the cards.

His head knew that. Unfortunately, his body hadn't gotten the memo.

Maybe he should call Antonia, a woman he occasionally saw in Nevada City in the neighboring county. She'd moved up to Gold Country about two years ago and owned a pottery studio on the main drag in town. He'd met her while browsing her shop for a gift to buy his secretary. In the looks department, she'd reminded him a little of Mary Ann. Blond, pale blue eyes, fair skin, rocking body. The similarities stopped there, though. Antonia was focused, rooted, and committed to the community. The previous year, she'd taken over the space next to her small store and expanded.

They'd had a nice thing going. No demands, no expectations. Just a monthly date in which Jace took her to dinner or in summertime, dinner and an outdoor concert. He enjoyed listening to her talk about art, which he knew nothing about. She pretended to be interested in ranching and Jace's sons.

Mostly, they enjoyed the sex.

But ever since Charlie had moved in, he'd stopped seeing Antonia. He didn't feel right about jumping into the sack with one woman while his mind was on another. Now, he questioned the sanity of that decision.

It was getting more difficult every day. Like the night before, when Grady had accidentally broken a water jug. The sound of smashing glass must've triggered a bad memory because Charlie went white as a sheet. It had taken the strength of Hercules to stop Jace from taking her in his arms and kissing away whatever flashback she was having.

Then, there were nights when the vision of her, sitting cross-legged on the couch by the fire with her dark hair loose around her shoulders, made him so hard he'd have to get up to leave the room.

But he wouldn't let things get out of control. Charlie was under his protection, for Christ's sake. As long as she lived under his roof, he wouldn't touch her.

Not unless she touched him first.

* * * *

The next morning, she waited in the kitchen for him with a thermos of coffee. It had become part of their routine. By the time he got back from checking on the cattle, she'd have breakfast made. The two of them would eat together and talk about their respective plans for the day until Travis and Grady dragged themselves out of bed.

It was Jace's favorite part of the day.

"It's not as cold as it was yesterday."

"March is almost here." He eyed her feet. Although she was dressed, she still had on a pair of fuzzy slippers. "You've been outside already?"

"Just on the back porch." She hugged herself and smiled. "It's shaping up to be a beautiful day."

It was barely light outside, but in Jace's experience a rancher could predict the weather better than a meteorologist. "This place is turning you into a cowgirl."

"You think?" The way her face glowed, she'd taken the comment as high praise.

"You want to drive out with me to the back pasture? We'll take my truck." Most of the time he saddled up Amigo, but Charlie didn't know how to ride. Someday soon, though, Jace would get her on the back of a horse.

"What about breakfast?"

"We'll make it when we get back." His eyes fell to her feet again. "Go put on a pair of boots." The only ones she had stopped short of her ankles and had probably been purchased in a high-end shoe store. But they were better than slippers.

"You sure? What about the boys?"

"They'll be fine. Now, giddyup, daylight's burning."

A few minutes later, she met him in the mudroom, raring to go. He helped her into the cab of his truck and they rode the short distance to the cattle barn in silence.

Jace killed the engine. "What are you sighing about over there?"

"It's so beautiful here." She turned sideways in her seat. "Did you always love it? Or did you dream as a boy of running off to the big city?"

He chuckled. "Never. From the time I was born this ranch was in my blood. Cash and Sawyer's too. Grandpa Dalton used to say it skipped a generation."

"Your parents didn't love it here?"

"They did. If my father hadn't been killed in the crash, he'd probably be running the ranch now." He paused. It had been more than a couple of decades since a drunk had plowed into his father's truck on Highway 49, but Jace still missed them every day. "Cash and Sawyer's fathers weren't into it, though. Uncle Jed and Uncle Dan weren't cut from the same cloth as Grandpa Dalton. Cash's dad wanted to be a cop." His lips tipped up. "Like I told you, I probably got that from him. And Uncle Dan…Sawyer's dad…owns a big PR firm in Los Angeles. They represent celebrities, rock stars, big athletes. Their specialty is crisis management."

"What's that?"

"Remember a few years ago when people were getting sick from contaminated orange juice?" Charlie nodded. "The citrus industry hired Aunt Wendy and Uncle Dan to rebuild consumer trust. That's the kind of stuff they do."

"They're the ones you don't want to take the money from to pay the taxes?"

"Not just them, no one. I pay my own debts." He reached across the cab and zipped her jacket. "Let's go."

She followed him to the barbed-wire fence and he held the middle strand up so she could climb through. "You got it?"

She made it to the other side with ease. "What do we do now?"

"Make sure the water trough's full."

"Okay, tell me how I can help."

She'd helped simply by spending the morning with him.

"Normally I'd check to see if any fences were down, but not on foot." He glanced at her shoes, which were now caked with mud. "We got to get you some real boots." Sometimes she wore red suede loafers, which were as practical for a working ranch as the ankle boots she had on.

She stared down at her footwear. "I didn't take many clothes with me when I left. I needed the car space for my sewing machines and supplies."

"Why don't you take a day and go shopping in Roseville? If you're nervous about Ainsley, I'll go with you." Shopping malls were the tenth circle of hell as far as he was concerned, and the likelihood of Ainsley finding her in a Sacramento suburb was pretty much next to nil. But better safe than sorry. "Have you thought any more about that restraining order we talked about?"

"Why? It's not like it would deter him from finding me. Or stop him from doing anything he wanted to do. Corbin doesn't believe he has to follow the rules."

"But I do, Charlie. Without a restraining order, he's not breaking the law if he approaches you in public. Help me do my job, here. Help me take care of you."

She gazed up at him. "I'd like to say I can take care of myself but ..." She sniffled and stared out over the horizon. "My sister, Allison, would never have let a man beat her up. We were raised in a gentle home, a good home. I don't know how I let this happen to me."

"Let's put the blame where it belongs, not on the survivor. And, Charlie, you can take care of yourself." Jace leaned against the barn, pulled Charlie against him until her back rested against his chest, and wrapped his arms around her waist. "The first step is filing that restraining order. Now tell me about this sister of yours. Don't know her, but I already like her."

"She's two years younger than me but a wise old soul." Charlie got quiet, then softly said, "We don't talk any longer and I miss her so much."

Jace felt Charlie shudder and knew she was crying. "Why don't you talk anymore?" He pulled her closer so she could lean the back of her head on his shoulder.

"She hated Corbin, despised him." Charlie's voice trembled. "I let him come between us. My sister, who means the world to me, and I let Corbin come between us. What kind of person lets a man drive a wedge between sisters? Family? Tell me that."

"Call her, tell her you're sorry. Then you'll have her back in your life."

"You make it sound so easy. Well it's not. What am I supposed to tell her? 'You were right, Corbin was the devil incarnate. Now I'm in hiding from him and I can't tell you where I am because I don't want to get you enmeshed in this mess.'" She turned around so she faced him. "I'm ashamed, Jace. I'm so ashamed."

"Shhhh," he whispered. "You've got nothing to be ashamed of. You're brave, Charlie. Only a brave person does what you did. File the restraining order. Call Allison. Take your life back."

"I'll think about it," she said, her voice tearful.

"Ah, don't cry, honey. It'll be okay. You're here now, you're safe."

"Safe? I'm not safe from myself. Look at the horrible decisions I made. Look at the awful man I let into my life. I let him destroy my business, my relationship with my family...my baby."

The crying started anew and this time her whole body shook with every wrenching sob. He pulled her into his arms and let her wail into his chest.

"Go ahead, get it all out." He held her tighter. "Let it go. I'm here for you, Charlie."

"Why? Why would you want anything to do with me?"

He rubbed his thumb along the side of her face and wiped away a tear. "Because I like you."

"I don't know why."

"Is that a way to talk?" His fingers subconsciously sifted through her silky hair and his voice grew lower. "You're an amazing, smart, talented woman, who was victimized by a human piece of garbage. You weren't the first—far from it—and unfortunately you won't be the last. But leaving him the way you did, that took real courage." He lifted her up into his arms. "Let's get you home. Sawyer can look after the cattle today."

"I'm okay. We can finish. Please...I don't want to pull you away from your work."

"We'll sit in the truck for a while and see how you feel." The cattle could wait.

He carried her to the passenger side and got in behind the wheel. It was chilly, so he turned on the engine and cranked the heat. He took off his shearling jacket, covered her with it, and handed her a wad of tissues from the dispenser on the visor.

"Better?"

"Yes" was all she said and for a long time they sat in the quiet of his truck cab.

The sun had finally made a full appearance, lighting up the sky like a giant orange.

"You'll be late for work and the boys are probably up by now." Charlie wiped her nose with the tissues and stared out the windshield.

"They'll be fine for a few minutes. Take whatever time you need." He reached over the console and covered her small hand with his.

"They should clone men like you, you know?"

He snorted. "God help us all if they did."

She turned in her seat to face him. "I'm serious. If it hadn't been for you, I don't know what I would've done. I probably would've gone crazy."

"Nah, you're a fighter and Corbin, he's a coward." A dead coward if Jace ever got his hands on him. Okay, Jace wouldn't really kill him but he'd like to make him suffer.

He leaned across the cab and kissed her. Just a sweet peck on the cheek, but Charlie turned and took his lips, cupping the back of his head with her hands to kiss him deeper.

Jace reacted and kissed her back. Long, slow, and thoroughly. When she didn't resist, he kept going, exploring her lips and licking inside her mouth with his tongue.

She tipped her head back against the seat and he went in for more, drunk on the taste of her. Her hands came around his neck and he pressed her deeper into the seat, bruising her lips with his, winding his hands through her hair. Kissing her into tomorrow.

He shouldn't have. It was wrong on about a thousand levels.

Yet, he couldn't seem to stop himself. She felt so good—curvy and warm and feminine—and responsive, returning his kisses with equal passion. He could make her feel good too. Take the hurt away if she'd let him.

He pushed his jacket off her and let his hands slide down her sides, pulling her into his lap. This time, he kissed her even more powerfully, devouring her mouth like he hadn't eaten in a week, his hands roaming freely over her sweater.

She made a sound, a whimper maybe. Jace was so lost in her he couldn't tell. But when she whimpered again it registered that he'd gone too far, that he needed to put the brakes on.

"Shit." He forced himself to pull away. "Ah, man, that won't happen again." He saw the chafing on her chin and rubbed the scruff on his face. He'd forgone shaving this morning to get more time with her before he had to go to work. Jeez, he was losing it. "I didn't scare you, did I?"

"Of course not. I started it." She traced his lips with her fingers. "And I don't regret one second of it."

He blew out a breath and lifted her out of his lap onto the bucket seat next to him. "Look, I don't want you to think this is a quid pro quo thing. Ah, shit, I'm not saying this right. We're friends…you're babysitting my kids…Ah, Christ, give me a second." He got out of the truck and walked behind the barn to gather his thoughts before he fucked this up any more than he already had.

The kiss had been forceful, even rough. God only knew what she'd been through with Ainsley. The last thing he wanted was for her to think she was expected to put out while she lived under his roof. The very notion of it made him sick. He wasn't one of those guys, he didn't want his sons to be one of those guys. What kind of message would this send to them?

"What are you doing?" Charlie came through the brush and tilted her head to the side.

Crap, maybe he'd been talking to himself. "Figuring out how I'm going to fix this."

"There's nothing to fix, Jace. We kissed. Not the end of the world. The fact is I quite liked it. And for the record, you've never made me feel like I needed to trade my kisses for your home or friendship. Never. You've been a perfect gentleman. I initiated the kiss, not you. And I initiated it because you make me feel safe, like you'd never take advantage. So can we please not make this a thing?"

"A thing?" He raised his brows. Had she just insinuated that he was acting like a high school girl? "As long as you're good, I'm good."

"I'm good. Better than good." Her face flushed red and she smiled. "Now, if we don't get back, Travis and Grady will think we've run off on them."

"Yeah, okay," he said but he wasn't okay at all.

* * * *

Sawyer watched as Jace's Ford F-150 pulled away from the barn, and gave his head a shake. The boy was getting himself in deep with his pretty houseguest.

He hiked into the pasture and used the hose from the water tank to fill a galvanized metal trough. It was still more than half full and the cattle preferred drinking from an irrigation pond a few clips up the road anyway. But they'd been filling that trough for as long as Sawyer could remember.

He shielded his eyes from the sun with his hand, having forgotten his sunglasses. Angus cows dotted the green hillsides. The rain this year had left the grass lush for grazing.

Sawyer hadn't bothered to saddle up Sugar or one of the other horses in the stable to check fences. Perhaps he'd take one of the mares out later, after he knocked out a few thousand words on his book. Nothing was better than a good brisk ride. With five hundred acres, he'd never run out of trails to explore.

First thing this morning, he'd put out a few calls about Angie's alleged co-op. Instead of sitting around, waiting for responses, he'd decided to stretch his legs and fill his lungs with fresh air.

He turned off the hose, wound it back up, and started to hike home when he turned in the other direction.

Ten minutes later, he lounged in a rocker on Cash's front porch. Technically it was Aubrey's, but after the engagement Cash and Ellie had moved in. Cash's old place was just across the creek and in the same state of disrepair he'd left it. Every time Sawyer saw the cabin he hummed a few bars of "Dueling Banjos."

Aubrey's cabin, on the other hand, was a showstopper. Flower boxes, great-looking screen door, and matching shutters all painted a forest green. The inside was even better and she'd done it all on a dime. No wonder she was one of the most sought-after interior designers in Gold Country.

The screen door squeaked open and Cash came out onto the porch. "You planning to sit out here all morning? Or were you expecting room service?"

"Why does everyone treat me like a profligate?"

"You get that off your word-of-the-day calendar?" Cash ushered Sawyer across the threshold.

"Nope, I just happen to have an amazing vocabulary. Where's Ellie? It's quiet in here."

"She stayed the night with a friend so they could work on a history project. Aubrey's in the bedroom."

Sawyer grimaced. "Am I interrupting something?"

"Let's just say your timing is better than usual. But I do have to get to a meeting that starts in an hour." Cash glanced at his watch. "What's up? Or are you here to raid the refrigerator?"

"Nah, I already ate. Coffee would be good, though."

Cash rolled his eyes but went into the kitchen to pour Sawyer a cup. Sawyer made himself at home at their dining room table.

"I went down to check on the cattle a little bit ago and found Jace in his truck making out with Charlie."

Sawyer waited for a snarky response about how he should mind his own business or that he was a voyeuristic bastard, but nothing was forthcoming. Just silence and a scowl.

Finally, he said, "I figured it was just a matter of time."

"It won't end well."

"What won't end well?" Aubrey came out of the bedroom in her work clothes, her hair wet.

"Jace and Charlie. I think they're a thing now." Sawyer sipped his coffee.

"Neither of them have said anything to me about it, but they're both adorable, so good on them."

Cash didn't comment, but Sawyer was pretty sure he was stifling another eye roll.

"She seems like a perfectly nice woman," Sawyer said. "But she's not for Jace. First of all, she's got a nutjob boyfriend with an influential father who can screw up Jace's chances in the election. Second of all, she doesn't strike me as a small-town girl. Last time Jace fell for one of those…well, we all know what happened."

Aubrey waved her hand in the air. "You don't know anything about Charlie. She's lovely and nothing like Mary Ann. As far as small towns, she seems to adore the ranch."

"Because it's serving as a safe house with Jace standing between her and the big, bad wolf. What happens when Ainsley isn't a threat any longer? I'll tell you what happens: Charlie resumes her life in San Francisco, leaving Jace and the boys in her rearview mirror."

"You're being completely unfair. Don't you think he's being unfair, Cash?"

Cash went into his signature silent mode again.

"You're both idiots. And I have to go to work." She kissed Cash and they wound up mashing lips long enough to make Sawyer blush.

"Jeez, get a room, people."

"We have a room but my pain-in-the-ass cousin decided to drop in uninvited."

Aubrey giggled, gave Cash another kiss, and planted a smooch on the top of Sawyer's head. "You're welcome here anytime, Dalton." She grabbed her purse off the hook by the door and blew them both a kiss goodbye.

"She likes me better than you," Sawyer said.

Cash went to the window as Aubrey's ancient Volvo came to life and watched her drive away. "Jace says some investigator has a lead on Angie."

Dry Creek Ranch may as well have gone back to the party line. Nothing happened on the ranch without it being telegraphed between the three of them. And now Aubrey.

"It's two years old, but yeah, it's something."

Cash frowned but remained mum.

"Just say what's on your mind." Sawyer got up and poured himself another cup of coffee.

"I don't have to say it." Cash found his boots by the door and pulled them on. "You know the drill better than any of us. I think you journalists call it skepticism. Take whatever this dude is telling you with a heavy dose of it."

"Yeah, I know." He squeezed the bridge of his nose.

Angela had been missing for five years now. One day he was talking to her on the phone, then, poof, he never heard from her again. It wasn't the first time she'd fallen off the map.

But they'd never been out of touch with her for more than six months at a time. When she failed to surface, Sawyer's parents spent tens of thousands of dollars searching for her. Private investigators, DNA databases, even psychics. In the last year, he'd taken over the search. And still, nothing.

"Maybe it's a good lead, Sawyer," Cash said. "I'm not saying it's not. But proceed with caution and try not to get your hopes up."

How was he supposed to do that? She was his sister, for God's sake. "Right. What are we going to do about the situation with Jace and Charlie or whatever her real name is?"

"Charlotte. And we're not doing anything. It's Jace's private life. 'Private' being the key word there."

"What if the ex comes sniffing around?"

"Then we'll back Jace up like he'd do for us."

Sawyer nodded. That of course went without saying. The issue was whether Jace was prepared for more heartbreak. "She wants to organize a fundraiser for his campaign."

"That's good. He could use contributions. Jolly's a joke, but according to the paper he's outraised Jace ten times over." Cash grabbed his hat off a peg in the entryway. "I gotta hit the road. Let me know what more you find out from this investigator. I've got a couple of comp days at the end of the month. If need be, you and I can take a trip to New Mexico."

"Thanks. I appreciate that."

Cash bobbed his head at the kitchen. "Help yourself."

Sawyer's lips slid up. "I always do."

After Cash left, Sawyer finished his coffee, washed his cup, and headed across the field to his place. If he stayed disciplined and kept off the internet he could make his daily word quota early enough to go on that ride and later rendezvous with the cute bookstore clerk he'd been seeing in Roseville. It was nothing serious, but she was nice company until he had to leave on another long assignment. The book sabbatical was only going to last so long. His editor at *The Atlantic* was already nagging him about covering some coup in Indonesia.

Last year, he'd barely slept in his own bed. Most of the time, he'd been in Afghanistan. His articles about the war and the Middle East had caught the attention of a couple of the big five publishing houses in New York and a book deal was made. It was his third in five years. Truth be told, he was starting to suffer serious burnout. But publish or perish, right? And Sawyer wasn't ready to disappear into obscurity yet.

He was halfway home when his cell vibrated in his jacket pocket. He tugged it out and checked the caller ID. It was a New Mexico area code.

Chapter 14

Over the next week, Charlotte planned Jace's barbecue fundraiser and continued to work on her projects in the old barn. She'd established a nice routine, including checking off her event to-do list before taking the boys to school, then spending a few hours in the workshop with her furniture. The only thing missing was her quiet breakfasts with Jace.

Ever since the kiss, he'd made himself scarce, finding every excuse under the sun to go to the office early. If it hadn't been for the not-so-surreptitious smoldering looks he sent her, Charlotte would've thought she'd repelled him that day in the pasture.

Frankly, she missed him and their mornings together to the point where she was ready to confront him about it and was just waiting for the right time.

He had been kind enough to escort her to a lawyer's office to file the domestic restraining order against Corbin and had held her hand as the attorney asked a million personal questions. It had been so sweet and considerate of him that she'd cried the entire drive home from Auburn.

According to the lawyer, Corbin was served on Friday. Here it was Monday and Charlotte was jumping at shadows. Even though the order did not contain Jace's address, it had been stamped with the Mill County Court insignia. Knowing Corbin, he was combing the entire region, looking for her at this very moment.

Everyone at the ranch—even the boys, who'd been told a pared-down version of the story—was on alert and the gate was kept closed at all times.

Still, her nerves were fried.

After dropping Travis and Grady at their schools, she'd come directly home and was now holed up in her workshop with a can of pepper spray.

To keep from going out of her mind, she tried to focus all her attention on a beat-up chair she wanted to rehabilitate. Someone had left the piece of furniture on the side of the road for large-item trash pickup. Other than the dated upholstery—green and orange floral flocked velvet—the chair had a lovely shape. Rounded arms, medium-high back, and a swivel bottom. With a touch of TLC, it would be as beautiful as it was functional.

She'd thrown it into the back of her CR-V and for the last few days had been sewing a slipcover to match the sofa she'd already finished. The two pieces could be sold as a set or individually.

Jace had constructed a sewing table in the barn for her, out of an old countertop Aubrey had donated to the space from a kitchen remodel she'd designed. And Sawyer had thrown in a couple of file cabinets he was no longer using, to store Charlotte's supplies.

She was finishing the zipper for one of the cushion covers when she heard a car drive up. Charlotte leapt for the pepper spray and her phone at the same time. She was just about to dial 911 when someone called out, "Yoo-hoo, anyone home?"

"Aubrey, is that you?" Charlotte opened the barn door a crack, just enough to see outside with one eye.

"It's me and I've got a friend with me."

Charlotte stuck the pepper spray under a pile of fabric remnants and slid open the door. A willowy woman with straight, long, blond hair alighted from Aubrey's station wagon in a pair of tooled cowboy boots and a suede jacket that made Charlotte's mouth water. The woman reminded Charlotte of Bo Derek.

"This is Dee Dee. She's one of my dearest clients. I told her about your studio and she was dying to take a look around."

Studio?

Charlotte patted her hair self-consciously. She hadn't even worn makeup today. "Sure, of course, come in." She immediately began to tidy up her workspace. "I wasn't expecting visitors, so it's kind of a mess."

She'd at least created vignettes with the pieces she'd completed. A bed with a handmade toile blanket and a pile of fluffy pillows. Next to the bed, she'd placed a matching red nightstand. At the foot, she'd stacked a few antique apple crates like a bench. And on the wall she'd hung a wooden sign stenciled with the words "My happy place."

The slipcovered sofa had been placed in front of old man Maitland's cast-off wagon, which Charlotte had turned into a coffee table. Behind the couch was a sofa table she'd constructed out of reclaimed barn wood and two rusted iron wheels that had been part of a produce cart. On each end of the table sat a lamp that had once been a pair of tattered cowboy boots. A chandelier made from the cut-off bottoms of wine bottles and white pillar candles completed the showcase. As soon as the chair was completed, she'd add it to the collection.

Dee Dee shrieked and bustled across the room to an ottoman Charlotte had found at a garage sale and had recovered in a cowhide Jace had given her. It was one of her favorite pieces.

"The den, Aubrey. Wouldn't this be perfect in the den?"

"It certainly would." Aubrey flicked a smile at Charlotte and held up a shelf rack made from deer antlers. The antlers had come from a church flea market down the road. "With this, don't you think, Dee Dee?"

"Yessssss! A hundred times yes. Add it to the list." Dee Dee bounced from piece to piece oohing and aahing, and within thirty minutes had put another half dozen pieces on the so-called list.

"Dee Dee and her husband just bought a mountain retreat in North Tahoe," Aubrey told Charlotte. "It's five thousand square feet and completely unfurnished. I'm helping her with that."

"That's great." Charlotte turned to Dee Dee. "Congratulations."

"Kale wanted it. He skis. I would've preferred the beach but whatever. The place is very rustic. Lots of wood, rock, and steel. I want to warm it up a bit but stick to the rustic theme."

Dee Dee plopped down on the sofa. "Ooh, this is comfy. It's a little more farmhouse chic than I want to go. But Sissy would go nuts for this couch, wouldn't she, Aubrey?"

"Totally," Aubrey said and got her phone out of her purse. "Now that you mention it, I'll send her a picture."

"Do you have anything else with cowhide?" Dee Dee asked Charlotte.

"Not yet, but I'm working on a few things." She wasn't really, but hoped Jace had more hides. She'd love to do a couple of chairs. "I could let Aubrey know when they're ready."

"What about wall hangings?" Dee Dee got up and started browsing some more.

"What did you have in mind?"

Dee Dee turned to Aubrey, who was playing around with a collection of candleholders Charlotte had made from old stair banisters, looking for the right height combination. "What kind of wall hangings are we looking for, Ree?"

Aubrey scanned the barn "Something like that." She pointed at a Zapotec rug that Charlotte had used as a moving blanket to cushion a couple of dairy crocks she'd inherited from the Maitland farm. The rug was missing some of its fringe on one end.

Charlotte took the rug, folded the damaged part under, and looked around the barn for something that could serve as a hanger. "I could sew the part I folded to create a pocket and use that"—she gestured toward a rusty branding iron she'd found discarded on the ranch that Jace said she could have—"as a rod. It's got that rustic vibe you want and I think the fact that it's a genuine branding iron will complement the theme you're going with."

"I love it," Aubrey said. "Dee?"

"Absolutely. Add it to the list, Aubrey."

By the time Aubrey and Dee Dee left, "the list" had grown to five thousand dollars' worth of merchandise. Charlotte could barely contain herself while Dee Dee wrote the check. Charlotte didn't have a bank account anymore, but she'd figure out a way to cash it later. The important thing was she'd had her first customer and Dee Dee had friends. Lots of friends with similar taste, according to Aubrey.

Charlotte was so busy dancing on cloud nine she didn't hear Jace's truck drive up, and jerked her head in surprise when he came through the barn doors. She quickly checked her watch to make sure she hadn't lost track of the time while Aubrey and Dee Dee were shopping and forgot the boys. But it was only one o'clock.

"What are you doing home?"

"Was in the neighborhood. I passed Aubrey on the way in. She said her client liked your stuff." He glanced around the barn before his eyes fell back on her.

"She bought five thousand dollars' worth of merchandise, Jace. Can you believe it?"

"Sure I can." He smiled. "Didn't you have sales like that when you owned your store?"

"Sometimes." She held her hands wide. "But this isn't exactly a boutique on a trendy street in the Bay Area. The best part is Dee Dee wants to bring some of her friends. They live in Sacramento and some of them own second homes around here and in Tahoe. Is it okay? I mean this is your ranch."

"You kidding me? Take their money." He winked and every one of her female parts stood up and did the wave. "Hey, remember we're keeping the gate locked for the time being. If I'm around I'll let them in."

She reached for his hand and slipped him the check.

"What's this?" He uncrumpled it. "You want me to cash it for you?"

"I want you to keep it."

"Charlie, you can get a bank account now. Ainsley knows you're in Mill County. You can only keep so hidden."

"I know. I want you to keep the money, put it toward the property taxes for the ranch."

He reared back, then handed her back the check. "It's your money, you earned it. I'm perfectly capable of supporting my family and this ranch."

She'd unintentionally hurt his pride, insulted him. With Corbin she would've cowered in the corner.

"This isn't because I think you're incapable of taking care of your own. It's rent for the use of the barn."

"Give me a fuh— a damn break." He looked up at the rafters, his jaw clenched tight. "I don't rent my barns. Keep the goddamn money." He started to walk away and she went after him.

"Jace, don't talk to me like that." She was shocked by the strength in her voice. Even more so, she was surprised she had the guts to challenge him.

He stopped and shoved his hands in his pockets. "You're pissing me off, Charlie."

"You're acting harsh. I don't like harsh."

Jace moved closer. "A man can be angry without hitting."

"I know," she said. "I know that you of all people would never do anything to hurt me. But can't you see how important it is for me to share this with you?" She held up the check. "Do you know how long it's been since I ..." She waved the check in the air. "This...I can contribute. Please let me contribute."

Her voice clogged and he pulled her into his arms.

"You contribute every day. My home, my boys...That's enough, that's all I need."

Apparently, that wasn't all he needed because as he held her a hard bulge pressed against her midsection and it wasn't his sidearm. She pressed back and heard him make a soft noise deep in his throat. He tried to let go but she wouldn't let him.

"Please," she pleaded, pretending to herself that she was asking for him to take the money. They both knew otherwise.

He stared into her eyes and she felt herself drowning in a sea of blue.

"I don't want to hurt you," he said, gently touching her hair.

"We've been over that." She laced her hands behind his neck and went up on tiptoes so the hard ridge in his pants could ride between the vee in her legs. "You would never hurt me."

"Not intentionally. But this"—he closed his eyes—"It's too soon after the...it's too much."

"It's been more than six weeks since the miscarriage." She said what he wouldn't. "Let me be the judge of what's too soon or too much." She kissed him and said against his lips, "I want to feel good again, Jace. I want to feel like a whole woman, not like a fragile victim." She stepped back and implored him with her eyes. "Please."

He stood there for what seemed like forever, warring with himself. Then in two long strides he was in front of her, lifting her off the ground. Charlotte wrapped her legs around his waist as he carried her to the sofa and gently laid her down. Jace came down beside her, dropping his hat on the floor. She leaned over, picked up the Stetson and placed it atop the wagon coffee table on its crown, like she'd seen him do a hundred times before.

He kissed her, sweetly at first. When she returned the kiss with fervor, he ramped it up, slipping his tongue inside her mouth. The way he moved over her with their mouths fused together was so erotic her entire body vibrated with want. Thank goodness the couch was deep enough to hold both of them.

His lips traced the side of her neck and he licked her throat. "You taste good. Sweet and salty. Tell me what you like. I want to make this good for you. I want to get it right."

"I like this." Her eyes fluttered closed and she arched her neck to give him better access.

He kissed her throat and tickled the whorl of her ear with his lips. Then he transferred his attention to her blouse, nimbly working the buttons open. She sent out a silent thanks that she'd worn her good bra. A black lacy one she'd bought years ago and had stuffed in her suitcase before fleeing San Francisco.

"Mm," he murmured as he laved attention on her breasts. He looked up at her, his eyes filled with so much naked desire she could barely speak. "This okay?" His hands moved to the front clasp on her bra.

She nodded and moaned as he freed her breasts, rubbing her nipples with his thumb.

"Oooh" was all she could manage, aroused by his large, calloused hands on her bare skin. Despite their roughness, he was gentle. And he moved slowly, drawing out every caress until she thought she'd scream in ecstasy from each touch.

Jace took one of her breasts in his mouth while he fondled the other.

"Oh, oh." She let out another moan as his mouth moved to her other breast, sucking until she thought she'd go mad with the brilliant sensation of it.

Her body bowed and she nearly came off the couch.

"Good?"

She didn't know how he was able to talk. Then again, he was doing all the work, giving her all the pleasure.

"Better...than...good." She slipped her hands under the hem of his shirt and felt his back bunch.

He sucked in a breath and pulled her against his rock-hard erection. The fact that she could do that to him was heady. Powerful.

Her hands slid over his rib cage and she rubbed her palms down his abs. She loved how the muscles in his stomach rippled.

He pulled the rest of his uniform shirt free from his pants and dragged it over his head, leaving him bare chested. He was beautiful. Bronzed, hard, and sinewy from working outdoors. Strong and powerful. She'd once watched him stack an entire truckload of hay.

Yet he only used his strength to give her joy, not pain.

Charlotte traced his happy trail with the tip of her finger, stopping at his waistband. She watched his eyes grow dark and heated and felt him shudder.

Rolling her on top of him, Jace made short work of getting the rest of her blouse and bra off. He continued to fondle her breasts, leaning up to kiss her. He cradled the back of her head while he devoured her mouth, making her even hotter than she was before.

She played with his fly, stopping short of unzipping his trousers. "I'm not on the pill or anything."

"I've got us covered," he said. "But it's up to you. We could just fool around if you want."

She pressed her breasts against his chest, loving the skin-to-skin contact, and inched her hand inside his pants. She didn't want to stop at kissing and touching, she wanted to feel him inside her.

Jace tugged her hand away and searched her face for an answer.

"Please," she said.

"Please what?"

"I want all of you."

He paused a moment as if he was waiting for her to change her mind. She worked his belt open, unzipped his fly, and touched him through his shorts. His arousal grew larger. Harder.

"Hang on a second." He lifted up, freed a wallet from his back pocket, and pulled out a packet of condoms.

"Do you always carry those around with you?" She was thankful he was prepared—she didn't think she could go a minute longer—but a part of her balked at the notion that there were other women. *What did you think, the man was celibate?*

He didn't answer, just fiddled with the closure on her pants and slid them down her legs. She kicked them off along with her ankle boots.

He rolled her under him, went up on both elbows and took a long leisurely stroll down her body with his eyes. She still had her panties on and he rimmed the elastic band with his index finger, then slowly tugged them down her legs. The sensation of the lace rasping against her skin made her whimper.

Somehow—she lost track of when or how—he'd shucked his own pants and underwear. He used his teeth to open the foil packet while he tested her with his fingers.

"You're so wet." He nuzzled her neck and continued to touch her center, rubbing until the friction made her crazy.

She arched up, a little frenzied. She couldn't remember ever being this desperate, this turned on. "Jace?"

"Charlie?"

"Yes. Please," she croaked, ready to beg if he didn't hurry.

He pushed up with both hands, captured her mouth with his, and entered her in one powerful stroke. He started out slow, letting her get accustomed to him. Charlotte spread her legs wider and he slid his hands under her bottom and cupped her butt so he could go deeper.

"This okay?"

"God, yes." She wrapped her arms around his neck and met him stroke for stroke.

"I want this to be good for you," he whispered in her ear. "Tell me what you like, what you don't like."

"So far, I like it all. Just don't stop."

He nibbled on her earlobe and kissed her neck, the whole time moving inside her. Pulling in and out in a steady rhythm that quickened with time. His hands moved from her butt to her breasts and his thumbs circled her nipples.

"You're beautiful," he said against her mouth. "So incredibly beautiful."

"So are you." She held each side of his face, staring into his blue eyes. "You're such a good man, Jace."

He didn't respond and Charlotte got the sense that he didn't feel like such a good man but had reached the point of no return. She gave small thanks because she couldn't bear it if he stopped. She wanted him to replace all the bad Corbin memories. But it was more than that too.

She simply wanted Jace for Jace.

He changed his position, pumping his hips harder. Faster.

She hooked her ankles around his waist, trying to keep up. "Oh, that's good. So good."

"Tell me when it's too much. I don't want to hurt you."

"I'm not a porcelain doll, Jace. I won't break. More."

"Yes, ma'am." He drove into her again and again, each thrust bringing her closer to climax.

"Jace! Jace!" she yelled out as she clenched and her breathing became ragged.

"Whenever you're ready, just let go. I've got you."

She clung to his shoulders while he reached between her legs and worked her with his fingers as he continued to thrust inside her. Charlotte ground into him one last time, called out his name and trembled with such exquisite release that for a beat she felt like she was floating.

Jace pistoned his hips a few more times, threw his head back, and grunted before collapsing on top of her.

They lay there for a long time, entwined in each other's arms. She buried her face against his chest and listened to his heartbeat as her eyes filled. The power of their intimacy, the sheer glory of it, had left her a mass of quivering emotions.

He gently lifted her face "Hey, hey," he said softly and wiped away a tear. "You okay?"

"I don't think I've ever been better."

He rolled them to their sides, keeping her enfolded in his arms. "Then why are you crying? Was it too soon?"

Not soon enough.

"No." She reached up and kissed him, running her hands through his thick, dark hair. Then she stared into his eyes, wanting to hold on to this moment and remember it forever. "It was perfect, Jace. You're perfect."

Chapter 15

Jace drove back to the station in a daze. He wasn't sorry he and Charlie had slept together—far from it—but it sure the hell did complicate things. Once wasn't going to be enough for him, not even close. It had only been twenty minutes since she'd left the house for town, and he was already hankering for her again.

But he was raising two boys, and jumping in bed with their live-in babysitter every chance he got wasn't exactly what he'd call being a good role model. Then there was Charlie, who still had her bags packed and her boots by the door. Once Ainsley was out of the picture, she'd leave, go back to San Francisco or Portland, and take up the life she left behind.

And where would that leave him?

History repeating itself, that's where. He was already more than infatuated and so damned tired of the people he cared about walking in and out of his life. Letting Charlie in too deep was setting himself up for more heartache. He just didn't have it in him to go through it again. Not with the tax bill due in April, a June primary on the horizon, and two boys who needed raising.

Nope, he had to keep her at arm's length, which meant no more sleeping together. *Yeah, right.* Even he didn't have that kind of willpower.

His phone went off, dragging him from his thoughts. When he saw it was Charlie his pulse picked up. Since the restraining order had been served, everyone was a little on edge.

He answered on Bluetooth. "You okay?"

"Travis isn't in school. The school secretary says I called him in sick this morning."

"We both know that isn't true. He ditched."

There was a long pause, then, "What if it's Corbin?"

"It's not Corbin." Jace didn't think Ainsley was stupid enough to kidnap a sheriff's kid. It would destroy his strategy of discrediting Charlie and making her look like a depressed nutjob who'd run off with his unborn child. "I'm wagering a guess that a certain young lady was also absent today. Are you still at the high school?"

"Yes. Grady is here too. And we're both sick with fear. He's never done anything like this before. Jace…"

"Hang tight while I make a call. I just pulled in to the sheriff's station and can be there in less than five minutes."

As soon as he got off the phone with Charlie, he called the school. As he suspected, Tina's "mother" had also called her daughter out sick. The question was where were they and why hadn't Travis shown up in time to be picked up? While Travis was a far cry from a criminal mastermind, he was usually better at covering his tracks.

He pulled into the school's circular driveway behind Charlie's Honda. Both she and Grady were standing on the lawn. The moment they spotted him, they came running to his window.

"What did you find out?" Charlie had lost all trace of her postcoital color. Before she'd left to pick up the kids, her cheeks had been rosy, like a woman well sated. Now, she was pale, like she'd just witnessed a longhorn gore a dog.

"He's playing hooky." Jace pinned Grady with a look. "You know anything about this?"

"No, sir."

Jace studied his son, searching for any guilty tells. "You sure?"

"Yes, sir." The boy couldn't lie to save his life and it was clear he was as worried about his brother as the rest of them were.

"Okay." He got out of the SUV and squeezed Grady's shoulder. "I'm guessing Travis lost track of the time." And when Travis realized he'd missed pickup he was going to have an oh-shit moment. Jace only wished he could be there to witness it. "Why don't the two of you go home. Travis can figure out his own ride." Which ultimately meant he'd have to call Jace and grovel.

"Shouldn't we look for him?" Charlie chewed her bottom lip.

"I've got some ideas." Jace had been a horny high school student in this town once too. "I'll take care of it."

"Are you sure?"

He couldn't help himself and pulled Charlie in for a hug and kissed her briefly on the lips. Either Grady was too consumed with Travis or was simply oblivious, because he didn't react.

"I'll find him," he said. "Go on back to the ranch."

Charlie reluctantly got in her car and Jace watched them drive off before getting in his sheriff's SUV. He nosed out onto Main Street and went in the opposite direction of the police station. From Highway 49 he hung a left onto Sweet Bay. It wasn't far from where he'd found Charlie seven weeks ago.

The two-lane road was flanked by forest on both sides and dead-ended at a trail that led to Dry Creek, where there was a sandy beach and a popular swimming hole. Jace parked in the lot at the trailhead. Besides an Outback with a ski rack and a Rav4 with Arizona plates, the lot was mostly empty. The state park attracted tourists and locals alike but was less traveled in the winter. Back in the day, though, it was where Jace and other kids went to make out, drink beer and party, year-round. It was a hike from the high school but definitely doable on foot if one was determined enough.

He took the trail for a half mile. A thick copse of redwoods blocked the sun and he wished he'd worn his jacket. But it sure smelled good. The wet bark, the crisp air, and the slight fishy odor of the creek reminded him of why he lived here. Why he never wanted to leave.

There was a rustling in the trees and he stopped to watch a doe and her two babies take off through the woods, then continued his trek to the swimming hole. A wooden sign with an arrow guided the way, but he didn't need it. The well-worn trail was as familiar to him as Dry Creek Ranch.

At the end of the road, the forest opened to a clearing where the creek widened and an outcrop of rocks formed a natural pool. There was a sign posted that cautioned visitors to swim at their own risk. Jace couldn't remember there ever being a drowning. The worst incident he could recall was a man who had suffered a heart attack and the paramedics couldn't get to him in time.

The beach was empty, save for two people lying on a woolen blanket at the other end of the beach. From Jace's vantage point he couldn't make out whether one of those people was Travis. He circled around, noting that the pair didn't move. As he got closer, he could tell it was a male and female but still had trouble identifying any of their features because their faces were turned toward each other and they were covered to their necks in jackets.

He did, however, recognize Travis's backpack. A black JanSport with a compartment for a laptop and a Future Farmers of America sticker on the front. Next to it was a tote bag with an iron-on emblem of a barrel racer.

Bingo!

He walked right up to them and toed Travis with his boot. No movement. Jace cued up "Reveille" on his cell phone and played it in Travis's ear.

"What the . . ? Shit!" Travis knocked off his jacket in an attempt to fasten his pants. The dim bulb had clearly forgotten to completely dress before he drifted off to sleep.

Tina came awake and in both their foggy states hadn't yet realized that Jace had caught them doing God knows what, though he had a fairly good idea.

"You've got ten minutes to get your asses to my SUV." He turned his back on them so Tina could straighten her clothes, or put them on. Jeez, he didn't want to know.

He could hear rustling in the background and started back to the trail. "Ten minutes," he yelled.

Not eight minutes later, they climbed into his back seat without saying a word. Jace started the engine and drove to the highway.

"Mr. Dalton...Sheriff...are you going to tell my parents?"

"Yep." He was keeping words to a minimum until he cooled down.

"They won't let her ride in the semifinals if you do," Travis said.

Jace presumed he was talking about a barrel racing competition. "Then you should've thought about that before one of you impersonated Charlie and Tina's mom, skipped school, and scared the hell out of us."

He gazed back at them through his rearview mirror. "Tina, do you still live on Honey Comb?"

"Yes," she said and exchanged a glance with Travis.

Don't look to Travis for help, Jace wanted to say. *He'll be doing hard time until he's twenty.*

He jumped onto the highway, passed a broken-down motorist, and called it in.

Tina's house was a white stucco ranch with tile arches that reminded him of a Mexican fast-food drive-through. There were no cars in the driveway and Jace remembered both her parents worked. Her mother was a real estate agent in Grass Valley and her father was an electrician. He'd done some work at the ranch a few years ago and was a good guy, as Jace recalled. He'd have to phone them later, when they got home.

Tina bolted out of the back seat as soon as Jace cut the engine. Travis started to follow her but Jace told him to get back in the car. Jace got out and followed Tina, who searched her bag for her key.

Tina's older brother, Donovan, opened the door before she found it. He stepped outside, took one look at his sister, and said, "Is there a problem,

Sheriff?" then craned his neck around Jace and Tina, spotting Travis in the SUV. Jace could see him putting the pieces together.

Tina dropped her gaze to her boots.

"Are your folks home?"

Donovan moved aside to let Tina go inside the house. "They're at work. You want me to have one of them call you?"

"That would be good. You'll keep an eye on her until your mom or dad gets home?"

"Yep, I'm off shift."

Jace had forgotten that Donovan was now a firefighter in Placer County. He still thought of the kid as the star running back at Dry Creek High.

"She's okay, right?" Donovan looked back at Travis in the truck. "Nothing big, just kids' stuff, I hope."

Is that what they were calling it these days?

Hell, Jace didn't know why he was being such a prude. He'd lost his virginity at fifteen with Barbie Russel underneath the Penn Valley rodeo stands. Last he heard, Barbie was married, had three kids, and taught science at a junior college in Southern California.

"They skipped school. Have your folks call me, okay?"

"Sure. Thanks for bringing her home." Donovan glanced at his watch. "My mom does a carpool with the Wagstaffs. Or a lot of times, Tina's got junior rodeo."

Jace nodded. No one was blaming Donovan for not keeping track of his sister. "Take it easy, Donovan."

Jace got back in the SUV. "Come up front, Travis."

Travis got out and came around to the passenger seat with his head hung low.

"Put on your seat belt." Jace backed out of the driveway. "I thought we talked about this. About you and Tina just being friends."

"We are."

Jace shot him a look. "That's not what it looked like at the swimming hole."

"Maybe not to you."

Jace didn't like the sharpness in Travis's voice. "You want to watch that attitude?"

"Or what? You're gonna ground me? You're gonna ground me anyway."

The kid had a point. He was definitely getting grounded.

"Look, Travis, I can't stop you from making bad decisions in life. We all make them. But there are consequences when you do." He slid his son a sideways glance.

Travis rolled his eyes. "Why do you have to make a capital case out of everything? If you tell her parents she'll get in big trouble and they probably won't let me see her anymore."

"That's okay, you'll be plenty busy for the foreseeable future, mucking stalls, soaping tack, stacking hay, and washing my truck."

Travis didn't try to argue, which Jace gave him points for.

"In the meantime, do we need to have another conversation about safe sex?"

"Give me a break, Dad."

Jace decided to spare him the talk. For now, anyway.

"Phone." Jace held out his hand.

Once Travis gave it up, they rode the rest of the way to the ranch in silence.

When he came up the driveway, Charlie and Grady ran out of the house onto the porch. Charlie's expression went from concern to relief the moment she spied Travis in the front seat.

Travis got out of the SUV, slammed the door, and made a beeline for the house.

"Where were you, Travis?" Grady trailed after him.

Charlie came down the porch stairs and looked at Jace questioningly.

"He was with Tina at the swimming hole, a spot in the state park where all the kids go. He's fine but his phone privileges have been revoked." Jace opened his door and held up Travis's cell. "And he's not to leave the house other than to do his chores."

"Thank goodness you found him and he's okay." She wrapped her arms around herself. "I was so worried. You must've been a wreck."

"Come here." He crooked his finger at her and pulled her into his arms. "Thank you for looking out for my kids."

She tilted her face up so they were staring into each other's eyes. That's when he kissed her. It was rushed because if he lingered there was no telling what he'd do. Carry her off to the barn again.

"I've gotta get to work," he said as he forced himself to pull away.

"Will you be home in time for dinner?"

"I'll do my best."

He watched her as she walked to the house, then hung a U-turn in the driveway and headed to town.

* * * *

Charlotte knocked on Travis's bedroom door. "Can I come in?" When there was no answer, she pushed open the door just enough to stick her head in. "You've been in here all afternoon. Are you hungry?"

"No." Travis was on his bed, his head propped up on a pile of pillows, staring at the ceiling.

She went in and sat on the edge of his mattress. "You want to talk about it?"

"You're not my mother, so quit trying to act like you are. Just because my dad looks at you all the time doesn't mean you're anything more than the babysitter."

She flinched. Where had this come from? While Travis could sometimes be surly, he'd always been polite.

"I thought we were friends," she said.

"Why? You're just going to leave as soon as my dad arrests your old boyfriend. Everyone knows it. Why do you think my dad's being such a jerk?"

"Because he took your phone? Come on, Travis."

Travis sat up. "Because he's gonna tell Tina's parents. They're really strict, they'll take away her horse, won't let her barrel race anymore, and they'll stop her from seeing me."

"That's on you and Tina, Travis, not your dad. You're the ones who decided to lie to school administrators, disappear for a day, and scare us all to death. He's simply doing what any good parent would do."

"How would you know? You're not a parent."

"No"—she stood up—"I'm not. But your father is and he's a good one. I think you know that and you're disappointed in yourself for disappointing him." Charlotte walked as far as the door. "When you get hungry come into the kitchen. I made beef stew." Travis might not like her right now, but he loved her beef stew.

Grady was sniffing the slow cooker when she went to set the table. "When are we eating? I'm starved."

"I was waiting for your dad." She glanced at the clock. It was seven. "But it's getting late. Come on, I'll fix you a bowl."

"What about Travis?"

"He said he wasn't hungry."

"He's in big trouble, isn't he?"

"That's between him and your dad. Now come sit down." Grady had a habit of taking a few bites, running around the kitchen, and returning for a few more bites. All that pent-up energy was exhausting, but she adored the boy.

"When's Dad coming home?"

"I don't know. Soon, I hope."

Travis came in and got a drink of water, trying to pretend the stew hadn't lured him to the kitchen. Charlotte went to the cupboard, got another bowl, and ladled him a serving.

"Bread's on the way," she said, and motioned for Travis to sit next to Grady.

He acted put out but dug into his stew.

She got the bread out of the oven. It was just a supermarket loaf but she'd brushed it with an egg wash. Warmed, the bread tasted as delicious as the ones she used to buy from the artisan bakeries in San Francisco. She cut off a good-sized piece and wrapped it in tin foil for Jace and sliced the rest for the table.

Grady shoved a hunk in his mouth and burned his tongue. Travis was still pretending not to be hungry, though he filched a slice of the bread when he thought she wasn't looking.

"Did you get restriction?" Grady asked his brother.

"None of your business, loser."

"Knock it off," Charlotte warned. "I want a peaceful dinner."

"You're the loser," Grady said. "I bet Dad won't let you go fishing with us at the lake this weekend."

"What did I say?" She passed Travis the butter and asked Grady, "How was school today?" She hoped he'd talk about something other than how Travis was "a loser."

"Good. I got an A on my spelling test." Grady's chest puffed out.

"That's great." Charlotte beamed. "Was it the one we did flash cards for?"

"Yep," he said in that laconic drawl that reminded her so much of his father. "Can I have more stew?"

"Of course you can."

While he got up for seconds, Travis leaned across the table. "I'm sorry about what I said before. Are you going to tell my dad?"

"Are you sorry that you might've hurt my feelings or are you sorry because you don't want your dad to know what you said to me?" She held up her hand. "Before you answer, you should know that my conversations with you are private, meaning I have no intention of telling him anything we talked about."

Travis's eyes dropped to his plate. He was deciding how to play this.

"I didn't mean to hurt your feelings…well, I guess I did," he said. "You're going to leave, aren't you?"

"Do I look like I'm leaving?" She hadn't really answered his question because she didn't know what the future held. She loved Dry Creek Ranch and there was no question she was besotted with its owner. But under no circumstances would she shake up their lives if Corbin became a threat, no matter how much Jace protested. And right now, she couldn't see a life without the specter of Corbin hanging over her.

She didn't need to share those thoughts with a fourteen-year-old, but at the same time she didn't want to lie to him either.

She suspected one of the reasons the boys had run off so many babysitters was to keep themselves from getting attached. Like Jace, they'd had a lot of loss in their lives.

Travis shrugged in response and went back to eating his stew. Grady carried his bowl to the table one-handed, sloshing sauce all over his placemat.

"I should've done that for you." Charlotte grabbed a towel and blotted the mess up. "Only a week until the cast comes off. Are you excited?"

"First thing I'm gonna do is scratch it." Grady held up his cast. It was covered in writing and stickers and was so soiled she wanted to scrub it with steel wool. "Then I'm gonna wash my arm."

One corner of her mouth slid up. It had to be pretty bad if Grady was talking about bathing. The kid couldn't sit still long enough to get in the tub and showers were too confining. He typically got more water on the bathroom floor than he did on himself.

The dogs started barking and the kids jumped up to see what was going on outside. A few minutes later, Jace's sheriff's vehicle came up the driveway.

"Dad's home," Grady hollered and bounced up and down at the window.

Travis quickly washed out his bowl, stuck it in the dishwasher, and took off to his room like the hounds of hell were chasing his heels. If Charlotte didn't know how gentle Jace was with his sons, she'd think the boy feared for his life. Travis simply didn't want to own up to his mistake.

Jace came in the door, looking exhausted, and Grady tackled him with a hug. For a house full of males—cowboys, no less—there was plenty of affection to go around. Grady was the most demonstrative, especially with his cousin Ellie and his Uncle Sawyer, who despite being a prominent writer was like a big kid.

"You guys eat already?" Jace got out of his jacket and hung his hat on the hook by the door.

"The boys did. I waited for you."

He let his eyes wander over her and for a second it was like they were the only ones in the room. Then Jace switched into Dad gear. "You do your homework?"

"I still have math."

"Then you better get to it, don't you think?" He scanned the kitchen. "Where's Travis?"

"He ate and went to his room," Charlotte said.

"Is he grounded, Dad?"

"Why? Are you taking after Uncle Sawyer and writing a book?" Jace squeezed Grady's head in the crook of his arm. "Go finish your homework."

The second Jace's study door clicked closed, he backed her against the center island, boxed her in, and kissed her. She returned the kiss with such fervor she even surprised herself. They'd only been apart six hours since Travis went temporarily missing, and she was starved for him. Her hands greedily slipped underneath his shirt and explored the hard planes of his muscles.

"Can I come to your room tonight?" he whispered in her ear.

Oh, she wanted that. Her body pulsed and she wasn't sure if she could even wait that long. "What about Travis and Grady?"

"We'll have to be discreet." He pushed away from the counter. "I should look in on Travis."

"He's worried about Tina's parents. Did you talk to them?"

"Oh yeah. Despite my pitch that kids will be kids, Tina's mom isn't taking it too well. I get the feeling they're pretty strict."

"That's what Travis said. Oh boy."

"They're fourteen years old. Call me an old man, but that's too young to be doing what they were doing."

Charlotte's mouth fell open. "I had no idea. Uh, I thought they were just having a ditch day."

"A ditch day with benefits. I'm holding out hope they didn't go all the way, but Travis doesn't want to talk about it."

"Go see if he'll open up." She gave him a little push and he grinned. "Yes, ma'am."

Chapter 16

Sawyer stared at the picture. If it was Angie, she'd changed so much he barely recognized her. It didn't help that the photo was grainy and the shot only caught her profile. But there were enough similarities—her small, turned-up nose, the structure of her cheekbones, a tiny beauty mark at the corner of her lip—to make him think it was her.

Granted, it was two years old. But this was the best lead he'd had since she'd disappeared. An actual location where she'd lived and a time frame.

A former member of the so-called co-op had returned his call and sent the picture. Unfortunately, the woman had been cagy about answering his questions. He wasn't sure if it was because she was trying to protect Angie's privacy or something else.

All he knew was that she'd become extremely guarded when he'd broached anything having to do with the co-op. Almost as if she was spooked about giving too much away. It reminded him of his military deep-throats, high-ranking brass in the Pentagon who would only share so much before they thought they were crossing the line.

He knew from experience that he'd have a better shot with her in person, but when he'd tried to pin her down on meeting with him she wouldn't commit. Sawyer had her address and was considering showing up on her doorstep. It wasn't always the best tactic, especially with someone who was already flighty.

But she knew more than she was saying, Sawyer had no doubt about that.

The buzzer rang and Sawyer called down that Jace could let himself up. After Grandpa Dalton died last spring and left them the ranch, he'd taken one of the rundown horse barns and converted it into a loft apartment.

He'd gotten a San Francisco architect to draw up the plans to juxtapose rustic with sleek modern design.

The bottom half, where the horse stalls used to be, was now a garage and mudroom with a staircase and elevator that ascended to the hayloft, where he had two thousand square feet of living space.

Except for his en suite and office, the rest of the rooms were open concept with cathedral ceilings that still had the original barn trusses.

It wasn't a huge apartment, but it had everything he needed.

In Los Angeles, he had his own wing in his parents' house. But since moving to the ranch, his LA quarters remained mostly vacant. Even while growing up in Southern California, Dry Creek Ranch had always felt like his real home.

Jace came up the stairs, took off his hat, and tossed his vest on the couch. "All right, let me see this picture."

Sawyer made room for him at the breakfast bar. "You want coffee?"

"Nah, Charlie's waiting for me for breakfast."

Sawyer tried to share Cash's butt-out policy. Jace was indeed entitled to a private life. But Sawyer would be damned before he let his cousin get hurt again. Mary Ann had done a real number on Jace—and the kids. He could count on one hand how many times she'd remembered to send a goddamn birthday card to Travis or Grady.

"You and Charlie seemed to have gotten pretty cozy lately."

Jace got up and poured himself a cup of coffee after all. "You got something to say, just spit it out."

"You want me to spit it out? Fine. Don't let your dick do your thinking for you. There are a lot of nice, single women around here without crazy ex-boyfriends whose fathers have tremendous political clout."

"Yeah, I'm not even going to dignify that by responding."

"Just saying." Sawyer threw his hands up in the air. "It's your job, your election."

"That's right. Let me see the fucking photo."

Sawyer slid the gritty black-and-white across the concrete countertop. Jace stared down at it for a long time.

"She looks different but I think it's her. Here"—Jace pointed—"around the mouth. And the mole. I wish the photo was color...the Dalton blue eyes. You show Cash yet?"

"Not yet. He's working a big cattle rustling case in Plumas County. As soon as he gets back."

"It's two years old, Sawyer." Jace huffed out a breath. "By now we would've heard from her, don't you think?"

"I don't know what to think. But this woman I talked to, the one who sent me the photo…she's hiding something."

"What makes you think that?"

Sawyer could see Jace's skepticism. Both his cousins thought he was looking for clues that didn't exist. But Sawyer wasn't a rookie when it came to reading people; his observation skills were top-notch. That's why magazines like *The Atlantic*, *GQ*, *Vanity Fair*, *Esquire* and *National Geographic* kept calling.

"She seemed frightened to say too much. Either that or she was covering for Angela."

But why? Despite Angela's quirky—and often high risk—lifestyle, she'd never been at odds with her family. While his parents disapproved of a lot of her choices and often voiced their disapproval loudly, they'd always been a tight-knit family.

"Did you get the impression she knows where Angie is now…or if she's even still with us?"

"No. I got the sense that after their time in the co-op they lost track of each other. It's the co-op she doesn't want to talk about or what Angie was doing there in the first place."

"Is this co-op a euphemism for a cult?"

"That was my thought," Sawyer said. "I did an internet search for cults in the Taos area in the last ten years, and nothing matched what the investigator or this woman described. They both made it out to sound like an organic farm, sort of like a kibbutz."

"What's that?"

"A self-sufficient community, usually based around agriculture." Sawyer had done a story years ago when he'd been based in Tel Aviv for the *New York Times* about how the old model for egalitarian communes was moving away from socialism and becoming popular with a new generation.

"It sounds like something Angie would go for, that's for sure," Jace said.

Sawyer agreed. His sister had never met an alternative living situation she didn't like.

"Hell, if she wanted to live on a farm she could've moved here and raised cattle," Jace continued.

"Too conventional, which isn't Angie's style. I'm considering going to New Mexico and pressing this woman for more info."

"Does she still live in Taos?"

"Santa Fe, according to what I found on the internet."

"You want me to come with you? I could probably spare a day or two."

"Cash made the same offer." Neither of Sawyer's cousins had the time, but they were like the Three Musketeers in that way. *All for one, and one for all.* "You two will scare the shit out of her." He gave Jace a playful punch in the arm. "But seriously, I can probably handle it on my own. If not, I'll call in reinforcements. I won't go before your barbecue anyway."

He had to hand it to Charlie. She'd taken his idea and had run with it. A couple of times she'd consulted with Sawyer to backstop the Tiffster, who didn't know jack about running campaigns but sure thought she did. From what Sawyer could tell, Charlie's heart was in the right place and she really did care for Jace and the boys.

But when the shit went down, which it ultimately would, where would it leave Jace? That was the bazillion-dollar question.

"I gotta get home." Jace put his cup in the sink. "Good work with that photo. It looks promising, but, Sawyer—"

Sawyer stuck his palm in front of Jace's face. "Don't say it. There's nothing you can say I haven't already thought of."

Jace nodded. "Whatever you need, you know we're here for you. Angie's the closest thing I ever had to a sister. I want her home too."

"I'll walk you down and hike down to the back forty, see how the cattle are faring."

"I'd appreciate that. I'm running low on time and have to get the kids to school today."

"Why's that?" Usually Charlie shuttled them to town and Sawyer wondered if the good senator's son had raised his ugly head in Dry Creek yet.

"Have to make a detour to the Klines' house. Travis has some apologizing to do."

Sawyer hitched a brow. "What's that about?"

"He and Miss Kline decided to ditch school and spend yesterday at the swimming hole over at the park."

"Oh yeah?" Sawyer laughed.

"It's not funny, asshole."

"Okay, but it kind of is. Tell me you didn't do shit like that in high school. I know I did. And Cash...on second thought, he probably never broke a rule in his life. I bet he used to stand at the corners of intersections and help old ladies cross the road."

"You finished?" Jace rubbed his hands together and stuck them in the pockets of his down vest.

It was March and still cold enough that Sawyer could see his breath.

"Why? You want to talk about something else?" They had a silent agreement not to discuss the taxes. Why beat a dead horse? Between the three of them, they'd figure out something. Hopefully.

Jace started across the field to the ranch house and waved his Stetson in the air. Sawyer went in the opposite direction. He had decisions to make about whether to pursue this newest lead on Angie or to accept the cold, hard evidence that his sister was never coming home.

* * * *

"The boys are getting dressed," Charlie told Jace as he came in the door.

He caught her around the waist and wrapped her in his arms. "Does that mean we have time for a quickie?"

"Didn't you get enough last night? And no, there's no time for a quickie." She pulled free and snapped him with a dish towel.

That vacant look she had in her eyes when he first found her was gone. So was her meek demeanor and penchant for constantly apologizing. Charlotte Holcomb had blossomed into a bossy little tiger. Best of all, she looked happy.

"Hey, I forgot to give this to you yesterday." He reached into his pocket for his wallet and pulled out five thousand dollars in crisp bills. "There's a safe in my study you can stash it in. But if I were you I'd open a checking account."

"How 'bout the safe for now?"

"Suit yourself, sweetheart." He took her hand. "Let me show you the combo."

She giggled like a teenager. "Is that code for something else?"

"You've got a dirty mind, woman."

Before they made it to his study, Grady bounded into the kitchen. "What's for breakfast? I'm starved."

"Starved? You had two bowls of stew last night and a half loaf of bread. How do chocolate-chip pancakes sound?"

"Score!" Grady pumped his fist in the air.

"Where's Travis?" Jace had had another talk with him last night and Travis had agreed that apologizing to the Klines in person was his best option. His other choices were to either write them a letter or call them on the phone.

Jace was proud that his son wasn't intimidated to look a grownup in the eye while asking for forgiveness. The Klines were good people. They wouldn't be too hard on him.

"Fixing his hair and hogging the bathroom." Grady rolled his eyes.

"Tell him Charlie's making pancakes and to get the lead out."

Grady ran off and Jace showed Charlie how to open the safe in his study.

"What's that?" Charlie poked at a stack of albums tucked at the back of the box.

"My grandfather's coin collection. It was something we used to do together." Jace had been thinking about the coins a lot lately. They were the only thing he owned besides the house and land that had any real worth. But like the ranch, the coin collection held more than financial value. They were pieces of his grandfather.

Charlie's face lit up. "Really? That's sweet."

"You're sweet." He backed her against the wall, his hands inching underneath her soft yellow sweater.

She swatted them away. "Breakfast, remember?"

He groaned. "Just five seconds of foreplay." He pulled her in for a quick kiss and swatted her behind. "Race ya to the kitchen."

Charlie started the pancake batter and Jace leaned against the counter to watch her.

"What do you have planned today?" he asked.

"A meeting with Tiffany at the coffee shop to go over some of the last-minute details for the fundraiser. Then I guess I'll work on my chair. Aubrey is bringing over one of her clients later this week and I'd like to have plenty of inventory."

"Thanks for organizing this shindig for me and thanks for putting up with Tiffany. I should be better at campaigning, better at the bullshit, but I'm not."

She reached up and took his face in her hands and kissed him. "I'm actually having fun. It's the first time I've felt useful in a long time."

"Ah, baby, if it wasn't for you and everything you do around here, my life would be in utter chaos."

She snorted. "Chaos? You seemed to have managed just fine before I came along, but I do appreciate the vote of confidence. And you should thank your cousin. The barbecue was his idea. Was the picture of Angela?"

"Yeah, I think so." He had mixed feelings about the photograph. It proved that two years ago Angie was alive, which gave him hope. But how many times had they followed seemingly good leads only to come up with nothing?

"That's wonderful, right?"

"It's an old photo, Charlie. We're no closer to finding Angie than we were five years ago."

Charlie got the griddle down from the pot rack. "Do you think she intentionally disappeared, like I did? Is there a chance she's running from someone?"

"I don't know. It's entirely possible. She kept some pretty weird company. But she was close to her family, all of us. By now I would think she would've reached out."

Charlie was quiet, then in a soft voice said, "I haven't. I've wanted to so many times but can't seem to dial their phone numbers, partly because I want to keep my parents and Al out of it. And partly because…"

He tilted his head to one side. "Because why?"

"The shame is unbearable. How did I let this happen to me, Jace? How did I fall for an abuser?"

"You ever think about talking to someone about it? A counselor or a therapist?" It was the second time he'd suggested seeking professional help. The first time, she'd brushed it off. But maybe with a little push she'd reconsider. "What happened to you wasn't your fault. No one thinks that. But maybe a professional could help you sort it out."

Travis and Grady came in for breakfast and the conversation came to an abrupt halt. The boys, absorbed in their own conversation, didn't seem to notice that the room had suddenly become quiet.

Charlie made them each a stack of chocolate chip pancakes. They were about the best thing Jace had ever eaten, yet Travis barely touched his. Jace almost felt sorry for the kid.

"Ready to go?" He gave Travis an encouraging pat on the arm.

"I am." Grady jumped up and hurried into the mudroom for his backpack.

"You sure you don't want me to take Grady?" Charlie flashed Travis a sympathetic smile.

"No sense in us both driving, not when I called in late to work. Grady can wait in the truck during our detour. Let's go, guys."

Travis gathered up his stuff as if he was about to walk to his execution. Jace didn't miss Charlie giving his son a reassuring squeeze as they filed out of the house.

He started to pull out of the driveway and threw the SUV into park. "I forgot something, be right back."

He jogged to the house and into the kitchen where Charlie was finishing the breakfast cleanup.

"Hey, you're back."

"I forgot this." He pressed her against the counter and took her mouth with his, kissing her with enough pent-up passion to start a bonfire. He couldn't seem to get enough of her. "See ya tonight."

"I could stop by the sheriff's department after my meeting with Tiffany and say hi."

"Yeah?" She'd never seen his office, not that there was much to it, but he was proud of the department he'd helped to shape. "I'd like that."

They kept kissing until he pried himself away. "Gotta go."

"Yes, you do." She pushed him toward the door and laughed.

It was in that moment that he knew he was in love with her. Not the same way he'd been in love with Mary Ann. That had been a desperate and lustful kind of love. Real at the time but without the staying power to last.

This…with Charlie…was a forever kind of love. Mature and passionate and desperate in its own way, but wholly different than what he'd had with Mary Ann. Because when Mary Ann left he moved on.

With Charlie he wasn't so sure he could.

Chapter 17

In a suit that looked straight off a Talbots rack and enough bling to fill a display case at Zales, Tiffany waved to Charlotte from across the coffee shop.

The place was already full and it wasn't even noon yet. In one corner, five tables had been pushed together to accommodate twenty diners. Judging by their cowboy boots, Wranglers, and Western shirts, they were cattlemen. Cash sat at the other end of the restaurant with a middle-aged man Charlotte had never seen before. They were deep in conversation and Charlotte didn't think Cash had seen her come through the door. Otherwise, he would've bobbed his head at her, the Dalton universal sign for a greeting.

A couple of the moms she'd befriended in the middle school pickup line were in a booth, drinking coffee. The two facing her waved, and she waved back.

Laney came out from behind the counter and gave Charlotte a big hug. "How are my boys? You must be keeping them well fed because they've upped and deserted me."

"We were here just a few days ago, Laney." They'd had steak sandwiches after Grady's soccer game.

Laney snorted. "They used to come three times a week and Saturday mornings. But that's okay. Nothing's better than home cooking." She nudged her head at Tiffany. "Miss High and Mighty's been waiting for ya."

"We're planning Jace's fundraiser. You're coming, right?"

"Wouldn't miss it for the world. Miz Bedazzled already hit me up for my black-eyed pea and bacon salad."

"Thank you, Laney."

Charlotte wended her way around the tables. Crazy, how in such a short amount of time the coffee shop, and all of Dry Creek for that matter, had become as familiar to her as the neighborhood where she grew up.

"I took the liberty of ordering you a diet cola," Tiffany said as Charlotte hung her coat on the back of the chair.

She didn't drink diet soda—aspartame left a strange aftertaste in her mouth—but started to take a sip to placate Tiffany because she didn't want to go against the tide. But as soon as the glass touched her lips, she changed her mind. "You know, I'd rather have ice water."

Tiffany raised her hand in the air to get the attention of a server and Charlotte said, "I'll order it with the rest of my meal." Later, it would occur to her that a few months ago she never would've interfered for fear that she would appear ungrateful or controlling, or high maintenance.

The whole time she was with Corbin, she let him order for her at restaurants or choose her clothing when they were out shopping, even if she wanted something else. Why would a person do that?

"Shall we get down to business?" Tiffany pulled a tablet out of her leather tote bag and booted it up. Her gold bangles jangled like church bells with every flutter of her hand. "Laney's supplying the salads, Pie in the Sky over in Chesterville is donating two dozen sheet cakes, and Ale Yeah, the beer."

"That's terrific. Adams Family Vineyards is good for the wine and the Nally brothers said in addition to sodas, chips, and veggie burgers, they'd throw in the paper plates, napkins, and compostable forks and knives. You think that's enough?" Charlotte wondered if they should have something besides burgers and dogs.

"I'll talk to Tony Sanchez about his taco truck," Tiffany said.

"Ooh, that would be fantastic."

Laney came to take their orders and wound up making herself at home at their table. "Let me try that on." She pointed to one of Tiffany's gaudier pieces, a cocktail ring with a cluster of garnets as big as a tangerine.

Tiffany slapped Laney's hand away.

"You want that last slice of chess pie, you let me try it on."

"Oh, all right." Tiffany slid the ring off her middle finger and handed it to Laney, who couldn't get it past her knuckle.

"Girl, your finger is as skinny as your ass." Laney put it on her pinky instead. "What do you think?"

Charlotte held her tongue. The ring was ugly as sin.

"It looks ridiculous there." Tiffany swiped it off her hand and nearly dropped it in her soda.

"Let me try on that necklace." Laney weighed the braided gold rope around Tiffany's neck in her hand.

"Get your own jewelry, Laney." But Tiffany took off the chain and popped it over Laney's head, flattening it over her apron.

Laney quickly took their orders. "I'll be right back. I want to show Jimmy Ray what I want for our anniversary."

She took off for the kitchen and Tiffany and Charlotte went back to planning. Tiffany wanted Jace to make a speech at the barbecue. Knowing Jace, Charlotte thought it highly unlikely he'd go along with the idea.

"He'd be more comfortable mingling," she said, and Tiffany studied her long and hard.

"What?" Charlotte stared back.

"The two of you need to go public."

"Public with what?" Charlotte's stomach dropped, fearing Tiffany had somehow found out about Corbin.

"That you're engaged."

"We're not engaged." Charlotte gulped. Where had Tiffany gotten that idea?

"It would be extremely helpful if you were. The rumors about him breaking up Aubrey and Mitch's engagement have never completely died down."

"Aubrey's marrying Cash, for goodness' sake." Charlotte looked around the coffee shop to see if Cash was still there, but he was gone. She'd never met Aubrey's ex-fiancé but the rap on him wasn't good. According to Aubrey, he'd narrowly escaped being brought up on conspiracy charges. Charlotte didn't know the whole story, but this talk about Jace running off with the bride-to-be was patently ridiculous.

"When did the truth ever matter? People believe what they want to believe. And Mitch's mother has a lot of friends in this county. Don't underestimate her influence."

Charlotte couldn't pick Mitch's mother out of a police lineup. She knew nothing about the woman. "What are you saying? Folks around here will vote for a completely inexperienced candidate because of a nasty old untrue rumor?"

"That's exactly what I'm saying. Look, all you have to do is hang on Jace's arm and act like the adoring fiancée during the barbecue. From where I'm sitting it doesn't seem like that much of a stretch. I mean, come on, the live-in babysitter who, like the sheriff, happens to be gorgeous, young, and single, decides she wants to plan a fundraiser for her boss because it seems like a fun thing to do. Really, Charlie?" Tiffany tilted her head and squinted one eye at Charlotte.

Jace Dalton had given her her life back. Planning his fundraiser was nothing in comparison, Charlotte wanted to say. But it was more than that. Much more. She knew that, but it wasn't a landscape she was ready to navigate. Not after her disastrous relationship with Corbin.

Laney returned with their food and Tiffany's necklace, saving Charlotte from committing to anything.

Tiffany didn't bring it up again until they were halfway through their salads. "Just think about it. I could even lend you a ring to wear on your wedding finger."

Charlotte already had one. It was somewhere at the bottom of her purse, where it would stay.

After the meeting, she drove the two blocks to the civic center. It was sprinkling. Charlotte found an umbrella in the back of the car and crossed the parking lot. The complex consisted of a series of 1920s white-brick buildings that housed the city hall, a few county offices, a small library, and the sheriff's department.

"Hi," Charlotte greeted a woman in uniform at the front desk. "I'm looking for the sheriff."

"Do you have an appointment?" the deputy asked and peered over the counter as if to see if Charlotte was armed. "Or are you here to bring baked goods?"

"Baked goods? Uh, no. I have an appointment. Charlie...Charlie Rogers."

"Oh." The deputy instantly appeared contrite. "I'll call Annabeth."

A few minutes later a well-dressed gray-haired lady came to the front desk to escort Charlotte to Jace's office.

"Lovely to finally meet you, Charlie. Jace speaks so highly of you."

"And of you too." Charlotte shook Jace's secretary's hand and they walked to the rear of the building. "Are you having a bake sale today?"

Annabeth appeared confused. "A bake sale?"

"The deputy at the counter asked if I was dropping off baked goods." Had Charlotte known, she would've made something.

Annabeth stifled a chuckle. "Many of the local ladies like to bring the sheriff cookies and pies and things from their kitchen."

"That's lovely." Charlotte marveled at how nice people were in small towns. "What a wonderful way of saying thank you for a job well done."

"Mm-hmm," Annabeth said and lifted one of her perfectly arched white brows. "He has quite a little fan club, our sheriff does. If all he needed was the single female vote he'd be a shoo-in to win the primary."

"Ahh." Now Charlotte grasped the situation. Some of these bakers were likely the coffee moms.

"And it's making us all fat." Annabeth snorted.

Not Jace. He didn't have an ounce of fat on him. At least he wasn't bringing the pastries home, flaunting all his would-be suitors.

Annabeth tapped on Jace's door and slowly opened it. "You have a visitor."

Jace was on the phone but he motioned for Charlotte to come in and shut the door. The office wasn't anything like his study at home with its rough-hewn log walls, woodburning stove, and high ceiling. This room was large but rather bland. White walls, a sofa and chair, a small conference table, a few certificates on the wall, and framed pictures of Travis and Grady on his desk and credenza. He needed a few more personal touches to warm the place up.

He winked at her and motioned for her to take a seat on the sofa while he continued his telephone conversation. Something about squad-car cameras and budgeting. He leaned back in his chair with his sleeves rolled up and his boots propped on the desk, looking thoroughly masculine. And her heart did a little hopscotch.

"How'd the meeting go?" He hung up the phone, got up and joined her on the sofa.

"Good, we're ready for Saturday." She intentionally left out the part about Tiffany's ploy for them to pretend they were engaged. "We're expecting a big crowd. How was Travis's meeting with the Klines?"

"It went as well as could be expected. They said he could do homework with Tina at the house two nights a week as long as an adult was present, which I thought was pretty generous given the stunt they pulled."

"Travis must've been relieved."

"Yep."

He moved closer and she suddenly felt like a giddy teenager, waiting for her first kiss. He did that to her even though she'd once believed she'd never have those feelings again. He reached in and pressed his lips against hers and every part of her body fired to life.

"I don't think we should be doing this here," she whispered against his lips, fearing that in another minute or so she'd be under him, naked, panting for more.

"Probably not." But he continued to kiss her. His arms wrapped around her, heavy and strong. "Want a tour?"

"Of what?" Her brain had trouble functioning while his tongue restlessly tangled with hers.

"The department." His hands had crawled under her coat and fumbled with the buttons on her sweater.

"This is not the way to win taxpayers over."

"You're no fun." He nibbled on her ear, his hands continuing to explore as her skin grew hotter and hotter under his touch.

"Give me the tour." She forced herself to her feet.

He tapped his head against the back of the couch and pinched the bridge of his nose. "You're killing me here."

They didn't have a lot of opportunities to be together, only during the nighttime, when the boys were sound asleep. And even then, they had to keep one ear open in case Travis or Grady woke up and went looking for Jace. During the day, Jace was usually swamped at work. It wasn't ideal, but their clandestine romance made her gloriously happy just the same.

"You'll manage to live." She offered him a hand to pull him off the couch. "Tour, please."

He tucked his shirt into his pants and took her down the hall to a large room filled with workstations. A few heads popped up from their cubicles.

"Hey, Sheriff." One of the deputies, a nice-looking man with blond hair and a ski-goggle tan, came over to where they were standing. He obviously wanted an introduction.

Jace draped his arm over Charlotte's shoulder, which surprised her. "This is Charlie. Charlie, Reggie, our watch commander."

She shook his hand. "Pleased to meet you."

"Not as pleased as I am to meet you." It was a cheesy line.

Jace thought so too because he rolled his eyes. "Don't you have work to do?"

Reggie grinned and went back to his workstation.

Jace watched him for a second and shook his head. "He loves to mess with me."

"Why's that?" She looked up at him.

"It's a guy thing."

Charlotte didn't sense any hostility between the two men. In fact, she got the distinct impression they were friends. Still, Jace had been openly proprietary, even though they'd never discussed the terms of their relationship. Jace's sudden possessiveness should've bothered her because of her experience with Corbin. He'd been jealous and controlling, constantly questioning her comings and goings, accusing her of flirting whenever she was remotely friendly to a member of the opposite sex. At one point, he even forbade her from talking to her male customers, demanding that her assistant do it instead.

The difference, though, was Jace wasn't a psycho and Corbin was.

He gave her a peek of the locker rooms and a walk-through of the tiny space they called a lunchroom. By far the most interesting part of the tour was the jail. Just a wing off the main building with four small cells. Though it was built in the early 2000s, it reminded Charlotte of the old West. Perhaps it was the pinewood paneling and the heavy iron bars on the cells.

Across the courtyard was the courthouse, a building slightly smaller than the sheriff's department. This one, though, was actually built in the old West at around the time of the Gold Rush. Charlotte imagined that the building had been seismically retrofitted and modernized many times over, including what looked to her like double-pane windows. But the brick, and the portico with its Western-style posts, appeared original.

There was a plaque on a brick pedestal at the entrance, describing the courthouse's history. Charlotte didn't take the time to read it because she didn't want to hold Jace up. Next time she was at the coffee shop, she'd make a point of coming back.

Dry Creek was drenched in Gold Rush history and Charlotte wanted to soak it up.

Jace peered at his watch. "I've got a meeting in five. Let me walk you back to your CR-V."

"I'm fine, Jace. I parked in the lot." There were plenty of people milling around, just like at the coffee shop. Corbin wouldn't dare violate the restraining order in front of witnesses.

"So." He hunched his shoulders. "I want to walk a pretty woman to her car."

"If you insist. I just don't want to interfere with your day."

They crossed the square and the parking lot, where he stood watch until she started her engine.

"You heading back to the ranch?"

She nodded. "I'll put in a couple of hours on my chair before I pick up the kids from school. Travis has junior rodeo this afternoon. Is he cleared to go?" Jace hadn't told her the terms of Travis's punishment other than he wasn't allowed to use the phone.

"Yeah, but that's it. No hanging out with friends afterward. Be sure to lock the gate when you get home."

Home? She didn't think of it that way. Everything still felt temporary, like any minute she might have to jump in her Honda and press the pedal to the metal.

Chapter 18

Jace crept across the hardwood floor, trying not to make a sound. He wasn't the lightest on his feet and tended to be a heavy walker. At least he didn't have his boots on. Sneaking around in his own home was beyond ridiculous. But he couldn't exactly preach abstinence to Travis while openly sleeping with Charlie, even if he was a grown man.

He was sorely tempted to send the boys for a sleepover with Uncle Sawyer sometime this week. Sawyer's book deadline be damned. There was always Cash and Aubrey, but their cabin was already tight as a squeeze chute. They didn't need two hyper boys making the place smaller.

Smack!

Ah, shit. He tripped over one of the dog's damn chew toys and slapped the wall to keep from falling and breaking his neck. Praying that one of the kids hadn't heard him, Jace waited a beat. When it seemed safe, he continued in the pitch blackness. No moon tonight and he'd forgotten to turn on the goddamn nightlight.

He felt his way in the dark until the hallway wall ended, turned the corner into the guest wing, and tapped lightly on Charlie's door.

"Come in," she whispered. She'd been waiting for him.

A smile blossomed in his chest and he got hard.

The door creaked as he opened it. Tomorrow, which was actually today, he planned to spray the shit out of the hinges with a can of WD-40.

He shucked his jeans, left them on the floor, and climbed into bed with her.

"What took you so long?" She had on an oversized T-shirt, which normally he would've found sexy. But right now, he wanted her naked.

"Grady came to my room about eleven and talked my ear off until midnight. I wanted to make sure he was fully asleep."

She muffled a laugh with the blanket. "All this sneaking around reminds me of high school."

"Really? You used to sneak around a lot?" He dragged the nightshirt over her head and planned to get rid of her panties as soon as he laved some attention on her breasts.

"No, but you know what I mean." She pulled him closer. "Kiss me."

"Yes, ma'am." He rolled onto his side and tugged her into his arms. Damn, she felt good. Her skin was soft, her breasts firm pressed against his chest and she smelled sweet, like soap and talcum powder.

The hot pull of her mouth made him a little crazy. He wanted to go slow, savor what was left of the night, but at this rate didn't think he'd last past the eight-second bell. She was so sexy, so supple, so freaking everything. His heart raced as she ground into him, pleading.

"Slow down, baby."

"Can't." She pushed him onto his back and straddled him, rubbing up and down his length until he thought he'd go off like a fire hydrant. "I've been lying here, thinking about this all night."

Her need and desperation made his entire body throb until he couldn't wait any longer. Jace clasped her hip with one hand and guided himself into her opening with the other. And with one sharp thrust he was inside her.

"Shit." He clenched his teeth and started to pull out.

"No, no." She arched up and pulled him back in, her warm tightness enveloping him like a glove.

It took every dint of his willpower to roll out from under her. "Condom." He hung over the bed and realized he didn't bring anything with him and muttered a curse. "Be right back."

She thrashed her head against the pillow in sheer frustration. "Hurry."

He didn't bother with his pants and ran from the guest wing down the hallway to his bedroom, naked, inadvertently kicking that goddamn chew toy against the wall where it made a loud *thwack*.

"Shit, shit, shit," he muttered aloud and stood stock still to listen. No one stirred and he resumed the race to his nightstand, returning to Charlotte a few seconds later.

This time, he locked her door.

One look at Charlotte lying on the bed, the blanket rucked around her hips with her amazing breasts bare, and his mouth watered. He ripped open one of the foil packets, suited up, and climbed back in.

He kissed her gently and let his hands wander over her breasts, then to the flat plane of her belly. Sliding down, he buried his face between her legs and felt her breath catch. She tasted sweet and musky and he couldn't get enough.

He used his tongue and fingers until he felt Charlie clench and her breathing quicken. Soon came a succession of hot spasms and a moan of such deep pleasure that it set Jace on fire. He couldn't remember ever wanting a woman this much.

"Oh, Jace." Her hands were in his hair.

He lifted his head up. "Good?"

She tilted her head back. "Mm" was all she could manage.

His chest filled with pride, knowing he could do this to her. That he could make her come undone.

He moved over her, kissing her breasts and drawing her nipples into his mouth. She cried out and he hushed her.

"As soon as we get this damn barbecue behind us, I'm taking you somewhere where we can be alone," he whispered against her ear.

He held her arms over her head and continued to feast on her breasts. They were flushed pink and so damn perfect they made him ache. Charlie ran her nails up and down his back, urging him for more.

He held himself above her and in one long, hard thrust was inside her again, moving. She whimpered and the sound, along with her heat, drove him wild. She pulled her legs up and planted her feet on the bed so he could go deeper.

He pulled out and entered her again with a powerful stroke that made her gasp. "Too much?" He stopped.

"No, no. So good." She ground against him, pleading for more.

"Oh, baby." He devoured her mouth as his thrusts quickened.

In a minute, he was going to lose his mind. He loved the way she responded to him. Every kiss, every touch, every stroke seemed to take her to new heights. And the little sounds she made. Whimpers, pants, moans drove him to the brink.

"You with me?" He hovered over her, looking down, not knowing how much longer he could last.

She closed her eyes and her lips parted, forming an O. "Yes…Jace…yes."

He urged her to wrap her legs around him and plunged into her deeper and deeper. Faster and faster. Harder and harder. She thrust up, meeting him stroke for stroke. Her body shook and he felt as if he were flying. Like he was soaring above the clouds and all he saw was her. Charlie.

She called out his name and broke apart, her body wracked with shudders.

He grit his teeth, trying to hold on and make it last forever. But he couldn't stop the tide pushing against him and he let it take him over until his mind went blank and his body erupted. Then he collapsed on top of her until he could steady his breathing.

He rolled to his side, taking her with him. She curled into his chest, tucking her head under his chin. Jace needed to get rid of the condom but he didn't want to let her go just yet.

He combed his fingers through her hair. "Did that work for you?" It was a self-serving question because he knew damned well that it had.

"Arrogant much?" She laughed and the sound of it made Jace's heart skip a beat.

"Give me a sec." He got off the bed and ducked into the bathroom.

When he finished disposing of the condom, he washed his face. Charlie kept the bathroom neat.

Too neat.

Her toiletries were tucked away in a cosmetic bag sitting on the corner of the vanity, not out on the shelves or in a drawer. Her soap, shampoos, and lotions were ready to go when she was. The implication of that stabbed at him. Don't get used to this, he told himself but couldn't stop from rushing back to her bed.

When he dove beneath the covers with her, she crawled under his arm and nestled into his chest. He pulled her leg over his and they slept like that until he woke a few hours later. One look at the clock and he got out of bed. Charlie was still down for the count. He tucked the quilt around her, kissed her softly, and returned to his own bedroom.

The sun was already coming up and shafts of early morning light made shadows on the walls. Instead of going back to sleep, he decided to saddle up Amigo and ride a few fences. He could be back in time to share his morning coffee with Charlie.

But that wouldn't be. His cell buzzed on the nightstand and he checked the caller ID. Duty called.

* * * *

Charlotte spent most of the day in her workshop. The slipcover for the chair was coming along nicely, and by the time Aubrey brought her client it would be done. It was getting time to do a little scouting at yard sales and flea markets. Between Dee Dee and Aubrey, who was in the middle of a big decorating project and had taken a few pieces on consignment, Charlotte needed fresh stock.

Jace had mentioned that a sheep ranch down the road had recently sold and the new buyers were tearing down the old barn to make room for a vineyard. What she wouldn't do to have a look around and see if there was anything worth scavenging. If she had time, she'd drop by the property on her way to pick Travis and Grady up from school. While Travis was at his Junior rodeo meeting, she'd promised to take Grady to the craft store over in Auburn for supplies for a project he was working on.

She played music on Jace's iPod while she sewed. All he had was country and western music, which she was quickly acquiring a taste for.

Twice, she'd picked up her phone to call Allison. If nothing else, she just wanted to hear her sister's voice.

Al owned a nursery in Portland and would be at work. Charlotte visualized her sister at her potting bench with her hands deep in dirt. While Charlotte liked to make old things new, Al loved growing plants and flowers. One visit to Dry Creek Ranch and Allison would fall hopelessly in love.

Charlotte wanted to tell her all about Jace. About Travis and Grady. But how absurd would it sound to her sister?

Hi, Al. I know it's been a while but you were right about Corbin. He was everything you said he was and more. I ran from him. Loaded up my car with as many things that would fit and drove for my life and for the life of the child growing inside me. But it was too late. I lost the baby, Al. I thought I'd lost everything. And then I met a man who made me believe in myself again. Who gave me hope and courage and safety. I'm here now, Al, with him and his two young sons. And I think I'm in love with him.

She closed her eyes because even to herself she sounded out of touch with reality. A complete wackjob. A weak woman, who'd jumped into the arms of a new man when she hadn't even recovered from the pain inflicted by the first.

There was a knock outside and she jumped. She was here alone and hadn't even remembered her pepper spray. Through the window she saw Cash's SUV and pressed her hands to her stomach with relief.

"Anyone here?"

She opened the side door and stuck her head out. "I am." That's when she noticed a second car—a Subaru Outback—had pulled alongside his truck and two women were climbing out.

"I found these ladies parked at the gate. They say they came to see your store." He raised his brows as if to say *what store?*

"O-h-h-h," she said, surprised. The barn was hardly a store, but she didn't want to dissuade the women from shopping. Charlotte just hoped she hadn't put Cash out.

"Thanks for letting them in."

He responded by folding his arms over his chest and staying rooted next to his truck.

The Dalton men were sticklers for security. She certainly wasn't complaining because they were doing it on her behalf. Still, the women appeared harmless.

"I can handle it from here. Thank you, Cash. I hope you weren't inconvenienced."

"Nope." He was a man of few words where she was concerned.

"Come on in." She greeted the women, who were staring at the barn as if they might have come to the wrong place.

Charlotte opened the big sliding door, letting the sunlight in. She expected Cash to leave. But he continued to lean against his truck like he had all the time in the world.

"How did you hear about me?" she asked the women, curious because she hadn't advertised, though it had become public knowledge that she regularly perused garage and yard sales between shuttling the boys to and from school and their activities.

"We're friends of Dee Dee's," the woman with the Hermès handbag said.

Charlotte had spotted the designer purse the minute she'd laid eyes on the two women. Dee Dee clearly ran with a well-heeled crowd, though these women seemed more subdued. Despite the fancy bag, the woman was in a pair of yoga pants and tennis shoes. The other woman wore leggings and a long sweater layered under a wool coat with a pair of Ugg knockoffs.

"Feel free to browse," she said. "Let me know if you have any questions."

While they explored her inventory, she joined Cash at the side of his truck, where she could still keep an eye on the barn if the women needed her help. "Sorry. This was not planned. I don't even know them."

"I got that. Sounds like word is spreading."

She couldn't tell if he disapproved of his ranch being invaded. His fiancée certainly approved. She was the one who'd gotten the ball rolling, which Charlotte was grateful for.

"They seem perfectly safe and I hate holding you up."

He didn't say anything, just continued to stand there like a sentry.

"I love this." The leggings lady held up a wine-bottle drying rack Jace had scavenged for her on one of his landfill runs. Charlotte hung a collection of enamelware coffee mugs from it that she'd found in a thrift store off Highway 49. "Do you have one that's smaller?"

"Sorry, no. I mostly deal in one-of-a-kinds." She went back into the barn. "What do you like it for?"

"Same thing you've done. Coffee mugs. But this would take up too much counter space."

"I could cut it in half and you could hang it flush against the wall." Charlotte demonstrated on the wood siding.

"Oh my goodness, I never would have thought of that. Sissy, wouldn't that look cute next to my pantry?"

"Darling. Maybe I should get one too."

She let the two women clamor over the drying rack and returned to Cash so as not to seem like she was hovering.

"I don't see a tag," Sissy said.

Charlotte hadn't thought about a price. Frankly, she still hadn't decided what to do with the bottle rack. "Uh, Two hundred as-is. Or a hundred and fifty for each half."

Cash made a low sound in his throat.

"It's a little more only because I'll have to hire someone to make the cuts," Charlotte explained. "It's pretty heavy steel. But if you have the right tools or can get someone to do it yourself, you'll save money."

"I'd rather you do it," Sissy said. "Wouldn't you, Mandy?"

"Yes." Mandy looked around, presumably for somewhere to stow the rack, and settled for Charlotte's sewing counter. "But can you put something on the back of it to make it easy to hang?"

"Absolutely," Charlotte said.

"Three hundred bucks?" Cash whispered. "Wineries throw them out when they get old."

"When was the last time you were in a gift shop or a kitchen store in St. Helena or Napa?" Charlotte had seen the racks priced at up to five hundred dollars depending on size and condition.

Cash let out a whistle. "I'm in the wrong business."

She chuckled. "I just have to find someone to cut it in half and add hangers, which I'm not exactly sure how to do." She'd been improvising when she'd made the suggestion to hang the rack on the wall.

"Jace has a cutting torch. You can probably screw some kind of holders onto the back with a standard drill. Jace will know how to do it. If not, there's a machine shop in Auburn."

"Perfect. Thanks."

"I love the couch," Sissy called to Charlotte. "Dee Dee told me I would and the pictures my decorator sent didn't do it justice."

Charlotte left Cash's side. Boy, would she love to sell the sofa. And the chair. It was taking up a lot of space in the workshop.

"I'm still working on the slipcover for the chair. It's a gorgeous set. Really good quality."

"I don't think both would fit in my family room."

Mandy strolled over from the pillows she'd been looking at. "It would if you got rid of Robert's recliner."

"We both know that's not going to happen. But maybe if I got rid of that big ottoman that we're using for a coffee table and got something smaller instead."

"That would work." Mandy walked around the back, taking in the details.

"How much do you want for both?" Sissy asked.

Charlotte did a quick tally in her head of how much the fabric and her supplies had cost. Without checking her receipts, it was a guesstimate but close enough to name a price that would ensure a nice profit. "Thirty-five hundred."

In one of the design showrooms in San Francisco, custom pieces like Charlotte's would've fetched twice as much. But because her sofa was refurbished and not brand-new, the price was fair.

Sissy looked at Mandy and said, "How soon until the chair is finished, and do you deliver?"

"I could have both wine racks and the chair by late next week." It was a stretch because she had Jace's fundraiser on Saturday and would have to divide her week between her workshop and organizing the event. But in her experience, customers weren't particularly patient and she wanted to seal the deal. "Where do you live?"

"River Park in Sacramento."

Charlotte had no idea where River Park was, but Sacramento was at least an hour away. She'd need to rent a U-Haul. "I'd have to charge you."

"Leo could do it for you in our toy hauler." Mandy lifted one end of the sofa. "Between Leo and Robert this should be no problem to move."

"All right, you've got yourself a deal." Sissy slid a credit card out of her wallet and Charlotte's heart sank.

"Um, I'm not set up yet to take credit cards." PayPal, Square, and any other mobile payment system had been on Meredith's "do-not-do" list because Corbin could use financial transactions to track her. "I'm so sorry for the inconvenience but right now I only take cash and checks."

Sissy chewed her bottom lip. "Really?"

Charlotte could tell she was wavering on the purchase. She didn't want to lose the sale, but what could she do?

"I'll have to think about it, then," Sissy said but seemed reluctant to let it go.

"I totally understand." Few people had thirty-five hundred dollars lying around.

"I'll take the drying rack, of course."

It was still a three-hundred-dollar sale, more than Charlotte had thirty minutes ago. And for something that cost her virtually nothing.

"Who should we make the check out to?" Mandy asked.

"Uh, Jace Dalton, please."

While the women focused on writing their checks, Charlotte moved the bottle rack next to the side door so she'd remember to take it up to the house, where Jace kept his tools.

"Do you have a few cards we could take with us?" Mandy handed Charlotte her check.

"Uh, that's another thing I don't have. Honestly, I've been focusing on building inventory and haven't officially opened yet." She used the word "opened" loosely because she'd never planned to go back into retail. But the idea that she was once again repurposing furniture and selling it to people who gave her pieces loving homes filled her with joy. "The only reason Dee Dee knew about me is through her interior designer, who's a friend of mine."

"Oh my gosh, we didn't mean to just show up," Sissy said. "Dee Dee made it sound like you were open for business."

"I'm thrilled you did, really. I just wish I was better prepared is all. But next time I will be, I promise. Would you like to come a week from this Friday to pick up your racks?"

"That would be great if it's not an inconvenience," Mandy said.

"Not at all." Charlotte shoved their checks in her pocket.

She was nervous that Cash was getting antsy. She could escort the ladies to the gate herself but would have to ride with them and walk back because she'd left her car up at the house.

Cash must've read her mind because he said, "I'll lock the gate after them."

"Thank you."

The women walked to their Outback with their heads together, whispering. Right before they got in the car, Sissy turned around and called to Charlotte, "What if I paid half now for the couch and chair and the other half when I pick it up?"

"That works," Charlotte said, a little surprised by the sudden turnaround.

Sissy returned with her checkbook. While she wrote, Charlotte mouthed to Cash, "Sorry."

He stunned her with a thumbs-up, which made her smile. It was a hell of a sale. Between Sissy and Dee Dee, she had a nice pile of cash. And she knew exactly what to do with it.

Chapter 19

Tiffany showed up at seven a.m. on the day of Jace's fundraising barbecue with a set of two-way radios—one for her and one for Charlotte—and proceeded to bark orders like a drill sergeant to anyone who'd volunteered.

Charlotte noticed that the only one immune from being bossed around was Aubrey. No one dared to tell her what to do. Aubrey had a way of raising one imperial eyebrow that instantly put Tiffany in her place. Besides, she had turned their banal white wedding tent into a red, white, and blue extravaganza complete with balloons, pinwheels, and giant "Jace Dalton for Sheriff" posters. To remind everyone that Jace had deep roots in the community, she'd scattered a few pictures of his late grandfather around the tent.

Jasper Dalton was a legend in Mill County; even Charlotte the newcomer knew that.

"Here." Tiffany pushed a ring into Charlotte's hand. "You don't have to say you're engaged but at least wear it."

Charlotte looked down at the emerald-cut diamond that set off a prism of color in the sunlight. "I hope this is fake."

Tiffany didn't say anything.

"Oh, for God's sake. What if I lose it?"

"You won't."

"This is absolutely crazy," Charlotte said because she was actually considering going through with this insane scheme if it would help Jace's campaign.

"People adore a good love story. And while everyone's talking about the gorgeous new woman in Jace's life, they'll forget about last year's love triangle."

"It wasn't a triangle, Tiffany." Charlotte nudged her head across the tent where Aubrey and Cash were exchanging what they thought was a private kiss. "If this town can't figure that out, they deserve Jacob Jolly. Besides, a candidate shouldn't lie to his constituents."

"Jace isn't lying. Come on, just put the damn thing on." Tiffany took the ring and shoved it onto Charlotte's wedding finger. "If anyone asks you about it be coy, say today's about Jace's bid for reelection."

"I can't believe I'm doing this." Charlotte watched as Jace lined up a row of grills across the tent. "Does he know we're doing this?"

"Of course not. Look, it's just a ring. You're entitled to wear anything you want. It doesn't have to mean anything."

"It just happens to be a diamond worn on my left hand." Charlotte snorted as she walked away, feeling the weight of the gold band around her finger.

Five minutes later, she bumped into Sawyer on the way to the house to grab a few things Aubrey needed.

He tipped his hat and kept walking.

"Hang on a second," she said, and he stopped. If she was going to pretend to be Jace's fiancée she needed to consult with someone other than Tiffany. Sawyer was not only a journalist but according to Jace, his parents were blue-chip publicists who specialized in rescuing politicians, celebrities, and athletes from ruin. He'd know whether Tiffany's political trick was a terrible idea.

She waved the diamond back and forth across his face. "Tiffany thinks I should wear this ring during the barbecue to give people the idea that Jace and I are engaged. She says I don't have to lie and that it's just a ring but that it'll give people something to talk about other than the"—she paused for a second because she didn't even know what to call it—"you know, the rumor. What do you think?"

He stood there for a few moments without saying anything. Initially, Charlotte thought he was angry. But on further reflection, she could tell he was weighing the pros and cons in his head.

"Don't lie. And whatever you do, don't tell Jace. He can't be part of this."

"So I should wear it?" She wasn't sure what he was telling her to do.

"If anyone asks you about it, blow them off. Tell them it was your mother's or some bullshit like that. They won't believe you. Everyone will think the two of you are engaged. But if things go sideways, you'll have cover. Seriously, Charlotte, this can't look like a publicity stunt."

"You don't think Tiffany's crazy, then?"

He let out a bark of laughter. "Oh, she's crazy all right. But let's just say this is one of her better ideas. Don't tell Jace, though. He has to have plausible deniability."

"Gotcha." She couldn't believe she was willing to be complicit in this farce. But to be Jace Dalton's fiancée, even for a day, didn't exactly suck.

Tiffany's voice came across the two-way radio. "Aubrey is still waiting for those tablecloths. Chop chop."

"I'm on it." Charlotte tilted her head up to the sky and prayed for patience. "I suddenly feel like a wedding planner."

Sawyer's lips curved in amusement and he headed off to help Cash with the chairs.

"Hey." Jace caught her around the waist and she instantly hid her left hand in the folds of her coat. "What were you and Sawyer talking about?"

"How bossy Tiffany is." The lie slid off her tongue and she felt a moment of guilt but reminded herself that the end justified the means.

"That it?" he asked, stuffing his hands in his pockets and rocking on his feet.

"We talked about you and how the barbecue was going to be a great success."

He quirked a brow. "Doesn't sound like Sawyer."

"Well, that's what we talked about." She reached up and tugged down the brim of his hat. "Looking good, Sheriff."

He might've blushed—Charlotte couldn't say for sure—but he definitely grinned and Charlotte felt that grin all the way down to her toes.

"If I don't get the tablecloths from the house, Tiffany will fire me."

Jace hooked his thumbs in his silver belt buckle and gave her a long, thorough once-over. "Maybe I'll come with you."

"Oh no, you don't. People will be here soon." She waved at the tent. "Time to mingle, big guy."

"What if I don't want to mingle?"

She grabbed a fistful of his shirt and pulled his face down so they were eye to eye. "You're supposed to be social at these campaign functions, Jace. That's the whole point. We're in it to win it."

"Where the hell did you come up with that—cheerleading practice?" His mouth quirked.

"Now you're just being ornery. Go kiss some babies, Jace." She jogged up the stairs to the porch, turned her head to find him watching her with that same silly grin on his lips, and she got those flutters again.

* * * *

Jace didn't want to kiss babies, he wanted to kiss Charlie. As often as she'd let him.

He walked toward the tent with a little more punch in his giddyup, even though he looked forward to this barbecue about as much as he did to getting typhoid fever. Charlie did that to him. She made him happy and steady and able to believe in love again. And he wanted to make her proud.

We're in it to win it.

He chuckled to himself and strode into the tent ready to take on Mill County.

Folks started pouring in around noon. Tiffany had wanted people to pay a hundred dollars a plate. But Jace had quickly nixed that idea.

"This ain't the French Laundry, Tiff. Dalton burgers are good but not a hundred-bucks good."

"They're not paying for the food," she'd argued. "They're paying to support the candidate."

"They can support me at the ballot box."

They'd settled on forty dollars a head, kids ate free. From the look of the crowd, forty bucks had been the sweet spot. Jace didn't take it for granted that everyone who'd come was here to support his bid for reelection. The good people of the county were always up for a party and Dry Creek Ranch was pretty damned hospitable.

Laney and Jimmy Ray waved as they got a couple of beers from the bar. Sam Gilletti, owner of Ale Yeah!, had volunteered to bring the kegs and run the taps. The Klines had come with Tina, which made Travis happy.

"Nice shindig." Randy Beals slapped Jace on the back.

"How you doing, Randy? How's things at the ranch?" Jace felt a wave of guilt for not having checked in with his neighbor. There never seemed to be enough hours in the day.

"Same old, same old." Randy frowned.

"You talk to someone about debt consolidation?"

Randy huffed out a breath. "What's the point, unless they can whittle my debt down to zero. Anything more than that, I ain't got."

Jace took a second or two to let that sink in. "What are you planning to do?"

"Sell before the bank takes it away, I reckon. I was gonna come over and talk to you boys about it, give you first crack at buying."

Jace's chest tightened. "Ah, Randy, I'm sorry. I wish more than anything there was a way you could turn this around."

"What about you boys? Can we work something out?"

Jace motioned for Randy to follow him away from the crowd and said, "We can't even cobble together the back taxes. No way do we have that kind of cash." Or credit. No bank would lend them the kind of money Beals Ranch was worth.

"I didn't think so." Randy lowered his head. "But your granddaddy meant the world to me and handing my land over to a Dalton would've taken some of the sting out of it."

Jace nodded. "I'm sorry, Randy. I wish there was something we could all do."

"Aw, hell, maybe it'll be nice not to have to work so hard. Marge wants to get a Winnebago, travel a little." Randy swung his arm over Jace's shoulder. "In the meantime, you've got my vote, son. Now I'm gonna get me one of those inferior burgers you're peddling and a beer."

The conversation had left Jace low, but he decided to wait until after the barbecue to tell Cash and Sawyer. No sense ruining the afternoon when everyone had worked so hard on his behalf.

"Who was that?" Charlie sidled up next to him.

"The neighbor from Beals Ranch I told you about." He gazed around the tent. "How do you think it's going so far?"

"Excellent, don't you?"

"I'm happy with it." He couldn't help himself and kissed the top of her head.

She smiled up him and straightened his collar. "Don't just talk to people you know."

"And you thought Tiffany was bossy?"

As if he'd conjured her with his little quip, Tiffany appeared at his right elbow. "I have some people I want you to meet." Before he could respond, she dragged him away.

She pushed him into Lionel Fisher, who owned a cement processing plant in Rock Bottom, an unincorporated area on the edge of Mill County, which had a population of less than five hundred. Fisher was a generous benefactor in the area and had built a couple of small parks with money out of his own pocket. Needless to say, his backing would go a long way.

"Nice barbecue." Fisher tipped his cowboy hat instead of shaking Jace's hand, old-school style.

"Thanks. Glad you could make it." Jace looked around Fisher. "You bring Barbara and the kids?"

"Nah, she's the 4-H horse leader in Rock Bottom and is up at that retreat at the Nevada City fairgrounds today. The kids' Saturdays are pretty packed. So it's just me. Came to hear what you have to say."

"I'm just looking for your vote, Lionel. It's as simple as that." Tiffany discreetly kicked him in the ankle, urging him to do the whole damn stump speech. "I've been a good sheriff," he continued, uncomfortable bragging about himself. But that's what Tiffany wanted him to do and on this score she was right. No one was going to toot his own horn for him. "I have more than a decade of law enforcement experience, including making detective on a midsize city's force. I believe…correct that…I know Mill County has been a safer place since I was elected sheriff."

"We had that biker murder two years ago and there's been an uptick in property crimes." Fisher was reading straight off of Jacob Jolly's talking points.

"Yep. We arrested two people in that biker case days after the murder. Both were convicted and got life in prison without the possibility of parole. I'd say that was a job well done. As far as the uptick in property crimes, that started before I took office. Take another look at those numbers, Lionel. You'll like what you see."

"You've done a good job, Jace. And I don't pay a lot of attention to rumors or sex scandals. But Jacob Jolly is offering a fresh perspective that I think will shake up the status quo."

Jace couldn't help but laugh. "I'm not arguing with you as far as shaking up the status quo, if you mean getting a guy in here with absolutely no law enforcement background. He runs a hardware store with two employees. I run a county department with a seven-figure budget and a staff of thirty. It's thirty because the first thing I did when I was elected was make good on my campaign promise to add ten more deputies to the department. Jacob Jolly is a great guy if you need a wrench. As the top cop in Mill County, not so much. I'd also be concerned that much of his contributions are coming from one special interest group and how beholden he might be to them in the future. I don't have half his war chest, Lionel." Jace made a point of drawing Fisher's attention to the crowd. "But every dime I've collected is from my constituents, not folks who live outside the county."

"All good points, Sheriff. All points I'll take into consideration when I go to the ballot box. Your grandfather was a good man and I think you're a good man. I also think Jolly's a good man."

"Fair enough," Jace said. "Get yourself a burger, Lionel, and I'll catch up with you later."

He walked away not feeling particularly optimistic about having won Fisher over. Tiffany chased after him.

"See, that wasn't so hard." She pulled him behind the bandstand, where a local bluegrass group was entertaining the crowd. "You were magnificent, by the way!"

"He's voting for Jolly."

"He was before you made your spiel. Now he's on the fence and I have the utmost faith he'll come around by the June primary."

"We'll see." Jace wasn't as convinced.

"Notice that the sex scandal came up again. I told you we had to mitigate that problem."

It was all Jace could do not to blow a loud raspberry. "I can't control ridiculous rumors. All people have to do is look at Aubrey and Cash to know that Mitch's story was bullshit."

"Jill's here, by the way."

"I saw her old man earlier. She's a neighbor, a constituent, what can I do?"

"Nothing." Tiffany gazed around the tent. The crowd had spilled out onto the lawn and everyone seemed to be enjoying the event. "We want her vote, Jace."

Jace didn't give a rat's ass about Jill's vote. As far as he was concerned she should be in jail, but Randy Beals had enough problems without having to visit his daughter behind a Plexiglas window. In the corner, near the bar, he spied Brett in his wheelchair and decided that whatever happened with the election didn't compare to having good friends. Great friends.

"Tiff, I see someone I want to talk to. Let's reconnoiter later." He squeezed through the crowd, shaking hands as he went.

"Hey, it's the man of the hour." Brett high-fived him.

"You came."

Brett threw his hands up in the air. "Of course I came. For you, bruh. And last I looked Sacramento was only an hour away and I'm still registered in Mill County, my friend."

"I heard you were voting for Jolly."

Brett flipped him the bird. "Jill's here along with the kids."

Jace nodded. "Anything new going on there?"

"She wants us to get back together."

"And?"

Brett shrugged. "I'm not ready yet. Fact is, I don't know if I can let what she did go, Jace. For the sake of the kids, I want to forgive and forget. But…shit."

"I hear ya." The whole damn affair was so freaking sad, Jace had trouble wrapping his head around it. Brett had given so much…to his country…to his community. Jill had been in love with him since she was a teenager.

And then Brett came back from the war a paraplegic and in the blink of an eye everything changed.

"I'd like to meet this babysitter you've been telling me about." Brett smirked. "Where is she?"

"Come on, I'll introduce you."

Guests cleared a path so Brett could get through in his chair, and Jace led him to the other side of the tent where Charlie and Aubrey had managed to make time for a burger.

"Look who I found crashing the party," Jace said.

"Brett!" Aubrey hopped in his lap and threw her arms around his neck.

Brett did a couple of spins in his wheelchair. "When's the big day? 'Cause I might steal you away."

"My fiancé will likely have something to say about that," Aubrey said. "June. You're coming, right?"

"I wouldn't miss it for the world."

Aubrey scooted out of Brett's lap and he extended his hand. "Charlie, I presume."

Jace made formal introductions, then got pulled away again by Tiffany. Charlie, Brett, and Aubrey stayed behind, talking. There was a photographer from the local paper milling around, taking pictures. Jace had seen him before at a couple of crime scenes and gave him a big hello.

"How'd you get stuck with this assignment?" The kid probably preferred real action, not a stuffy campaign function.

"It's not so bad spending the day on an awesome ranch." The photographer smiled. "Can I get a shot of you standing next to one of your campaign posters?"

"How 'bout I flip you a burger, instead?" Tiffany perked up at the suggestion, probably liking the folksy appeal of the sheriff standing over a barbecue.

"That would be awesome." The photographer got his camera ready, clearly jazzed about the photo op.

But Tiffany's smile faded as soon as Jace slipped a "Mr. Good Lookin' is Cookin" apron over his head and she stared daggers at him. Apparently, it wasn't the image she was going for.

The apron had been a gift from Aubrey and it's what he wore when he did all his backyard grilling.

Just keeping it real, Tiff.

The photographer ate it up, though. "Turn a little to the left so I can get the apron." *Click, click, click.*

"How do you like your beef?"

"Medium rare." The camera man kept shooting pictures.

"A man after my own heart." A burger should never have an internal temperature of more than 145 degrees as far as Jace was concerned. He slapped a slice of cheese on top of the patty, waited for it to melt, and served it up with a toasted bun. "Here you go. Take a load off and grab yourself a beer."

Jace took off the apron, much to Tiffany's relief, and she led him off to another Jolly supporter, who'd probably come to the barbecue on a reconnaissance mission for Jace's opponent.

Whatever. Forty bucks was forty bucks, regardless. And by the end of the event, schmoozing everyone old enough to vote, he had more than earned every cent they brought in and then some.

Chapter 20

Sunday morning Tiffany called, barely able to contain her glee. "Have you seen the paper yet?"

Charlotte was in the midst of making crepes, with the phone clasped between her shoulder and her neck. "No, why? Is there a positive mention of the fundraiser?"

"Better than positive. Go look. I'll hang on."

"Jace," Charlotte called to the dining room where the entire Dalton gang had descended for breakfast and to do a postmortem—Sawyer's words—of the event. "Tiffany is on the phone. She wants you to look at the paper."

A short time later Jace came into the kitchen, took the phone from Charlotte and said, "Tiff, I have to call you back."

He hung up with a solemn expression on his face.

"What's wrong? Tiffany said the coverage was good."

He took the batter bowl from her and put it down on the counter. "Come in here for a sec."

She followed him back to the dining room, where the local paper was spread out on the table. There was a picture of her up on tiptoes, straightening Jace's collar, the fake engagement ring twinkling in the flash of the camera's strobe.

Charlotte's first thought was that Jace was furious about the ring. Very quickly, though, she saw the real problem.

"Oh no." She put her hand to her heart. "How did this happen?" It was a ridiculous question. There were at least three newspaper and TV photographers at the event and lord knew the number of attendees taking pictures with their phones to post on social media. "I'm such an idiot." She squeezed her eyes shut. She'd inadvertently left a road map for Corbin.

"Nope, that distinction goes to me," Jace said and wrapped his arms around her. "I'm the cop, I should've thought about pictures, about the security issues they posed."

"Ainsley already knows you're somewhere in Mill County." Sawyer hitched his shoulders. "And if he sees the picture in the paper, or online, he'll know you attended a campaign fundraiser for the sheriff. Doesn't seem like the end of the world."

Cash slid the paper across the table under Sawyer's face. "What does that picture look like to you?"

Charlotte didn't have to take a second look. How did the adage go? A picture's worth a thousand words. She and Jace were staring at each other with such heat in their eyes that she was surprised the newspaper hadn't spontaneously combusted. Throw in the sparkling diamond ring and Corbin was bound to form his own conclusions and go crazy with possessiveness.

Oddly, no one had mentioned Tiffany's diamond ring, not even Jace. She certainly didn't feel the need to bring it up. The situation was bad enough as it was.

Sawyer took a long look and grimaced. "Yeah, I see what you mean." He pushed the paper back at Jace.

"There's not much we can do about it now," Jace said. "The truth is I've been waiting for this thing to come to a head. We'll just have to be more vigilant about security when Charlie's here alone. And when Ainsley comes, I'll be ready."

"We'll be ready," Cash corrected.

Charlotte didn't want this. She didn't want to disrupt these good people's lives or ruin Jace's chances at reelection with yet another scandal. Most of all, she didn't want the stink of Corbin to touch Travis and Grady.

Her stay here had been a dream, and leaving Jace and his family behind would be like driving a stake through her heart. But the time had come to return to her original plan. She didn't even care about her own safety anymore. She cared about protecting the people she loved.

After breakfast Jace found her in her in her bedroom.

"You okay?"

She sat on the edge of the bed, fidgeting. "I guess in this day of social media and phone cameras it was inevitable that a picture of me would eventually surface. I just wish you hadn't gotten caught up in it."

He leaned against the dresser and his gaze slipped to her left hand. "What was up with the ring?" So, he had noticed. Charlotte felt a bead of perspiration trickle down her neck.

Jace's expression remained neutral and she couldn't tell whether he was angry. For a second, she considered lying but there'd been enough of that already. Jace deserved the truth and she deserved his rebuke for being duplicitous, even if she'd only had his best interests in mind.

She cleared her throat. "Tiffany thought if I wore the ring people would think we were engaged and it would put the old rumor about you and Aubrey to rest, or at least give everyone something else to talk about. Ultimately, she thought it would help your chances for reelection."

This time, she saw anger flicker across his face and Charlotte braced herself for his temper.

But he didn't move from the dresser and in a low voice said, "And you thought that was a good idea?"

"I didn't think it could hurt and…I wanted to help you." She shoved her hands under her legs to stop them from shaking. "Please don't be mad." Even to her own ears her voice sounded weak. Pathetic.

"I am mad, Charlie. It was a lie designed to manipulate voters. It's everything I'm against and you of all people should know that about me."

She did and yet she'd worn the ring anyway. "I…uh…wasn't thinking."

"No, you weren't." He turned on his heels and started for the door.

"Jace," she called to him. "I'm sorry. I'm terribly sorry."

He whirled around and she flinched.

"I know you are," he said. "And I know you were only trying to help. But I wish you would've talked to me first."

He walked out of the room, leaving Charlotte alone on the bed.

He was furious. Very, very angry, which he had every right to be. But he hadn't hit her or even raised his voice.

* * * *

Sunday passed in a blur. While Tiffany and Jace's family had deemed the fundraiser a rousing success, he wasn't so sure. He'd talked to at least a dozen people at the barbecue who said they were leaning toward Jolly.

"No offense. You've been a great sheriff but maybe it's time for new blood," Mercedes Aguilar, Mitch's secretary at Reynolds Construction, had told him. Of course, she was devoted to Mitch and still nursed residual resentment over Aubrey and Mitch's breakup and Mitch's subsequent arrest. But she'd once been a loyal member of Jace's fan club.

Jace supposed he should take solace in the fact that people like Mama, the owner of Mama's Towing and one of his toughest critics, was continuing to stand by him.

Time would tell. But at least he had the barbecue behind him. And Corbin Fucking Ainsley in front of him. It didn't take an FBI profiler to know that the ring Charlie had worn in the picture was like throwing down the gauntlet to a man like Ainsley.

Oh well, it was done now. And Charlie's heart had been in the right place. She'd worn the ring for him. For the sake of his reelection. He'd forgiven her. But Ainsley…Jace was looking forward to meeting the sumbitch face-to-face.

He looked up at the clock on the wall and got to his feet. On the way out of the office, he told Annabeth to hold his calls and walked to Mother Lode Road.

April was just a few days away, but the temperature hadn't gotten the memo. Jace zipped up his vest and pulled his hat down low.

Cash and Sawyer were waiting for him at the coffee shop at their usual table, where a pitcher of sarsaparilla and a fresh decanter of coffee waited.

"We took the liberty of ordering for you," Sawyer said. "Cash has to be in Placer County by two."

Jace took off his hat and hung it off a steer horn on the wall. "What's going on in Placer County?"

"A couple of drive-by shootings. Some idiot or idiots are picking off sheep in the fields." Cash poured himself a cup of coffee.

"You talk to the sheriff over there? He's a good guy."

"We're working it together," Cash said. "So far, no suspects."

"What kind of asshole does something like that?" Sawyer reached across the table for the coffee decanter.

"Don't know, but I hope you catch whoever's responsible." Jace poured himself a glass of the sarsaparilla. If he had another cup of coffee he'd be bouncing off the walls.

"I don't have much time either. Grady's getting his cast off this afternoon." Charlie had volunteered to take him, but Jace thought he'd make a surprise appearance at the doctor's office and take everyone out for dinner after the big reveal. "So let me get right to the point." He'd put off telling his cousins long enough. "Randy Beals told me he's selling his ranch."

"Ah, shit." Sawyer rubbed his hand down his face.

"I guess it was inevitable." Cash, always the pragmatist. "Does he have a buyer yet?"

Jace shook his head. "Doesn't sound like he's listed it and has given us first dibs. I told him we couldn't even pay Grandpa's back taxes. Where we at on that, anyway?"

"I've got my end covered. Just sold the foreign rights on my last book. My agent's still working out the details but it should be a decent payout. I'm willing to put any extra toward your end of it." He looked first at Jace and then at Cash.

"Congratulations on the foreign rights," Cash said. "But no one expects you to carry all three of us. I talked to an investment broker about borrowing against my 401(k). Right now, it's looking like my best option."

Cash's gaze fell on Jace, who only had one possession worth anything that would even come close to paying his share. It would hurt to part with it. But it was that…or nothing.

"I've been doing some research on the internet," he said. "And it looks like Grandpa's coin collection might be worth something."

"He left that to you," Sawyer said and jabbed his fork in the air. "That was something you two did together. He wouldn't want you to sell it."

Jace was a kid when he and his grandfather had started going to coin shows together. They'd even gone to the New York International Numismatic Convention at the Waldorf Astoria Hotel. It had been Jace's first trip to the Big Apple, which had made a lasting impression. Never in his life did he want to live in a big city. Too many damned people.

But the convention had been exciting. Coins from all over the world, many of them ancient. He and his grandfather had been blown away by the history in that room. Jace would always remember the experience.

"The coins were a hobby, the ranch was Grandpa's life," Jace said. "It'll be sad to give up that piece of him, but I can live with it if it means holding on to the land, holding on to our legacy."

"Even if we manage to pay the arrears and the regularly scheduled payment this time, we'll have to pay again in November," Cash said.

"So? No matter where, unless we plan to rent for the rest of our lives, we'd have to pay property taxes, Cash."

"Not on five hundred acres of prime real estate worth a fortune. But you fucking well know that, Jace. All I'm saying is that if we're committed to keeping the ranch we have to come up with a plan to support it, not fly by the seat of our pants. We need to have a slush fund so we don't have to beg, borrow, and steal every time a property tax or insurance bill comes due."

"Fine, Cash. What's the plan?" Jace knew he sounded like a dick, but it was his default when he was clueless about what to do. The cattle operation was a nice side-hustle that paid for itself with a little left over for small upgrades on the ranch. But it didn't pay the big bills. "I'm open to anything you've got."

"What if, instead of selling off some of the land, we develop a hundred acres ourselves. Big lots, maybe five acres each, with nice houses that we can sell for a hefty price. We could start a trust with the profits that'll tide us over for at least the next ten years."

"Nope." Sawyer was adamant. "We've been over this. We're not breaking up the land. Come up with a better plan."

"Ditto to what Sawyer said," Jace seconded. "Not happening, Cash."

"Okay, then let's hear your ideas." Cash looked at his cousins.

"Buy Randy's land and grow the cattle operation." Sawyer grinned. "Go big or go home, right?"

"You're delusional."

This time, Jace agreed with Cash. Sawyer lived on an alternate planet from the rest of them.

"I say we focus on paying the tax bill for right now, then come up with a plan for the future." Between Charlie's situation and the upcoming primary, Jace was mentally tapped out. But he had been giving a lot of thought to Charlie's idea about developing a ranch-related business besides raising cattle to support the land.

"I second that."

Their food came and they ate in companionable silence for a while, each man lost in his own thoughts.

"Maybe we should do what Charlie does and sell junk," Cash said as he finished his sandwich. "You know how much she pedals that stuff in her workshop for? A small fortune, that's how much."

Jace's lips quirked. "It's not junk when she gets through with it."

"Aubrey's bringing over two clients today with deep pockets." Cash scratched his jaw. "I don't get it."

"What's there to get? Charlie's a good businesswoman. She's as clever as she is creative." Beautiful too. In the months she'd been living at the ranch, she and Jace had become a true team in every sense of the word.

"Shit." Cash caught the time and reached for his wallet. "I've gotta go."

"I'll take care of the bill," Sawyer said. "You can get me next time."

Cash took off, leaving Jace and Sawyer to finish their sandwiches together.

"Anything new with that woman you talked to about Angie and the co-op in New Mexico?" Jace asked.

"*Nada.* I'm still deciding whether to go in person. My head's been in finishing the book and the foreign rights sale on the other one."

"Pretty impressive." Jace leaned across the table and smacked Sawyer upside the head. "You're a freaking rock star. Grandpa would've been so damned proud. We all are, you know?"

Sawyer seemed mildly embarrassed by the praise. "I wish Ange was around. She was my biggest cheerleader, used to call me Mr. Fourth Estate. I got a big kick out of that."

"We all wish she was around, Sawyer. You writing today?"

"Every day." He drained the rest of his coffee and flagged the server for their bill. "Grady's getting his cast off, huh?"

"Yup. He was bouncing off the walls all evening, excited about seeing his actual arm again. It's just a matter of time before he breaks something else. The kid doesn't know how to sit still."

"He's hyper all right, but he hasn't scared Charlie off."

"Nope, she's tougher than she looks."

Sawyer perused the long row of credit cards in his wallet before choosing one. "She did a nice job with the fundraiser. I wasn't too sure about her in the beginning, but I think she's good for you. That smile you've been sporting ever since she showed up is starting to get nauseating, you know?"

"I wish Ainsley wasn't hanging over her head."

"Maybe he isn't. Since she filed the restraining order it doesn't seem like it would've been that hard to find her. Mill County's tiny and people here like to talk. Any investigator worth his salt would've located her in ten seconds. And someone like Ainsley could afford the best, which makes me think he's not looking."

Jace thought about it all the way back to the office. Sawyer had good instincts about these kinds of things. Ainsley had to be concerned about his legal exposure. Criminal juries didn't like defendants who kicked and beat their pregnant girlfriends. Why show up and make more trouble for himself?

By the time he left for Grady's appointment, he'd halfway convinced himself that the threat level had dropped to low.

* * * *

Charlotte had made another sale, this one her largest of all. One of Aubrey's clients whipped through the barn like a tornado, buying everything in sight.

The iron-gate-turned-headboard, the wagon-wheel chandelier, the trough garden fountain, the wheelbarrow planter, the barn door, and a number of other items Charlotte had picked up here and there and repurposed along the way.

The client had recently purchased a vacation home on a private lake near the Nevada state line and wanted to get it onto Vrbo as quickly as possible so it could start paying for itself. And the place needed to be completely furnished.

She and Aubrey were coming back with a moving truck on Tuesday and had already given Charlotte a fat check made out to Jace Dalton. It was currently tucked away in Jace's safe with the rest of Charlotte's earnings. Now there was hardly anything left in the workshop, just a lot of odds and ends that Charlotte had collected along the way but had no plans for.

It was good, she told herself. She'd accomplished her goal of repurposing everything she'd taken from old man Maitland's barn and then some. Friday, Sissy was coming to pick up the chair and sofa. So when Charlotte stole away Saturday morning, no one would be able to say she hadn't fulfilled her commitments. Instead of one week, she'd given Jace two months.

Two of the best months of her life.

She dried her eyes and ordered herself to grow a spine. When Corbin came she would no longer be here. That way, he couldn't complicate anyone else's life.

Jace's reelection bid was precarious enough. A showdown with the influential Ainsley family was the last thing he needed.

Meredith had instructed her to leave as soon as possible, but Charlotte had to get her ducks in a row first, starting with Jace. She wasn't going to tell him she was leaving but wanted to make sure he and the kids were taken care of before she hit the road.

Those were her thoughts as she left the ranch to pick up the boys in time for Grady's appointment. He wanted that cast off in the worst way, and Aubrey's client had held Charlotte up.

She raced to the gate, wishing she didn't have to spend the extra time getting out of the car to open and close it. It was a gorgeous day. So sunny, she'd been fooled into not wearing a jacket. For the first time this month, it felt like spring. A crop of poppies and lilacs had started to bloom in the fields and everywhere Charlotte looked she saw bursts of color. Even the air smelled fragrant with flowers.

She breathed in the glorious scent, swung the gate open and drove to the other side, then rushed back out to relock it. The boys liked to hop on the bottom rail, push off with their feet, and ride the gate closed. Though tempted to try it, Charlotte lifted the heavy iron just high enough to keep the bottom from dragging in the dirt and quickly shut it behind her.

She got in the driver's seat, locked her door, and turned onto Dry Creek Road. That's when she felt it. A swish of air on the back of her neck and something cold and steely against her skin.

"Keep driving." The voice was low and cruel and the last time she'd heard it she was on the floor, battered and broken from being repeatedly kicked.

"Corbin…no…for God's sake don't do this." Her eyes darted to the passenger seat, unable to remember if her phone was out or still in her handbag.

"What are you looking for, Charlotte?"

She didn't respond, just scanned the road hoping to see a familiar car and somehow send out an SOS. Cash, Sawyer, anyone.

They were only a short distance to the highway and with every mile marker her chance for rescue or escape diminished. By the time the boys realized she wasn't coming for them, Charlotte could be anywhere.

"A restraining order, Charlotte? I could be disbarred for the shit you're accusing me of. Do you and your fucking *fiancé* want to get me disbarred? Huh, Charlotte?"

"No, Corbin." He liked her submissive, and if she was going to come out of this, she'd have to play the part. Even if it made her gorge rise.

She considered jumping out of the vehicle but was afraid she'd either kill herself in the process or Corbin would shoot her before she got both feet out the door. She was sure it was a gun she felt on her neck.

"Corbin, just let me go and I'll withdraw the restraining order."

He laughed. "Too late for that now. Besides, we've got a lot to talk about, a lot of lost time to make up for. So you're engaged, huh? I could've given you everything but instead you settle for some hayseed sheriff in the middle of nowhere. What the hell's wrong with you, Charlotte?"

He smelled of alcohol and she'd never known him to be a heavy drinker. Then again, she hadn't known a lot of things about Corbin Ainsley. Not until he'd managed to control every aspect of her life.

He shoved the hunk of steel harder against her neck. "Up at the highway make a right. Away from that little shithole town where your boyfriend the rent-a-cop is."

She felt relieved and petrified at the same time. *Leave Jace out of this.* "Where are we going?"

"Charlotte, Charlotte, Charlotte. Always with the questions. You think you would've learned by now."

"Why are you doing this, Corbin? Why are you jeopardizing your career, your father's career?"

He laughed again. "Since when are you concerned about my career? You go off, lose our child, and hook up with the first guy you meet. What kind of woman does something like that, huh, Charlotte? I wanted to give you my name and what did you do? You played me, you threw me over like a chump. And now you're flaunting your goddamn engagement in my face."

Corbin was slurring his words and Charlotte feared he might be on something besides alcohol. She also worried that after he was finished with her, he'd exact his revenge on Jace.

"I don't know what you're talking about. I'm not engaged. Please, Corbin, just let me go," she pleaded.

"You're never going anywhere again, Charlotte. You think I'd let you get away with taking my kid away from me? What did you do, get rid of the baby on purpose? We were supposed to be a family."

They'd gotten to the stoplight at the intersection of the highway and Charlotte prayed that a neighbor would pass by and see her. Then again, what good would it do? Corbin was crouched down in the back seat and this was the same route she took every day at this time to pick up the boys. Nothing to see here.

"I told you to go right," he commanded.

But the light had turned red and there was oncoming traffic. This was her last chance. Once they hit the highway, she'd be completely at Corbin's mercy. If she wanted to escape she had to do it now.

Jump and run.

She reached for the door handle but Corbin snaked his arm around her throat and pressed cold metal against her larynx.

"Don't even think about it."

"Please," she whimpered.

The light was green.

"Turn!"

With no other choice, she did what he said. "Where are we going?"

"Do you ever stop talking, Charlotte? God, you used to give me such a headache with your endless nattering. Your fucking store. No one gave a shit about your fucking store."

"Where are we going, Corbin?" she asked, and this time her voice was strong. Her fear had collided with anger. Why had he searched her out? Why couldn't he just leave her alone?

Men like Corbin can never let it go, Charlotte. They always have to win.

That's what Meredith had told her in those first few frightening days when Charlotte had planned her stealth getaway. It had been both a warning and a pep talk to leave, to move far, far away.

He cackled. "Where do you want to go, Charlotte? How about straight to hell?"

She drove, wishing she could flag down one of the motorists headed in the opposite direction. But they whizzed by her in a blur of color, oblivious to her plight.

She passed the motel where Jace had brought her that first night. Past the Dutch Bros. Coffee kiosk where an endless line of cars waited. Then the urgent care facility where she'd been treated after the miscarriage. The same hospital where she'd taken Grady for his broken arm.

It was surreal watching all these places whir by in her rearview mirror while Corbin held a gun to the back of her head. Soon, they'd be approaching the entrance to Interstate 80. What would Corbin do then?

At some point, the boys would notify Jace that she hadn't picked them up and he would eventually alert the Highway Patrol to be on the lookout for her Honda. The interstate would be her best chance for rescue.

But Corbin wasn't an idiot. Certainly he knew they'd be easier to spot on a major interstate.

"Keep going," he said when they came to the on-ramp, and what little hope she had plummeted.

They crossed the freeway and Charlotte was lost. She'd never been south of Auburn on Highway 49 and had no idea what lay ahead.

They drove for what seemed like miles. And the farther they went, the curvier the road got, with hairpin turns and sheer drops into a river much larger than Dry Creek. Charlotte was petrified, her foot riding the brake and her hands squeezing the wheel. But Corbin was losing his patience.

"Pick up the pace," he said so close to her ear that it made her jump in her seat.

She weighed the possibility of driving off the mountainside but didn't like her chances. The drop would likely kill them both.

She needed a better escape route.

After twenty minutes of twists and turns, the road became flat and straight and much more manageable. If not for Corbin sitting behind her, she would've found her breath.

They sped by a cluster of old Western-style buildings and continued past signs advertising white-water rafting tours and adventures. The drive seemed endless. And to nowhere.

"Pull in here." Corbin ordered her down a turnout that was little more than a dirt road.

She followed his command until they came to a fork in the trail, where Corbin told her to take a right onto a bumpy lane that was no more than a car-width wide. The area was wooded and there didn't seem to be a house for miles.

Ahead, she made out water, and the closer they got to it she realized it was a river. Likely the same river from where they'd come. In the distance, there was a large trestle bridge but Charlotte couldn't tell how far away it was. It appeared to be close to the little Western town they'd passed, but fear had thrown off her sense of direction.

"Stop here."

Her car, along with her heart, skidded to a halt.

"Where are we?"

"Your final resting place." Corbin stuck his head up front and the smell of liquor filled the cab as if it was emanating from his pores. He must've been on a bender for days. "Get out of the car."

She wanted to stall, find her phone or anything she could use as a weapon, but Corbin jammed the barrel of what she could now plainly see was a pistol against her arm. Slowly, she opened the door and slid out, trying to get her bearings.

"This is crazy, Corbin." She wanted to say that he would never get away with whatever maniacal plan he had in store but she was wrong. No one would ever find her here. He could dump her remains in the rushing river, dispose of her car, and make up an alibi. No one would ever be the wiser.

"We've got a lot of talking to do, Char. A lot of catching up."

"Oh God." She shuddered. Before, Corbin had always seemed sane, just mean and controlling. Now she swore he was completely off his rocker.

* * * *

Jace was going out of his mind. He had two technicians tracing Charlie's GPS: the one in her vehicle and the one on her phone. Earlier, he'd put out a BOLO for Charlie's CR-V.

"Jace, is there a chance she just left, went to Colorado or somewhere else to hide?" Cash asked on the other end of the phone.

"She wouldn't have done that. What did Aubrey say? Was she there earlier?"

"Yep, brought a client and says everything seemed normal. She locked the gate on her way out."

None of this made sense. If Charlie planned to leave she wouldn't have taken off in the middle of the day, leaving the boys stranded. And he'd like to think she wouldn't have taken off without at least saying goodbye.

"Sawyer went to the house. Her suitcase, her clothes, everything is still there. Her sewing machines are in the workshop. She wouldn't have left without them." Or without at least leaving a note. These last two months had to have meant something to her. "This doesn't smell right, Cash. Ainsley saw the picture, figured out where she was, and now he has her, I feel it in my gut."

"I'm on my way back from Placer," Cash said. "Try to stay calm."

Easy for Cash to say. It wasn't his woman.

Reggie came into his office. "Jace, we may have gotten something."

"Cash, I've gotta go." Jace gave his full attention to the watch commander.

"No luck with her phone. It's probably turned off," Reggie said. "But her car has HondaLink, which has an OnStar-type service that can track the location of her car. We're talking to an adviser from the company, trying to determine whether we need a search warrant."

"A search warrant?" Jace's head was about to explode.

Reggie held up his hands. "Jace, we're operating on the theory that her ex abducted her. There's no evidence that that's the case. Come on, man, think like a cop. Think about HondaLink's exposure here."

Jace counted to ten, trying to hold himself in check. Screw privacy at a time like this. He knew in his heart of hearts that Ainsley had her. And every second they spent jerking off was critical.

"Annabeth," he bellowed. "Get the Rosie the Riveter Foundation on the phone. I want to talk to Meredith." Jace didn't even know Meredith's last name. But the organization had been used as a shill to purchase Charlie's car, and perhaps Meredith could talk some sense into Honda or whoever the hell owned the car service application.

Annabeth appeared in the doorway. "Deputy Anderson just called. He found a Porsche Cayman hidden in a grove of trees just off Dry Creek Road, about a half mile from your ranch. Plates come back to Corbin Ainsley."

Jace pinned Reggie with a look.

"I'm on it."

"Send HondaLink a copy of the goddamn restraining order," Jace called to Reggie as he jogged down the hall.

Ainsley was sloppy. You'd think a guy with a freaking law degree would've planned this out better. Jace should've been elated by Ainsley's mistakes. Instead, it scared him to death. The man was operating like he had nothing to lose, which in Jace's mind could only mean one thing.

* * * *

Corbin dragged Charlotte by the back of her collar to the river's edge. She patted her pockets, foolishly searching for her phone.

Corbin laughed. "You left it in your purse on the floor of the car, Char. Hope you don't mind but I took the liberty of chucking your battery into the woods while you were screwing around with that piece-of-shit gate. Besides, who you going to call? Nine-one-one? Think they'll find you in time?"

She couldn't even tell anyone where she was. *Near a river.* There were about half a dozen in Mill County alone. She shivered, thinking about how isolated they were.

"Oh Charlotte, Charlotte, Charlotte." He glanced her over. "Should've worn a jacket. Then again you never had the sense God gave geese, now did you?"

Corbin looked disheveled, like he'd slept in the same clothes for a week. Charlotte remembered how persnickety he used to be about his suits. God forbid the dry cleaner used those tiny safety pins to tack his pants to the paper hanger. He'd fly into a rage, threatening to put them out of business.

"By the way, your dyke sister's been looking for you. There's another one who's dumber than a doornail." He shook his head. "What am I going to do with you, Charlotte, huh?"

"Corbin—"

"Did I ask you to talk?" He pushed her onto the hard ground. "Do you know how much I loved you? How much I wanted to take care of you? Always with that shop. That ridiculous shop. Here I was, giving you a house in Presidio Heights and it still wasn't good enough. Anything you wanted, I gave you. Anything. But none of it was good enough. Not my name, not my child, not my love. Not a goddamned thing."

She felt around her for a fallen branch or a rock, anything with which to hit Corbin over the head. "I loved you too, Corbin. Maybe we could start over again." The idea filled her throat with bile.

"I wouldn't take you back if you were the last woman on earth. You're a disloyal bitch. And a fucking drama queen. You'd think I'd chained you to the wall and forced you to eat cockroaches the way you ran from me. You know how many times I had to lie about you to my father?"

"Where's Charlotte?"

"She's in Portland, her mother's sick."

"How come Charlotte's not here?"

"She's under the weather."

"Did Charlotte leave you, Corbin?"

"What are you crazy? Charlotte and I are forever, Dad."

He looked down at her on the dirt, drew his leg back, and kicked her in the side. Hard. Charlotte doubled over.

"Get up."

She was trembling now. Not from the cold but from his flinty stare. His eyes were like dark quartz. Hard and unyielding. He lifted the gun and she froze.

Oh God, this is it.

"I said get up!"

Even from where she lay sprawled on the ground, she could smell him. Booze and desperation. His hand shook ever so slightly. And for a second, she thought, *Just kill me. Get it over with and put me out of my misery.*

Just as quickly, a red-hot rage overtook her. This man had held her hostage long enough. He'd irrevocably changed her life. And why? Because she'd loved him and hadn't been strong enough—or smart enough—to realize that love shouldn't be binding. It shouldn't control a person. It shouldn't make them bleed and turn black and blue.

He was yelling now. His face red and puffy and distorted. Her anger, rushing through her like a torrent, drowned out the sound of his voice. It was as if he'd become a character in a silent movie. All his movements exaggerated, but no words.

You're brave, Charlie. Take your life back. Jace's words roared in her head.

Charlotte didn't think. She didn't allow fear to overwhelm her. Pretending to get up, she hurled herself at Corbin's legs, knocking him on his back. The gun fell out of his hand and skittered a few feet away.

She didn't bother to scoop it off the ground—and wouldn't have known what to do with it even if she had—and ran as fast and far as she could go. She blindly headed in the direction of the road, hoping she could flag someone down for help. But the keys to her Honda were still in the car.

She had no delusions that she'd permanently incapacitated Corbin. He wasn't a particularly large man but he was strong. And crazy. At best, her attack had only momentarily thrown him off guard. Once he recovered, he'd have the advantage in her CR-V.

She changed direction, running as fast as she could while searching for a good place to hide. Up ahead there was a dense thicket of pine and blue oak trees and she veered for cover. The wind whistled through the branches, making an ominous sound. At first, Charlotte thought it was Corbin coming after her. She turned to look over her shoulder, stumbled over a rock, and tumbled into a ravine covered in leaves.

Her heart stopped. Had he seen her fall? Had he heard her? She crawled behind the trunk of a fir tree and listened. Nothing besides the sound of rushing water and the rustling of trees.

But Corbin was out there somewhere.

She waited for a beat, her pulse quickening. Somewhere along the way, she'd lost a shoe and her foot was bleeding.

A twig snapped and she held her breath, wondering how visible she was. She had on a red cowl neck and blue jeans, not exactly good camouflage colors.

Please be a forest creature, she prayed.

The area didn't seem well traveled by humans, at least this time of year. Perhaps it got more visitors in summer when tourists came to play in the river.

After what seemed like an eternity, she shuddered with relief. The noise hadn't come from Corbin.

Still, he was searching for her, she knew that instinctively. He'd wait her out and no one would be able to find her to come to her rescue. If she had even a slight chance of surviving this, she needed to do more to conceal herself until she came up with a plan to get to the main road undetected.

She buried herself under a mound of leaves with just enough space for a clear airway so she could breathe. The sun was starting to set and she could feel the cold air bite through her clothes. In the distance, she heard something crackle and closed her eyes, waiting for it, helpless.

Something or someone was coming closer.

Chapter 21

El Dorado County sheriff deputies swarmed the South Fork American River, a short distance outside of Coloma. This was their jurisdiction, their show. But that didn't stop Jace from rocketing ninety miles an hour across two county lines with his lights flashing and his siren blaring.

He wasn't a religious man, but he prayed the whole way there.

This was his fault. He'd talked Charlie into the restraining order and promised he'd protect her. A fat lot of good he'd been. Ainsley had picked her off right outside his goddamn gate in broad daylight. If he ever got his hands on the prick he was going to squeeze the life out of him.

The problem was they hadn't found Ainsley, only Charlie's CR-V. HondaLink had given them the coordinates and the vehicle was right where they said it would be, along with Charlie's purse.

Jace paced where deputies had cordoned off the car. "You're burning daylight," he shouted at the lieutenant in charge of the search.

"We're doing the best we can, Sheriff."

"Not a lot of places they could've gone from here on foot." Jace scanned the area. Just the river, a dirt road, and a hell of a lot of forest. "When are the dogs getting here?"

"Any minute." The lieutenant brushed by him, barking orders at a couple of deputies.

"The son-of-a-bitch has her." Jace squeezed the sides of his head with his palms. "Every second here is critical and we've gotta wait for the goddamn dogs?"

Jace felt a hand on his arm.

"Not helpful." It was Cash. "Let them do their jobs."

"Where'd you come from?" Last he talked to Cash he was headed back to Dry Creek.

"I came straight here when I heard they located her car. The boys are with Aubrey and Sawyer."

"I'm losing it," Jace said. "She's out here somewhere, she's gotta be, and he's got her. The son-of-a-bitch has her."

An El Dorado County sheriff's van drove up and two K-9 trailing dogs jumped out of the side door with their handlers. Jace had used dogs before in lost hiker cases but Ainsley wasn't lost, he was hiding. And Jace considered him dangerous. Best case scenario: He was holding Charlie captive in a hidey-hole somewhere in the woods. Which meant there was no room for screwups.

"My guys and I want to go with one of the teams," Jace told the lieutenant. Charlie's abduction took place in Jace's county, his department had a right.

Cash didn't say anything but Jace could feel his disapproval through his flak jacket. *You're too close to the victim.* Too close? He was in love with Charlie. If he didn't go in, if he wasn't a part of the search, he'd go out of his mind.

"All right," the lieutenant agreed and eyed Jace's team's tactical gear. Everyone was suited up and ready to go.

The handlers were letting the dogs sniff the interior of Charlie's car and the contents of her purse. They had no scent article from Ainsley except maybe a hit from the CR-V. The going theory was that Ainsley had carjacked Charlie as she was shutting the gate and had forced her to drive here. The river was one of the most popular recreational spots in Northern California, so it didn't surprise Jace that Ainsley would know about it. What did surprise him is that Ainsley had found a spot this remote. He either scoped out the isolated segment along the eighty-seven-mile-long river or he knew the area inside and out.

Jace and his team went with the dog named Jenga, a black Malinois. Jenga sniffed the air and the ground and trotted off in the opposite direction of the water's edge. A rush of relief swamped Jace. The river in this part of the fork was rough and treacherous. Even a good swimmer wouldn't stand a chance.

But the terrain was steep and thick with trees and underbrush. A person who knew what he was doing could go without detection for days here. Jace had no idea whether Ainsley had any kind of wilderness training. From his pictures on the internet he looked like a slick city lawyer. There'd been nothing in his bio about past military service or outdoor hobbies, just a lot of crap about Ainsley's degrees and pedigree.

What worried Jace the most was Ainsley spooking from the swarm of cops who had descended and doing something desperate. The problem was they didn't have a lot options in a scenario like this. Either way, Charlie was in imminent danger.

Jenga took a couple of winding turns and seemed to pick up a trail. But Jace wasn't an expert on search dogs. He just knew they were the best tools in these kinds of situations.

Soon, it would be dark. The dogs could search in the night but without light it would make it more difficult for him and his team. Everything seemed to be working against them.

They followed Jenga as he swept through the forest. The other dog, Curry, wasn't far behind. Fifteen, twenty minutes went by and Jace was starting to fear that Ainsley wasn't here, that he'd taken Charlie somewhere else entirely.

Then Jenga stopped suddenly and began to circle a mound of leaves. Jace's men fanned out, rifles raised.

The handler kicked away some of the leaves, revealing a red suede loafer. He signaled to Jace to come forward.

He crouched down to take a closer look. It was Charlie's, he was sure of it. When she wasn't wearing her ankle boots, she wore the red shoes. They had a gold chain across the top and a small wooden heel.

Jace's heart sank and it took every ounce of his resolve to stay calm. She was out here somewhere. Hurt, helpless…Jace wouldn't let himself think anything else.

He nodded to the deputy. Someone photographed the shoe and bagged it. Jenga had already shot ahead, on to something new. And they were off again, following the dog as he took them on a circuitous route across the forest floor.

Jace didn't like it. It seemed far afield from where they'd found Charlie's shoe.

"I'm going to circle around," he told one of his deputies and doubled back to the way they'd come.

The air smelled like wet compost, pine, and fear. His fear. There was a noise and his head shot up. A squirrel scurried up a branch and Jace felt himself relax.

Up ahead, something caught his attention and he used a couple of big trees for cover as he hiked toward it. At first, he thought his eyes had been playing tricks on him. But as he got closer, a piece of torn fabric waved from a branch in the breeze. He radioed the team and without touching the cloth, made a more thorough examination. It was blue and looked to Jace like nylon. Like maybe it had come from a jacket. Charlie had a camel-colored wool coat.

He scanned the area, theorizing about what direction the person was headed when he or she got snagged on the tree limb. North or south? East or west? Jace dropped his eyes to the ground, looking for tracks, but the leaves made it hard to see possible footprints.

Then there it was. Three feet away he spied what looked like a fresh imprint of a tennis shoe. Maybe a men's size ten or eleven.

He lifted his gaze. About half a football-field-length's away there was an outcropping of large rocks and Jace's heart hammered in his chest.

"What do you got?" Jenga and his handler were back.

Jace pointed to the navy fabric and watched Jenga circle the tree and make a zigzaggy trail toward the rock outcrop. He gestured to his deputies and in formation they moved out, encircling the area.

With his rifle raised, Jace yelled, "This is the Mill County Sheriff's Department. We know you're in there, Ainsley. Real slowly raise your arms and we'll talk this out." Presuming Ainsley was actually hiding in the rocks, there were about a million ways this could go wrong.

El Dorado County had a hostage negotiator on hand, but Jace wanted to confirm they had Ainsley first. Jenga continued to wind around the rocks, his ears pricked forward. His handler called him back and nodded to Jace. It seemed they'd found their quarry.

"Ainsley," Jace called again.

No response. Jace was getting a bad feeling.

"Someone call for the negotiator," he said. "The rest of you cover me. I'm going in."

It wasn't protocol. In fact, it was felony stupid. If Cash wasn't back at the command post he would've done everything short of shooting Jace to try to stop him. But leaving Charlie to fend for herself until they got a negotiator in here wasn't an option. Not where Jace was concerned.

"Sheriff, stand down," one of the El Dorado deputies said.

He ignored her and crept around the periphery of the outcrop, hoping he could sneak up on Ainsley and take him into custody without incident. His heart thudded against his chest. He'd pulled off some crazy shit in his time but never when the stakes were this high.

Be okay, Charlie. Please be okay.

He caught a flash of blond through the crevasses in the rocks. Ainsley. Charlie had to be in there with him.

Don't think about her now, just keep your eye on the target.

Jace slunk behind one of the boulders and listened hard, trying to pinpoint Ainsley's location. All he heard was the pounding of his own pulse. There was another flash of color, this time blue.

Ainsley was on the move.

Jace snuck around the outside of the rock cluster, looking for a way to get in, undetected. It was like a cave inside, flanked by walls of granite. He was just about to slip between two rocks when he came face-to-face with Ainsley.

Jace had ditched his rifle with the team, favoring the lightness of his Glock. He raised the semiautomatic and leveled it at Ainsley's chest. "Show your hands! Take them out of your pockets. Slowly!"

Ainsley jerked out a pistol.

"Drop it! Drop it now!" Jace shouted as he took cover behind one of the large rock formations and fingered the trigger on his own weapon.

He could hear movement behind him. The troops were converging.

"I told you to drop it, Ainsley."

Ainsley put the barrel of the gun inside his mouth.

Ah, Jesus. Jace came out from behind the rock. "Don't do it, Corbin. Drop the gun and we can talk. Tell me where Charlotte is."

Ainsley's hand shook and his trigger finger twitched. From where Jace was standing it looked like Ainsley held a Sig Sauer. It had enough firepower to get the job done if Ainsley wanted to off himself. Jace's stomach churned. A suicidal suspect held all kinds of implications, none of them good for Charlie.

Jace came closer, taking one hand off the grip of his Glock to hold it out to Ainsley. "Don't do this, man. Give me the gun and tell me where Charlotte is." He was trying to keep his head while his throat closed up on him. "Where is she?"

It happened so fast Jace didn't see it coming until the muzzle flashed. A pain seared through him and he felt himself falling backwards. In the foggy distance someone yelled, "Man down."

Then everything went dark.

Chapter 22

Charlotte managed to dress herself for the first time since Monday. For two days she'd been lost in a world of what-ifs. If she hadn't stayed at Dry Creek Ranch, she wouldn't have brought terror and misery with her. If she had only left, Corbin never would've come.

He was in the hospital now, awaiting a bedside arraignment. According to the prosecutor, they had enough charges to lock him up for a lifetime. Even his father, the senator, had distanced himself from his son, refusing to come to the hearing. Without Charles Ainsley's money and name, Corbin was on his own. As it turned out, the "affable" high-powered Corbin didn't appear to have a friend in the world or any influence without Daddy.

She was truly free of him now. But at what cost?

Sawyer, Cash, and Aubrey had rallied behind her but there had to be recrimination too. How could they not blame her? The boys had been so quiet that the house felt like a morgue, everyone tiptoeing around her.

She checked the bandage on her foot and tried to move her shoulder, which she'd either pulled during her flight from Corbin or while hiding motionless for hours in the dense grove of trees. A search-and-rescue dog had ultimately found her buried under the mound of leaves. By that time, Corbin had been hauled off to the emergency room with a bullet in his arm. And Jace…she couldn't bear to think about it.

She put on a thick pair of socks and slipped her feet into her brown leather ankle boots, testing the sole of her scraped foot. It didn't feel too bad. Her hair was wet and instead of blowing it dry she twisted it into a thick knot and clasped it with a barrette at the back of her head.

In the bathroom mirror, her cheeks were still pale and when she turned to look over her shoulder at her reflection there was a black-and-blue mark on the back of her neck where Corbin had pressed his gun so hard against her flesh it had bruised the skin. She undid the barrette and lowered her messy bun to cover it.

Tomorrow, she planned to pack. It was safe to return to San Francisco and try to restore the life she had before Corbin. But oddly, she had no desire to go back there. That was the problem, she didn't know where to go or who to be. Was she Charlotte Holcomb or Charlie Rogers or the woman who let Corbin Ainsley take everything from her?

What she did know was she couldn't stay here. The ranch had become a beautiful crutch, but now she had to stand on her own two feet. And though her business was starting to take off here, living in Mill County was out of the question. Everything about the place would remind her of Jace.

And her heart would break when she needed it to heal.

"Hey, you're up and dressed." Jace took her into his arms. "You look good, baby."

She pressed closer and saw him grimace. "Sorry, sorry."

"It's okay." He lifted his shirt. At the last minute, Corbin had turned his pistol from himself onto Jace. The impact of the gunshot against Jace's bullet-proof vest had left a purple bruise that was well on its way to turning a sickly yellow. "See, much better."

"What about your head? How's that?" The velocity of the bullet had knocked Jace backwards and he'd hit his head on a rock. He was lucky he'd only received a mild concussion.

"Still hard as ever." He tapped the side of his noggin with his fist, then kissed her on the side of her neck. "I've got a surprise for you."

"You do?" She hadn't told him she was leaving yet and had hoped to do it this morning, right after breakfast, before she made up excuses to herself to stay on a few more days.

"It's in the living room. You ready?"

"I suppose." The truth was she wasn't so big on surprises. She'd had enough to last her for a while. But Jace was obviously excited about this one and she didn't want to disappoint him.

He led her down the silent hallway. The quiet was eerie and she wondered where Travis and Grady went. To the coffee shop for waffles with one of Jace's cousins, perhaps, then off to school. For the past two nights they'd broken protocol and Jace had slept in her bed, holding her until she fell asleep. Neither one of the boys had said anything, accepting the sleeping arrangements as standard operating procedure.

They'd been so sweet, even bringing her breakfast in bed one morning while Jace was out checking on the cattle.

Her heart twisted. After tomorrow she wouldn't hear them running down these halls at breakneck speed, yelling at the top of their lungs. Or see their shining faces first thing after school. She'd promised to make Grady a quilt with the logos of all his favorite baseball teams. Charlotte would send it to him, she promised herself. Wherever she was, she'd make the blanket and pop it in the mail.

"Close your eyes," Jace told her. "I'll lead you the rest of the way."

"Well? Can I look now?" she asked after Jace had guided her into the living room.

"Yep."

She opened her eyes slowly. Morning light filled the room, dappling the wooden floor with sunshine. And sitting on the big leather and kilim sofa sat Allison. Charlotte blinked twice just to make sure her sister wasn't a mirage.

Charlotte's throat clogged and her eyes filled.

But it was Allison who was up on her feet, flinging herself into Charlotte's arms, first. "Charlotte. My God, Charlotte."

They hadn't spoken a word in months but their love for each other had never waned.

"Mom and Dad?" Charlotte sniffled.

"They're missing you like crazy. They wanted to come but...we've all been so worried, Charlotte. Sick with fear that that awful man brainwashed you."

In a way, Corbin had. He'd convinced her that cruelty was what passion looked like. And that controlling someone was the same as devotion. And anger was love, the true kind.

"Not anymore, Al." But how had she let it happen in the first place?

"Jace told me what that man did. Oh, Charlotte, I'm so sorry."

They went for a walk, just the two of them, and Charlotte told Allison the whole story: Meredith and her foundation, how Charlotte ran away, the baby, the miscarriage, Jace, his sons, and Dry Creek Ranch.

Allison cried with her as they stared out over the land.

"It's beautiful here." She rested her foot on the bottom rail of the fence and watched the horses graze in the field, then turned to study Charlotte's face. "And Jace... he seems like a good man. When he called he only gave me the barest of details. The cousin...Sawyer...told me on the ride from the airport that you've been living here. Are you two—?"

Charlotte looked away, afraid her sister could read her every emotion.

"Charlie?" It had been a long time since Allison had used Charlotte's childhood nickname, not since they were girls. "Is there something going on with you and the sheriff?"

"I babysat his children, Travis and Grady. In return, he let me stay here...helped me file a restraining order against Corbin." At least that's how it started.

"It seems to me like more. The way you were holding on to each other when you first came into the living room. The way he looked at you afterward."

Charlotte squeezed back tears. "There can't be more."

"But there is, isn't there?"

"Oh, Al." Charlotte tilted her head back. "What's wrong with me? What the hell is wrong with me?" She swiped at her eyes with the back of her hand.

Allison cradled Charlotte in her arms. "Nothing's wrong with you. You're the sweetest, kindest person I know."

No, she wasn't. Because for the last six months she'd lain in her bed at night, hoping that Corbin Ainsley would die.

"You knew, Allison. Right from the get-go, you knew what kind of man Corbin was. Why couldn't I see it? Why was I so blind?"

"Because you wanted to believe. We all want to believe in love, Charlotte. That's how we're built."

"Can you ever forgive me? Can we ever go back to being the family we were before Corbin came into my life?"

Allison looped her arm through Charlotte's. "There's nothing to forgive. If anything, I wish I would've been there for you more. I feel like I let you down, Char. That you were in trouble and I let my frustration with you pull me away. Instead of giving up, I should've come to San Francisco and demanded that you leave him."

Charlotte wiped a tear away. "There was nothing more you could've done. What's important is that I have you back in my life and I'll never let you go again." She wrapped her arms around her sister. "I love you, Al."

"I love you, Charlie."

They stood there a long time, holding each other, hugging. Having her family back meant everything to Charlotte.

"Come see my workshop," she finally said, wanting so much to share with Allison the magical world she'd been living in, thanks to the Daltons.

She knew Allison would eventually circle around to the topic of Jace again. But Charlotte needed time to sort out the confusion of the last few days. Hell, the last year.

They crossed the field through a bed of wild poppies to the old barn. She slid open the door and watched Allison take it all in.

"Wow," Allison said in awe. She stared up at the rafters, then gazed around the building, letting her eyes linger on Charlotte's sewing station. "This is freaking fantastic." She rubbed her arms. "A little chilly though."

Charlotte turned on the space heater Jace had lent her from the house. "I've sold most of my merchandise."

"What about this sofa and chair?" Allison ran her hands over the slipcover admiringly. "This is so you, Charlotte. It's fantastic." Her lips curved, showing off her dimples, and a warmth flowed through Charlotte like sunshine.

Jace had given her back her little sister. What a precious gift it was.

"It's sold and getting picked up on Friday," Charlotte said and had to look away. The couch held too many memories of that first time with Jace. Jace.

He'd done this for her. He'd reunited Charlotte with her sister, then gone off to the office, even though he was supposed to be taking the week to recuperate, so the Holcomb sisters could have time and space to catch up. And catch up, they did.

She and Allison spent the entire day together, talking and making plans. In the ranch house's enormous kitchen, they made tea while Charlotte worked up the nerve to call her parents.

"They only want to hear your voice," Allison said. "Let them know you're okay."

The call was emotional and for a long time Charlotte and her mother just sobbed. When she hung up it was with the promise that they would all be together soon and Charlotte would tell them everything.

That evening, after Jace and the boys got home, they grilled, treating Allison to the ranch's homegrown beef. Because it was still too cool to eat outside, Charlotte set the dining room table as if they were having an indoor picnic. Allison made a floral arrangement from wildflowers they had picked earlier. The cheery colors helped dispel the somber mood.

After dinner, Grady asked Al to sign his cast. With everything that had happened, they'd had to postpone his doctor's appointment. Allison signed it with her usual flourish, drawing a border of flowers around her name.

The boys went off to do their homework. And when the last dish was dried and put away, Allison excused herself, feigning exhaustion so Charlotte and Jace could have the rest of the evening together.

"You have a good visit with your sister?" Jace came up behind her, caught her around the waist, and tenderly kissed the bruise on the back of her neck.

"It was wonderful." She turned around, reached up to bring down his face and kissed him softly on the lips. "Thank you. It was the best surprise anyone could've given me. I missed her so much, Jace. My parents too." She buried her face in his chest so he wouldn't see her crying.

He caressed her back, giving her the time she needed to pull herself together.

"How was work?" she asked, her mouth muffled against his chambray shirt.

Jace lifted her face, his blue eyes shining. "According to Tiffany, getting shot has done wonders for my poll numbers. Her only regret is that it didn't happen closer to the June primary."

He was making a joke but Charlotte didn't find it funny.

"You could've been killed," she said. "That's the horror I take to bed with me every night. God, Jace."

He held her close, sifting his fingers through her hair. "But I wasn't, Charlie. I have too much to live for."

And just like that her heart melted. Leaving him, leaving here, made it difficult to breathe. But staying…She had to be on her own. She had to figure out why she'd been complicit in her own tragic story.

"Could we go for a walk?" she asked him. "There are things I'd like to talk about."

They hiked across the field with no direction in mind, winding up at the big cattle barn. The sun was setting over the hills, painting red and purple streaks across the sky. Somewhere, out in the distance, a cow bawled.

"I'm leaving on Friday," she blurted in the most artless way imaginable after rehearsing it a dozen times in her head. But this was Jace. Plain-speaking Jace, and there would be no way of sugarcoating it with him. "I need to spend time with my folks. I need to reboot."

He leaned against the barn, folded one leg at the knee, and planted the sole of his cowboy boot against the wall. "Okay. Have you booked a flight yet? I can take you to the airport."

"I'm driving with Allison." She held his gaze, her bottom lip quivering.

She saw when it suddenly hit him. The light went out in his blue eyes and there was an imperceptible twitch in his right cheek.

"What are you saying, Charlie? Ah, Christ." He pushed off the wall and walked a few feet away with his back to her. "I'm in love with you. I think I fell for you that first time in the kitchen when you sewed Grady's shirt."

His voice was low, as if he was still working it out in his head. He slowly turned to face her. "I realize you're not ready. I know that, Charlie. But why can't you stay? Why can't we go on like we have been? You can build your business and when you're ready...and if you decide I'm the one ..." He trailed off and turned again to stare off into the distance. "Ah, Jesus."

She went to him and twined her arms around his neck. "I love you, Jace. My heart is so full that sometimes I think it'll burst. Just explode in my chest. But I have to go. It's not that I'm not ready yet, it's that I don't know if I'll ever be. I can't move on until I heal and I can't heal until I figure out who I am and why I let myself be a human punching bag for love. Until I do that I'm no good to anyone."

"Charlie...I'll wait." He held her so gently, so hopefully, it made her ache inside.

She put her hands on the sides of his cheeks. That face. That amazing, beautifully rugged face. How she would miss that face. "Don't wait, Jace. I've made so many mistakes, so many bad decisions, that it may take me a lifetime to understand why. Just know that you...Travis and Grady...this ranch brought me back from the dead. But the work to make me healthy again has yet to begin. Thank you, Jace. Words cannot express how thankful I am that you came into my life." Her voice trembled. She was crying hard now. Big, wet, sloppy tears and a wet nose that wouldn't stop running. "And know that I love you. I will always love you."

Chapter 23

Friday evening Jace stood in Charlie's bedroom, staring at the empty space. The furniture was still there, but she was gone.

He sat on the edge of the bed, where her scent still lingered, and inhaled it as if it would bring her back. It hadn't even been eight hours, yet he felt the loss of her deep down in his bones.

"Dad, look what Charlie left me."

Jace's head came up. "What do you got there, buddy?"

Grady held up a patchwork quilt. Every square had a different baseball team logo. The Giants, the A's, the Padres.

"It's great." Jace reached out and touched the blanket.

"She made one for Travis too. It's on his bed. You want to see it?"

"Nah, Travis should see it first. It's his gift."

"When's Charlie coming back, Dad?"

How was he supposed to tell his boys she wasn't? They'd already been through this once with their mother. "I don't know, buddy. She's going home to her family. They need each other now."

"But she's our family too."

"Yep," he said, trying not to choke up. "But the three of us, we're good as long as we have one another."

Grady sat next to Jace on the bed. "Are you sad, Dad?"

"Yep." He ruffled Grady's hair. "It'll pass. You got homework?"

"It's Friday."

"Why don't you get it over with so we can spend the rest of the weekend playing? What do you say?"

"You're not going to work?"

"Nope. Maybe the three of us should go to the lake, pitch a tent, and do some serious fishing. How does that sound?"

"Good, I guess." Grady shrugged. "Travis might want to spend it with Tina." He made gagging noises.

"It's just a hunch, but I bet he'll choose fishing. Go finish your homework while I make dinner."

"Can we have that monkey bread stuff Charlie bakes?"

"I don't know how to make it, buddy. But I'll do a little research for the next time." He got to his feet and Grady followed him to the kitchen, where he grabbed his backpack from the mudroom and took it to Jace's study.

Travis would be home from junior rodeo practice in an hour. Jace went through the motions of getting dinner started. The kids had to eat and he had to do something to keep his mind off Charlie. He'd picked up the phone at least twenty times today to call her to see how the drive was going... and to beg her to come home.

At least she had her sister and wasn't making the trip alone. Portland wasn't so far anyway.

"Hey." Sawyer came through the door and immediately stuck his head in the fridge. "What's for dinner?"

"Burgers and mac and cheese." Jace found a package of ground beef in the freezer and stuck it in the microwave to defrost. While he waited, he grabbed a grill pan. He didn't feel like dealing with the barbecue.

"We gonna talk about it?"

"Nope, nothing to talk about. She's gone."

"Jace—"

He held up his hand. "What part of no don't you understand?"

"I wouldn't be a very good reporter if I let everyone who didn't want to talk shut me down, now would I? The good news is you don't have to answer any questions, just listen. Charlie isn't Mary Ann. She's crazy in love with you, Jace. If you don't believe me, ask Cash and Aubrey. We're all in agreement that she's nuts about you."

"I'm glad you could all take time away from your busy schedules to discuss my personal life. Why don't you try getting one of your own?"

"Why don't you pull the stick out of your ass and get on the phone. Tell her you love her. Tell her you want her back."

For a supposedly smart guy, Sawyer was a moron. "I told her that already."

Jace watched Sawyer process the information. It would've been funny if Jace's heart wasn't in goddamn pieces.

"You did? Then why the hell isn't she here?"

"Because she's got issues to work out. Trust issues."

Sawyer reeled back. "Come on! You're the most trustworthy dude in the world."

"Not me. Her. She has to learn to trust herself."

"Give her a few weeks, then go get her."

Jace shook his head. "Nope. If you love someone, set them free."

"Are you actually quoting a fucking greeting card?"

Jace didn't know where the saying had come from but in this case it applied. "I love her, Sawyer, but it has to be her decision. Otherwise, I'm no different than Ainsley."

"Ainsley is a sociopath." Sawyer jabbed his finger at Jace. "You're not. Are you really willing to let her go without fight?"

"If I thought fighting would win this, I'd fight. I've got to give her time and space. She's got a lot of things to work out and I'm not going anywhere."

"You're just going to wait?"

"What choice do I have?"

Sawyer studied Jace. "Don't wait too long, Jace. The saying is bullshit. Absence does not make the heart grow fonder."

* * * *

By April, Jace was starting to think Sawyer was right. He hadn't heard a word from Charlie. She'd texted Grady, who had sent her a picture of his arm with his cast off. It had taken everything Jace had not to respond. The relationship she had with his kids was between them.

If she wanted to contact him independently, she knew where to find him.

He fell into his regular routine of taking care of the ranch and going to work, missing her more every day. Sometimes, after the boys fell asleep, he'd wander into her room, close his eyes, and pretend she was there. For a second or two, he'd feel at peace and then his heart would fold in half.

Antonia had called twice, once with an invitation to attend a pottery show at her studio and the other an invite to dinner at her place. Both times he found convenient excuses to bow out.

About the only good thing he could say about the month was someone was interested in buying Grandpa Dalton's coin collection. They'd settled on a fair price, even though the amount fell slightly short of his share of the property taxes, which were due in four days.

He'd decided to take a cash advance on one of his credit cards. It would jam him up financially—the interest rate was like 18 percent—but he'd run out of solutions. And come December he'd be in the same financial straits again. Although they wouldn't have the back taxes hanging over their heads, the regular taxes on a property this size were truly more than the three of them could handle without more income. Charlie was right. They needed to come up with a way for the ranch to generate revenue in addition to what their small cattle operation brought in.

Time for another family meeting.

He went to the safe to retrieve the coin collection and give it a good dusting before shipping it to his buyer. Next to the coin collection was a stack of bills and checks. Charlie's money. She'd forgotten her earnings from the furniture she'd sold. On the top of the pile was a note.

Jace, there are no words to describe my thanks for all you've done. You, the boys, and Dry Creek Ranch were my salvation. Please take the money and use it toward the taxes. Before you let your macho pride get in the way, think about how important this is for me. You gave me the chance to start over again, to do the work I love most. The workshop in your barn was the first step in taking my life back. Dry Creek Ranch—and of course you—put me on the road to recovery. Knowing that I can make this contribution is part of my healing. Please don't take that away from me by rejecting the funds. I love you!

Yours truly,

Charlie

He read the note over and over again. He could almost hear her voice saying every word. And for a long time, he sat there, his insides hurting. Finally, he returned the money and the note to the safe and locked it behind him.

* * * *

June came with its mercurial weather, which perfectly reflected Jace's mood. Gloomy. There still hadn't been any word from Charlie. In a moment of utter weakness, he'd called Allison to check in. She'd said Charlie was getting counseling and facing her demons and not much more. Jace didn't push.

He often scanned her Facebook page to see if she'd opened a new store. But the last post on the page was from more than a year ago.

There was talk that Ainsley had agreed to a plea bargain, which meant Charlie wouldn't have to come back to testify. It was the best possible outcome. Charlie wouldn't have to relive any part of her life with Ainsley. But it also meant she had no reason to ever return to California.

As the days drew closer to summer, he was starting to accept that she was gone to him.

"Are you listening?"

"I heard every word." Jace lifted his face from staring at his plate and looked directly at Tiffany.

"Then what did I just say?"

"Okay, I lied. I'm all ears now." He toyed with his steak sandwich.

"That reporter from the *Call* wants to follow you to the ballot box on Tuesday and watch you cast your vote. I told him that was fine."

"Thanks for asking." Jace planned to take Travis and Grady with him and didn't want a reporter tagging along.

"This is just in case you tie with Jolly and have to go on to the general election. It never hurts to curry favor with the press."

"Fine," he said and pushed his plate away.

Tiffany leaned closer and whispered, "I'm hoping you'll flat out win this."

Jace hoped so too. He was tired of campaigning, while Jolly seemed to relish the attention. And why not? Jolly was a personable guy and Jace had a hunch that campaign functions appealed to him even more than being sheriff. If nothing else, Jolly's candidacy had been a boon for his hardware store.

"You think you can make it two more days without stirring up some kind of controversy?"

"Like what?" Why did Tiffany have to be so freaking dramatic?

Tiffany threw him a heavy dose of side eye. She was more nervous about Tuesday than he was, even though it was his ass on the line. "I just wish Charlie was here. You two looked good together and everyone adored her. Sally Reynolds is still telling everyone you broke up her son's marriage."

"Sally Reynolds is lucky her son isn't doing three years in Folsom."

"Just don't make any headlines before Tuesday, unless it's to save a cat or a little old lady."

"What about getting shot? You want me to do that again?" Ah, crap. He was in a foul mood. Tiffany didn't deserve his sarcasm. Jace reached across the table and placed his hand on her arm. "You've done a great job, Tiff. Thank you for being my campaign manager, putting up with my shit, and caring so much about this community. Whatever happens on Tuesday, know how much I appreciate everything you've done."

She held up her hand. "Save it for when the polls close and every vote is counted." She flagged down Laney for the bill. "Now I'm going to enjoy the rest of my Sunday."

"You don't enjoy hanging out with me?" He winked.

"Perhaps if you were twenty years older and not such a rascal." She winked back.

"Go on and git. Say hi to your husband for me and I'll take care of the check." He fished his wallet out of his jacket pocket, squared up with Laney at the cash register, and went home.

The house was empty. Travis was at Tina's, studying for finals, and Grady was at a friend's. He thought about wandering over to Cash and Aubrey's cabin, but they spent most of their weekends finalizing their wedding plans. Sawyer was up to his elbows in revisions on the first draft of his book. That left Jace to entertain himself.

He decided to pay Amigo a visit, sliced an apple and hiked down to the horse barn with the dogs. Sunflower was the first to greet him, sticking her face over the corral gate, looking for either a treat or a scratch on the nose.

"Here you go, girl." He fed her a piece of the fruit he'd brought and whistled to Amigo.

The gelding lifted his head from the grass and strolled over to the fence. Jace scratched his head, climbed through the space between the railings, and checked his gelding's hooves. Travis was doing a good job mucking stalls.

After feeding the horses the rest of his apple, Jace took the trail with no place in mind and wound up at Charlie's old workshop. He hadn't been inside since she'd left, sparing himself visions of her hunched over her sewing machine, or cutting a piece of thread with her teeth, and a flood of other memories.

He wandered around the mostly empty space. On the wall was a weathered barn-wood sign with white letters that spelled out "My happy place" and his throat clogged. This had indeed been Charlie's happy place.

The sewing counter they'd set up was still there but her machines were gone. The space heater he'd dug out of the basement sat in the corner. The rafters she'd once knocked clean were back to being covered in cobwebs. He looked around for a broom and found one leaning against the back wall.

"What are you up to?"

Jace jumped. "Why the hell did you sneak up on me like that?" The damn dogs, who'd stretched out in a sunny spot on the floor, were useless.

Cash cocked a hip against one of the posts. "Didn't mean to. I was headed over to Sawyer's to borrow a sleeping bag and saw the barn door open."

"What do you need a sleeping bag for?"

"Ellie's going on a camping trip with the Millers as soon as school lets out."

"I've got three. You could've borrowed one of mine."

Cash shrugged. "Sawyer offered first. What are you doing in here?" He took in the broom and hitched a brow. "Spring cleaning?"

"Nah, just looking around."

"You nervous about Tuesday?"

"Tiffany seems to think I'm in good shape, but who knows? Jolly's got a good following. Truth is, if I hadn't gotten shot saving one of my constituents, he probably would've beaten me."

"Constituents?" Again with the raised eyebrow.

"You know what I mean."

"How is she?"

"Her sister says she's doing okay." Jace sat on the sewing counter and rested his heels on an old vegetable crate. "I haven't talked to Charlie, though."

"No?" Cash was doing that silent interrogation thing he always did.

"Haven't talked to her since she pulled out of here in March." He wasn't telling Cash anything he didn't already know. "I'm giving her space to do what she needs to do."

Cash pinned Jace with a look. "It's June. It's Mary Ann all over again, Jace."

"I only waited for Mary Ann for the boys' sake, not because of any misconceptions that we were still in love. That ship sailed the day she walked out on us."

"What about Charlie?"

She wasn't coming back was what Cash was trying to say in the nicest way possible. Jace didn't answer at first, trying to come to grips with the reality of the situation. Cash was right, Charlie wouldn't be returning to Dry Creek. She'd mistaken gratitude for love and had realized that as soon as she'd gotten to Oregon.

To be frank, he'd known that in his heart of hearts the day she'd left but hadn't wanted to face the bleak truth of it.

"Nothing," Jace said. "It's time for me to move on."

"You got a plan for that?" Cash joined him on the counter.

"Win the primary on Tuesday, figure out a way this ranch can bring in more income, be best man at your wedding, and watch our new crop of calves grow fat. You got a better suggestion?"

"How about dating?"

"Yeah, that too." Jace had zero interest, but maybe if he got out there he would.

"It's time, don't you think?" Cash squeezed Jace's shoulder. "I've got to get that sleeping bag." He looked around the barn. "Don't spend too much time in here, looking backwards."

"Yup," Jace said, but when Cash left, he stayed behind to hold his own private memorial for what could've been.

Chapter 24

Tuesday morning, Jace stared at the red striped tie he planned to wear to cast his vote at the grange hall on Dry Creek Road.

"Screw it." He tossed the tie on his bed and rummaged through his drawer, finding what he was looking for. Grandpa Dalton's lucky bolo tie. It was sterling silver and turquoise and definitely louder than the simple bolos Jace wore. But today he could use an extra boost of good juju.

The old man used to brag that wearing the bolo tie outside the delivery room had gotten him four healthy grandchildren. And the night he'd worn it to the annual Cattlemen's Association dinner, he'd won Cattleman of the Year.

Grady burst into his bedroom. "Travis says we don't get to vote."

"Hey, pardner, what did I say about knocking?"

"Sorry. Is it true?"

"Yep, not until you're eighteen. But I'll let you two help me fill out my ballot."

Grady sat on the edge of the bed. "Can Ellie come too?"

"Ellie's coming with Uncle Cash and Aunt Aubrey. Uncle Sawyer too. We're all caravanning together."

"Do I have to go to school?"

"Yep, right after breakfast at the coffee shop. Mrs. Kerr will pick you up this afternoon."

Grady groaned. "D-a-a-a-a-d. Why does she have to be our babysitter? She smells like onions all the time."

Because she was the best he could come up with after Charlie left. "She's a nice lady and you guys remind her of her grandkids who live on the other side of the country. Can't you cut a grandmother a break?"

"I guess. Why can't Charlie move back?"

"Because she lives in Oregon. You know that." They'd been over it more than a dozen times and he really didn't want to discuss it again. Not now, when he had enough on his mind. "Where's Travis? I want to talk to you guys."

"I'll get him." Grady ran out of Jace's room, shouting at the top of his lungs for his brother.

Jace slipped the bolo tie over his neck and adjusted the braided leather cord under his collar. He took one more look in the mirror and decided he was presentable enough. He'd gone back and forth on whether to wear his uniform and decided to go with plain clothes. Because no matter what happened today, he'd always be a rancher.

"Grady says you need to have a talk with us." Travis stood in the doorway of Jace's bathroom, Grady crowding behind him.

Jace gave both boys a once-over, grabbed a comb from his vanity drawer, and ran it through their hair.

"Ow," Grady cried.

"So this is the deal," Jace said. "A newspaper reporter is coming with us to the grange hall to watch me vote. So mind your p's and q's."

"What does that mean?" Travis asked.

"Be on your best behavior. No fighting, no burping, no foul language. Got it?"

Both boys nodded and he smothered a grin.

"Okay, let's do this."

"Let's do it," Travis and Grady said in unison and bumped their fists with his.

Jace gathered them up in a bear hug and dropped a kiss on the top of each one's head. Outside, a horn tooted. Tiffany sat in the driveway at the wheel of her Mercedes with the reporter, who hopped into the front seat of Jace's truck. Tiffany and the rest of the gang followed him to the grange hall in their respective vehicles.

There was a small crowd assembled near the entrance to the polls, talking and drinking coffee out of travel mugs. They applauded as Jace and the rest of the Dalton clan crossed the parking lot to cast their votes.

"Go Sheriff! Go Sheriff!" Ruben's mom, Kelly, chanted.

"I think she's single," Sawyer whispered in Jace's ear.

Jace ignored him and went over to the group to shake hands. The reporter snapped a few pictures.

Jace broke away from the crowd and joined the rest of his family in the hall. Mitzi Lerner, Jace's former first-grade teacher, sat at a table, checking names on a registration list and handing out ballots. She greeted the Daltons with a big smile.

"We're a little crowded right now. The booth on the end is open, though."

"You take it, Jace." Cash said.

Travis and Grady went with him and he let them mark his name on the ballot.

"Like this, Dad?" Grady asked as he colored in the line with pencil.

"Yep. That right there is the lucky vote. Why don't you guys go outside while I finish up here?"

He cast the rest of his votes and met his cousins at the door. "Why don't you and the boys go on ahead to the coffee shop," he told them. "I'll meet you there as soon as I finish up here."

Tiffany hung back to make sure he stayed on script—whatever the hell that meant—and to shuttle the reporter back to his car after the interview.

"Let's go over to the side of the grange hall where it's private, so Josh here can finish up without any interruptions," she said.

They followed Tiff to a secluded corner of the building where the reporter did a Q and A.

By the twelfth question, Jace was starting to get antsy. One of Jimmy Ray's waffles was waiting for him. "We good?"

"We're good, Sheriff." The reporter stashed his pad and pen in his back pocket and Jace watched Tiffany talk his head off on the way to her car.

Jace started for the parking lot, only to be stopped along the way by more well-wishers.

"Atta boy." Dougie Sampson, the local backhoe driver, high-fived Jace.

Mama tapped the horn of her tow truck a few times and stuck her hand out the window to give him a thumbs-up.

Twenty handshakes later, Jace made a beeline for his truck, hoping to avoid getting further waylaid.

And that's when he saw her.

She was on the outer edge of the parking lot, standing next to her CR-V, with a tentative smile playing on her lips, as if she didn't know how she might be received.

He squinted a few times to make sure his eyes weren't playing tricks on him. But it was her.

Charlie.

He froze, trying to absorb the shock. He wanted to go to her but his feet wouldn't seem to move.

When he continued to just stand there she said, "I voted," and pointed to the red, white, and blue sticker on her blouse. "Uh…I used your address to register online…I hope you don't mind."

The soft breeze blew her dark hair around her face. And he could've sworn he'd forgotten how to breathe, let alone walk. She was so astonishingly beautiful that he continued to stay rooted in place, just staring.

She'd changed since March. Her hair was shorter now, falling in soft waves around her face. Her brown eyes sparkled. And the gaunt planes of her body had been replaced with soft curves. Gone was the haunted look he remembered so well from the first time he'd met her.

"So you came back to vote?" He was still trying to process her presence.

"To vote and to see you and the boys, if that's okay."

He sucked in a breath, not knowing whether he could survive another goodbye from her. But if all she had to give was a brief visit, he'd take it. And cherish every damned second he had with her.

His legs began to move and the next thing he knew he was lifting her in the air.

She laughed, and the sound of it was so joyous that heat radiated through his chest. He put her down and she went up on tiptoes and spread kisses across his face.

A part of him wanted to hold on to this moment forever. No questions, no worries about tomorrow. There was only today. There was only now.

But for his own sanity he needed to know. "How long are you staying?"

"How long will you have me?"

He pulled away and looked at her. Really looked. "Forever," he said. "I want you to stay forever."

She threw herself into his arms. "I thought maybe you'd forgotten about me by now…that you had someone else."

"Never. There's only you. But I thought …" He backed away just far enough to peer into her eyes. "How are you, Charlie? Why the change of heart?"

"My heart never changed. It was always set on you. It was the rest of me that needed healing."

He tilted his head. "Has that happened? Have you healed?"

"I had a lot of time to reflect, if that's what you mean. It was good to be with my family. Good to come to the realization that I would never let another man, or anyone else, come between me and them again. I saw a therapist while I was in Portland. A really good therapist. We worked through a lot of things."

"I'm glad." He stroked her face, reveling in the softness of her skin. "Are you ready to be with me, Charlie?" Jace held his breath. If she said no, he'd figure out a way to persuade her to stay.

"So ready," she said, her voice shaking. "I missed you more than you can imagine. You're the best thing that ever happened to me. I just needed time to trust my feelings again."

He lifted her chin with his finger. "You trust 'em, then? Because I won't let you down. I might make mistakes but I would never intentionally hurt you, Charlie. I'll work every day to make you happy, the happiest you can ever be. That's a promise."

"You've already made me happy." There were tears glistening in her eyes. "I love you so much, Jace."

"Not half as much as I love you." He kissed her, losing track of time and everything around him. For him, there was only Charlie.

"Uh, I think we're making a bit of a spectacle of ourselves," she said against his lips and reluctantly broke the kiss.

"I don't care," he said, and glanced up to see a few passersby who'd come to vote, staring. "But if you want, we can sit in my truck." He didn't want to let go of her even for a minute.

"Let's go home," she said. "Let's go home to Dry Creek Ranch."

His breath caught in his throat. She was coming home with him, this time for good.

Epilogue

"It was the most beautiful wedding I've ever been to." Charlotte swung Jace's hand as Travis, Grady, and Ellie ran to the ranch house ahead of them. Ellie was staying with them for a week while Cash and Aubrey went on their honeymoon.

"You pick up any ideas?" Jace asked.

"For ours?" Charlotte glanced down at her engagement ring, a one-carat asscher cut that Jace had found in an antique store while she was trolling for goodies to restore. "I want it at the ranch too. I want my sister to do the flowers and Aubrey to do the table settings. Like Allison, Aubrey's got an amazing eye."

"Have you thought any more about Aubrey's business proposal?"

"It's a go." Charlotte beamed. "We shook on it at the rehearsal dinner last night. I can't believe she's willing to risk leaving her lucrative job at the architectural firm to pair up with me, especially because I don't have a dime to put into this venture. But I'm crazy with excitement about it."

They'd reached the house and Charlotte suggested they sit on the front porch and watch the sunset. "I love it here." She sighed. But she suspected she'd love any place as long as she was there with Jace and the boys.

"I'll be right back," Jace said.

"Do you need to call in?" The hours of a country sheriff were unpredictable. And after getting 80 percent of the vote, it looked like this was going to be his career for a good long time.

"Nope, I've got something for you."

She couldn't imagine what. He'd already given her everything she could ever want. A house, a family, a place for her business, and enough love to make her the happiest woman in Mill County.

He returned with a white envelope and handed it to her.

"What's this?" She opened the flap and looked inside. A stack of bills peeked back at her.

"I sold my grandfather's coin collection to pay the back taxes. That's the money you earned from your business. You should use it for your and Aubrey's store and design studio."

"Oh, Jace, I wanted you to put it toward the ranch." She pushed the envelope back at him. "Please, this is important to me." Corbin had turned her into a kept woman and she never wanted to be in that position again. Couldn't Jace understand that she needed to hold her own?

"Ultimately, it will be for the ranch," he said. "Remember how you said we needed to figure out a way for the land to support us? This is that way. The shop and studio, Charlie. If it thrives, we thrive. And maybe along the way we can house a few more small businesses. I have no idea what kind yet, something agricultural, I hope."

She did a double take because it was perfect. "Leasing out business space...What an inspired idea. You could rent to places that would complement Aubrey and my shop. A country mercantile for instance. Or a café where we could serve Dalton beef. And a—"

"Let's not get carried away just yet." Jace's lips slid up. "When Cash and Aubrey get back from Hawaii and Sawyer from New Mexico, we'll all sit down and brainstorm."

Charlotte rested her head on Jace's shoulder. "Sawyer decided to go, huh? You think this woman will give him any more information about his sister?"

"I don't know. I guess if he didn't go, we'd never know for sure. But my gut tells me that whatever he learns won't be good. I don't think Sawyer—or any of us, for that matter—are really prepared to find out what happened to Angie."

Charlotte knew Angela's disappearance had taken a toll on the Daltons. And while Jace stood tough, he'd suffered enough loss.

But today had been Cash and Aubrey's wedding, a time of joy and new beginnings. Tomorrow they could talk about Angie. Tonight should be about their bright future together.

"I'm excited about your ranch idea," she said and laced her fingers in his. "You're a brilliant man, Sheriff Dalton."

"Me? It was your idea." Jace pulled her out of her rocker and onto his lap and wrapped his arms around her waist.

She cuddled against his chest and listened to the steady beat of his heart. "Good thing you decided to marry me, then."

"Decided?" Jace hitched a brow. "I'll give you credit for the ranch idea. But marriage, that was my idea, woman."

"But I said yes."

"And what a wise choice that was, because I'm the love of your life."

"Yes, you are, and I'm yours."

His mouth captured hers in a kiss that went from sweet to needy in under a second. "What do you say we watch the sunset from the bedroom?"

"I say that's an excellent idea."

He lifted her like a bride and carried her inside.

Printed in the United States
by Baker & Taylor Publisher Services